Birds of a Feather

Birds of a Feather

Fred Ephraim

53775

ACKNOWLEDGEMENT

Author photo by:
Kelsey Edwards

To Liliana as always through your love and devotion I flourish.

To my brother Stanley and my sister Frankie who would both have loved the story and the character named after their brother Albert. Albert I hope you enjoy your namesake.

And to Dawn and Jason read it and smile.

Hi, MA and Maise.

CHAPTER I

The day I finally learned to fold the warden's king-sized fitted bed sheets in a nice, neat square was the happiest single day I spent in my two-and-a-half to five years in prison. It was just the way he liked them, and I had paid dearly to learn this laundryomatic secret from a departing inmate.

Warden Brandeis—no, not from that famous judicial lineage of (Louis Dembitz Brandeis.) This warden, Arnold Brandeis, was truly an ersatz and shameful figure if in fact he was at all related; but he was a stickler about his laundry being done correctly, and I dutifully obliged him, for I longed to keep this, the cushiest job in the entire cellblock, until graduation and freedom from this insane world.

It was a horrible, animalistic world so different from the one that I had not so long ago blithely, foolishly, and thoughtlessly jeopardized, and now so desperately long for the simplest place to live in it and among the normal again.

I have yet to reach a state of exhaustion from the amazing jolts that I feel every time I am privileged enough to receive them. These humanistic jolts of which I speak are at first the products of real epiphanic imaginings in human form; they are real ideas of substantive man in real time in the real world, which in my more lucid and tranquil moments of uninterrupted meditation I am disposed to accept. In their glorious favor, I receive them directly through flashes of blissful thoughts, through enter-cranial spasms that jump vivaciously, vigorously, and heartily across the synaptic gaps firing their new impulses of never-ceasing knowledge, reminding me daily of the peace and value of small and simple things. They chill, thrill, and dither me with ominous forebodings and lung-vibrating shouts to warn me away from breathing too deeply in my daily accumulation of dosages from the pervasive and airborne disease of ennui. Their timely alarms guard my mind against desultory and idle wondering too close to complacency's cliff edge, where the high risk of prison life's fatal fall into the abyss of doldrums' bottomless pit is always at risk. It is indeed a conundrum, a contradiction of sorts as to why the awakening of my once—lethargic and careless mind only comes from the monotony of prison's confinement, and after the soul-shattering loss of one's personal freedom. Or is it not but my own stubborn refusal to have borne live witness and testament to my own life, while living it so blissfully well and secure in freedom's arms, that had brought me tumbling ass over dingleberries down.

I am a light-skinned black man, an oxymoron if I've ever heard one, who, sadly, had committed a white-collar crime—not something violent or seedy, dirty, or even dangerous in the wide variety and scheme of things and crimes. It was a pure crime, as crimes go, and as clean as the colorful paper it had been written on: a bad check—it even had pictures of clouds and the sun shining on them, on it's face. But alas, and so sadly for me, that very skin is why I spent two and a half years in Sing Sing, a maximum-security prison in beautiful upstate Ossining, New York, instead of some relatively posh white-collar prison farm in an equally bucolic setting somewhere else. I guess they got confused when they saw me, and my sorta, kinda black face, and they just thought to ship me off to the place where even my diluted visage was more common than not rather than to the minimum-security prison where my staple of white counterparts—white-collar criminals—are in the majority.

Actually, the whole debacle, it was bittersweet as it was just a little over an hour—once she had boarded the train at Grand Central Station—for my mom, Gladys, to pull up in the prison bus at my front door, all the way up from the Big Apple. She would never accept a ride in a car from a friend; it would have been far too mortifying to be dropped off at the front gates of Sing Sing Correctional Facility to ever live down in two lifetimes. It was bad enough that everyone important to her knew that I was boarding there; she wasn't about to have them bear witness to it as well. The whole fiasco damned near broke her heart and mine; I love her so much.

Before my arrest and disgrace, everything was rolling along just fine, thank you very much. I was riding high, but, all of a sudden—through bad acts of my own perpetration—the world that I had built along with my mother's aide and love all just seemed to cave in all around me and mine.

The Lawrence Travel Agency was doing fabulously well; I had two offices going, one uptown in Harlem and one downtown in Heaven—as

I always called the Upper East Side of Manhattan—and I was aiming on opening a third office on the Upper West Side. The economy was booming and when that happens, New Yorkers, like most of the world, travel a hell lot more than when things are tight. We had survived a two-to-five-year downturn, depending on your particular business. During the difficult days, Mother always cautioned me not to worry, but it became increasingly difficult for me to see my business drying up. During this period, I had stupidly and ill-advisedly kited a check or two to cover gaps and shortages in my liquid cash flow, but it always worked out; anyway, it was just for short period of times that I would pull this risky maneuver. And of course, I didn't think I was hurting anyone, and I know I wasn't the only small business doing this during this and even in more prosperous times. But alas, I was the one who later got busted; looking back, I've got to be cool with that because going into it, I knew I was doing something illegal. But here and upon this rueful opportunity for reflection and truth, I was just being greedy; I was doing well enough to have waited my proper turn to expand—it was coming.

As I said before, the economy was booming at the time, and I wanted to take advantage of the upswing for selfish reasons, and to quickly recover my losses, and, at the same time, to shoot way ahead, you know, the American way . . . expand, expand, expand. I didn't have the capital—my books showed bad from the less-than-prosperous times, so I couldn't get the financing from the banks. I did what I shouldn't have, and it was seventeen years ago tomorrow that I finally walked out of Sing Sing a free man. By that time my life had been ruined, or, more precisely, I had ruined my own life. That's when Mother stepped in—that gracious old lady—she got me this job in her building as a concierge and doorman.

You might think, at first, that's quite a ways to fall from owning your own business, and you would be right. Whether you think it served me right or I got a bad break, it was still quite a fall from grace and incipient wealth. After what I had been through, I was happy to have it. Now, you have to understand, this doorman gig, well, it wasn't just any job, and it certainly wasn't just any building; the exposure of the two is why there's any story to tell at all.

In the first place, the building is on Fifth Avenue. Now, for you the uninitiated, Fifth Avenue, across the road from Central Park—yes, the Frederick Law Olmstead Central Park in the middle of Manhattan—is one of toniest addresses in the history of Western civilization, and most of the people living there know it and act like they know it. Now, picture me. I know that might be difficult since I haven't yet told you what I look like, except that I am black, a male, now in my late thirties.

Well, in the beginning, in those Lawrence Travel Agency days, I was fresh out of college, a month over twenty years old, precocious and very entrepreneurial. I had no idea what I wanted to do. I could have gone to law school, but I knew that I didn't want to go out and work for somebody just so they could boss me around and tell me what to do at some law firm, hoping to make partner in less than five years, for eighty hours a week; I just wasn't made that way. So Gladys, my mom, she grubstaked me the money to open my first travel agency office; the second came within the first year. It was scary at first, but after I took my first junket and got the hang of the travel business, it felt as smooth as a greased hand sliding into a pigskin leather glove . . . it was like butter, and I was having a really good time, women—all kinds of women—parties, limitless traveling, and such. I was young and having a really good time.

The biggest problem, although I didn't see it at the time, was that I was so young, too young and inexperienced for the vicissitudes of the roller coaster of entrepreneurial enterprise. I wanted to be a huge success at any cost, and the two years' downturn in the economy knocked me for a loop. When things got good again, I wanted to secure my future success right then and there by developing a cushion against future economic unevenness. But now, almost a two full decades later, I'm working forty-hour weeks doing what someone tells me to do . . . but wait, it gets really interesting from here.

This building—I don't want to give you the address because I don't want you to come snooping around looking for people. These people, who by the time I'm finished telling you about them, will become all too familiar to you, and you might start to act like you know them or some such thing, and that just won't do. But suffice to say it is one of the more prestigious addresses in a less-than-one-mile stretch of some of the planet's most prestigious addresses, and it's a co-op. A co-op on Fifth Avenue, you know the kind of residences with boards that will meet to consider your application whenever it suits them, and who will turn you down if your name isn't in the right social register, or if you don't belong to the right club, know the right people, or if your summerhouse is on the wrong South Hampton Street. It is just another way these privileged few to say if you don't share the pedigree, the money, the connections, then take a Polaroid because that's the only way you'll ever get to hold a piece of this real estate in your grubby little hands.

Each building on this grand avenue is lined so perfectly straight with the one that precedes it and follows it along the avenue—that standing in-line with the doorway with my uniform and hat on. All I need to do is lean six inches forward and turn my head in either direction, and I can see clearly for the total length of this urban enclave of the super wealthy in either direction . . . anal, ain't it? Well, that's what they want you to think. Like the perfect building façades all lined up neatly would have you believe that nothing untoward or untidy goes on in these environs . . . well, forget about it.

I'm here to tell it's a lot different than it looks.

I stand there in front every morning, and I have a beautiful uniform—that's if you, in the first place, are enamored with the uniform thing as you have already probably guessed I'm not. Well, it's gray in the fall and winter, and green for the spring and summer, and their respective weights are significantly different enough to make me more comfortable one season from the other; in fact, I think the spring outfit is just a tad heavier than the winter one. You know it's the park and everything; it's important to blend in. Since I've been here so long, I have seniority; the fellow that I replaced seventeen years ago, he had been here for thirty-five years before he retired—or was it they retired him.

Anyway, in the mornings, I work the door and the concierge desk since there's just no need for two of us; there's not that much going on then. Besides, the elevator guys are always around the lobby. The building has three sets of elevators. Two sets, which open up into the grand foyers of each apartment; there is a larger freight elevator in the rear of the building for moving in and out and for large deliveries—or deliveries that, if they cannot be carried and delivered by the fingertips of an old woman's hand, they must be hauled in through the freight elevator. The building is very prissy in that way. The third elevator goes exclusively to the penthouse triplex; it's a baronial eighteen-thousand-square-foot apartment. It was the home of the original builder and owner of the building, some late nineteenth-turn-of-the-twentieth-century Gilded Age industrialist whose name I've never cared to know. That apartment, by the way, is where my mother, Gladys Lawrence, lives.

Now, just wait a second before you start not believing me. Gladys lives there with her long time . . . I pause here because it's exceedingly difficult, to put into words, just what to call these two women. So maybe I should spend a little time telling you a little about the two of them. Mildred Smith—that's the other woman's name; or the name of the other woman who lives in the palace at the top of the building. The building, I must say, that is more like a person, a woman, than a thing.

Anyway, Mildred Smith is the widow of Richard Smith, the late billionaire real estate developer; he's been dead a long time. Well, they—my mother and Mildred—they have been together since I was a little kid. I know she helped us out a lot when I was little. I mean she paid for my education while my mother was working for her that's why I was able to attend prep school up at Hotchkiss and college at Brown; she's always been so very good to us. Well, when I left for Hotchkiss, my mom moved in with Mildred full-time, and they have been inseparable ever since. So to make the mistake and call them friends, or anything else, would be in a word to reduce all that they are to each other; they are the most together, in all ways, old ladies.

As I was starting to say about the building, it's alive, it has a kind of heart and even a soul. How could something built by men not take on the qualities and the attributes of man—think about it. The elevators and the stairs are the arteries and veins, the bricks and mortar are the skin, the windows are the eyes, all of the various vents and ducts are the endocrine system, and all of the apartments are its organs, the people are its organisms—the life that flows through the body. And me, well, I don't know what you'd call me; I haven't figured that out yet, even after all of this time. I guess, you'll have to decide.

As I was starting to say before, the word *façade* is totally *apropos,* as things are not always what they seem. Sitting here in my office with my hard hat in hand, waiting for my brother. I remember—it was about this time last year. I had just changed from my gray to green uniform; it was a welcomed change, because the gray one can get kind of depressing after a while. Well, I was standing early one morning when a familiar yet unwelcome sound greeted my ears.

I don't know exactly how to describe it—the sound, that is; it's the sound of something boney falling from aloft, some 140 feet aloft. Let's cut to the chase: it was a rat's severed head. Surprised, aren't you? It wasn't one of those undersized white farm-raised lab rats that some miscreant Fifth Avenue rich kid had gotten bored with and decided, for a sick joke, to behead and throw it down at me from his apartment of privilege; no, it wasn't that. Because this rat's head, as usual, was from one of those cat-sized, incinerator smoke—gray, incisors size of switchblade knives Central Park rats that no child, however mischievous, would ever go anywhere near without a cocked and ready twelve-gauge shotgun and a native guide. And there was no human being disgusting enough to want to touch it with their hands in order to throw it down at me; in fact, it wasn't thrown down at me. Although it had come from above, it wasn't thrown down.

Let me give you a little hint; you've probably heard something about us—us being my building. We're the one that's been in the news for years. We're the one with the big bird living on the ledge. And that's who dropped the rat's head down next to me. She does it from time to time. Most people don't know this, but falcons are messy eaters, especially when there is food in abundance as there is right across the street in Central Park—, all kinds of rodents like the aforementioned fat catlike rats. She fits right in with the other inhabitants of this wealthy enclave, where waste makes room for more waste.

It's not always heads that she drops; sometimes it's a foot or a leg. Once she even dropped the entrails of a gray squirrel. I thought at first it was a snake; it scared the hell out of me. I almost lost my breakfast right then and there.

"You know, you could use some table manners. It's like chewing with your mouth open. Nobody needs to see what you're having for breakfast."

I mouth a yell up as I shake my white-gloved fist in disgust toward the falcon's nest; there's no sense in me actually yelling as all the negative attention would then be cast upon me. I harrumph in mock annoyance—as you may have already inferred, this was not the first of my dealings with this untidy situation—after that is when I headed inside and retrieved my carcass-removal equipment from the small broom closet next to the concierge. It's just a regular tidy-up kit, *des rigueurs* for this part of town. It's all chrome and shining, a long-handled calf's leather grip one-piece broom and dustpan set; I took it and a plastic bag to remove and dispose of the rat's head. I am always glad—as so far it has not occurred even once—that no one else is standing beside me whenever this kind of hideousness occurs because they would undoubtedly expect me to solve what is an intractable problem. Not the removal of the falcons, mind you—that act would disturb many to no end—but to somehow take flight and catch the debris before it hits the ground to disturb their delicate sensibilities. You see this peregrine falcon has become a city pet and tourist attraction.

Every day of the year, and I do mean every day, rain, snow, sleet, hale, or sun shine—the more inclement, the better it seems—it's like the bad weather brings out the maternal instinct in people as if these birds haven't spent centuries learning how to take care of themselves. There are always people who literally stand loitering all hours of the day across the street at Central Park craning their necks to the point of disabilities trying to catch a glimpse of the falcons; there are two of them as you might suspect. There are even some who come every day to take pictures and write stories about this diurnal bird. So to interfere with it would be to do something that would incur the wrath of an untold number of people. And I for one am not in the least bit interested in being the one to cause that kind of tumult.

This building, as I'm sure all buildings are to some greater-than-lesser extent, is as provincial as a small town. City people don't like to hear the word *provincial* used in any descriptions of themselves—especially New Yorkers—but a city, especially a city the size of New York City, is just a bunch of small towns all crushed together, block by block, town by town. The entire place is nothing but a hotbed of small towns, some wealthier than others, all different from each other. As a regular New Yorker would say, "*Over there you got your Irish, and up there you got your Puerto Ricans, and your high society on Fifth and Park Avenues, and your derelicts, and every other conceivable group known to man everywhere else.*" Now that's what New York is made so exclusively of. And they all pretend, and even boast, that they could live very well, each group without the other group, especially when one of their groups are parading up Fifth Avenue on their special celebratory day; but that'll never happen. It's a colorful town all made up of street fairs and pumpkin festivals, presided over by a plethora of community associations, neighborhood associations, block associations, and co-op boards, all to keep control of their little fiefdoms. And under the overly labored guise and palaver about egalitarianism, someone is always at the head of the table or at the top of the food chain. And, as is always true in small towns, everyone knows everyone else, and everyone else knows everyone else's business or at least pretends that they know.

Although there's a lot of money in this building, and I do mean a lot of money, the Smiths alone are reported to be worth in excess of ten billion dollars. People here act like people everywhere, no matter how many toys they have. Money does not ever trump humanity; it just makes the playground and the toys more expensive.

Take John Smith, for instance; he belongs to Mildred and is around my age. He's got more money than God. He controls the Smiths' real estate development empire, and yet he is unhappy and angry with only God knows what. Like the other day, he and Brutus—that's his Jack

Russell terrier—they go walking in the park, which they do every day like clockwork. I'm sure while he walks, he's thinking about work, you know, like how high to build his next skyscraper or how much he can get away with charging for his exclusive condos. Anyway, he goes walking while Brutus runs off leash. On this day out of nowhere—it's not really out of nowhere because after all, this is Central Park, a veritable magnet of every kind and level of humanity—that's when these two fellows approach him. I use the term *fellows* loosely.

Now, look, I'm not saying that these two fellows were top-drawer kind of guys. They weren't in suits and ties taking the shortcut through the park on their ways to business; they were bums, okay.

But this is New York, where every other person is either a bum or looks to most like a bum. But, just so we get this straight, these two fellows, they were bums, young, but bums all the same. Well, one of them—I'll call him Amos—he walks up to John Smith. Now John Smith is nattily attired in his Savile Row purchased Gieves & Hawkes suits; he actually flies there to have them fitted and made; he thinks it's the only way, the extravagant way that is. So he is walking with his head held so high it's a miracle he didn't graze his nose on the low-slung tree branches that grace this jewel of urbanity, but that's exactly when Amos asks, "Hey, Slick, can you help us out with a little somethin'-somethin'?"

It would have done well enough for John Smith to make a better, a more thoughtful, even a more civil choice in his response; it would have been far simpler and far more efficacious. But oh no . . . he decides to be belligerent, as exampled by his risky retort to these definite bums, soon to be turned into marauding thugs.

"What . . . ? Get a fucking job . . . Slick."

If he had been one of their homeboys, these words would probably just have rolled off his tongue and bounced off their backs. But John Smith—he was not one of their homeboys; he was a wealthy white man in a Savile Row suit, walking his rat dog off a leash, and the dog was now barking at them as if he knew—better, it seems, than his master—that they were up to something no good. The other man of the two young black derelicts had been facing the other direction when all of this talking was taking place between John and Amos. I'll call him the other young man, Andy. Now Andy is alerted, and he turns to face the commotion spurred on in part by John Smith's poorly timed recriminations. Now Andy gets into the act; you can plainly see that he's all-swollen with bluster and admonishment toward his compatriot.

"You see, motherfucker? I told you not to ask this tight-ass motherfucker for no money. Didn't I, stupid?"

Now, Amos has to make a decision whether to pursue the matter, or to turn and leave with Andy.

They seemed at once content with the outcome:; Amos had made his request and had been in no uncertain terms rebuffed. While Andy had voiced his disapproval of his friend's solicitation of the uptight stranger, and he had made his position and point of view crystal clear to them both. And they both did demur; they both turned to walk away, but for some reason known only to John and God if known to anyone, John turns around as both he and the two young men are now walking in opposite directions from each other, and he says over his shoulder as if it's a thought coming from another man's mind, for why in God's name would he have said what he is about to say. "Anyway, who the hell are you calling a tight ass?"

Andy, once the levelheaded one of the two bums—he turns and walks strongly and menacingly back toward John Smith, and this time he is nowhere near as conciliatory as he was in the first go-round. He gets up in John's face as he readies to talk eye to eye with him. Andy stands on his tiptoes as he straightens his back for emphasis—it looks kind of silly as he is a head shorter than John Smith—like a cat staring in a mirror at himself; they almost touch noses. Andy's breathing is heavy, huffing and puffing; he then wheezes through his nose without saying a word, all this for a long second. He holds his stare, and then finally he says, "What?"

He sprays his one word defiantly—it was a street version of the word *what*, as in, what are you going to do about it now that I'm standing here wolfing you in your face?—John Smith stands his ground, and then he inexplicably repeats himself in just about the same tone and tenor of his first mistaken retort, "I asked, who 'Who are you calling a tight ass?"

In truth, Andy really didn't want to go any further with this scenario,; but he had to make it look good, for his manhood had been besmirched in front of homeboy witness, who would go and tell on him if he did not defend his mythological street creds—a true conundrum (a damned if you do, damned if you don't scenario). He's now—at least in his mind—stuck in mid-step between walking away back toward Amos and doing something further against John Smith. In the world of his testosterone-driven mind, there's no graceful exit; he can't just back away, no, not from this sartorially splendiferous white Fifth Avenue boy. There was no chance in hell of that occurring, short of the cops showing up right then; he wasn't backing down.

It can't end here like that, and, besides, John Smith is feeling very superior now—he can sense Andy's hesitation—and so he won't back down, and he won't let it go either. He is really feeling his Wheaties as he escalates his attack and continues to berate the two men, "Why don't both of you take a bath, stop soliciting strangers in the park, and get yourselves gainful employment."

Maybe John Smith, in a moment of secret and well-hidden altruism, was about to offer the two young men jobs—as he in his position could well do that very thing—and that this charade of revulsion and disgust was just his comical prelude to doing just that; we'll never know. For alas and sadly for him, those last acerbic words had completely tipped the scale to release the pent-up insanity that resides in the hearts, heads, and loins of all men that, in the case of these two Neanderthals, was skimming ever so closely to the surface, waiting to unleash itself in an explosion of violence. And that did it; they had both had enough of John Smith's rich white mouth spewing one-sided truths, far different from the way they two most certainly viewed the world—and, by the way, the world viewed them. For in the skewed logic of their troubled minds, it was now time for a regular beat down—an ass whipping, as it were. So Andy finally pushes his face against John's, and it, in the street vernacular, was on. He unabashedly jumped on him, followed closely by Amos, who seemed totally surprised at this unwelcome turn of events; in the blink of an eye—or, more appropriately, in a New York minute—he quickly found himself lying on his back, being pummeled, punched, and kicked by Amos and Andy. All while Andy yells, "We got us a job now, you bigmouth asshole, and that's kickin' yo dumb white ass, you stupid motherfucker!"

Times are not often that good things can be said about the strident yapping of a little rat dog, but this time, fortunately for John Smith, is one of those rare times. The short attention span that seems bred into these desultory canines—who, during the verbal part of the argument, disinterested, had wandered off to parts unknown. He now comes rushing back, finally seeing his master lain out on the ground being roughed up by the two misguided souls. He begins doing what comes very naturally to him; he barks, and bounds up and down repeatedly like a wild jackrabbit. Finally, he yaps, barks, and bounds away the two men as they scurry laughing and howling away through the park.

John Smith finally makes it back to standing on his feet. And now, from the beating, he's tattered and torn and a little worse for wear, and he was considerably larger than either of the two men, and there were no weapons used—thank God.—Pphysically he seemed all right. And, as he crosses the street and walks toward the building, I spot him.

Now, I can see from the distance that he's holding his savior, Brutus, in his arms. Ms Under normal circumstances, he would never let that dog touch his finery, so I sense instantly that there is something amiss. But as he draws closer, I can tell from his altered and disheveled appearance that he's not fared too well in what is obvious to me has been some sort of skirmish. I may have graduated from Brown University, but I know what the end of a beat down looks like; it looks just the way John Smith appears—disheveled, as he is certainly the worse for wear—as he's about to cross Fifth Avenue.

At first, when he's still on the other side of the street and about fifty yards north of the building, I think of going out to meet him to make inquiry and assist him, but I thought the better of it. I decided to wait; he was walking and moving just fine, and I didn't want to draw any additional attention to him and make a scene. I suspect he would have liked that even less than he had cherished the beat down.

Finally, John Smith is at the building; as he had gotten closer, he was looking worse the closer he came. So I walk out a couple of feet to meet him.

"What the hell happened to you, Mr. Smith?"

I'm being a bit disingenuous here; please, let me clear things up a bit for you. You see, I don't like John Smith, and he doesn't like me now either—I say now because I'm anxious to tell you why; let's wait on that—but his mother likes me, and his wife likes me as well, a lot. Yet even with that set of circumstances, it's not like I'm standing here thinking, *well, well, somebody finally kicked his behind.* No, not at all, that's just not what I'm thinking at all. But I can guess why he got his behind handed to him. I'll give you one guess . . . he mouthed off at someone that doesn't work for him or live in one of his buildings. You know, someone that doesn't know or just doesn't care about how highly he regards himself. But he's hurt, and he's a human being in need of some compassion, and, lastly, I know him. So I walk forward, and solicitously I offer my hand in assistance. He offers me this as he pulls abruptly away from my offering hand: "What does it look like, Albert? I was mugged by two of your people."

This is the point where all people, especially for those who are clear, conscious, and cognizant of who they are in their own minds, are acutely aware of what someone else is trying in this particular kind of moment to do to them. In short, someone is trying to reduce you. I could have been quick on the draw to squeak the name of that odious malignancy that resides in all of us and call his attitude and comment racist; but I prefer not, for I know him well enough to know different. I'll just chose to call him an intolerant, frustrated idiot. It's not about ethnicity; it's all about elitism, money, status, and class. He comes from a family worth ten billion dollars; he has a house in the Hamptons, a yacht with a helicopter, and a private jet. He grew up in a penthouse triplex on Fifth Avenue, and he still lives there in the same building, and you, and people like you and I don't. It's a simple point of fact; everyone that does not live like him is not like him. Yet and still, knowing him, and maybe because of knowing all of this, I won't give him an inch.

"My people?" I say with only the barest hint of sarcasm. He pauses for a brief moment to utter another absurdity as he brushes past me.

"Why weren't you there to stop this outrage? What is wrong with you people?"

It was just another thing to ignore. So I took another tact.

"Would you like me to get the police, sir?"

He harrumphs indignantly, and then he turns with that silly dog of his looking as befuddled as I was about to be by his next request.

"You know what I'd like, Albert?"

I wanted to answer him, but I dared not; I figured he needed to blow his entire wad of pent up frustration right then and there; and thinking that his wife, Nancy, is still upstairs, maybe if I gave him enough room, he could excoriate some of that venom before he had to face her. So I waited for him to say his piece.

"I would like for you to get the scum who just did this to me, that's what I'd really like. Will you be doing that, Albert? Now, will you?"

I wasn't surprised by the request, only the sincerity with which it had been delivered.

"I'm sorry, sir. I have no idea who did this to you, sir. I'd better call the police, sir."

It only took him a moment to respond, and he wasn't happy at all. In fact, I sensed that he was really now getting angry with me, as if I really had something to do with it after all. It was absurd, but who can really tell how someone else's mind works, especially when they are unable to distinguish simple truths from mental mythology.

"Yes, you do that, Albert. You go call the police. Meanwhile, your friends can be miles away when the police finally arrive, just like always."

He had finally hit that nerve he had been digging so furiously away to hit. And before I knew it, I had responded. As he was already on his way to the elevators, I found myself walking behind him to say my piece, "I beg your pardon, sir?"

Again with the last word, he just can't help himself. As he steps toward the elevators, he turns for one final salvo.

"You can beg all the pardons you want, Albert, but I know you know what I'm talking about. You're all in this together."

He turns away again and walks toward the elevators, and the operators intercept him and start making a big fuss over him. He's much more conciliatory toward them. I don't know if it's because they are white, or maybe he's just run out of steam. Anyway, as he steps inside the elevator, he turns to face out and gives me a final look of remorse, as if to say in frustration rather than in apology that his mouth has again gotten the best of him.

"Do what you must, Albert. I'll be inside."

This has been the worst of the many abrasive moments we, John Smith and I, have shared through the years with each other; this one has really put me in a morose mood. Some time passes, and as I am standing contemplating the logic of my life, who else but the other half of John Smith's marriage approaches me. It's Nancy Smith, in all ways the opposite of her husband, John—a common occurrence in this dwelling, as you will later be exposed to. She is so different from him; she's vibrant, sunny, and full of energy. She is friendly, fit, and attractive, whereas he is dour, hostile, and a bit on the chubby side. She has always befriended me, and I've really, really always tried to show my appreciation in any way that I could.

"I understand that my husband tore into you for no good reason, Albert. I don't know what the hell's gotten into him lately, he's become increasingly moody."

This was not one of my finer moments, and, besides, I wasn't expecting her to do what she was in the midst of doing. I really didn't want her to be licking my wounds for me like some friendly puppy. I know many women don't understand this, and it's difficult for us men to tell them in which situations this is consistently true; it's a timing thing, you know? But it suffices it to say sometimes a man wants to be alone to stew in his own juices. I mean, that's how we figure things out; that's how we grow. It's sometimes painful, but that's the only way. It's not so much that we don't need you around, but at these times it's better that you let us alone. I would have preferred to work this momentary grieving out on my own. Questions and answers were just not, for the moment, my cup of tea. But, you see here, this is difficult, because I'm standing there in the lobby in my spring uniform, which means that I work here, and everyone in this building is my boss; I am a servant, and, as such, it is my job to serve the whims and moods of my many benefactors.

So I attempt to split the difference between work and familiarity. I soften my stance and decide to use behavior rather than words in an effort to give a clear message of my desire to seek momentary solitude. I tried various mimes that I know she understands; I suck my teeth and roll my eyes toward the ceiling in an effort to try and indicate some sort of nonchalance and indifference. Sadly, I failed abysmally. She responds quickly, as is her way ever so consistently.

"Stop pouting, Albert. I've already used up all of my patience for that behavior at home with him."

Maybe she is aware of something that forever escapes me because words leak out of my mouth like drops of water from a hole in a bucket before I knew I was saying them.

"He thinks we all know each other."

I heard the words, but they feel like they've come from some other place or person, but I know in truth that they've come from me. It seems that Nancy has gotten the response she was looking for as she immediately engages me, "We, who is this we, Albert?"

She can see that I'm annoyed. I just didn't want her or anyone coming to me and breaking down my thoughts. I wanted to have them to myself, to keep my own counsel as it were. This is obviously going to be impossible now. So I look straight at her and say, "You know what I'm talking about . . . Mrs. Smith."

This is not the first time we've, Mrs. Smith and I, had this conversation.

"Yes, as a matter of fact, Albert, I do know exactly what you're talking about. But God forbid, if I had said *you guys* to include all blacks, you would have bitten my head off for being insensitive, even racist. But when you say *we*, it's acceptable. I still don't get it, Albert."

Let me say here and now that I know exactly what's going on; it's been going on for years, and the pattern is exactly the same. Now, I told you before that the façade is not reality, right? Now, this woman, I've known her for seventeen years, and, except when she's been away on vacation, I've seen her every day. I've done her favors, and she, no doubt, has done me favors; and I've kept her secrets. I know this woman well. This morning she's sitting all fit and tight in her workout tights, with her hair pulled back, on her way to Pilates and yoga classes; I don't know what she's feeling, but I know that she's reeling me in, and, in this determined state, she is not to be denied, She doesn't countenance denial very well, especially from someone like me.

I try to distract her from her intended purpose and have a serious conversation, thinking that maybe she'll reciprocate.

"Well, that's just the thing, Mrs. Smith. Your husband acts like all black men are criminals, and on top of that, he seems to think that we all know each other."

It's exceedingly clear what she's going for, and she just can't resist the opening.

"Well, don't you?" she says, and then she smiles flirtatiously, and that's when the elevators guys begin clearing their throats in mocked amusement. That is, until Nancy Smith turns and gives them the scarlet stare, a stare that could set the park across the street on fire if she had a notion to direct it toward its trees. They, the two elevator operators, immediately find something else to do. You know, that's the thing about wealth; it becomes a license, a sort of carte blanche on selected behavior, and others' opinions and judgments just don't matter. In fact, if your tenure is valued, it—your judgment, good or bad—necessarily needs to be suspended in the face of staunch retribution. It is in that way that Nancy is very much the same as her husband, John.

But I don't always adhere to my own advice. I retort, "Yeah, very funny."

Sometimes I just can't help myself, but it is clear that Mrs. Smith takes offense to my tone, as she snaps seriously and shoots back condescension, "Decompress, brother."

You see, what I've just done here was to skate on the outer edges of her tolerance for inferiors. You can see it in her physical posture that she is raising the haughty wall of position, status, and station to shield herself from the emotions of feeling equal and vulnerable. But I dance lively, I halt the wall's ascent with a mere smile, and she quickly rescinds the order. She really wasn't that committed to it in the first place; it was just a conditioned response. That's all she really knows, having used this same hackneyed behavior to the detriment of all other more fertile options. Her reaction is sudden, like pressing the brakes in the car; she twists her face and looks bemused. She's no dummy, she understands what just happened, but her retreat is complete.

"Look, Albert. Come on, he probably did something to incur their wrath. Those two men didn't just simply attack him for no reason."

I quickly find her words very curious; they seemed personal and even a little angry.

"He thinks he can boss everyone around . . ."

She is angry with him.

"And say unkind things to them without a negative response, or some kind of retribution. Look, they didn't even rob him. He had hundreds in his wallet, and they never touched it. And that yapping rat dog of his certainly would never have deterred a real thief the way he believes it did."

I didn't want it to seem as if I hadn't been listening, so I threw in, "Well, I'm sure he won't think so."

She was still down on her husband, having let all but the tail of the cat out of the bag. She was clearly on a different journey, and it was clear that she hadn't yet reached her destination.

"Who cares, Albert?"

Here it comes; I can smell it.

"Really . . . do you really care what he thinks, Albert?"

I try to look sad; I'm begging here. Maybe she'll think I'm tired and that I need to go home and rest. But it seems she gets the wrong signal.

"Albert, you're so sensitive. Now, isn't that attractive."

That's it; I'm dead in the water. She leans in close to me and pinches me on the behind.

"Why don't you come up later and we'll see if time and attention can mollify your battered sensibilities."

It is far too late in our clandestine relationship to decline such an invitation. Don't get me wrong; on the street, this is a hot woman, hands down. It's not at all difficult to be with her, no no no. But in this worn-out scenario, I've got no juice. I work here, and she's just playing around, and even though my mom is strong with the Smith family, John Smith is still the president of the co-op board. It's just not a good thing. But as I already said, I'm in much too deep to pull out now. No pun intended.

CHAPTER II

Gladys and Mildred, Mildred and Gladys—that's how I think of the inseparable duo; they fit together like a hand in a glove or two peas in a pod, because they are so well—suited for each other, and what a pod it is up there in the sky somewhere near heaven. Near heaven, I say, not because of their height—nothing here on exclusive Fifth Avenue from Central Park South to the low nineties—and I'm being very generous at the higher-numbered streets' want for equal exclusivity as the ones below seventySeventy-Second Street. But none of the buildings are nearly that tall as to even want to reach heaven. I say near heaven because of the riches and wealth of the place. It's a mansion inside a building. There was a time, I guess around the time that this building was first built, that no one who hadn't been inside the place would have any idea what a place like this could look like. But now, with the Internet and all kinds of real estate shows on television, all you have to do is to tune in, and you can see some of the most outstandingly lavish places from all over the world.

Still, comparisons and exposure do nothing, nothing at all to diminish the sheer overwhelming majesty of this place; it's not only huge. Its appointments are still—after careful, spare, and meticulous restorative freshening-ups-top-shelf. This place was built when artisans were still doing everything by hand; there is nothing in the place that wasn't made expressly for this place and this place only. For some, it may be old school—all that wood and ornate hand carving, the hand-painted murals on the ceilings, and original imported Italian frescoes hanging or ensconced in uniquely-placed alcoves throughout the apartment. To hear about it, it might sound like too much, but not when you get up close to it and marvel at the detail and care it took to put this place together; it's fabulous . . . no, it's more than fabulous, close to heaven—it is simply heavenly.

And you know I have not even begun to talk about the furnishings. No, they are not the originals, but they will do just fine, thank you very much. Everything in there is older than the two women who inhabit the place, and that would make everything there an antique—just kidding. Ancient Persian rugs, original Lalique vases, one-of-a-kind Tiffany lamps, hanging crystal sconces, and crystal chandeliers. Original artwork, paintings, and sculptures fit for any museum. Twenty-two-, twenty-, and eighteen-foot-high cordoned ceilings in every room, including the closets, foot-thick mahogany crown moldings throughout, Jesus. Sometimes when I'm up there, I'm afraid to say his name for fear that he just might descend the stairs, and I wouldn't know what next to say. Having said all of that, the two women—Gladys and Mildred—are anything but haughty and pretentious; they are more naughty and adventurous than anything else. They have a ball, the two of them, and they top it off every evening with brandy, a very French cognac, an Armagnac from Auch, and of course, the *pièce de résistance*, real Cuban cigars; those old gals are a hoot.

Every night after dinner they sit in their incredible library, mellowing out as they talk about the day's interesting events, the stock market, real estate, or anything else that suits their moods and fancies. They are like the FBI, the CIA, and Women's Auxiliary all rolled up into one; they've got eyes and ears everywhere. You wouldn't know it to look at them, but they know everything about everyone in the building. The two of them are actually not that old; Gladys is sixty-one, and Mildred is a little older at sixty-five, but they're both very quiet, which makes them seem smaller, if not older. Mildred is old-school. She actually has blue hair; it, her hair that is, really looks like some kind of bird feathers, all teased and bouffant. And Gladys has what black folks used to call "good hair," and she wears hers teased as well; but hers is jet-black, every last strand of it. And they—the both of them—are broomstick thin; they fit well the saying that you can never be too rich or too thin.

Mildred Lawrence—Lawrence is her maiden name—hails from the Midwest around Kansas City, but she's been in New York ever since she graduated from Barnard College; she's never lost her Midwestern values. Actually, that's where she met Richard Smith, up on Broadway at the Library, a restaurant and, at the time, a well-known hangout for locals and university students; he was in his last year at Columbia Law when she was just a freshman at Barnard. Gladys, on the other hand, just barely squeaked through school with a commercial certificate from the now-defunct Commerce High School in Harlem, but she is smart as a whip. While I was away at Hotchkiss and Brown, my mother, with Mildred's insistence, went to Hunter College, mostly at night, for six and a half years, to get a degree in business and computer science. They never told me anything about it; the two of them were, and still are, very secretive about things. I found out quite by accident.

I love my mom very much; she's been terrific with me, and she's always been there for me.

One day, a couple of years back, we were walking through the park; it's her absolute favorite place to be in the world. I think it was over a weekend, but no matter. We were walking arm-in-arm while laughing and talking. At one point a woman passing us by takes an extra long stare, and then she stops and blurts out my mother's name: "Gladys, Gladys Lawrence, is that you?"

My mother smiles as she seems to also recognize the woman. Then, they both stepped toward each other and greeted each other with pleasant words, hugs, and smiles. They looked to be around the same age. Let me think now; this happened around ten years ago when I was twenty-nine. My mother must have been around fifty or fifty-one then. So let's say they were both in their fifties. So they finish hugging and stuff, and this woman says to my mom, "I haven't seen you since graduation, Gladys. How have you been?"

Now, I'm looking at this woman. She's well-dressed, as is my mom; she's well-spoken, as is my mom, but she's white. Now, my mom went to Commerce High School, almost forty-five years ago, and there were no white people there; I know that because she told me so. And this woman is clearly the same age as my mom.

"This is my son, Albert, Martha . . ."

Martha and I shake hands, and they say their good-byes. We, my mother and I, continued to walk. After a couple of moments of deadly silence, in which I was waiting for her to explain what had just happened, I couldn't wait any longer; I thought I would burst.

"Mother, who was that woman?" She doesn't answer me, so I say sternly, "Gladys?"

She's funny, my mother—sometimes she's like a bank vault with legs; she can hold things in until the right documents are furnished before anyone is allowed to extract them. I guess I now had the right document. So she answers me calmly and matter-of-factly as if she was quoting the day's weather report. Actually by this time, I had garnered from their conversation that my mother was some kind of wiz, and an A student no less, and that this Martha had been one of her professors at Hunter College. I could hear them referencing these facts throughout their brief yet full conversation—but now, I wanted to hear it from Gladys. Well, even though I had already heard most of it through listening to their conversation—I know it was rude, but I couldn't help eavesdropping. But standing there, it still didn't ring all the way through to my brain until my mother tells me everything herself; after that, you could have knocked me over with a feather. I was elated, and so very, very proud of my mom; I said, "Mother, Gladys, I am so very proud of you. I'm sorry you felt the need to keep it a secret from me, but that still doesn't diminish my happiness and pride."

It saddened me when I realized why she hadn't told me. You see, she hadn't attended college for six and a half years consecutively. She had started taking a course here, a course there, after she finally knew that I would be all right at Hotchkiss; then in my last two years at Brown, she became more intense. When I was working at the travel business, she was there every day helping me out in any way she could—now I finally realized why she was so good with all the computer stuff—I had no idea she had put off her college classes again for me. Really, I had no idea; I was too wrapped up in myself. But it was when I went to prison that she finally completed her course work and graduated—with honors. And that's why she never told me about it; she was always thinking of me. And there I was, sitting behind bars, wasting one of life's golden opportunities, handed to me on a silver platter by Gladys and Mildred; I had squandered it. My selfishness had landed me in prison. A more impossibly embarrassing and frustrating situation for our family I could never imagine; in that circumstance, she wasn't about to tell me about her triumphs and successes.

She has way too much class and love for me than to do something like that. Come to discover, there were a whole lot of things my mother kept from me until my maturity and personal growth could present her with the right documents to open her vault of surprises. I wished I could have been a fly on the wall while listening to many of their conversations, their conversations, meaning Gladys and Mildred.

As they sit sipping their Armagnac, the smoke and unmistakable fragrance of their Cuban cigars waft ever so gently through the higher reaches of this cavernous yet extremely elegant library; the two ladies' voices' squeak with laughter like little girls at a sleepover. All day from their various sources: a deliveryman here, a maid there; they have gathered every line of gossip, every story, and every rumor afloat in their building and from elsewhere in their very posh neighborhood. It is part of their daily recreation.

Mildred puts down her snifter to pick up her cigar from her ornate Lalique crystal ashtray. She takes a deep breath and exhales as a cloud of smoke momentarily obscures the features of her angularly attractive white face.

"Our boys had a little spat today it seems Ms"

Gladys likewise takes a drag and puffs a cloud from her Havana as she sighs reflectively.

"Yeah, they are both like their fathers, you know, Millie. John, he is hot-tempered like Richard. He's always blaming everybody for everything, like he's the king of something. And Albert's like my Wayne was, he's probably got his insides all tied up in a knot now, and won't be able to go regular for the rest of the week."

Again Mildred takes a puff, blows some more smoke, and then she too pauses contemplatively. She is clearly thinking about their not-so-ordinary familial relationship. As she ponders her thoughts before speaking, they both take another sip of their Armagnac.

"You'd think they'd act more alike given that they've got the same blood running through their veins. You know, as close as they are in birth, they couldn't be farther apart in life."

Gladys's reaction is much more clinical than emotional as she ponders the vicissitudes and the variables of each of the boys' individual personalities.

"I guess it's all about male dominant genes, Millie. Hell, I bore them both, but if the two of them don't act just like their fathers, they couldn't be more like them. It's amusing, don't you think?"

Mildred smiles softly and takes another sip from her sifter, and then she offers, "I wonder how they'll both take it when they find out the truth, they were once like two peas in a pod. The good old days, huh?"

Gladys is quick to challenge the notion of old days being good, saying, "The only good thing about the old days, Millie, is that it's good they are gone." They both look at each other and laugh their silly adolescent laughs, more like cackles than anything else.

Every morning like clockwork, just as I move inside to the concierge desk, my mom comes down to see me. She is the happiest person I know. She never slips into any sort of complacency. I mean, it seems that every moment of her life has particular meaning. Maybe I'm not being very clear here; let me explain. We all, me included, go through our lives treating each day the same, as if there is no difference in the value or meaning of the moments that each day is an accumulation of; we glide through one day after another after another on automatic pilot. We wander, sometimes aimlessly trampling on the very nuanced aspects of life, never thinking about the moments that make up the life of the day. Now, I'm not talking about the to-do—list kind of day, in which we go from one thing to the next thinking about that particular task, and when done, crossing it off the list—no, not that at all. I'm talking about the individual moments as they all accumulate to pass what we arbitrarily call time. Lest we see the oppressive yet invisible hand hovering to contrive and manipulate the beauty of life itself into cold and mechanical measurements of time: the second, the minute, the hour, and the day; then we fail to see the moment as life. As Gwendolyn Brooks, a masterful thinker, writer, and poet—she was President Clinton's poet laureate—put it so succinctly yet magnificently, "Exhaust every moment."

That's my mom in a nutshell. Although she's not perfect at it yet, I can see her constantly working at doing it better, even after all these years. She is aware of things, she takes time to notice, she's not always perfect in her reactions or responses, but who is; and besides, I think in this case that perfection is imperfection. She notices everything, and about everyone there is always something that she sees that it seems no one else either sees or cares enough to see. She has a reverence for time and an instinctive understanding that time is the sole component added to any equation that can completely change that equation. This morning, as with most mornings, she brings that same awareness to me; as with the arrival of every morning that came before this, I am excited to see her.

"Good mornin', Albert."

It's funny thing, Mom was born in Harlem, but she has a Southern accent. I asked her once why she still has it, and she told me that her mother had a Southern accent, and that was the way she kept her mother alive inside of herself. Her radiant smile is like a mirror for me, seeing her face, my face can't help but reflect what I see. I straighten up when I see her.

"Mornin', Mother . . . I mean, ma'am."

Her eyes immediately pierce through my fake countenance and find their ways to my heart.

"What's the matter, son? You seem a little edgy this mornin'. Is this whole thing with John upsetting you still?"

Even knowing what I know about my mom, her percipient nature and all, I still succumb to the compulsion to deflect my true emotions. As I answer her, she stares at me, but the insipid words flow habitually easily from my all-too-compliant lips.

"Oh, that. He's probably sitting on some kind of big-money deal, and he's just a bundle of nerves now."

Mother stares at me for a while; she studies my face with intense interest, almost like she is trying to determine the appropriateness and weight of her coming response. Then she says something—part of it hits me strangely and stays with me for the rest of that day: "If only that were true . . ."

She says with a knowing nod, "It's still a poor reason to treat you badly. You've really made a nice recovery, Albert."

Now that's the part that really threw me; I wasn't sure what that meant. "Thank you, ma'am.

I needed to put some distance between the comment and my emotions, or else we were going to end up having a private family conference in public. She stares at me as her brow slowly furrows in displeasure. I've never understood how she does that; it's so singularly isolated from the rest of her facial muscles, it seems.

"You stop calling me ma'am, Albert. How many times do I have to tell you that? Everyone knows I'm your mother. Trust me, Albert, your time will come. Remember, even God has to cook the pot of soup once he puts all the ingredients in it."

Boy, she's really something. Sometimes she can be as cryptic as hieroglyphics. I smile, somewhat exhausted from this mornings exchange, but nonetheless ebullient for having had the opportunity to spend time with my mother.

It's been about a week now since John Smith's incident in the park. He has not apologized for his harsh words to me, but contrition has been in his behavior toward me of late, I'm sure. If talking more to me is a sign of contrition, then he has in fact been asking for forgiveness daily. The incident in the park has changed his sense of safety, and for that I am indeed saddened. But after all is said and done, we do still live in New York, a town beset with all kinds of adversity. With that understanding, Mr. Smith has decided to increase our security presence in the form of a burly, swollen brother named Windler; he's ex-military. He's like a walking tree stump, and every time I see him, the only name I can think to call him is Stumpy. He has positioned him in the corner of the office next to the elevators so he can be close by if needed, but he really hasn't yet learned when to pounce and when to chill. Like this morning, for instance, what happened with the deliveryman Jose' could easily have been avoided if he had been assigned to me as I had requested. I hadn't requested him at all, but I knew, now that he was here, that his leash needed to be a short one. But, alas, that decision was not in my the purview of my meager powers. I had offered once and was at once rejected by the board president, John Smith; but as the lobby staff was under my supervision, once he was there, I had tried to have him likewise supervised by me. At first Mr. Smith declined, and later he relented, seeing the sense of it.

However, this morning as he was still learning his position, he almost scared José to death. José came in carrying his little brown bags of whatever and headed for his usual destination when I looked up and saw him.

"José weren't you just here an hour ago?"

José smiled broadly at me. I don't know why he always smiles so broadly at me when he sees me; maybe he finds me funny or funny—looking in my uniform. Anyway, it hadn't been him before who made the delivery; I had gone to the WC and had returned only to see the back of a delivery person exiting the building, and I made the erroneous assumption that it had been José.

"No, sir, Mr. Albert . . . I'm José, Jesus make the other delivery before, he deliver the lady's breakfast, but she not get enough."

I'm thinking two things, neither of which did I think appropriate to share with José': One of them was that I hadn't noticed the difference in the two deliverymen; I didn't want to say that to him and risk it sounding condescending and racist as if to insinuate that because he's Latino, I think they all look alike. The simple fact is that I was busy doing something when Jesus had come earlier, and I hadn't taken full notice of him. And the second thing, well, you'll see later what I'm talking about; but if the destination of his delivery, which is always the same, hasn't had enough, well, she must be in her sin this morning.

"I'm sure you're right, José."

Try as I might to cover my thoughts, JoseJosé' gets a whiff of them anyway.

"*Con el permiso*, Senor Albert?"

All of the delivery guys have been trying to teach me Spanish, and sometimes they'll test me with Spanish phrases. I can understand José well; they are all good teachers, but right now, I don't want to delay his arrival any more than necessary with my self-congratulatory preening and idle fawning over my bilingual self. I know that his summoner anxiously awaits his timely arrival. So I sent him forth without further delay.

"Oh yes, José', go right up."

José looks at me curiously; we both know that he was begging my pardon about my last inference and not begging his leave. But we both also knew that I was not going to respond specifically to what could prove to be my embarrassment over an egregious and erroneous inference—that they all looked alike—and that this conversation had run its course. So José smiles and nods and heads for the elevators.

I see it out of the corner of my eye just as José crosses the imaginary extended line of the office door and into the eyesight of our new security. The pall of security in its all-too-frequent manifestations always seems to make me feel uneasy and even less secure than before its institution; it feels rather fascist.

Anyway, as José crosses that imaginary line, Stumpy literally rushes him and almost makes him drop his delivery. This building's lobby up until now has been a very peaceful environment. It is built like a fort. Everything is soundproof, at least, east to west it is; noise diffuses south to north from the stairwells. But generally, all human exchanges are at a low-decibel level, like in a church or a closet full of winter coats, stuffy and quiet. Talking about destroying the solemnity of the place.

"Where do you think you're going?"

An ear-wrecking, nerve-shattering dither is his voice; it indeed sounds like the voice you'd expect would likely emanate from such a fortress-like body.

It was as if he had hit a wall; in mid-stride, José reversed his forward motion and took a step back to before he entered the alarm zone. Thankfully, the lobby was empty other than the five of us servants: José; the two elevator operators named Gus and Nathan; and Stumpy, the growling-bear-voiced insecurity guard; and me. JoseJosé' starts to shake; Stumpy's voice almost scared the English out of him. But José' recovers quickly. He's no punk; he was just caught by surprise.

"I go see the lady, Mrs. Peters. I have delivery."

I started moving forward to intercede before this unwanted and unnecessary scene escalates into something untidy, as if it hadn't already breached that territory. As I step in between the two, I really can't think of his name. I guess I could have elected not to call him anything at all as we all have occasion to doing when we've misplaced some new acquaintance's name or in this case a new coworker; well, I didn't make that choice. I just went right ahead and called him Stumpy; he didn't like it, not one bit, and it showed on his face immediately.

"It's okay, Stumpy, he's okay."

Everything stopped—all talk, all motion—as we all cleared our minds to allow for a change in direction. José seemed to instantly relax as he nodded in my direction and takes took a step toward the elevators while Gus and Nathan—the two elevator men—smiled, as the brief moment of excitement quickly passed back to the humdrum of the morning. And who but Stumpy knows what was going on in his mind. As I was already turning back toward the concierge, Stumpy barks at my back, "I told you, my name's not Stumpy."

His words hit me in the back of the neck like a brick, a soft brick that is, not enough to hurt me, but enough to warn me that a heavier one could just as easily be thrown and land as accurately if I persisted in violating his birthright to be called by his given name. I get it. So I turn back as smoothly as I can to face him. As I turn, my computer-like brain is tumbling through every name I've ever heard, trying to come up with the one that belongs to this foreboding presence. Thank God I got it before I am all the way around facing him again.

"I'm sorry, Windler, I keep forgetting. It's just that you look so, so—."

Windler is clearly not happy; he has taken great offense, and, frankly, I'm a little intimidated.

"So what? So Stumpy," he says. Is this his humor I'm hearing? I can't be sure. The words seem humorous, but he's not smiling. I scramble for safety and sanity, allowing that either is still possible.

"No, it's just that you are so strong, just like a tree stump. It's hard to think of anything else whenever I look at you, that's all. It's really not meant as any kind of an insult, really."

And it really wasn't. Maybe there was even some envy in there someplace—I don't know. He looks good if you like that kind of body, really; I wasn't trying to be hurtful. I can do better than that. All the while I'm thinking, Stumpy . . . I mean Windler is thinking too. He looks incredulous and then a bit bemused.

"Really."

I think he likes it, my explanation that is, if not the moniker. I think I'll wait for him to request it before I use it again.

"Yes, really, Windler, really."

Upstairs now, José enters the Peters apartment. Every apartment in this building is something out of *Architectural Digest*, I swear, and the Peters place, for my taste, is the best of the lot. It's obviously not the largest apartment, but we are speaking in very relative terms, as their twelve rooms encompass just a little under six thousand square feet. If I put together all of the apartments I've ever lived in, they would hardly reach a total of six thousand square feet. The Peters' apartment, like the Peters themselves, is very different from most of the apartments in the building. Old money tends to like and smell alike. There's a certain kind of unanimity of presentation, as if they as a group were trying to not only hold on to the money but also hold on to the past, whereas the Peters break the mold. They are old money, at least, she is. She was named the debutante of the eighties. Him, I know less about, but he's loaded as well. Anyway, their place is this shrine to the modern. They must have more Warhol, Rauschenberg, Lichtenstein, and Hockney, with some Picasso, Giacometti—including some of his priceless sculptures, and Pollack thrown in for good measure, than most museums; it's a mid-century modern heaven of originals. And they have twice that amount on loan to museums around the world. And the furniture, it's all Bauhaus, Mies, and Gehry originals, down to obscure no-name future superstars; it's eclectic, like her tastes.

Her tastes—Mrs. Peters's—you wouldn't believe. In fact, it really isn't that difficult to believe, Puerto Rican men are as desirable as any other men, Sarah Peters is really Hog's ass after them to the exclusion of all others—including her own husband, it seems. So as José enters her apartment, the chase, as it were, is about to commence. José' stands in the vaunted foyer; immediately his mouth is agape, and his eyes bulge in astonishment. He seems to recognize the based-displayed Giacometti sculpture ominously posed on one side of him. And as he turns his head, there is a Zoran Music self-portrait hanging on the other side. With his food delivery in his hands, he shakes his head in amazement as a "Wow" shapes his lips. He takes a deep breath, but that doesn't clear his overwhelming nervousness.

And as he attempts to speak, he still stutters too out loud his mission, "Hello, missus, I make delivery."

He waits nervously for the shortest moment on record when his trembling mouth shapes itself to call out once more. But before he can vocalize again, in walks Mrs. Sarah Peters. Now, let's paint this picture. The reason why Sarah Baron was crowned the debutante of the eighties was not because of her money; they all have money, and many of them have more than her. It was, however, because of her beauty; she was stunning. I say *was* because that was almost thirty years, twenty pounds, and a thousand bottles of tequila and five hundred lemons ago. Come to think of it—maybe that's why she lusts after Puerto Rican men so much, but to follow that logic, then, it would be Mexican men. Anyway, now don't get me wrong; Sarah Peters is not bad to look at, not at all. And when she walks languidly into the foyer all dolled up, looking slender and seductive in her floor-length see-through red Trashy Lingerie robe that she picked up in LA, with nothing on underneath, the scene just about melts away that tequila marinade and the extra weight. After all, there's something very tempting about being the object of a sexy woman's desires; it makes one feel kind of special. Well, that's true of men today. Anyway, it's not to be today, and it's not to be José. We see that especially not today as Sarah gets close to him.

"Put that silly brown bag down, and come over here to me, my little greasy spoon. I need a taste of something dirty in my mouth."

José doesn't respond right away; he's in shock—the entire scene, the glorious museum-quality artwork, the overwhelming wealth and breathtaking ambiance of the apartment, and, of course, the naked seductive woman, and him standing there with greasy brown delivery bags. The entire scene is brimming with contradictions. This, of course, is not the first time some lonely woman or some woman just out to shock a deliveryman has come to the door nude or half-dressed; the guys at the deli talk about stuff like that all the time. But he can tell that everything about today is going to be different; he can just feel it. The moment passes, and then, finally, his nervous lips vibrate out a sentence.

"*Con el permiso, señora.* I make delivery, yes?"

Maybe she thinks he's playing a game of hard to get, and this little charade turns her on at first—that is, until she realizes it's no game at all.

"Yes, my little cockroach, yes, yes, you make delivery, yes. Now, release yourself from those delivery rags and come make your delivery and spread some hot sauce on your momma. Come, come with me," Sarah says as she walks sultrily and seductively toward where the bedrooms or some other comfortable place must be, but when she turns around, José is nowhere to be found. She quickly grows impatient with this cat-and-mouse game. If it's about money, all he has to do is produce, and he'll get the money that is coming to him, she thinks. But this present delay is making her lose her steam.

"Where the hell is he?" she says as she turns around and finds him not two steps behind her, as she normally expected. No, he wasn't; in fact, he was not standing there at all. Sarah Peters quickly steps back to the foyer, where she finds José still standing like an effigy of Lot's wife, a petrified pillar of salt in the same place where she had just left him. She gives him a stern look, and he responds with, "I make delivery, no?"

That's it; she's had it. This is not at all what she had in mind. Jesus had delivered earlier and had done it so well that she was now moaning for more. Jesus was her deliveryman; several times per week, sometimes even on consecutive days, he delivered breakfast and more in the way of dessert to Sarah Peters, like clockwork. It's clear that he had little or no problem with it, and no complaints either. Sometimes, once in a great while, she calls him back for a second visit, for what could be called brunch. Today the deli was extremely busy, and when she called for a second order, she assumed, as usual, that they would know to send Jesus. She didn't ask for him; she just assumed that it would be he who would show up. When it turned out to be José who came instead, she assumed that he somehow knew the deal, and it also seemed that she was cool with José as stand-in, as at first she made no objections. It was, in fact, a whole lot of assuming for a woman who wanted such specificity in her orders from the deli.

"No, no, you don't make delivery, José."

Frustrated but undaunted by the wait or the task of baptizing the uninitiated José in the flood of her lusts, she reaches out and takes José by the hand and begins to guide him in the direction of her desires and her bedroom.

"You come with me. What's your name, José?"

She asks in a flippant, sarcastic, denigrating manner, something in the vein of *They all look alike, and they're all named José.* But his name is José, and he is only slightly confused, if at all. It's not like in a job such as his, in a city teeming with all sorts of a bias, slights, thoughtlessness, and outright bigotry, that he hasn't been on the receiving end of such reduction before this moment.

So he smiles ever so slightly as he stiffens and says, "*Sí, señora.*"

And at this point, Sarah Peters is on a mission to having her way no matter what it takes, and this name confusion is not about to derail her plans if she can help it. So she stops for a second to clear it up.

"No, no, *sí, señora.* What is your name?"

Still standing rigidly in that very same spot, José, who is taller than Jesus—still not as tall as the five-foot-nine-inch Sarah Peters—nods his head; and now he himself begins to seriously engage in his own rescue without losing his much-needed job, a delicate surgery indeed. He sees that Sarah Peters is very frustrated, and he's heard the talk around the deli about Jesus and Mrs. Peters, but that's not his thing. And no, he hadn't talked to

Jesus before he had come to make the delivery because Jesus was already out on another delivery, or else, it would have been he standing there right then taking care of his usual business.

It is exceedingly clear that Mrs. Peters doesn't know, and she doesn't care anything about this JoseJosé' as a person. But this José is actually a very devout Catholic and a very bright, hard working young family man, who is working his way through night college. He is not Jesus, he doesn't even look anything like Jesus, and here and now he refuses, in his own very quiet, shy way, to be objectified by this upper-crust predator on Fifth Avenue.

"José, *señnora*. José is my name like you say, missus."

It is clear in her body language and in her tone that she is just about out of steam; this difficulty and level of ordeal was farther from the anticipated event that she had in mind than she could have imagined. As Sarah Peters peters out, she listlessly responds, "Oh, okay, so your name is José, yes?"

She tugs one more time, but even she is no longer into it. She is feeling somewhat sad and forlorn as all the energy seems to drain from her countenance; her head drops, and her body goes a little limp. José now senses victory in this battle of his faith over her will. He knows that he cannot say what he'd like to say to her, even though she has totally disrespected him as a man and as a human being with equal rights to hers. He knows that he would probably be reported and lose his job and that she wouldn't get it anyway, way up there where she lives. But he feels it's a victory all the same.

"Yes, missus. My name is José, and I make delivery."

He finally pulls away from her now-flaccid hand, and he looks hard at her as he takes small steps toward the elevator door. In a final act of quiet defiance, this art history major puts his paper delivery bags on the base of the Giacometti sculpture as he rings for the elevator.

"I go now, *señora*, yes?"

As the elevator door closes behind José, Sarah stares hard and in frustration. Exasperatedly she throws her hands up into the air and screams to no one in particular as the apartment is completely empty now that José has left.

"I can't believe this shit! My own husband won't touch me, and I can't even give this shit away to a fucking delivery boy. Oh, goddamn it!"

After a second and seeming alarmed by something, Sarah stomps over to a nearby telephone and dials the concierge. She knows, of course, that it's I who will pick up the telephone, and she seems, by her attending behavior, in a rush to speak with me. I'm not standing behind the desk when the phone rings, so it takes me until the third ring to catch it.

"Albert, could you take care of José when he arrives down there, please. When you've done that, and you have a free moment, would you come up here, please. I would really like to speak with you about something."

Scant moments later, the elevator's door opens, and José walks quickly past everyone as he almost runs out of the building; I run behind him to the street. José doesn't see me when he begins to break into a nervous jog, but I call out to him as I run behind him.

"José! José!"

José's mind must have still been upstairs, as he goes several more steps before he finally hears my screeching voice. Finally, he stops and turns around, and as I catch up to him, I'm panting and out of breath. I take a look around at the people passing by. Recognizing that this is just the kind of scene certain to draw attention on staid and curious Fifth Avenue, and not what I'm in the least bit intending, I try to calm the watching eyes by acting very friendly toward José in an effort to defuse the unwanted attention. It works, as the people who have started to watch just walk on by like New Yorkers most often tend to do. Before I can say a word, José complains as the recent embarrassing incident still dominates his frantic thoughts; he says, "That white lady, she's naked and crazy. I don't want to make deliveries there no more, she's sexy crazy." I looked quickly around to see if his words have caught anyone else's attention; I really don't want to see this thing escalate. At this point, I am very curious about exactly what went on upstairs in the Peters' apartment, but I'm not about to ask the nearly hysterical José.

I try to calm the young man down, "It's okay, José, it's okay."

It's exceedingly clear that I'm going to need something other than words to calm this young man down—as he is highly agitated, although I think he is on some level trying to play me. My quick change in strategy works, as I reach into my pocket and pull a bill away from the roll of bills in my hand, José's eyes give him away as they stretch with desire's lust.

"Here, take this. Now, I want you to forget about what just happened here today, you understand?"

The monetary gesture at first quiets José, but when he finally takes a look at it, he explodes, this time gleefully.

"*Dios mio*, a hundred dollars. She's a very expensive lady, Senor Albert, yes?"

José smiles, of course; he can use the money, and he's done nothing to be ashamed of. And, besides, it's me giving him the money, not the naked and horny Mrs. Peters. But it is I, I must admit, that is now more panicky than José as I go the extra length to explain my surprising largess., "No, no, José, that's for not talking about what happened here today, you understand, José? You say nothing to anyone, or you'll lose your job. Do we understand each other, José?"

I can kick myself still every time I think about that day. I look back at myself, and even I condescended toward José ; I treated him like a child, or worse yet, like an idiot—just because he has an accent—as if he couldn't or didn't understand the simplest thing. He was just a good, hardworking Christian man who didn't want to get mixed up in some ugly stuff. I'll have to admit, though, that José seemed okay by the time he skips away down Fifth Avenue and turned the corner headed back to the deli.

CHAPTER III

I returned to the building; and to my delight, one of my favorite people on earth, Amy Dillon, is there in the lobby. She is all dressed in her school's gray and navy uniform and backpack, all bubbly, smiling, and full of youthful energy. As she comes skipping toward the concierge, she seems to have something on her mind.

"Good morning, Albert."

Amy always brings the energy back to this sometimes-gloomy lobby. She often brings my dormant sense of play bursting proudly and happily out of me.

"Morning, Little Ms Sunshine. I started to call up for you, but I got distracted. Aren't you way past getting to school on time?"

I smile because I know she's going to react smartly to my comment. We have this long-running game between us. It's become my job to remember everything about her—au contraire, it is indeed my pleasure to remember anything at all about this wonderful young lady, whom I adore—since I'm always telling her that I do. I've known her all of her life, since the day she was born. And this has become our occasional game in which she tries to stump me sometimes to see if I indeed remember everything; so far, I'm batting a thousand.

"You forgot, Albert, we're on a special schedule this week."

I smile and laugh, and just when she thinks she has a victory in this little game of ours.

"I was just kidding you, Amy. I knew you wouldn't be coming down until now. This is the week your school celebrates its founder, Herman Williams Smith."

Amy's not even a little surprised as she walks closer to the desk and stops; she turns to see if anyone else is near enough to hear what she has to tell me, and when she spots Windler, a little too close for her comfort, she waves me down so she can be close enough to tell me her secret in my ear.

"Are you on this afternoon?"

She knows that I am; she knows my schedule as well as I do, but I play along and grunt, uh-huh, thinking that she may be nervous about what she has to tell me.

"I want to bring Rufus by before my father gets home."

I smile supportively; she hasn't yet told me much about this Rufus fellow, and I know how she trusts and relies upon my judgment advice and counsel. Since her father's body and mind are mostly absorbed in business and only God knows what else, he's rarely there for her. And her mother is off somewhere in Africa on safari trying to find herself, and asked me to keep an eye on Amy while she's away. I already feel obliged to take special care with Amy. It's not like this is something new, I've always had a good relationship with her anyway. We've been fond of each other for years. There has been many a day since she was a little thing that she and I have spent hours upon hours right here in the lobby talking and laughing about everything under the sun.

"I'll be here, miss."

Now I'm very curious about this Rufus fellow; she never mentioned him before now, and yet she's bringing him by to meet me; that in and of it self is very revealing. This is clearly a big moment in her young life and a sure test for all of us. It has been well established through the years of knowing her so well and closely as I do that although Amy Dillon is just a young pup, she is a very thoughtful and methodical person about her movements, choices, and decisions—not unlike her mother, Jessie. Sometimes, even when I at first might question them, in the end, they turn out pretty darn well, so I smile, knowing that there's a surprise in store for me later today.

"Good, I'll catch you later."

Amy turns and starts her walk toward the door when she turns all the way back around to look at me with what I can only call a contemplative look on her pretty young face.

"You know, you are my best friend ever, Albert. I love you."

And then she, with a jaunty little skip in her step, waves and leaves the building for school a short walk away. This is not the first time she has told me either of those two things, that she loves me and that I'm her best friend, but this is the first time that I can remember that she was so serious when she told me. I took a mental note, and then I proceeded to get on with my day.

It seems that everyone is running late today, as Dennis Dillon steps off the elevator just moments after Amy exits the building. Looking forever distracted, his mind and vision elsewhere. I swear if this man had a seeing-eye dog, he would never actually have to know where he was. All he would have to do is to let the dog guide his body while his mind stayed totally preoccupied. Sometimes it seems that the only reason he talks to anyone in the lobby is because the furniture gets in his way, and then he becomes lucid.

This morning, as what happens on many mornings, he literally bumps into the concierge desk, and that seems to alert him to what to do and say.

"Good morning, Albert."

I guess I'm more than a little swayed by my feelings for Amy; she deserves a better father, if not better, at least one who is more attentive—you think that especially now that her mother is away for so long. If I in fact am sounding a little harsh about Mr. Dillon, that for sure must be the motivation behind those sentiments.

"Good morning, Mr. Dillon."

You see, he's not even looking at me when he talks to me, or worse, even when I speak to him. How rude.

"Did Amy get off to school all right, and on time?"

I'd like to smack him to maybe wake him up.

"Yes, sir, she did." While talking, he begins fumbling around in his pockets for something. This multitasking stuff is distracting and annoying; either talk to me or feel yourself up, but not both at the same time.

"Good. She's been acting strangely lately. I think she may be up to something. Have you noticed anything, Albert?"

What a moronic jackass. Doesn't he have the sense, the common sense if not the fatherly instinct, to even ask her what's going on? Even though I am close with Amy, he's her blood—he's her father. What the hell is wrong with people? That's exactly why I never got married or chose to have any children; you've really got to want to be a good father first before you go and have children. Just because you can have them doesn't mean that you should have them; you've got to want them, and then it's still a great challenge.

"Oh, look. Jessie sends her regards, she's in Kenya now," he says as he fumbles a postcard from his pocket.

I take the postcard from him. I want to shake him, but instead I look at the card; I've seen it before.

"That's nice, Mr. Dillon."

I go to hand it back to him, but he waves me off.

"Oh no, Albert, you keep it, it's for you. She didn't send me anything."

What a rube, a rube in the city, living on Fifth Avenue no less—he hasn't got a clue about anything, any of the important stuff that is, or at least that's the way it has always seemed with him. I take the card, open the drawer, and put it in with an identical card and a letter from Jessie Dillon telling me about her sojourn to Africa. I close the drawer and look at Dennis Dillon; he's still looking the other way off into space somewhere, and he begins talking to me again, "Listen, Albert. I want you to do me a favor. Since this merger deal, I've had to put in more time at the firm, and with Jessie away, I wonder, if you could keep . . ."

I couldn't stand to let his feeble mouth finish his beg. What a nincompoop. That's what my mother would have called him. I, on the other hand, have far saltier words for what I think of him, but you get my meaning without them, I'm sure. So instead, I finish his sentence, "Keep an eye on Amy, sir?"

He finally, for the first time this morning, turns to look at me. It was only for a fleeting second, made significant by the act, not the duration. But he turns away again as he begins to speak, "Yes, that's exactly it, Albert. How many times have I asked you to do that in her sixteen years, Albert?"

He should be ashamed, embarrassed, and mortified to be having this conversation with me, but obviously he's not. It pains me to be civil to him; I find him so lacking, but alas, I am but a servant and he the master. And it's his life and his daughter, not mine. Besides, whether he asked or not, I would always keep an eye on Amy, and that's because of Amy and Jessie, not him. This fact, and the fact that I had already assured her mother that I would do the same, allows me to soften, somewhat, my response to his query.

"Oh, about sixteen hundred times, sir."

He barely, if even, heard me; as I smile, he is already way lost in thought and already heading for the exit and to parts and places unknown.

After about another two weeks of the usual days, something else bubbles up at our dwelling. I was standing at the desk as usual when Mr. Smith disfavors my ears with a cranky query, "What the hell is going on out there, Albert?"

As I am fully ready to tell him that there is quite a swell of people out there directly across the street from the building, it's clear to me and

45

everyone else why they are there—clear to everyone else save for John Smith, that is.

"Oh that, sir. They've been out there since dawn."

Smith contemplates in silence for a moment, and then he looks to the crowd and then at me again.

"For what reason, Albert?"

I feint surprise to cover my annoyance at Smith's obvious lack of connection with the world immediately around him. For years people have stopped right where the crowd is standing to look up at the falcons, the now-world-famous Fifth Avenue falcons, who have been nesting on the ledge of our building for at least ten years. They have been filmed for television, appeared in movies, written about in magazines, and talked about by passersby loud enough to hear their words from across the street. Now, how could he have been unaware of all of this; I conclude that he isn't. I have concluded that he is just an arrogant, selfish, self-absorbed son of bitch; that's just in name, not in truth, because his mother is actually a saint. But of course, I stick to the role of a servant and submerge my feelings of frustration beneath my duty and answer with the facts as they stand.

"Old Blue Eyes, sir. They are here to protest your decision to remove the falcon's nest from the ledge of the building, sir."

Instantly I am glad that I didn't allow my own feeling to get wrapped up in my report. This way I was able to watch him react, knowing that I hadn't in anyway influenced his reaction; it was priceless.

"You've got to be kidding?"

Yep, that's what he said—what an idiot. The word *clueless* must have been created for him; totally clueless he was. But it's not clueless about the events. I know he was aware of the hype around the falcons; he would have had to be dead not to be aware. But it is the people that he is so oblivious to—just like in the park, when he set off Amos and Andy. It was like he was begging them to attack him and beat him down; he just can't read people, or he just doesn't care. And I think that he thinks that he is so far above the ordinary guy, that the ordinary guy just doesn't matter. It's beyond run-of-the-mill racism and bigotry; it's classism. It's the way of royalty; no wonder there was a French Revolution. Inside, my heart is shaking its head in total disbelief.

"No, sir. I'm as serious as a heart attack."

Smith then turns his wrath on me as he looks at me with that look of imperious distain; clearly he's been pricked by my comment, a flippant comment, I admit. It was one that I had taken strains to avoid, but, alas, even with my extreme effort, it still slipped out. Sometimes it's just too difficult to hold your tongue.

"What is that supposed to mean, Albert?"

Now, I just can't help myself. All I want is for this stick up the ass man . . . for Christ's sake—he's younger than me, and yet he's as stiff as an old board; it's no wonder his wife acts the way she acts. I know he can only stand so much; he's no idiot, but I can't help poking at him a little. So I offer, with my tongue planted firmly and squarely in my cheek, "What, sir? What is what supposed to mean?"

I told you he was as stiff as a board; listen to what he says, and he is as serious as cancer when he says it: "As serious as a heart attack. Is that not what you said? Are you hoping for me to have a heart attack, Albert?"

Jesus Christ! What the hell is wrong with this man? I am, or someone is going to have to loosen this man up before he literally brakes in half. I am completely dumbfounded.

"Sir?"

It is all I can manage to say. Now thinking back, maybe it was he who was pulling the joke on me, you know? Anyway, when Mr. Smith finally deigns to walk outside the building, the people across the street seem to recognize him—God only knows from where they recognize his sourpuss. All I can guess is that someone must have tipped them all off as to his identity. Whatever the case, all I know is that as soon as they saw him, the decibel level increased tenfold. There's a limo waiting, as usual, to take him to his office. I thought, wrongly, that maybe with all the ruckus across the street, he would have tried to be more discreet and quiet; well, it was a hopeless and wasted thought. He might as well have thrown his fist into the air in some kind of anarchist salute as he pauses outside of his limo to defiantly stare the crowed down. But this is New York, after all, and New Yorkers are not easily intimidated; in fact, they holler at him even louder than before as he gets in the car and finally he drives away. It might have been all well and good that the traffic was so heavy, or else, some of the protesters may have found their ways across the street to confront Mr. John Smith on a more personal level, and I for one am glad that never happened.

All day, the protest ebbed and flowed, mostly it ebbed. The gathering stayed about the same size as some people left and a new group of people took their places; it was like they were taking shifts, but there wasn't nearly as much noise now. Windler and I watched until evening when John Smith returned home. It had seemed, thinking back, that the protestors were gathering and waiting for him to return, as if they knew his schedule. Just about an hour before he arrived, the crowd got bigger—, the largest of the day, in fact.

As John Smith exited his limo, they all start up again, shouting, "Put the nest back!" at the tops of their voices. I'm ready to leave for the day; actually, I should have been gone by now, but I lingered just in case I was needed. I had already changed my clothes, though; I didn't want to appear to be angling for overtime. He already thinks they pay me too much. Windler is standing next to me as Smith makes it to the building.

"Has this been going on all day, Albert?"

I wanted to explain the day, how the crowd seemed to have been waiting for his arrival, but I thought the better of it; it would probably have led to an unnecessary and fruitlessly boring discussion. So I just answer his question as if I were taking a deposition, "No, sir, it just started when your car appeared."

He frowns.

"Can't we do anything about this, Albert?"

I know that I do, in fact, have an answer that will suit his desires, but not his fancy, so I digress to a more manageable alarm.

"Oh, by the way, sir, the Audubon League president stopped by to see you earlier. She left this envelope for you."

Smith continues to be clueless, or just plain arrogant, as he grumbles.

"What the hell does the Audubon League president want with me?"

Of course, he knows what they want; doesn't he realize what all the hubbub is all about, or is he really just that self-centered and egotistical? Well, it's his problem, not mine, and he's the one that's going to have to deal with it. So after a slight pause for thought, I said, "I'm sure I wouldn't know that, sir."

There's humor in everything—my mom has always assured me of that fact, even when I got arrested for kiting checks; after looking back at it, I have to laugh about the utter stupidity involved in actually doing the deed. If, at the time of writing the checks, I could have looked into that ubiquitous mythical crystal ball, I would have had the full knowledge of the consequence of my behavior, you know, the knowledge and feeling of what it would be like to spend time in prison for any reason, let alone for writing a couple of words on a small piece of paper—I would most certainly have found another and much better way. But, alas and sadly, I didn't have that knowledge until after I had gone to prison.

Do you know how significant that act was? I'll tell you how significant; at first—and that was for the first ten years or so after getting out of prison—I had said often to myself and anyone who would listen that the misdeed had ruined my life. But I have mellowed much in the intervening years and have come to the conclusion that it—that same misdeed—has changed my life, and that alteration, although not nearly as ruminatively beneficial, has its positive attributes as well. Experience is truly the very best teacher. Sometimes, in remembrance of that experience, I guess I have to laugh to keep from crying. I try to see the value and truth in everything and allow others to do the same—unless they specifically ask, and, even then, it's debatable whether to give my two cents is a good idea. I've long since learned that telling people what their problems are and telling them what to do about them are both a colossal waste of our time. Everyone should be afforded the equal opportunity to travel their own journey on their own road, and at their own pace; in short, they must be allowed to fail.

No person is all one thing; I mean, no one is always good or always bad, or always anything. We are all human beings, subject to the vicissitudes of life that failure and opportunity force us all to face. Our character is shaped by and is the residue of that very struggle—and it is a continuous, lifelong struggle as life itself struggles to sustain itself through each breath of air it takes. If you don't believe me, hold your breath for just one minute. Our character struggles just the same; it struggles quietly to retain its uniqueness. Character is a life force.

As I had already dressed to go home, Windler had donned a uniform to stand his turn at the door. Smith looks over to him, never seeming to pay much attention to him; it was surprising to hear him reference the man at all.

"Don't we have anything that fits you better than that, Windler?"

I have to admit that Windler was a sight to behold; he is a huge man, the kind of man that nothing off the rack—any rack, that is—would ever fit. Standing there in front of the building next to Smith and me, Windler looks like some kind of giant sculpture from the Metropolitan Museum, which is just up the street from here—he really does. Not a classic sculpture—if he were naked, I'm sure he would rival any sculpture done by Rodin, but in his uniform, he looks more like a pile of boulders stuffed into a cloth sack as he bulges and stretches the compliant yet stressed fabric every which way. Windler is almost as shocked as I was that Mr. Smith was addressing him directly, but still, it didn't take him long to respond.

"This is the one he gave me," Windler says while looking over at me. "I thought maybe it was all you had left in my size, Mr. Smith."

Smith can't help but smirk; it seems he was forced to use a considerable amount of self-control not to laugh out loud. As his body shook, he tried to hide his reaction to the way Windler looked by coughing instead of by laughing; but I know him too well, and it was obvious to me that he was cracking up with laughter inside.

"Well, that's not even close to fitting your swollen, lumpy body."

He let's out a snicker and coughs again to cover it up.

"Albert, measure him and order him a uniform that fits, will you?"

I couldn't laugh for two reasons: for one, I didn't want to embarrass Windler, and the second, I didn't want Windler to punch me in the nose for laughing at him. I never can anticipate what John Smith will do next; even after all of these years, I really can't figure him out.

"I would have, sir, but I wasn't sure of just how long you were going to keep him around for security, sir."

Smith looks hard at Windler before he answers. This time he does permit himself to smile.

"Well, I'm not sure either, Albert. But he sure as hell won't be staying very long looking like this."

I was glad to have had the conversation; I liked Windler, and his company was a far cry and a great diversion from the usual ho-hum fair and monotony of the co-op lobby. And, oh, by the way, if I had gone ahead and ordered a new uniform for Windler without having had this very conversation, you can bet that Mr. Smith would have found a way to make me pay for it. Oh well—I just smiled and said, "I'll order one tomorrow, sir."

There is a board meeting planned for tonight; I sometimes attend if my mother or even Mildred Smith requests me to be there, but this time neither has. I was glad because I wanted to run some errands this evening.

"By the by, Albert, have people started up to my mother's for the board meeting?"

Oh no, I hope he doesn't ask me to go. I'd really rather not.

"Yes, they have, sir. The penthouse elevator is unlocked and ready to receive guests as Ms Mildred has left instructions to do so, sir."

Oh no, here it comes. I can tell by the look on his face that he has been told, by one or both of the women, to personally invite me.

"Have you spent any time with your mother recently, Albert?"

I knew it; I should have left when I had the chance.

"Oh yes, sir, and Mrs. Lawrence is doing just fine, sir."

I knew it—here it comes, the coup de grâce.

"I know how she's doing, Albert. I'm sure that I get to see her more often than you. The question asked and answered was if you had spent time with her lately."

That's it; I'm going to have to put my errands off until later or tomorrow. All this arrogant jawboning is John's way of telling me to come to the board meeting to visit with my mother, the same woman who raised him and whom he loves and respects as much as he does his own mother.

After the board meeting, during which I sat with my mom, I kissed her and Ms Mildred and quickly left to run the errands that the remaining business time permitted while the three of them—John, Mildred, and Gladys—remained to talk among themselves things they would never dare speak about in front of the other board members. It seems, by the tone of their ensuing conversation, that they had indeed discussed at length the Old Blue Eyes situation. The three of them sit in the library as Gladys, Mildred, and John imbibe, pleasurably absorbing their nightly cognac and Cubans, when Mildred's mood and words shift to the evening's hot topic.

"How could you do that without consulting the two of us, John?"

Immediately John is set back on his hills by his mother's pointed and unexpected query. She had not voiced a dissenting opinion during the board meeting; in fact, if John had even thought about it a little, he would have noticed that she had been unusually quiet. He slowly pulls the sifter of Armagnac from his now-nervous lips.

"I thought . . ."

Mildred has quickly gone from zero to sixty.

"No, that's exactly what you didn't do, John, you didn't think at all."

Mildred is really upset. John thinks that her aggressive tone is clearly disproportionate to anything that he could have done. In fact, he doesn't recall having done anything at all wrong; he again is clueless.

"You didn't think, John, you acted out of some kind of frustration or anger. Now, look at what we have across the street."

John's body heats up instinctively, a knee-jerk reaction and defense from his being attacked; in his way of thinking, it is not germane. Actually, it is unimportant whether the attack is righteous or not; the fact is that he's being attacked at all, and he's not in the habit of tolerating such perceived abuse.

"Anger over what?"

The tone of his retort is more than a little huffy. As Mildred seems eager to retreat to a safer place, she fires a weaker shot than the first one.

"John, I have no idea from one moment to the next what makes you angry."

John's anger has piqued as he barks back at his mother, "That's nonsense, Mother. You know very damn well the kinds of things that make me angry."

Gladys has seen and heard enough. During their first few moments of combat, she peacefully sat there, sipping her brandy and puffing on her Cuban, seeming oblivious to the rancorous tête-à-tête taking place scant feet from her peace. She now gently puts down her cigar and sifter and slowly turns her wiry frame to face John and Mildred. And now in a soft yet resolute voice to match her disturbed mood, she clears her throat, and the room turns suddenly quiet.

"Excuse me? Whom do you think you're talking to like that?"

It's as if an anvil had fallen from the ceiling and hit him on the head, you know, like in those old cartoons. John's head dropped what seemed like a full foot from its once-lofty, haughty perch; at first, you could barely see his eyes until he looks up and shamefully mumbles through his crestfallen contrition, "I apologize, Mother Gladys."

It was like flipping a coin while being very familiar with the face up—side; you have not the foggiest notion as to what will appear on the tail side. That's how surprising it is to see John Smith reflect this new and unexpected attitude and posture. Mother Gladys, as he calls my mother, is like his Yoda—she really is. She raised him from the time he was in diapers just like she raised me. I watched her because I was there next to her for most of that time. I practically lived here from the time that I was a little boy until I went to school; I spent all of my time here in this baronial penthouse with my mother and the Smiths. We had an apartment uptown, but we were rarely there; mom and Mildred were rarely apart, and they did everything for each other. They could teach most people a thing or two about friendship and loyalty.

By the time I started school, down at the Little Red School House, in the Village—mom picked it, but Mildred paid for it. John was just beginning to walk then; it worked out perfectly. She could spend most of the day mothering John while I was at school.

At first, we would spend most of our weekends uptown; I could always tell that everyone was sad about that arrangement. It was not until after Mr. Smith died that Mom and I moved in for good, but, by then, I was already in high school at Hotchkiss, in Connecticut—again that was mom's choice—while John attended Collegiate, right here in Manhattan. I never knew why she always seemed to separate us in the world. It was her doing, I know; she ran the house. She taught us everything just alike, and for a long time, John and I were close, but he's never forgiven me for messing up and going to prison; he knows as well as anyone that I broke my mother's heart, and he's never forgiven me for that. It suffices to say their love runs deep for each other.

"Don't you Mother Gladys me, boy. I know I taught you better than that."

While John's head is down, totally out of respect, not fear, Gladys and Mildred give each other a quick glance and a smile.

"Now, John, you need to find a way to put back that blue-eyed falcon's nest. You hear me?"

There was no wiggle room left in this conversation, no room to negotiate a way out of this papal bull from on high; the penthouse pope had spoken.

"Okay, I'll get started on it tomorrow."

Reduced and defeated, John leaks a last whimper, like a little puppy, he whines his final limp complaint, "But you two don't have to put up with detritus falling on your heads."

Emboldened as always by Gladys's intervention, Mildred lofts a final response on the topic, "Oh, stop exaggerating, John. And besides, whatever falls from there is not a good enough reason to make those beautiful falcons homeless, you understand?"

John had not received the double-barreled attack in years, and now he's really smarting; they are quite a dynamic duo—those two a regular one-two punch. Defeated and subdued, John responds passively, "Yes, ma'am."

Both old girls smile at each other as a rejuvenated Mildred sends another ponderable in John's direction, "Now, what about Mrs. Tinkerton and the Russian?"

A new topic and new concerns, and an instantly revived John shifts gears smoothly like a Ferrari, and he goes from first to second without the slightest shift shock; it's business, of course, and John loves nothing better than doing business, of course—he's revived.

"Well, he wants to give her twenty million, two million over the eighteen million that she's asking for the unit."

This is a new topic that Mildred has a keen interest in; she is the building's largest stockholder by far, and it makes her quite a bit more than the building's titular matriarch, if you will. As such, she, along with John, wields an overwhelming majority of the co-op board votes, as the building, once owned by the family, turned co-op under her husband's astute and forward-thinking leadership, leaving her standing alone with 51 percent of the shares. With the addition of John's shares—and he because of their dominant shares is the permanent board president—virtually every decision made concerning the building's business had to flow through and be approved by them. It's not as if there is any history of divisiveness or dissension on the board or in the building because there hasn't been any of that; it's been pretty peaceful up 'till now.

Mildred is especially keen on this particular piece of business because she hasn't liked Margaret Tinkerton for some time now—actually, she hasn't liked her from the beginning, when she and her husband first moved into the building; she had nothing to do with that decision. Margaret Tinkerton was once a big Hollywood star, and her loud-mouthed, pipe-smoking husband—well, they're just not her kind of people. They had come into the building while Mr. Smith ran the show; he and Mr. Tinkerton at that time had a close business relationship and a friendship. So Mildred, as a dutiful wife, was obliged to tolerate them at that time, but her tolerance had long since worn way down after her husband's death. Now the two families were on the lukewarm cycle of their friendship—you know, the civil hellos and good-byes and the pleasant-have-a-nice-day kind of greetings, but nothing more than that.

"We know that, John, we were here at the board meeting to hear that same bit of news that you heard. But what we're asking is, what are you going to do about his threat? What was that she said, Gladys?"

And that's when John—already feeling a bit pummeled by the two partners in crime as they fed strongly off each other—stutters to give a decisive and convincing answer. Instead he whimpers and whines apologetically.

"It wasn't a threat, Mother. All Mrs. Tinkerton had said—and that by the way was even before the vote was cast to turn the Russian down, led by me I must add—was that he would be very unhappy if he were turned down. I didn't sense a threat, only that he would be disappointed. And besides, Mother, who wouldn't be disappointed to be turned away from our, the finest co-op anywhere."

Gladys gives a look skyward as she rolls her eyes and head back, taking a deep breath and counting to ten to keep from overreacting. While Mildred, this time the calmer of the two ladies, engages her son more directly, "Excuse me, but it certainly sounded like a threat to me—maybe it was nonspecific, but it made me sit up straight. John, you need to be careful, especially with that entire racket going on across the street at Central Park. We've really had enough celebrity brought to our home already with that movie actress living here; we really could use some time out of the spotlight. So two things: One, you need to get the falcon's nest back up or, in our case, back down there where it belongs. And the second thing, you must take care of this Russian-Tinkerton situation quickly before it mushrooms out of control as well."

All the while Mildred is scolding John, Gladys is nodding her head in rhythmic agreement and moans and hums uh-huh to signify her support. Clearly, these two distaff mentors have humbled John, but it's okay as they two are and have always been his rocks and greatest supporters. As he gathers himself from his comfortable chair, he rises and walks over to give both of his mother figures kisses on their respective cheeks; he loves them both dearly, and they clearly feel the same way about him. As he is leaving, he seems instantly better within a couple of steps from them, and as he turns, John says, "Again, thanks for dinner, ladies. The chicken stew was the big—hit surprise, but all the food was wonderful as usual."

Gladys laughs out loud.

"Well, we had to do something with all that chicken—it would have gone bad after a while; you can only keep it frozen for a short time before it's no good for man or beast. We should throw a party whenever we need to clean out that big old freezer that your father kept his venison in. That thing is so big, he used to keep a whole buck frozen in it and used the saws and carcass-hacking cleavers to cut and chop it into smaller sections. I miss his venison."

Gladys pines effusively; yet Mildred, on the other hand, is not quite as sentimental, and good feeling about her late husband as upbeat Gladys is, not nearly so; she chimes in corrosively, "Yes, well, that's the only thing worth missing about him."

Mildred's acerbic retort takes John by surprise.

"What was that, Mother?"

Mildred recovers quickly as it was clear she had disturbed John, and she wasn't in any mood to be traveling down a rock-and-pothole-strewn memory lane road with him, not now at least. He knew little about his father's secret abuses that the two women were themselves too well acquainted with, but this wasn't the time for that particular skeleton to be yanked out of their dark and cluttered closet.

55

"Oh, nothing, son. I was just thinking out loud."

John begins again to walk toward the elevator when he turns abruptly to toss a final query at the two women, "I thought you two had gotten rid of that old freezer, and those hideous carcass-carving tools . . ."

John shivers to think about them as he is standing there traveling down his own separate version of memory lane.

"When I was a boy, those things used to frighten the hell out of me, especially the way he used to whale away at those needlessly slaughtered animals. It's not like we were pioneers, and we needed to kill for food. It was gruesome, the way the blood splattered all over the place. It was so very gross. Eek! And besides, with that rubber apron and that noise from the cutting, sawing, and chopping, it was like something out of a horror movie."

As John walks the rest of the way to the elevators, neither Mildred nor Gladys responds to his query concerning the freezer. Finally, he presses the button, and the elevator door immediately opens; he enters, turns, and waves good-bye. As the door closes, the two women stare softly and wordlessly at each other, each one knowing far too well the other one's secret and being quite sanguine and sated in that fact. And now John, alone in the elevator and alone with his own thoughts, ponders his missions as directed by his mothers.

At the Plaza Hotel, in one of its most expensive suites, one male, one female sit, one facing the other in this exquisite yet formidable setting, and where the baron can view clearly through the large windows of his lofty rented perch facing Fifth Avenue, the building and home of his future desire across the street and slightly up the road a piece. It's he and Mrs. Margaret Tinkerton, setting tête-à-tête, one aggressive, the other cloaked in guile, both wanting.

"Oh no, Baron, you have been more than generous. This is not some ploy for more money. As I told you at the beginning, the sale would be upon condition of the board's approval. Believe me, I am more than a little unnerved by this result. I had no idea that they would react this way, but, damn it, my hands are tied unless we can somehow get them to reconsider."

The Russian is not amused; this is America, and money changes everything. He stares a long, harsh stare at Mrs. Tinkerton as he ponders his next words and future move.

"Yes, yes, I hear you, Mrs. Tinkerton, but you said that the board's vote was just a formality."

Mrs. Tinkerton thinks fast; she knows she must come up with something. Hoping to put the onus on the baron, she alludes to an untruth.

"Yes, Boris, but they didn't like what they turned up . . . huh, I mean come on now, Baron. Baron?" she squeaks the last *baron* with the shrilled voice of incredulity.

The corpulent yet wily Russian is a sly dog, and an old dog at that; he's full of tricks and guile and has no compunction to restrict his acquisitions or the nature that stimulates them. Me thinks that's called greed. He looks Mrs. Tinkerton right square in the eyes, and without as much as a blink, he says,

"What's in a name, Mrs. Tinkerton? You were once a whore, but this America, where everything is possible, yes?"

Margaret Tinkerton is shocked, but she is quite the dog herself, a fox, I think we'll call her; she coolly stiffens in her seat.

"What do you think you know about me, Baron Romanovsky?"

She almost chokes as she says his bogus name with a new resolve while she herself is now skating on the thin ice of total exposure and its commensurate embarrassment.

The Russian is about to crown himself king in a game of chess, for which Russian's are known worldwide for their mastery. He smiles demonically at the point of checkmating his overmatched foe.

"It is my business to know everything about the people I am to do business with, Carol Perkins. I mean Mrs. Tinkerton. You were a Hollywood street hooker before Mr. Tinkerton, who's no Peter Pan himself, picked you up off the street and groomed you into a soap opera sitcom legend. As I said, it's my business to be well-informed. Shall I go on?"

For the first time Margaret or Carol or whatever her name really is—she looses her cool as she reaches up and flips her four-hundred-dollar straw hat back on her head. The gloves are off, but it's clear she's got the smaller fists. Margaret sits back in her seat; she takes a beat like a good actress should before saying an important line.

"All right, so I'm no Virgin Queen, but, Boris, you're no baron either."

Boris lets out the most milk-curdling sinister laugh you've ever heard, but it is clear he is only half-amused. He too adjusts in his seat as he turns to look out over Fifth Avenue at the co-op of his dreams, his dream at least for now. He stares quietly for maybe a minute, and then he turns back to Margaret Tinkerton; he stares at her with his cold, dark, Russian eyes, then he clears his throat, and says, "Look, Margaret, I want your house and you need my money. I know about your husband's gambling debts, too . . ."

He laughs again—this time it's derisive. He knows she's in a bind, and she'd like to make this deal with anyone sooner or later, but the sooner the better as was just revealed in the Russian's disclosing her husband's thought to be secret gambling indebtedness. And Boris is, right now, the only player in the picture for her expensive abode.

"Now, how are we going to make this deal happen? This whole thing is really . . . what is it that you Americans say?"

He thinks for a moment.

"Oh yes, I now know what it is they say . . . they say that this thing is really starting to piss me off."

CHAPTER IV

The Fifth Avenue traffic below is muffled out of existence by the height of the room from the street, the thickness of the walls, and, yes, the latest in soundproof energy-efficient replacement windows. And, in the quiet of her bedroom, that's not the only thing that has been muffled out of existence. Here now are two that have muffled trust and loyalty out of existence; Nancy Smith is lying naked in bed with me, Albert Lawrence. Our frolicking is often the very thing that fuels the rage behind many a domestic murder—I'm all too certain of that—and the lack of discretion flaunting, at least on Mrs. Smith's part, with a very careless devil-may-care attitude every moment is begging to be caught. Now, where does that leave her, dupe, me, Albert Lawrence? She, Nancy Smith, her billions withstanding, on the street would be called a hottie; so there's no question that she could have her pick of men—and that leads directly to the reason, I, Albert Lawrence, got leveraged into this tryst in the first place. I was thinking that one day with the one-track mind of Little Albert from down there in his basement boiler room of over heated pipes, instead of the Albert from the penthouse, who sees and thinks much better, and whose powers of discerning are much more mature and developed—but yet now the words whimper in this bed of lust turned bed of tears. "I've had enough. I can't do this any longer." Her voice rang this singular alarm.

It seemed that my time was up for this encounter, so I rolled over to the edge of the bed and sat as my feet dangled over the side of this lofty mount. For me, this little diversion had gone on quite long enough; in truth, I really don't know how I allowed myself to get in this far. It's been . . . now let me think. I guess it's been about a good ten years since that first time; I remember it now as I close my eyes, thinking back. It was springtime; I know because I had my green uniform on. Her limo had pulled up at the front, and I had walked out to give her a hand with the car door, of course, and it turned out that she had gone shopping, a lot of shopping, and there were packages everywhere. I didn't know why since there were so many that she hadn't had them delivered any way. There were, of course, more packages and bags than she could handle herself, and before she could even ask, I had offered to take them up to her place myself; she said yes.

So finally, I get all of the packages up there; I couldn't believe one person could shop that much in one afternoon, but then I figured she must be bored, as her husband, John Smith, was out of town on an extended business trip; it was a big, important real estate acquisition he was doing in Florida—Mildred and Gladys had told me all about it.

You see, although John and I had grown up together—literally, until I went off to high school at Hotchkiss—we were actually pretty good friends for a while back then. But after my stupidity with those checks and my ultimate imprisonment . . . after that, he would have nothing to do with me, absolutely nothing. It wasn't for such a bad reason either—because with all my shenanigans, I had hurt others along with myself, probably some more than myself, if that's possible. And the person that he himself first witnessed that I had hurt the most was my mother, whom he calls Mother Gladys because she's always been like a mother to him. In fact, if truth be known, she raised him; she raised us both. She probably, in her own inimitable way, raised the entire family of Smiths and Lawrences.

Well, that's why in a nutshell, we, John Smith and I, have the relationship that we have, or the lack of a relationship; we are by no means strangers to each other. And so on this day, I am standing in his apartment; it's beautiful like every other apartment in this oasis of luxury on Fifth Avenue. It is, however, much more on the eclectic side, and I think I must attribute that to Nancy more than John. John only thinks about work, building, and buying, while Nancy thinks only about . . . well, let's put it this way: Nancy is a twenty-first century hedonist. She only thinks about things and people that pleasure her.

So now I'm standing there in their foyer, piling packages chest high on top of each other, when she comes out of the kitchen with a tray filled with drinks; I thought that at first a strange sight. But Nancy Smith is all smiles and cheer.

"Oh no no no, Albert, you can't leave them here, who's going to carry them into the closet where they belong?"

It seemed at the time a not-too-curious observation for which I felt reasonably compelled to rectify. So I began taking them toward, actually, in the direction that she walked still holding the tray of drinks. Now that was even more curious as she never mentions them; she just carries them like some pet lapdog out in front of her chest. Let me say now, and I'm sure that most men will understand that this is a fine woman, a fine-looking and high-quality woman. She moves like a woman should, she smiles like a woman will, and in the confines and environs of a quiet and beautiful apartment like this, and on Fifth Avenue too, well, let me tell you. All the images of chase and conquest, love and lust begin to rumble in my primitive belly as I follow behind her sultry feminine form, and as her behind moves and fluffs gently like little soft pillows beneath the curved lines of her dress, she must know what she's doing to me—she must know that. And as I peek around from behind the packages and boxes to make certain that I don't lose the trail, my body heats up from the exertion of carrying the weight and her presence in front of me in this now-very-provocative setting. I knew then that if she wanted me, I was easy prey; and as it turned out, both things were as true as she is beautiful.

I had felt it from her for some long time going into this moment. She was that kind of woman. She made every man want her; it was her cachet, her web, her self-assigned greatest appeal—which in getting to know her, this truth was far from her only or best truth, but on this day it was indeed all I valued and all I could think of when walking behind her.

As we finally turned into the closet, I inadvertently bumped into a Giacometti statue—what is it with wealthy people and their Giacomettis, are they *des rigueur*? Anyway, I bumped into this millions-dollar statue, and she doesn't even bat an eye. When she finally stopped and nodded, I knew she meant for me to rest the boxes where she indicated, and as soon as I did, she in turn placed the tray on top of the boxes. As she did, and without as much as a word, she takes my hand, she lifts it to her chest, and places it upon her firm yet unenhanced breast. I thought I would melt, oh yes, Jesus—there is a god. From then on, we were closer in all ways than we had been at any time before this time.

And now it's this time again, and my feet are about to hit the floor. I was never one to assume that a single gift was an endowment for life, and even though this gift—giving has lasted this long, its termination was a certainty. If this was the moment, then I was sanguine and thankful for her largess. So as I heard her words, I would not be telling the truth if I said I was not for the moment surprised, but my life had prepared me for sudden changes, especially when tenure is denied.

But as I slide compliantly forward to walk away, get dressed, and take my leave; Nancy grabs me by the shoulder, and with her athletic grip—born of weight training, yoga, and Pilates—she slams me back down on the mattress of her king-size bed.

"Albert, where are you going?"

I was shocked, attacked from behind; she hadn't been this playful in months. Now I'm looking up at her. Her face is in my face, and she's not smiling; in fact, she had her serious hurt face on, and it was then that I knew that I had misjudged the moment. But I didn't want to deal with whatever was behind that sharp look on her face; I really didn't want to hear it. Yes, see, as I said before, I have no tenure here, and sometimes that's good. It's like two nations—say the old Soviet Union and the United States—they build these huge nuclear arsenals as mutual deterrents; it's not about getting married, or even harmony, but it is about keeping the other one honest, if not actually peaceful. That's what being in an affair and having no tenure is all about, and I wanted to keep my arsenal that supports our permanent détente—no insurmountable hostilities on either side, as it were and has been for ten years now. So with that in mind, I answered her with what I do admit now was a kind of fraudulent naiveté.

"You just said you had enough," I said, but instantly I could feel her body quicken with a kind of irritated stiffening, and as it began to squirm with discomfort, it was clear that I had taken the wrong tack. I was escalating when what I really wanted to do was to extinguish the mounting tension between us erstwhile lovers; our time has passed, and what remains is just a ritual of lust's boredom and habit. She's still a fine-looking woman—there's no question—but her mind has long since gone elsewhere. It was hot in the beginning—I could feel it then; it was exciting for both of us. When we'd meet at different out-of-the-way places for our rendezvous, it was storybook and steamy; that was all in the beginning, though, at least five years ago now. But, sometimes, when a woman gets going on one of these emotional excursions, the best a man can hope for is a safe ride and to hold on for the unpredictable journey; it's not really the ride that's so unpredictable because with a woman a man is always on a ride for sure. But it is the destination that often remains in question, and this time, really, I had no idea where we were headed.

So with that, she rises up and slides closer to my still-unclothed body; I for certain feel exposed because her moving closer was clearly not for amorous purposes or intent.

"Albert, what the hell is wrong with you? I wasn't talking about you leaving, don't you get it? Don't you know what's going on here?"

Now it's my turn to stiffen up; I don't think I like where this fast-moving train is headed. It's taking an old turn, so old that the tracks are rusted over as the concomitant squeaking increases. I needed to bail.

"Look, Mrs. Smith, I am your doorman, and I___."

Men are fools, and I freely admit my birthright to this particular flaw. What more insulting, degrading, reductive, and humiliating moniker to attach to a lover—even if, in fact, it does belong to her, this is not the circumstance in which she needs to be reminded of that. Mrs. Smith—what an idiot I am. This is what running for cover induces from the weak. I just grabbed the first thing I could think of as I tried to flee the inevitable. I called her Mrs. Smith—what a fool. But that's why I postulated earlier that you never know what the destination is, and sometimes the destination shapes the journey.

She all but ignored my obvious faux pas; I hadn't called her Mrs. Smith in private in ten years, in fact, not since that day in her closet when I, in the heat and throes of passion, repeated it over and over—"Oh, Mrs. Smith, Mrs. Smith, Mrs. Smith!" But now she had her sights on a different destination, and she was not going to be denied because of my nervousness with the approaching terminus right up ahead.

Nancy, the name I most frequently called her now—in more heated times, I called her more heated names; but now it was Nancy or nothing, just grunts or throat-clearing affectionate animalistic growls.

We were used to each other. Now, don't get me wrong—I was still, and always thought I would be, quite fond of her. I'm sure if I had gone to a psychiatrist, a psychologist, or someone who understands these things, they would have immediately pointed out that this relationship, almost from the start, was some kind of warped play against my once good friend, John Smith, who, because of my misstep, had all but totally abandoned me. I, of course, would have at first denied any such notion; I was clearly above any such kind of feral retribution. But there was that evidence always lurking about. She was his wife, and he had rejected me.

But she is on a mission now, and even I can't get in my own way to save myself. Then, all of sudden, Nancy pounces; she literally takes one big bounce on the king-size mattress, as if hurdling from a trampoline, and she lands squarely on my chest. Now she's really looking down on me. This is really strange, because you'd think that, from her actions, she would be more animated afterward, but she's not; well, at first she wasn't, but then after sitting there on my chest for a quiet moment, she begins to pick up steam as she points her little finger directly at my nose.

"Albert, you are a fool, you know? A big fool you have been, and you have been a fool for the last ten years. Haven't you been paying attention? For the last ten years you have been the only man in my life that's given a hoot about me, and that's the absolute truth. You know everything about me—you know my schedule, my favorite outfits, you even know all of my favorite things. You remember my birthdays, always, and you never fail to pick me up when I am down. You are my best friend, Albert. What do you think, do you think that after all we have shared together that you are just my fucking doorman?"

I couldn't help smiling as Nancy growled that last part. I guess it was rhetorical as her quixotic patience wore suddenly out as she growled again, "Well, do you?"

I wanted to say do I what, but I dared not. Sadly and in truth, nothing more substantial did come to mind.

"Well . . ."

That was all I could muster as I stared back into her now-bulging eyes; her mood suddenly changes. She bursts into laughter at her own humor as she rolls over and off my chest.

"My fucking doorman . . . you get it, Albert, my fucking doorman?"

Nancy is real clever. I knew that she didn't think that "my fucking doorman" comment was all that funny, but she was trying to lighten my mood, seeing as I had gone all shucks on her. I just stared back at her. I wasn't about to give her what she was angling for; this was not the first time she had gone through this poor-me charade, and I didn't want to get caught up in it. She's done this trip before; it must be that time of the month. Finally, the truth comes rushing back when I don't take the bait and as she turns serious again.

"Well, do you, Albert?"

I stutter, "Well___."

She jumps all over my pause.

"Well—what, Albert? Do you think I care what you do for a living? I'm already loaded. I don't need you to support me, Albert. I care about who you are, and you've proven for ten long years what kind of man you are. Don't you understand, Albert? I need you to take care of me, like a man takes care of a woman. This is not some schoolgirl crush, or some floozy's fantasy. Is that what you think it is, Albert?"

I know what's coming next; she's going to question my sanity in some way. I watch her as she clears her throat; she's not finished yet.

"Don't tell me you didn't know or suspect this, Albert."

Bingo, she's right there on time with it, and now I have to play along. Once, some years ago, I made the mistake of telling Nancy that she had gone through this and had said all of this already. What a huge mistake; she blasted me. I've since learned that this emotional thing she goes through is very real to her; it's like some kind of purge, a self-exorcism, if that's even possible, but she goes through it cyclically. I never know when it's coming, and sometimes it is more intense than at other times. So I play along.

"Mrs. Smith, you've never said anything before."

She quips back instantly, "Said anything? Albert, who do you think I am? Do you think I haven't thought about this for years now? What did you expect me to do? Did you expect me to rattle around like a penny in an empty shoe box every time something shakes me? Well, did you, Albert?"

Remember, I've been through this before, many times. So I say, "But you never said___."

"I've given this moment years of thought, Albert, and I'm bringing it to you now. Albert, you're the man, Albert . . . right? Or aren't you?"

This was the perfect time for me to make my exit; timing is everything. So I sit up again—while she contemplates something extraterrestrial—and I put my uniform back on while she stares at me. She's not really seeing me. I know that look of hers; her mind is already elsewhere. I feel like such a whore now as I walk toward the bedroom door; I'm feeling like I really don't want to be doing this anymore. I walk through the door and leave without another word being spoken between us.

Some few days later, as I was standing in the lobby behind the concierge, Dennis Dillon comes walking in many hours earlier than usual. He's obviously coming from work because he has his briefcase at his side. I'm really not that fond of Mr. Dillon, as I've already stated my reasons; but he is, after all, one of the stockholders in this building, and I must treat him with the accorded respect as I do everyone else.

"Good afternoon, Mr. Dillon, home early today?"

My voice lilts naturally at the end of an inquisitive sentence, and he clearly mistakes it for a pleasantry and a prelude to welcomed conversation, which it indeed was not. But it was too late as he—in his all too high-toned voice—proceeds to tell me his reasons for being home this early. I listened respectfully.

"Yes, Albert, I thought that I would surprise Amy. It is her birthday today, did you know this, Albert?"

I, of course, knew it was Amy's birthday. I always make sure to give her a little something on her birthday. So I answer him more subdued than I'd really like to answer him; with a fake smile of acknowledgement on my face, I say, "Yes, I know, sir."

You know, I say that I don't like him, but it's really because of the way he neglects his family. It's not even because I think him an odious and genetically bad person; it's just that . . . well, he's so goofy it's difficult to hate on him.

"I know you know, Albert, it is really all of your fault in the first place, Albert."

I'm surprised.

"I beg your pardon, sir."

"No, Albert, it is a good thing. I saw the birthday card and flowers that you bought for her yesterday. You see, I never had to remember her birthday before; Jessie always took care of that. But now that she is traveling the world, things fall through the cracks. I have ordered some balloons and clowns to surprise her. They should be here before she gets home from school. I called them to learn what time she gets out, I did not know that either, I guess I could have called on you for that information as well, couldn't I have, Albert. Let me know as soon as they arrive, Albert, all right?"

I must admit I was very surprised that for an almost total incompetent, as far as a father and husband were concerned, this was in fact quite a nice thing he was doing—none too late—for his daughter's birthday. This time I smiled genuinely; it was going to be great for Amy to experience this from her father, no matter what the source of the stimulus was.

"Yes, sir, Mr. Dillon, I'll let you know as soon as they arrive."

I have to admit that I was now jittery standing there waiting for the balloons and clowns to arrive. And when they finally did, they looked great, but then I thought that maybe they were a bit old hat for a sixteen-year-old girl—but you know, what do I know? It is crystal clear that I don't understand older women, or women my own age, so what in the world would make me think that I know what's going on in a young woman's mind? Anyway, I called up to Mr. Dillon.

"Yes, sir, Mr. Dillon. The clowns are all here, shall I, shall I send them all up now?"

I had done it none too soon, for merely minutes later, into the lobby strolls Amy Dillon, arm in arm with her beau Rufus. They are always so happy together. I don't have to ask because Amy long ago already told me that her father doesn't know about her boyfriend, Rufus. Amy is all smiles, and as I've met Rufus sometime ago, he too gives me a cheerful hello.

"Good afternoon, Little Ms Sunshine."

"Hi, Albert," she says as she only half-sees me; she is too, too taken with Rufus. But I need to warn her; it's this loyalty thing, you know. I feel very, very loyal to Amy and her mom; they both deserve better, and if I—as I now do—see a danger approaching, I am obliged to give a heads-up. So I motion Amy over to the concierge—she leaves Rufus's side for the moment—and I lean over to tell her what's in the offing.

"What's up, Albert?"

I speak softly so as not to alarm her or Rufus. I'm not trying to start anything; I just don't want there to be any unnecessary bad emotion-laden feelings bandied about before cooler heads can prevail, if I can help it.

"Your father's home. He's waiting for you upstairs with a big birthday surprise."

Amy is instantly surprised, and she recoiled as if she's been shot out of a circus cannon.

"What could be a bigger surprise than him being home, Albert?"

She is quickly away from the desk and at Rufus's side in a flash; she grabs his arm and begins to tug him toward the door.

"Thanks, Albert, don't tell him that you saw me, okay . . . Let's go, Rufus."

Rufus quickly glances at me, and he gives me that "What did you say to her to make her react this way" look. But then, the young man stops the show. He's an athletic and rather muscular young man, and Amy is no match for his superior strength; he stops and stands still, and finally she stops trying to move this immovable object.

"What's going on, Amy?"

Amy's charade at keeping her father and boyfriend apart has met for the first time at the juncture of Prolonged Deceit and Moment of Truth—two normally divergent roads; she knows now that she has to choose her next steps carefully.

"My father's upstairs now; he's waiting for me with a birthday surprise."

If Rufus was so cool, it would have been a stretch to say he was gleeful, but in point of fact, it was clear that he was pleased to hear that Amy's father was finally at home when he had come to visit; he had wanted to meet him. Rufus smiles, but you can tell that it's a hesitant smile because he senses a shoe is about to drop and spoil his premature joy. He flashes a look at me, and then he turns again to Amy.

"So what's the problem, Amy?" he says with an edge of knowing anxiety, the kind of educated anxiety that comes from having had similar experiences that come with the black territory that his visage consistently confines him to. Amy turns red as she is about to reveal what may be a costly secret. It was clear from the first when I was introduced to Rufus that they were both very fond of each other, and so it would follow that any indiscretion, however minor, emanating from either side was bound to hurt quite disproportionately to its size; that's why the red face. I could tell—as I had known her since birth and had experienced her every mood—that Amy was now experiencing a lump of guilt caught in her throat. But to her credit, red faced, guilt-ridden, and all, she spoke right up, "He doesn't know about you yet, Rufus."

Rufus—in an action contrary to what Amy might have thought his reaction would be—then smiles, and he takes her hand; the young man is very smooth. But it's Amy that shows her age, or better yet, her fear as she pulls away from Rufus.

"What do you mean, Rufus?"

Rufus's attitude changes abruptly; as Amy pulls away from him, he senses a moment of rejection. He seems to swell in his muscular young frame as he takes in a full breath and readies himself to speak to answer Amy's query, "What? You don't think I knew you were trying to hide me from your folks by telling me they were on safari in Africa?"

Amy's defensive position is suddenly shattered as she acquiesces. She comes back with a somewhat tepid yet witty rejoinder, "Well, that was half-true, my mother really is on safari in Africa."

Kids in love are something, a model to us all, I'm sure; if we'd only take a closer look at them sometime we'd see the utter freedom in which they live. The two of them care so greatly for each other, and is it clear that prolonged anger is just not one of their options; I see this quite apparently in the speed with which they return to harmony. Rufus smiles broadly and says softly as he again reaches out for Amy's hand; she, this time, lets him take it as they squeeze them together.

"Yeah, but not your dad, right?"

Then Amy, like a little bird, warbles a wonderful high-pitched trill and a characteristic unmistakable giggle—that she's possessed since she was a baby in her mother's arms—follows closely right behind it; I know them both so well because it shocked me the first time I heard them.

"That's right, you busted me. My dad's not on safari, he's upstairs waiting to spring some sort of pathetic birthday surprise on me. He only knows it's my birthday because of Albert, who never forgets. Come on, Rufus, let's go, Rufus."

Amy attempts to pull Rufus from the lobby, but the rock will not budge.

"No, no, it's not going to be like that . . ."

Rufus pauses for a moment as if he knows to cool his roll, like the old-timers used to say—to slow down and stop wolfing the young lady. It's clear Amy has quite a decision to make here and now, and he intuits that he should not push too hard on her. When he starts up again, he is much calmer as he knows what's at stake. "It's your choice now, Amy, because I'm not hiding out from your dad."

Amy harrumphs.

"What is that supposed to mean, Rufus?"

Even the change in his tone did not elicit the exact response he was looking for. But Rufus stays calm as he smiles his toothiest smile yet.

"You know what it means, Amy. We need to face this together."

I know this little passion play probably doesn't mean much to those of you on the outside of this little lobby scene, but to these kids, and on this day, this is their whole life. Everything that they will, going forward, feel about themselves will flow from how they each handle this very moment. I know it must sound a little far-fetched, but it's moments like these—especially when we're young like Rufus and Amy—that determine how we deal with a whole host of situations and moments for the rest of our lives; not immutably, but quite defining and determining. Amy then hesitates long enough to make a quick yet resolute decision; she turns around and tugs Rufus's arm toward the elevator. And as she walks away, she takes a quick glance in my direction as our eyes meet; she smiles softly as I nod my head approvingly. And then I hear her mumble to no one in particular,

"Well, I guess we're all going to have big surprises on my birthday."

CHAPTER V

I t's a tall Mies van der Rohe-inspired glass and metal midtown Manhattan office building, a perfect setting for a John Smith kind of man, all business he is. It is the end of another successful day of business—well, at least the office part; he will likely continue on late into the night on the phones and computer, speaking, text messaging, and e-mailing to Europe, Asia, and other parts of North America, making deals well into the wee hours 'till the next morning. He's like the Napoleon Bonaparte of the world of real estate barons; he sleeps very little and is always on a campaign to conquer and change the pieces on the Monopoly board to his favor. As he exits the elevator at the street level of this modern monument to austerity, he and his entourage of assistants and vice presidents trailing him to the lobby of one of his many properties, whose environ is as unadorned as he is fastidious—it too is neatly furnished with strategically placed Mies Barcelona table, chair, and ottoman sets of varying colors: red, white, and blue—four sets to be exact.

As he passes effortlessly, yet characteristically determined through the medium-size lobby, he eventually sheds his faithful entourage as he finally exits alone through the revolving glass doors. On the other side of the revolving glass door, at the curb, sits a large black car, where three men sit in wait for someone. They are three rather foreign-looking men, and two of them are larger than the third; they two are of the hulking bodyguard variety. From inside the car, the smaller, but not small man of the three foreign-looking men speaks. "That's him, Oleg. Go and tend to him."

And that's when one of the two hulking men exits the front door of the large black car, and he walks over to where John Smith is now standing. He looms so large over John Smith that he creates a shadow of shelter from the sun like a big shade tree would if it had been planted there instead of him.

Smith is surprised, but his natural haughtiness does not let him give in to this fleeting emotion. The large man leans slightly forward as he bends to ask, in his deep, heavily accented, Russian bass voice, "Sir, you are Mr. Smith, yes?"

John Smith is surprised in an arrogant sort of way as he throws his head back at an angle, which raises his chin on an angle—even from his higher position, it must feel to the Russian that Smith is looking down at him. It takes but two words for Smith to gain the upper hand: "Who asking?"

The large man is taken aback for a second as his body actually shifts and then tilts backward, but then he quickly recovers as he announces himself, "I am Oleg Demetriyevich, and I am asking for Baron Romanovsky's."

As he turns his massive body toward the large black car, he—with his outreached hand—shows John Smith the way to the car. Mr. Smith doesn't give up that easily, and he acts as if no motion has been made toward the car; he then pretends not to have seen his action as he answers only to Oleg's spoken words. He smiles arrogantly as he finally answers to Oleg's assignation, "So you know my name, lots of people know my name, it's not that difficult to learn. I don't know any baron____."

Smith pauses as the name rings a bell in his head.

"Oh, wait . . . Baron Romanovsky."

Smith then looks toward the car for the first time as Oleg smiles happily.

"You do know the baron, yes?"

Smith then bends slightly at the waist to better look through the rear window of the big black Rolls-Royce, and the baron then lowers the rear window to expose his face from behind the obscurity created by the tinted glass. Smith nods as he walks over to the car.

"Okay, okay, I'll play along. Nice car, Baron. How can I help you?"

Then from behind, Oleg walks over and opens the rear door to the car. From inside, the Baron Romanovsky sits imperiously, which must suit John Smith just fine, as there must be an instant haughty kinship immediately established between the two self-important men. The baron—sitting on the far side of the rear seat—leans ever so slightly forward, and speaks. "Mr. Smith, I would very much like to have a few words with you, sir, if you have a moment."

Smith hesitates, not out of fear, for there is nothing to fear, but as he is always on his way to doing something else, he is acutely aware that this little detour is certain to put him off schedule. But after a moment of thought, he considers and accepts the offer.

Smith steps forward and gets into the backseat of the car; and as he does, Oleg quickly—or as quickly as a man his size is able to move—slides in beside him, sandwiching him between himself and the Baron Romanovsky. Now for the first time, John Smith is nervous, or at least he's uncomfortable enough to realize that he's not in control of this situation.

In the lobby, Albert calls out to Amy just before she enters the elevator with Rufus.

"I'll have to call up to tell your father that you're on the way up so he can have everything ready for you."

Amy for some reason stops in her tracks. It seems like she thought that maybe she could surprise her dad first before he surprised her.

"Do you have to, Albert?"

Rufus has no intentions of letting this moment past as he quickly pulls Amy into the elevator.

"Come on, girl, let the man do his job."

Inside the Dillon apartment, Amy's father, Dennis, puts down the house phone as he hurries the clowns to their stations. There are multicolored balloons everywhere, bumping into all of the hanging and standing art on every wall and in every corner like some kind of art gallery museum. They are all standing there, ten feet from the elevator doors with their makeup and smiles on their faces and balloons in their hand. When the elevator door opens to a cheery greeting of surprise by the clowns and Dennis Dillon and as Rufus and Amy exit the elevator, they are shocked by the presence of such a colorful cadre of folks. But they both know that this is the surprise that Albert has already warned them about, and indeed, there is no faking here—they really are surprised.

It is very noisy now, and everyone is all smiles: the clowns, Amy, and Rufus, and at first, standing in the back of the clowns smiling along with everyone else is Dennis Dillon himself.

But then his point of view, everything abruptly changes, and his toothy smile gives quickly and suddenly way to an unexpected sight; it is surprising, but it is in fact his daughter, Amy, having already exited the elevator and is now standing there in the middle of the foyer, but she is not alone. In fact, she is with a person that he has never seen before. This scene in and of itself is not so very strange, but it is clear from their proximity to each other—the two of them standing so closely together—that they are more than just school buddies or friends. Amy is holding tightly on to Rufus;

clearly they are more than just friends. Dennis is instantly unhappy with this scene, and he is determined to get to the bottom of it right then and there. So he puts an instant halt to what is to him a clearly indiscreet and unwelcome relationship that has appeared without notice right there in his own house. He acts quite emotionally, given the situation; his outburst could have easily waited and taken a temporary backset to the birthday festivities.

"Wait. Stop! Stop! Stop! What's going on here, Amy?"

He literally yells at the top of his incredulous voice, and all the festivities—the smiles, the laughter, the singing of "Happy Birthday"—they all stop suddenly and at once. The clowns then pivot to their rear with their now-turned-down smiles, and as they stare at the emotional Dennis Dillon, he without hesitation or discretion, takes several steps between the cluster of balloons and clowns toward where the shocked Amy and Rufus are standing. Dennis Dillon stops two full steps in front of the couple. Leaving room for late-found discretion or the fact that now he can see the muscularity and athletic build on Rufus, he has smartly shied away from putting himself so close to possible physical danger in the form of this young black man's possible retaliation against his all-too-verbose antics. He looks straight at his daughter this time when he speaks: "Explain this to me, Amy. Who is this boy, and what is he doing here with you like this?"

Rufus is not impressed by the man's anger, nor is he in the least bit afraid of it; the proof of that fact is immediately on exhibit as he steps forward one strong step and offers his hand to the distraught father of his girlfriend. Rufus, in fact, towers over the smaller white man; as he gently yet confidently extends his large black hand, Dennis Dillon is pained to reject it—coming from this highly mannered world, although his outburst would have just signaled for the moment the contrary. All motion stops as the balloons—seemingly in a timely salute to the dramatic and conciliatory gesture of the moment—float silently up to the high ceiling. The clowns look on, like the happy faces of a Greek chorus, as all attention and sound are held in abeyance awaiting Dennis Dillon's next move; but it's Rufus, not Dennis Dillon, who breaks the stalemate of silence, first with his best toothy smile and then with his words.

"Hello, sir. I am Rufus Kingston. It's so very good to finally meet you, sir. Amy couldn't wait for us to get together. She has told me so much about you and Mrs. Dillon. I hope her safari is going well. My mom went to Kenya on safari last year, and she really loved it."

Now the balloons are not the only things dangling in the rarified air of the Dillon foyer as all eyes turn again to the father awaiting his attitude and response.

The black car has left the city in silence, and as they drive in the late-afternoon/ early—evening traffic along the Palisades Parkway, looking back and across you can see the beautiful New York City skyline passing along the other side of the Hudson. John Smith has become a veritable Russian sandwich as he sits squished between the two Russians, Boris on the one side and the massive Oleg Demetriyevich on the other side, who actually, because of his girth, causes John Smith to move even closer to the menacing Boris Romanovsky. Wise is the fool who knows enough to keep his mouth shut, and that's exactly what John Smith has done ever since he determined that he had been a fool to have ever entered this den of menace on very expensive wheels. Finally, Boris breaks the long uncomfortable silence, "We know about Gladys and Mildred, and a__."

And then the driver, Borga, interrupts and adds his two cents: "And we even know that your son, Jeffrey, he's away at the Andover school, yes?"

John Smith tries to maintain his composure, hoping to get calmly through this litany of pronouncements that so accurately delivered arrows to pierce his family's safety, or safety no more, as it were. As he stiffens in his seat, he thinks for sure that if they know this much about him and his family, how much more do they know; and, more to the point, what is it that they plan to do with this knowledge? And lastly, as if to nail the final nail in his all-but-sealed coffin, Oleg, sitting next to him, nudges him with one of his huge elbows, and, as if they are buddies sitting together chatting in a steam bath, he leans into John Smith as he smiles through his days-old beard stubble that renders his face darker and more foreboding than ever necessary given the ridiculous scariness of his massive bulk—. He speaks by far the worst English of the three Russians.

"Oh yes, and the lovely Nancy Smith, your wife, she take every morning, like the clock, she goes to her yoga classes in her tights at ten o'clock. She looks very well, your wife, she does, yes?"

John Smith can hold on to his cool no longer; he lurches forward trying to clear himself from his pinched-in position. And as he frees his shoulders, he slides to the edge of the seat and turns to face their leader, the Baron Romanovsky. And that's just what he calls him, being careful so as not to cause a rift where there is none. But his tongue at first runs away from his good sense as he spouts out, "What the hell do you want from me and my family, Baron Romanovsky? I'll pay anything you want, just leave them all be."

His plea invariably gets a rise out of the Russian, who laughs deeply and loudly, followed closely by similar outbursts from his two henchmen. Smith is shaken as he can immediately see that his offer hasn't impressed them in the least.

"Oh, Mr. Smith, do not become nervous. We can make more money in one year than you can make in a lifetime—we pay no taxes. Besides, Mr. Smith, we make good neighborhood even better for you and your family."

That was it; suddenly, it hit him what they really wanted, and it has nothing really to do with his family and really little to do with him personally. John Smith realizes, in truth, and at least for the moment he is relived by his percipient discovery, as he blurts out unabashedly,

"The Tinkerton place. You want the Tinkerton place."

Baron Romanovsky nods affirmatively, and like a chameleon he emerges childlike; he turns on the charm that is so well—hidden beneath his menace. As he gestures softly with his large, outstretched hands, it is clear that even with his not-so-veiled threats looming over their near—kidnapping of Mr. Smith, it is in the end John Smith who holds the final power over who gets into the building. He begs.

"Please, Mr. John Smith, we are asking you to reconsider my application and very fair offer for apartment. I still pay top dollar, yes? I promise we make better neighbors than enemy."

Smith, forgetting his compromised circumstance, is seductively pulled into a rhetorical conversation with his captor as he expresses, incorrectly, his lack of power in this situation, "But I can't make that decision on my own."

Boris smiles broadly as immediately the conversation moves in his favor.

"You, Mr. Smith, you can do just what you want to make everything more pleasant for all. I have very good imagination for bad things to happen to people who displeasure my good moods."

As all of the blood instantly leaves his head, Smith's face turns completely white, and then just as quickly, it fills again flush and red with a jolt of angry blood. He now can't look at either man for fear that his anger-laden fear will get the best of his mouth and he'll end up saying something that will get him even further into this fix, or whatever it is that he is actually into now. So he turns awkwardly to peer out behind him through the rear window of this elegant car as New York disappears in the distance. Even if he doesn't mean it, he knows now that his agreement to let them into the building is the only thing that's going to get this car turned around and headed toward home again. This time, as he turns back to allow his mind to reengage his imprisoned body, and as his normal color returns to his cheeks, he nods in a tacit approval of the baron's request. But the Baron Romanovsky just stares incredulously at the squirming John Smith; for Smith's nod is but a wordless indication, and it clear what the baron wants to hear is Smith's words in place of his approving and somewhat noncommittal nod. Then John Smith, reading the baron's mood, speaks, "Okay, okay, if that's all you want, I will do what you ask, but you stay away from my family."

Smith's remonstration is a useless exercise in toothless anger, and he and the baron both know this, but what else is he in power to do; he had not gang of men to protect him and his family from this ruthless Russian's wrath. And what about the authorities? He thinks. But what evidence of a crime is there? And even after reporting what has happened, who is in the position to stop the Russians from doing any number of things to hurt him and his family, and just as easily to any number of other people that he cares about. There is more than sufficient evidence that the Russians know about his colleagues from work, as they first picked him up from there. Nothing—that's what it would do, absolutely nothing. These are the thoughts that are running through John Smith's mind; he's knows he's in quite a fix.

After his pithy little speech admonishing the bad big baron to stay away from his family, Smith is out of steam as he literally sinks down between the two Russians. The Baron Boris Romanovsky then smiles victoriously, he exclaims with a thinly veiled yet boisterous and passionate rebuke.

"Oh, Mr. Smith, you make everything so simple, you make very wise choice, yes," Boris says as he reaches out and pats a defeated John Smith on his slumped shoulder. And almost as an after thought—but you could tell without laboring to figure things out that it was all part of the plan—he slyly calls up to Borga, the big Russian who is driving the beautiful Rolls-Royce.

"Oh yes, Borga, we go back now. Call Ivanov. Tell him we will not be coming this time, that he put the tools away for now."

I was made aware that a change of heart had taken place in regard to the Russian. At the time I had no idea what had taken place between him and Mr. Smith, but from the first, when the Russians moved in—and I do mean Russians plural, because they always seemed to arrive and depart in bunches—I sensed an abiding tension between the two men. Or, let me be clearer: the tension was always there, but it really mostly, or completely, emanated from Mr. Smith. Actually, it manifested—the tension, that is—in a very strange way from Mr. Smith.

As you must have already gathered from my descriptions and characterization of John Smith's demeanor, you can easily tell that I think he is a tight ass—the tightest I've ever seen, with the exception of my freshman English literature professor at Brown, that is; you couldn't squeeze a worn-out thin dime between his butt cheeks on a million-dollar bet. But it was that character backdrop that made it so apparent that he seethed whenever he was in proximity to the baron, an occasion that he almost completely avoided. You could easily witness this phenomenal character transformation as when juxtaposed to his oft times dour demeanor, he was somehow transformed into whenever the two of them were present in the same place at the same time. Mr. Smith would awkwardly force a toothy, insincere smile, and genuflect toward the baron and behave in an obsequious manner akin to the way an old plantation-house slave did with his erstwhile master—the phrase *who's your daddy* always comes to mind whenever I think of the two of them together. It was by this that I knew the tension, and, therefore, the animus was well established between the two men, and more to the point, it was Baron Romanovsky that had the upper hand in this war between two strong wills, for now, that was; through all of this, though, I always felt that Mr. Smith was lying in wait for his moment to reestablish his position at the top of the heap of egos and authority again.

CHAPTER VI

Let me say here and now that at this time, I didn't have any idea or premonition as to how topsy-turvy the building would soon become. It was exceedingly clear that John Smith was not happy about something, but that in and of it self was not especially noteworthy; these days more than ever before, he was just an all-the-time bad-tempered fellow.

There were not many who had ever left this building, not since I've been working here; it was only death that had emptied an apartment, and that might have occurred a half-dozen times in my tenure. And so with this recent sale of the Tinkerton apartment, the building was all abuzz, and even Gladys and Mildred figured in the ubiquitous chatter called gossip.

It was amazing to see how fast these Russians worked to change their apartment into something different. When I say something different, I am really being excessively generous in my kindness. They and their Russian workers—who, by the way, only spoke Russian—worked like beavers days and nights remodeling their very spacious duplex. But they worked fast and were done in what must have been record time for that size job. I was invited to peek in several times by the gregarious baron as he checked up on the progress of the renovation daily, or else I would have had no idea what was going on up there. Let me say this here and now: it was different, very different; and, oh yes, it had an appeal—that is if you lived in the old French Quarter in New Orleans, or maybe even some obscure part of a Las Vegas hotel made to look garish and timeless.

A bordello is the word I would use to accurately describe this expensive yet bawdy renovation, if the two adjectives are not mutually exclusive. In a word, it was fabulously, decadent, yes, but fabulous, nonetheless. And when I say old French Quarter, I meant old as in time, years back in the past. Not knowing much about the formal language of architecture such as what period and style he was doing the place in, I have to rely on my association and comparisons to pictures that I've seen, and from that, I would say that it looks like a Victorian bordello.

With that finished, it wasn't long until the festivities would begin, and it was on one particular evening that it all started to get out of hand. After work and after having run some errands, I had stopped by late to see Gladys and Mildred while John was out of town on business. It was always that way; it was much easier and tension-free for me to go there for my longer visits when he wasn't around to throw cold water on it with his constant and pervasive chill. Well, anyway, I was through visiting with them and was downstairs in the lobby, and as I was headed out to return to my Upper West Side apartment—I had stopped off for a while to check up on things downstairs. I was standing by the concierge thinking; my mind must have drifted off a bit.

It had become quite a frustrating period for me lately, as I was getting older—not old yet, mind you. But I was beginning to feel a certain kind of emptiness. I am a December baby, and, if you believe in astrology, or any of that kind of stuff, that makes me a Sagittarian—Sagittarians are notorious late bloomers. And I, through my missteps and foibles, had certainly not fully blossomed into what had been expected of me, or into what I had expected of myself; simply put: so far, I was a colossal failure. Yes, it was a fancy building; and yes, it was on Fifth Avenue; and yes, it paid reasonably well, with benefits and all; yes, it was an easy job; yes, yes, and yes . . . but I was going nowhere. What is the difference between all the people who live in this building and me? Let me offer up an answer to my self-imposed query, that is, before you think too hard on it. Nothing, there is no difference; I know this because I've spent all of these years here, right here among them, and I'll tell you for certain that there is no difference in them and me, or them and most of you, for that matter. Think about it for a minute, okay. For instance, if you take away all of their privileges like better services, a higher standard of living, and access to . . . well, access to everything imaginable, leisure time, travel to anywhere on earth at any time, exposure to the best of everything: schools, clothes, transportation, doctors, health care, cultural awareness, safety and security; and yet with all of these so-called advantages, their lives are—excuse my French here—but their lives on an individual basis are just as fucked up as the next guy who doesn't have a tenth of their advantages. I know this; I am in the best position to know this because I am—and have been since I was a child—in the middle of this uniqueness, the only position to witness the real truth. They fail and flounder as much and as often as the next guy, but they cover better because they live in the rarified air of twenty-four-hour protection from us peons; think about who controls our access to them. They control all communication mediums: newspapers, radio, television, the Internet; really, we only get the access that they allow us. Think about it; these are the people, and other people around the country just like them, who run this nation through their banks and multinational corporations. Not American corporations, mind you—these corporation are nations unto themselves, be aware. Just because they have American and American-sounding names, it doesn't mean they wake every morning with the Pledge of Allegiance anywhere near their lips or in their hearts. And look at us, how well have we've fared in their money-grubbing, avaricious hands; have they made many mistakes: the mortgage crises, the wars we engage in, global warming, the immigration crises, the embarrassment of our public education system, our lack of national health care, childhood poverty, crime and drugs stranglehold on our youth, childhood poverty, senior citizens' rampant neglect, and on, and on, and on.

My brain's rambling didn't stop there, because I was really most concerned in the present moment with my own failure. You see, as you already know, I had many of the same advantages; yeah, yeah, yeah, I know I'm black or African American—now that's just too many words for me to use just to describe the color that I am. Who thought up that moniker? Because, in all honesty, it doesn't really describe much else about me or anyone else. African American—what a joke—most blacks can't find Africa on the map, and those that can have little or no interest in their so-called motherland. Let's keep it real, brother; we are, most of us anyway, are thinking about our daily survival, not our neighbors, let alone someone that looks like us but lives thousands of land miles away from where we live and millions of miles away from what we are thinking. Only people like the God-kissed Oprah and the magnificent Angelina Jolie have that luxury.

I had the advantages of access, and that's big; I went to the best schools, I am an Ivy League graduate, and I blew it—that's on me. And now I am lamenting my wasted opportunity. Standing here in my fog, I am pondering a move to something more entrepreneurial.

When I finished my mental walkabout, I stepped to the front of the building to leave, and, at the same time, several stretch limos pulled up in front of the building; even before they had pulled up and stopped, you could hear the parade of music preceding them down Fifth Avenue by a block at least. Well, there's no mystery there; Fifth Avenue is a public thoroughfare in the middle of New York City—Manhattan is New York

City. The boroughs and suburbs, i.e., Queens, Brooklyn, Westchester, are just that—boroughs and suburbs. The city can be a very noisy festive place on any given night; all you have to do is to give someone a reason to party, and it was on. Anyway, the noise and the fanfare aroused me—because the music was really thumpin'—and my curiosity got the best of me, so I stopped to watch them pass; only they didn't pass.

The limos were full of women, one or two of them—I couldn't tell how many as it was quite dark—were hanging out of the sunroof, a pretty common Manhattan occurrence. I was ready to get going—it had already been a long day, and I was quite weary—I should have stayed over with Mildred and Gladys. They always offered; in fact, they both thought that I should be living with them anyway. They had already asked me a hundred times over to do just that.

Well, the limo slowed as it approached my building—I sometimes call it my building; I know it's quite proprietary, but I've been here so long. What else would you have me call it—perhaps the building where I work all day and where my mother lives. Would that name suit you better? Not me—it's far too long and cumbersome. So they slowed and finally stopped at my building, and as the doors open—no one waited for the chauffeur to run out and open the door for them, these beautiful women, one more beautiful than the next—they all started to fold out of the limos. The funny and amazing thing was that they were all dressed to party, but *dressed* is the active word here. They were dressed like Victorian hoes—I mean hookers and prostitutes; they were corseted and bustled with ribbons and lace and parasols and flounced hats and laced shoes and garters. They all looked very, very authentic, and I thought then, *I know where they are going, they're going to the Baron Romanovsky's Victorian bordello.* Well, I be damned, all of a sudden—this building is going to flip out. That John Smith is out of town, we won't get the full brunt of the hysteria, but . . . well, I couldn't go home now, not now seeing all of this in front of me; I stepped aside and let the women pass. I was not on duty, and if they were going where I thought they were going, I was sure that the Baron Romanovsky had already taken care of their announcements to the building. No no no, I decided that I was just going to watch this very interesting show.

I stood aside as the women—I believe there were twelve of them in all—walked into the building, and they piled into the elevator. They were a friendly lot, each one of them spoke and smiled as they passed me by. Windler was standing by at the security office door lusting after them when I approached and asked him what was up. It was then that he told me it was the Baron Romanovsky's housewarming party Russian style; he also said that the entire building had been invited. I couldn't resist, so I boarded the next elevator to the baron's apartment. I was both nervous and excited as I rode up on the elevator; I must admit I felt like a little kid going to his first boy-girl party.

When finally the elevator door opened into the totally transformed apartment, I was instantly transported into another world and time; except for the music, everything was circa late 1800s. The foyer resembled nothing short of a saloon—a pretty large saloon lounge at that, complete with a bar with glass liquor bottles lined up on long glass shelves backed by a huge wall mirror. An open, double-curved, railed stairway centered the room leading to the balconied second-floor party palace where every bedroom has a different theme. All of the guests, including the men, were dressed in period costumes—although I must admit many of their costumes were clearly not of the same period as the twelve fillies that had come by way of the stretch limos. There was a live band playing loud music on each floor; one was playing rhythm and blues covers and the other rock covers. When I entered, Baron Romanovsky was sitting at the bar with one of his henchmen, Borga. He didn't notice men in all the commotion, even though I sat close to them at the bar, but even with the noise, which really wasn't that loud after all, it was just the surprise of it at first that had made me react to it. I could almost hear the two men talking, but not clearly.

Boris was oblivious to any eavesdropping on his conversation with Borga, and if one could have heard them, they would have known more about their intentions for the co-op.

"Borga, this Fifth Avenue is American icon. It means much to them. It is like a highborn Russian noble's estate in St. Petersburg, yes? We will never suffer in the cold of a Russian winter ever again, or any such place ever again."

Borga's large frame barely fits on the comparatively small barstool, but he is nonetheless very comfortable with their discussion as he smiles broadly and happily with his new bounty and life. But his response reveals more unhappiness than his smiles offer evidence to. "Yes, Boris, this all sounds good, but only you are here now."

A rather sullen and ungrateful remark you might think from a man that seems ostensibly to be nothing more than a lackey for the baron. But in truth, it is these three men,: Borga, Oleg, and Boris, brothers they are and more, who have crawled their ways out from the harshness and

BIRDS OF A FEATHER

savagery of the Russian gutter to now reign together over a multifaceted criminal empire that has spread its tentacles far beyond Russia's boarders, throughout Europe, parts of Asia, and the United States. You name it—from oil, diamonds, technology, to drugs, gambling, real estate, to outright straight-up thuggery—they are involved happily and competitively. And Boris is sensitive to his brother's concerns; even though he, Boris, is the mastermind, he could not have come this far without his family of brotherly thugs.

He smiles a half-faced, half-inebriated smile as he replies sincerely to his younger sibling, "Not to worry, Borga. We will soon have it all to ourselves. The old women who sit on our heads, they will soon be covered by more dirt than diamonds. Then we will take next the top-three floors. Once we have them, we will force our weight on all the units below until they all belong to us, yes." Boris smiles again as two of the Victorian-dressed women walk over to the two men. The revelry continued into the night, but I had to get some much-needed sleep. It was a good party, though, something very new for this building, and I wondered what the repercussions were going to be. I didn't see any of the other owners from the building at the party, at least not while I was there, and I only stayed long enough to look around; probably hardly anyone even knew I was there. I wonder then what John Smith will have to say about it—but since he's not around for the time being, it'll be awhile before anyone knows what he thinks, or will say about it, that is until he returns.

Several mornings following that raucous party, Mildred and Gladys are walking arm in arm taking their daily constitutionals through Central Park when Mildred, still disturbed by the goings-on in their building, says, "For the life of me, Gladys dear, I still can't understand why John changed his mind so abruptly and decided to let that low-class Russian and his gang of thugs purchase that floozy's unit. It was a silly thing to do; he merely ended up exchanging one degenerate for another. Anyone these days can have large sums of money, I guess, and now we're stuck with them."

Gladys, the taller of the two women, but both of them are as wiry as young maple trees—she leans in close to her companion in all things mortal, and she agrees wholeheartedly with her, not that she always agrees. Gladys has a mind and thoughts of her own, but here she does agree unabashedly.

"Yeah, he did a total about-face on all of us. One day he was dead set against it—even refusing to check out his bona fides—and next he welcomes that scoundrel in with open arms, or at least that's the way it feels to me. But then to top it off, after he lays this egg on us, he takes off on an extended business trip. I don't understand him sometimes, Mildred, really I don't. As Albert would say at a time like this, 'What's up with that?'"

Mildred leans in to her rock of a friend—she would be absolutely lost without her; she has never been a very strong woman, but together in their seamless relationship, they make one hell of a team.

"I don't know, darling, but we really need to get a hold of John, this situation, with all the partying and noise, and the strange people coming and going has really gotten out of hand."

Over the next several days, it was true. The Russians were very busy with guests from all over; they were mostly foreign-looking people—mainly Russians, to be more specific. And they did come and go at all hours of the day and night. It wasn't so much that they did anything in particular, or for that matter, anything out of the ordinary. I mean they, for the most part. were just like anyone else that would or did arrive at the building during this time—strangers, I mean. They weren't excessively loud, or even discourteous—the baron must have warned them to be nice—but there were just so many of them, I suppose, is what raised the ire of the tenants. And the fact that they didn't look like the rest of the tenants;, they were peasants in suits—Russian peasants at that. To paraphrase an old axiom, you can take the peasant out of the gutter, but even in a suit, you can't take the gutter out of the peasant. This address on Fifth Avenue didn't then, and doesn't now, suffer inferiors well—the only thing that could have been worse, in my experience, is if they had all been black men instead, constantly parading through their exclusive lobby.

Well, this all didn't sit well with the haughty, and indeed something had to be done about it, and John Smith was away—and he was to blame for this invasion of Russians, he was the one who was going to have to fix the mess. I'm certain by this time he had been contacted, probably through his business or through Mildred and Gladys, but however it happened, he returned sooner than he had ever expected. It, however, was not for several weeks, and then one evening, while I was still on duty—I was taking the late shift for a while—I looked up and there he was standing right in front of me. And like nothing, he begins his conversation as if he had left in the morning and had just returned in the evening.

"Good evening, Mr. Smith. You've finally returned. It's good to see you back and looking healthy," I said in my best concierge voice over my own voice, for in my real head, I was yelling, *You idiot, where the hell have you been with everyone here clamoring for your attention, where have you been?* But he in his ever-haughty demeanor, at least on the surface, seemed unfazed by my greeting or the thinly veiled negative thoughts in my head. He as usual was outwardly undeterred by what others thought, and I know I run the risk of being hypercritical here, but I've thought for a long time that this veneer of confidence and austerity was always just a front for his innate insecurity—after all, I knew him way before he started acting this way, way back when he was a silly, skinny, scared kid, whom I would always protect from the bullies.

When we were kids, and often we'd go across the street and play in the park together—he was younger, and he used to follow me wherever I went—I used to like to hang out further uptown than our parents knew we were playing; the kids were rougher uptown. We never really lied about it because we very rarely left the park, but still we knew what areas were off-limits. It's obvious that one of us is white and the other one is not, but I had my own troubles as well—high yellow and tan man were some of the names that the uptown "brothers" called me because my skin is light. But it didn't take long for me to get my props after several flailing-fist run-ins with the toughest one in the bunch. But John, on the other hand, no matter what, was still white, and a couple of times I had to take up for him, but it all worked out in the end when we just stopped going uptown.

Then, when our parents sent us to separate schools, or actually, while I was away at Hotchkiss, they enrolled him at Collegiate; I never understood that, but that's when we started to grow apart. Back then, he was never haughty; in fact, he was quite shy, but after eight years of almost complete separation from him, we totally lost our rhythms with each other. And of course, after my arrest and prison . . . well, you know the rest. And now, to me, he's a totally different person, but I know deep down inside—and probably not that deep down—he's still that little scared kid who used to follow me around. And now, Mr. Haughty finally in obvious disdains, John finally deigns to answer me. This after looking around the lobby suspiciously with his pink nose sniffing and all turned up as if he had stumbled on to a foreign scent of some kind.

"Yes, Albert, it's good to be back home. How are things?"

I wanted to say to him that he knew very well how things were going, and that's the reason why he has cut his trip short, but I would never say that in public for others to hear; so I did my concierge's usual and swallowed whatever real personality I possessed as I gave him my brief yet accurate recitation of the status of our building.

"Well, Mr. Smith, things have been quite different here lately."

If his chin were raised any higher, it would have hit the chandelier hanging from the center of the lobby's ceiling. But with very little change in the tone or the very studied inflection in Mr. Smith's voice, he continues in his impeccably implacable manner.

"According to my mother's e-mails, your assessment of the present state of our building seems grossly understated." And then with just a hint of personality, Mr. Smith clears his throat.

"Why don't you give me your honest impression, Albert? You always have a unique point of view, and a way of stating things that seems to shed the correct shade of light on things."

Now I'm wondering, is he asking me for my opinion, or is this his warped way of asking me for my advice? I hesitate. "Well . . ."

But he is on me in a flash, quite out of character for the usually reserved Mr. Smith, as he almost blurts out, but he catches himself. And again in a more subdued tone, he states his words more carefully than at first his increasingly agitated temperament had desired too.

"Come out with it, man, I've never known you to be shy with your opinions before, Albert."

Given our history, that was a very revealing thing to say to me. Maybe no one else within earshot would have recognized it; probably no one else besides our mothers would have known what was really being stated here. And I must say, this is a first, because in all the time that I've been here, and I do mean for the fifteen, sixteen—oh my god, I've been here for over seventeen years. For over seventeen years, this man who was once like a brother to me, and me to him, he has never referred back to that time when we were kids together. No, not one time—even though at first, both our parents begged him to let go of his anger with me for what I had caused my mother to go through—he had never made reference to that time, not ever; but he had now. It was a real breakthrough for us, and I was stoked.

"In truth, John—."

In my exuberance I had blurted out a forbidden cordial; we were not—the servants that is—no matter how friendly we had become with the tenants—ever to use their first names. But I was so excited that this little tête-à-tête had harked back to our former relationship that I forgot myself; either that, or subconsciously I was furtively testing the old-relationship waters. But I caught myself, for it was truth that for whatever reason I had done it, it was still—according to the rules—inappropriate. I quickly corrected myself, and without apology to draw even more unwanted attention to my *faux pas*, I continued quickly forward as I self-corrected.

"In truth, sir, the place since you were last here . . . has gone to hell, sir."

I'd swear on a stack of King James versions of the Bible that he smiled; for a brief second I saw an unmistakable former presence in the form of a smile appear on John's face, but, alas and so sadly, it disappeared even quicker—like frightened mouse darting back into the safety and comfort of his hole—than the mere moment that it took to present itself in the first place. And then that other dour, sour stoneface reappeared with a vengeance, almost in a reaction to erase the memory of that lighter, more amiable countenance.

"Well, that's honest. What are the particulars, Albert?"

And again he lightens up just a little, but I'm not falling for it this time—fool me once, shame on you; fool me twice, shame on me. He continues this way for just a dramatically perfect sentence.

"Come on, tell me exactly what you mean."

I pause, and then I let him in on the goings-on.

"Well, sir, our nobility___."

In trying not to laugh, Mr. Smith clears his throat. His antics of these last several moments have been meanly out of character, or at least out of the characterization that has possessed him for these last seventeen years, and I am acutely aware that this has not been an accident. Maybe his time away has led him to reconsider our relationship; I would have no idea about such things, but suffices to say, I'm not going to jump into this by myself without invitation, no matter how seductive and appealing he chooses to be. No no no, I need more proof that he is willing to change and thaw the icy buildup between us two. So I too stiffen up.

"Well, sir, our nobility has turned this place into a saloon with constant partying and rowdiness at all hours of the day and night."

It's clear Mr. Smith found my characterization of the Russian's very amusing.

"By nobility, I must assume without too much of a stretch of my mental faculties that you mean the Baron Romanovsky?"

Getting likewise caught up in his abounding stiffness, I answered him succinctly, "One and the same, sir."

Mr. Smith nods his head affirmatively, and then he answered me with inside information that I suspected—because it came at this point in our conversation—as it was just a short time later confirmed that he indeed had been previously furnished with, when he admits, "My mother has told me as much. And what about the other tenants, Albert? What are they saying?"

I must admit that Mr. Smith seemed uncharacteristically reticent to act on his own emotions as he is well-known to doing without hesitation; it was clear that he was upset by what he knew full well was going on in the building. But for the life of me, I couldn't understand his hesitancy to deal with this situation forthwith. Even when he was a boy, he had more heart than that, and that was even when he knew he would receive an "ass whipping" from one of the bigger boys in the park uptown. Never in the past has he given a hoot about what the other tenants thought, especially if it was something that he wanted to do—he'd just go and do it. This building is like his little fiefdom on Fifth Avenue, so his anemic reaction—or, more precisely stated, his lack of action—makes me concerned that there is something untoward and hidden going on between these Russians and Mr. Smith. The talk in the building, while he was away, did sometimes negatively swirl around that fact, the fact of him having allowed the Russian to purchase the Tinkerton unit in the first place; he hadn't confided in anyone as to his reasoning behind the mood and decision change. As I stared at him for a fraction of a second, all of this had gone speedily through my head. I intuited, he did want an answer, didn't he? So I furnished him with one—given his present state of mind—that he could readily handle.

So I said.

"Well, the walls in this building are very thick, sir. So they are split in their assessment of the noise factor. On the one hand, sir, some of them are barely aware of his shenanigans, while others are like chimneys stoked up with frustration and anger, spewing constant complaints, sir."

I waited but he didn't say anything; I could see that he was thinking, but it was frustrating seeing him like this. Finally, I interrupted his silence with a reminder. Gladys had called down earlier as they knew he was due in this evening, and she told me to inform him then that his mother wanted to see him as soon as he arrived.

"Your mother is expecting you directly, sir."

He didn't seem surprised; in fact, he seemed all out of surprise for the time being. All he did was to look at me with a strange, totally unfamiliar look—and here I was thinking that I had seen all of his looks. And then he just says, as if an, oh by the way, or simple afterthought, "I know. Thank you, Albert, for your insights."

And then he just walks off without another word. I almost had to yell out after him, as I modulated my voice upward just a tad, "Not a problem, sir."

CHAPTER VII

"Can you hear that?"

By the time John arrives to his mother's penthouse apartment, she had been stewing literally for days over the ruckus below. She was like a possessed feline scratching at the wall where the mouse escaped into a hole; she was not about to give up her verbal assault on the Russians' occupation of the unit just beneath her, even if the noise below was more sedate than it had been in days. The truth was that you would have been hard-pressed to hear anything. You had to be very quiet—even totally quiet, not breathing—before you could hear the music from below. This is a pre-prewar building, built like Fort Knox it was, seeming almost to be hand-carved from a mountain of granite, it was so thick. She was straining to hear anything, but her nerves and patience had already been disturbed past settling, and she wanted something done to soothe them. John's ever-present haughtiness had not abandoned him; as he entered the apartment his mother, Mildred, had verbally pounced on him. As she asks the question, if he could hear anything, John pauses in his tracks and listens hard before he answers.

When he finally makes out the music, he comments, "Yes, and it's rather nicely done. It's Tchaikovsky, isn't it?"

Like Queen Victoria herself, Mildred and Gladys both were not amused. Gladys harrumphs and clears her throat while Mildred, shocked by John's cavalier and inaccurate response, gasps indignantly. John stiffens and stares at them in a defensive posture—because that's what it is, they both know him all too well to mistake it for anything else. His insensitive behavior is a quick pricking thorn to Mildred's already-fragile nerves, as she has had enough of this Russian situation, a situation that he alone is responsible for having created. She flares up as she corrects his erroneous assertion about the music.

"No, it's Mozart's 'Quartet in C Major' for strings, John. Is that supposed to be a joke, John, is it now? Well, it's not in the least bit funny—this Russian horde below us has been terrorizing us for weeks now, with their parties and floozies. It's just gotten to be too much; it's appalling, John, just appalling."

John quickly loses his haughty edge as he feels the eyes of the family's enforcer, Gladys, weighing down on him. He is pained to hear her words, which he knows are brewing under the shadow of her very serious scowl, and as she walks over to him, he visibly cowers. It is instantly clear old habits die hard, and Gladys's potent and long-standing role as family enforcer has not diminished over the years, as his supplicant's behavior is a clear and present testament to. There is nothing physical going on here; John has the utmost love and respect for the woman that raised him and who has been there for him every step of the way throughout his entire life. But it's clear now at this moment that he has incurred her wrath, and as she stands there next to him, he submits to it. Standing over him, she excoriates in her own very inimitable way.

"Boy . . . you need to get serious because he is that Russian baron, or whatever he is supposed to be, he certainly hasn't been acting very noble. He's even asked us . . . I mean your mother, if she wanted to sell this place to him. The words were asking, but you know, come to think of it, the attitude was more insistent than that, John. You know what I'm saying, boy?"

John reflects quickly and is aghast by what he is hearing from Gladys and from the inference he gathers from Mildred's attending behavior as well. He had sat down while Gladys was talking, but her last words made him pop up out of his seat like a jack-in-the-box when the music stops. And just as Gladys finishes her speech, John remonstrates with a loud, "What!"

And then Gladys has the audience she was angling for; she jumps on it right away.

"I see that got your attention, John, now didn't it?"

John has lost his cool—as he, in his agitated state begins to pace and fidget like rarely ever before—and it's clear the two ladies are not used to seeing him this way. But what they don't know about is the thinly veiled threat that slithered from the mouth of the sly Baron Romanovsky, who has kept John back on his heels ever since that drive up the Palisades some long weeks ago. But even with this private knowledge and obvious concern, he can't hold back on his anger.

"What do you mean he's been asking you to sell him this apartment? When did he . . . what did he say? Tell me, Mother, what exactly did he say?"

You can see that it's Gladys, not Mildred, who wants to speak at the sound of the gavel, but it's Mildred who stutters first, "Well, he said . . ."

But Gladys, always the more outspoken of the two—she takes over after Mildred's first pause.

"I'll tell you exactly what he said, son . . ."

But here, for some unknown reason—after she calls John son—she pauses uncharacteristically. She flashes a look at Mildred; they make eye contact, and then after they nod toward each other and continue staring into each other's eyes for a long moment. John takes great notice of this little hiccup, but he doesn't let it distract him for the moment; he instead mentally stores it away for later as he is immediately interested in what Gladys has to tell him. When she pauses, John waits for an anxious second, and then, "Yes, Mother Gladys, go on. I'm listening."

Then Gladys's eyes break away from her locked stare with Mildred's eyes as she, more thoughtfully now, it seems, continues her account of the baron's offer to purchase their apartment.

"We, your mother and me, were walking in the park . . . Was it two weeks ago, Millie?"

Mildred smiles, and then she nods to affirm Gladys's memory and other things taking place between them and at the time unbeknownst to John; Gladys smiles back at her, and then she continues as she recalls the entire episode that occurred in Central Park some two weeks prior.

"We were walking our normal daily walk through the park, the morning walk, not the evening walk. In fact, we were returning home. Is that right, Millie?"

Mildred nods, and John sighs impatiently, but Gladys flashes him that "Don't you rush me, boy" look, and he settles down immediately. Gladys smiles and continues her story at her own pace.

"Let's see, where I was . . . oh yes, we were on our way back home. As you well know, John, the park can have its intrigues, but this one was more excitable than usual. Off in the bushes, off the road up near the stoned wall on Fifth Avenue, there was this rustling and yelling. It was bad enough that they were yelling, which was already enough of a distraction to ruin a very pleasant walk, but half of the yelling was in another language, which until recently had been pretty unfamiliar to our ears."

Gladys stops talking and takes a long admonishing look at John.

"I guess you know where I'm going with some of this, don't you, son?"

John knows instinctively that she's not happy with something that he's done, and it's no stretch to figure out that it has something to do with the Russians.

"Well, yes, it was Russian being bellowed loudly and raucously, and there was English as well, not English from the building, but street words, from street voices. It was two men that were being beaten by four oversized Russian-speaking bullies. Now, I don't know what those boys had done to provoke those Russians, but whatever it was, it was clear that they had already been beaten up enough for having done it. You understand where I'm coming from with this, don't you, son? I'm getting a little ahead of myself here. Well, we came walking up, Millie and me, and then before we knew it, the Russian. You know, the one you let purchase the Tinkerton place, yeah, well, he comes slithering up like the snake from the tree of life to offer us an apple. He's a low human being, John, very low. And now he's sidling up next to us, Millie and me. Now, mind you, the Russian thugs are still whaling away at the boys in the bushes, but when he came close, and I turned to look at the bushes where the action was taking place, it was then and only then that he waved his men off to stop the beatings. Now mind you, we can see what his men are doing to those young men, whether they deserved to be punished or not, I wasn't then nor am I now able to say, but clearly it had been overdone.

"But what I want to say about that is he acted like nothing had happened, nothing at all. He's just a career thug, John, that's what he is, and I don't care how much money he has.

"'Good day, Mrs. Smith and Mrs. Lawrence, it's nice to see you both out and about.'

"Can you believe the nerve, the audacity of that Russian thug. And he knew us, John, he knew us by name and everything. What else does he know about us, John, what else? We—I wasn't buying any of his smarmy charm—I said to him, 'What happened over there with those men?' And it knocked him back on his heels for a second. I'm sure he thought that these old ladies still have some spunk and weren't impressed or afraid of his thuggery. When he recovered, he says, 'Oh, that. Don't trouble yourselves with that, ladies . . . right now, ladies, I would like to invite you to my home. It is just below your home, I believe.'

"What nonsense, he believes it's right below our home. He knew darn well where it was. I couldn't believe the way that Russian snake slithered, and in the sun too. And that's when Millie says, 'Oh my . . . so you're the Russian.' Didn't you, Millie?"

Mildred had been quiet until then, but it was clear that she had been enjoying Gladys's recitation of that day's events; she perks up to join her friend's rendition, "Oh yes, and that when I said that must be the new owner of the Tinkerton apartment, and that he had the advantage on us as we've never been formally or otherwise introduced."

And indeed that's what she had said, which seemed to tickle the Russian, and with his endless obsequious smarminess, he oozes.

"Guilty as charged, Madames Smith and Lawrence, guilty as charged."

"But I wasn't giving up on him, he was smooth all right, but my days on the street, no matter if it was a long time ago, some things you never forget, and when you pick up a snake, to be safe, you've got to take it by the head so it won't end up taking a bite out of you, so I said poking at him a little, 'You seem very well-informed as to who we are, aren't you?'

"The baron then stares curiously at me for a moment, and then he offers up his name and title, 'As always, madames, I am the Baron Boris Romanovsky, at your service.'"

"Ha-ha, that was funny, Millie, when you said."

"I know, when I said, 'Had I known we were in the presence of royalty, I would have curtsied.' Yes, I remember that as well, Gladys dear.

"And then that buffoon, not sensing that he was being laughed at—, or maybe he did know and he just didn't care—then he says, 'No need, madame, I am very informal. It is a fact that if you were in Russia, you yourselves would be bowed to as it is clear you two are also royalty of our castle.'"

"He is a sly one, that Baron Romanovsky is—fact, that just what I said, isn't it, Millie?

"Yes indeed, I did say it right there in front of his face, John, didn't I, Millie? I said it right to his face. 'He's a smooth one, ain't he?' I said.

"And then everything went all quiet between us three, we all just stood there uncomfortably looking at each other for a brief moment. He knew we had made him, you know, like they say on the police programs, so we just all stood there for a moment. And then, that's when it happened.

"'It is my intention to buy your apartment unit from you two. You only have to name your price, but no matter, I'll soon have it, I will.'

"As bold as a king striding to his throne through a crowd of his subjects he was, and like a peacock, all proud and confident, he just said it to our faces. That man has no couth, no shame at all, but I knew he was serious, and I already knew that he was dangerous, the way he had his thugs beating up on the young men in broad daylight and all. But that's when Millie—you know how hard it is to get Millie all stirred up—well that got her going. She says, 'Well, I never . . . ,' and that's when I grabbed her at her arm to pull her away. I pulled her away, but the Russian seemed amused at the entire scene as he smiles his evil-leering smile at us. As we walked away, he calls out, 'But you will sell it to me, and soon, too.'

"I pulled Millie, and we hurried home."

John is beside himself with upset, but he too knows that the Russian is an odious, dangerous, and evil character, and that his *modus operandi* is to first proffer a thinly veiled threat—just as he had been with him when he and his thugs took him for his little ride up the Hudson—was consistent with his own experience. And now they had multiplied; there were even more of them than before. He was feeling the danger increase, but he would have to be very calculating in his response lest he lose his only leverage, and that was the element of surprise in whatever he chose to do to counter this Russian menace.

CHAPTER VIII

While all of this intrigue is going on upstairs throughout the building, I'm still holding forth downstairs in the lobby at the concierge. This afternoon, I am standing there as Amy Dillon enters the lobby hand in hand with Rufus; I must say that I was surprised to see them together after the excitement of her birthday some weeks ago. I hadn't asked, after that day, any questions; as usual, I had seen Amy every day since then, but it wasn't my place to pry. And as my curiosity had peaked and subsequently waned during that time, I must say that with all the other distractions—although I wasn't personally involved in them—I could feel the rhyme and rhythm of the building had changed demonstrably; consequently, my focus had wandered elsewhere. But this afternoon as she walked into the lobby with Rufus, my mind was again at full attention to their story, but still, I couldn't ask.

"Good afternoon, Ms Dillon, Rufus," I said, and then I remembered—I hadn't thought about it since he'd given it to me early this morning, but Dennis Dillon had given me an envelope to give to Amy when she returned home from school this afternoon, so, I called her over. And as I was taking the envelope out of the drawer, I then remembered what he had told me to tell her.

"Here, your dad left these tickets for you. He told me to tell you to have a good time, and that he'd see you later."

It was clear that the tickets pleased Amy, but I didn't sense that she was all that surprised.

"Oh, thanks, Albert," she said pleasantly and quickly as she turned to walk away, but then she stopped because as she looked up from the envelope, she must have caught the look on my face; I'm sure it registered an all-too-telling expression of curiosity, if not surprise. Amy had walked several steps away from and back toward Rufus by then, so on her little journey back, I tried to compose myself. It didn't work at all. She is so smart that, Amy Dillon is, she didn't come at me directly and accuse me of being curious—no, that's not what she did; she came at me from the side as she inquired about my health with a question that is bound to elicit more in the answering than the question itself.

"What's the matter, Albert, aren't you feeling well?"

I couldn't just lie. I knew that if I answered yes, she would stop everything to attend to me as she always had. Ever since she was little girl, Amy Dillon would play nurse to me, even to the point—a couple of times—of taking me upstairs to their wonderful apartment and making her mother put me to bed in one of their many guest rooms until I had recovered. It was on those occasions that I had bonded with her mother as well. Once a couple years back, I was indeed really sick—I had a bad case of the flu—and they, the two of them, took the best care of me; it was really great. So no, I wouldn't dare tell Amy that I wasn't feeling well and run the risk of that kind of treatment, which would have been totally inappropriate because I wasn't now ill. So I told her the truth, which then totally exposed me to further inquiry.

"Oh no, Amy, I'm just fine . . ."

I should have left well enough alone, but I reflexively added the nervous, and in this case the interrogative, adverb, which turned itself back on me, when I added, "Why?"

Yeah, *why* is right. Why did I add *why*? I could have escaped with my curiosity intact, and without further inquiry from her. It was not necessary to know at that precise moment. I could have waited until later; she for certain would have told me everything then. I didn't have to know what was going between her and her father and, of course, with Rufus at this very precise moment. Yes, Rufus was, is, and always will be black like me, and therefore subject to all the inherent societal and familial tendencies to disregard our equal humanity; but apparently, he—for some reason not obvious to me—has a particular kind of resiliency, and maybe some secret clout. I sensed that her father, Dennis Dillon, would not be overjoyed or in the least bit happy with their romantic association, and that was because he was black; but here today, they were both as obvious as day not hiding or trying to hide their relationship, and I was curious how they had pulled it off. But again, I hadn't meant to be that obvious in my outward reaction and response to my innate ignorance. But here she comes; I've seen that coy smile she's flashing—it had appeared on her face too many times before this moment, moments in which I know that she, like her mother, is going after something that she is determined and hell-bent on getting to her satisfaction.

She pauses and then she starts in on me: "Oh, it was just that you were looking kind of strange, that's all, Albert. I thought that if you weren't ill . . . well, I thought that maybe you had something on your chest that you wanted to get off."

It's a funny thing about men and women in relationships, especially when they care strongly for each other or are in love. What I'm trying to say here is that they sense each other's moods and requirements for space. Here we are the three of us.

Rufus, because he had walked over with Amy when she had returned to the concierge, Amy, and me—we are all three of us standing there in this tight little triumvirate. However, when Amy's final query is launched from her inquisitor's lips, Rufus peels off slowly and walks over to visit with Windler in the security office. I knew that he knew that Amy was on a path seeking truth to reconcile her momentary angst. And I knew that he knew that I didn't want to be outed while he stood there in front of me watching my humiliation, which it would have been if he had stayed, so he left us alone. Cool, the young brother is very cool.

Okay, the jig was up, and I had to come clean. She had rarely if ever caught me this way. I don't know; maybe it's the topic—because this whole thing is indeed about race, isn't it? Or maybe—as I momentarily delude myself into hoping—she's just getting older and smarter and becoming more of a woman. And maybe, just maybe, all are true. But here I am standing being gently yet clearly confronted by a young lady whom I held in my arms as a child more than once. She is clearly now not a child, and maybe it's time—like right now—that I realized that fact.

After I fumbled around for the right words, finally I began to string together a few cogent and truthful offerings.

"Amy, I don't mean to pry—."

But before I could get my next words out, she was all over it. She had grown up right before my eyes, and I had missed the transformation from little girl to young woman. I, like so many others, had missed the moment, and for sure it hadn't happened in just one moment. I had missed the change, her metamorphosis, the signs of this type of maturity's arrival; and I must call it a type of maturity. Amy was serious. When I say serious, I don't mean the morose or dour type of attitudinal changes that so many of the young folks in this building and on this street have and do go through. It's a sort of air, a coat of funky and haughty air, if you will, that they put on to convince the world that they have arrived and that they are now adults to be taken seriously—or, in the cases of the children on this block. It is now that they are now people to be reckoned with; it's their birthright as taught to them by their parents and grandparents before them.

She too had arrived, but she, if I may, had taken a different transport; it should have been obvious before now, if not before Rufus, then definitely after him. He is a young black man, and no matter who he is, she is a white young lady from Fifth Avenue, and, historically, their worlds would and could never be one. So it would stand, as par for the adolescent course, that she might have a curiosity fling on the side somewhere at a table in the corner in the back in the dark so to speak, but you never bring the forbidden fruit home, not in the light of day—not on Fifth Avenue, you don't. But she did; yes I know she balked once, I know, but wouldn't you? Putting yourself in her position; if you were about to default on both your history and your vaunted birthright position in this, the greatest country in the world, in this the greatest city, on the best block, wouldn't you think twice before doing it? I'd say, you'd bet your sweet ass you would, more than once I'd be willing to wager. But Amy balked partially only once, and with Rufus's strength—and we must all know where his strength comes from—whatever happened upstairs . . . well, the proof, they say, is in the pudding, because here she and they are again.

No, she has not taken the road, the beaten path to comply with her surrounding ethos; she had set out on her own, and there now standing before me is that young woman. Yes, she's young, but she is seriously living HER life—in capitals. She then steps on my words with her own percipient words.

"Sure you do, Albert, but go on and do your thing."

With my two large black hands, I had to pick my fallen chin up off the counter of the concierge. But it wasn't a sad chin; it started out surprised as it fell from my face, but by the time it hit the desk, it was as happy as a pig in slop to witness the girl, Amy Dillon, for the first time as a young woman. I must tell you it was like she was my own daughter standing there, strong, protective, and defiant; and it was then that I had a sense of what had taken place upstairs on her birthday. No, I didn't know the particulars, and I didn't need to know them—I am no gossip. But what I knew without having to witness the event was that I was so proud to stand witness to the victor. She was the victor because she has endeavored to undo the pervasive racist insanity that engulfs us all.

But still, I had not witnessed the scene, and she and I knew that I had no idea who she had become—if I had, I wouldn't have been so predictable in my surprise with Rufus being back here in the light of day, as it were. She knew that because she knew me, and I was not going to try and hide my shortcomings and pretend that I knew any better at all.

"That's okay, Ms Dillon, that's okay, it's just fine, I was out of line."

And then, Amy is back to her old self again—we after all have been friends forever. She smiles at me, but it's a weak smile full of concern, not of happiness.

"I'm sorry, Albert. I didn't mean to be aggressive with you, but I kind of know what's on your mind. And frankly, I'm tired of dealing with the subject matter. People are so dishonest, and I'm tired of talking to their lying faces. If Rufus weren't Harper Kingston's son, my father would have probably disowned me by now. So if you're surprised that I'm not really that surprised by the tickets, well, you're right, I am not."

I wasn't that surprised about the tickets, but no matter, it's nice to have her back; it's not that I don't like the changed woman that she's become, but I don't know her well enough yet—the new woman that is—to have our regular conversation with her. What if this new persona is presently angry with me, you know, for not anticipating her change better? But now that she was sounding like herself again, I was more confident to be my old self with her; I was so happy that I blurted out, "Who the hell is . . . Harper Kingston, did you say?"

I had said his name—Harper Kingston—in a less modulated tone than this staid building's lobby normally tolerated without rancor, and immediately all heads in the lobby turned to look in my direction, and that included the head of Rufus, who peeked out of the security door along with Windler's big head. Amy immediately caught Rufus's eye and waved him back into the security office, which he and Windler quickly retreated back into their comfortable little hole. Amy smiled her lovely, warm smile at me, which immediately put me back at ease, as I had become just a little jittery after my unanticipated outburst had garnered such wide disapproval. It wasn't but a moment until Amy rose to my rescue.

"Oh, him . . . well, I'm kind of glad you don't know who he is, Albert, but my father certainly does, and maybe it serves him right, the hypocrite that he is."

Again I was confused by the inference and the reference made to her father, Dennis Dillon, him being a hypocrite and all; and I guess that again it showed on my very emotional and revealing face. But this time she didn't smile; she just stared at me as if she was thinking intensely about something, but only for the moment, and then she continued, "You know that big merger that swallowed up Dad's law firm—you know, the one he's always talking about?"

Of course I knew; I was so tired of hearing about it every day. Rich people are not so unlike everybody else, except for that one salient difference that makes them totally different from everyone else—at least in their eyes it does—and that difference is money; they have a lot of it, so much so they are not even called rich anymore. They are referred to as 'the wealthy'; they even get a definite article place in front of their status: the wealthy, where it used to be just rich people.

Dennis Dillon was such a stiff and arrogant human being; he was so often the most difficult of the owners to stomach. I don't know, but maybe it had something to do with how fond his wife and daughter were of me—and me of them—maybe he was jealous of me or something. I must cast a serious pall of doubt on that. He was seldom talkative; I mean he'd talk, but he wouldn't really ever say anything of substance besides to give me instructions about this and that or to tell me to look after his daughter, a task for which he already knew he never had to ask. But it was and had been different for the last little while—two months maybe. He was, or rather he had become, totally obsessed with his law firm. It had been his father's law firm—his father had started way back in the Twenties with some very famous partners—in fact, his father had been John Smith's father's lawyer; that's how he ended up in the same building as the Smiths in the first place. This entire building is so nefarious and familial that way, every family here—until recently that is—is related in some way to every other family, either by favor, blood, or money; it's so immoral and incestuous, and yes, there are some not-so-distant cousins living here as well, all done to keep the money close, if not actually in the family. And that's the white part of why Rufus's presence here is such an enigma—that sound is so unpleasantly close to a slur it makes me blush to say it. That and the fact that he is black is really a conundrum; however, that very confusion is about to be dispelled and exposed for what it really is: a huge falsehood is what it is. Here I am trying to understand what is going on here, and all the time secretly hoping—in my heart of hearts, the silly black man that I am, always hopeful—that something positive has taken place, maybe something like people are becoming more open, accepting, and fair-minded, ha. After thinking through her query, I knew what to answer my little trouper.

"Yeah, well, of course, I know about that, that's the only thing on his mind that he ever talks to me about lately. Every day he mentions it, and that's not the strangest part because before that, he didn't bother to talk much to me about anything substantive, so, Little Ms Sunshine, what's up with that?"

Finally, I had touched her heart; we were back to where we once were, friends again. I could tell by her smile that she wasn't going to be angry with me anytime soon. I could tell she was ready to confide in me now, as before.

"Yeah, you have gotten that right, Albert . . . Well, Harper Kingston's law firm is the firm that bought up my dad's law firm."

She pauses to think, and then she looks toward the security office, and we can both hear Rufus and Windler laughing inside the security office, and their laughter brings a warm smile to her face. That's when Amy Dillon turns to me, but I already knew what she was going to say; I could feel it in my bones, in my heart, in my head ringing like a church bell on Sunday morning. So I stuck my foot in it; I wanted to hear more, but I knew that I was going to have to let her know that I knew what she was going through, and that was by exchanging an immediate sense of understanding that I knew what she was facing.

"And Rufus is Harper Kingston's son, and your father's new boss."

I had taken a chance, but I was right in my calculations because Amy's face lit up like a firefly glowing at night in the middle of Central Park's Sheep Meadow.

"Bingo, Albert, you hit the nail on the head, they are father and son, and it wasn't until he made that discovery, or better yet, it was not until that discovery was thrust upon him in the form of "'Do you even know who this young man is?' that he became so attentive and compliant, and it was Rufus, not me, who chilled me out about him, and guided me in how to use my advantages and gifts. Rufus is the one who made me understand that my anger was counterproductive, and that if I persisted in being angry, that I would, in the end, lose the moral high ground to battle fatigue. It took some doing, Albert, as it was bad enough, Albert, that my father is a racist, that I could never abide, but I was made to understand how he became that way. As a product of this very environment, Albert, it would have been very difficult for him to have avoided it. He's not one you would ever mistake for a revolutionary."

I was so pleased and shocked at the same time; I didn't really know what to say. Well, that's not completely true. I had an awful lot to say, but this was neither the time nor the place to be saying it. I was still just the doorman, and I had to keep my place. So I dribble out an anemic retort to her deluge of thought.

"Rufus is a fine young man, withstanding his advantaged birth."

Amy again smiled at me.

"Why yes, he is, Albert, thanks for that. You can see that, can't you, Albert?"

I didn't want to seem like I was piling on, even though I thought that her father was definitely bigoted, but he was biased against many things, and race was just one of them. So I thought I'd offer something more conciliatory, as it was clear that Rufus had guided her well in other things of a more intellectual and dialectic tone. I did it again, clearly and thoughtlessly misstep because she almost blew a gasket in her fiery response.

"All my father can see is the money, Albert. Why do you think my mother's alone somewhere in the middle of the jungles of Africa without him anyhow, Albert?"

I don't know why, but I continue to play the peacemaker. I'm guessing that if I don't, I might be in danger of revealing too much about my own true feelings for her and her mother to her.

"I'm sure there's more to it than that, Amy."

Amy wastes no time in returning a comment., "You'd be surprised, my friend, you'd be very surprised."

I had lost my resolve of diplomacy; it was time to fold up my tent and get off this battlefield as my losses were mounting and my pursuit of a win now would only prove at best to be a wasteful and pyrrhic victory. And with one retreating salutary remark, I endeavored to cut my losses by half as I spoke my only remaining truth uncluttered by obvious intentions to dissuade an angered young lady, "Well, Amy, you win some by inches, and some you win by miles. Take the win, Little Ms Sunshine, they are far better than the losses, yet sometimes not as meaningful. You've got a good heart, little girl, now you stay strong, you hear me?"

Amy then smiled an incomplete, thoughtful smile as she slowly walked away from the concierge desk toward the security office to fetch her hard-fought-for beau.

"I hear you, Albert, thanks," she says over her delicate young shoulder as she steps slowly away.

As if on a discordant cue, her entrance changed the quiet ambiance of lobby's slow-moving air from warm, intimate, and serious to frivolous and chaotic as Nancy Smith comes striding through the front door of the building. I quickly busied myself behind the desk, hoping against hope that she was still too annoyed with me to bother me with her romantic travails, but my hopes were quickly dashed when I heard the very distinctive shrill of her high-strung, impatient voice wafting speedily across the lobby to assault my ears and disturb my momentary peace. But there was not any longer to be peace; Nancy Smith was about to see to that.

Unlike for the past several weeks, she was no longer content with ignoring me; this time instead of heading away from my desk, she headed straight for it and me. I'm looking down, massaging my mind with a wasted yet hopeful illusion that she would read my wants and wander kindly and gently away, but that was all to no avail.

"Albert," she says, crisply in her squeaky voice, but I played dumb like I hadn't heard her; then she says again, "Albert."

I couldn't—well—I didn't think it was fair to run the risk of really making her angry or, in fact, embarrassing her by ignoring her in public, so I lifted my head to find her face in my face as close as a postage stamp is to a letter. This time she modulates her voice to a softer, almost-sad whisper; I almost felt sorry for her. Although I knew, and in fact always knew, that she was selfish, I also knew that some of that very selfishness came from her pain of being ignored by her husband.

You never really know how something's got started; all I know is that she had cornered me into a clandestine relationship with her, and that, if I am completely honest, I must admit that at one time right at the beginning of the affair, say the first couple of years or so, the whole thing, the idea and the romance, was quite thrilling—maybe because it was good or maybe because it was new. But now, both of those things had passed, good and new, and I really didn't want to continue in it; besides, and I know it's a little late for this pithy revelation after ten years, but it's not the right thing for a good man to do. Besides, her husband's right here. I have to put myself in his place; how would I like it if some man was having an affair with my wife, and I had to look in his face every day. He knew, of course, he knew—at least I think he knows.

But here she is standing in my face nose to nose.

"Why have you been avoiding me, Albert, have I done something to offend you?"

I thought that a strange query, but it really wasn't that strange for a woman; women are wired differently than us men, and it causes them to often say things that we have no facility to understand. They understand each other, but far be it from any man alive to understand them. I think they all secretly know this; I mean, they tell us this all the time—you just don't understand me—but we rarely, if ever, listen. I mean we listen—we do—many of us listen intently, but still truth, facts, and the understanding, too, too often escape us by the bucketsful. That's why that on a first date, if a guy even mentions that he understands a woman, there will always be a hopeful—on her part—second date. To answer Nancy's question, in my head only of course, *Of course I've been avoiding you, you have run me down, woman, and I am tired. Why don't you make an effort to have a better relationship with your husband? Hell, I have no idea how you should go about doing it, but do something, for Christ's sake.* But, of course, I can't say that to her here and now, so I lie.

"Oh no, you have done nothing to offend me, Mrs. Smith. But I am afraid that I am short the number of apologies needed to make up for my own offense to you."

I had laid it on thick, thicker than I would have advised another man to do, but I was nervous and caught off guard after dealing with Amy Dillon just moments before Nancy had entered the lobby, and I wasn't prepared to deal with her angst. But she didn't know or care about my state of unpreparedness; she was loaded for bear, and she must have calculated this moment and was not to be denied.

Then, finally she removes her face from my face—by only an inch or so—and then she blows, still modulated and controlled, which to me made it all the more potent.

"Nice words, Albert Lawrence, but they're wasted, you're using them on the wrong woman. That stuff is way too light for me, my brother. Do you really think you're going to get off that easily now, do you, Albert? Come on now, have you not contemplated our last discussion? I am not just going to go away now, Albert. The cat is out of the bag, and it's a woman. Now, Albert, you are the man, so be the man that we both know you are, and you step up and do your duty. You know you want to be with me, Albert, so do your duty."

It's amazing what a few well-placed words can do; she had nailed me, not necessarily with what I wanted, but she did make me question myself. Sometimes it's not so clear what you want or don't, or sometimes you don't want it all the time. There was a time that I did indeed want her—Nancy that is—just the way she's saying right now, and I remember that time, but not now. People grow up, out, and apart, and I guess that's what happened to us; besides, that illicit relationship was so circumscribed that there was never any room to grow into a real relationship. Sneaking and creeping around do not make for the best foundation to establish a lasting relationship. There is no wonder that she feels that I have felt that way about her because I did, but that time has passed for me, and maybe it has passed for her as well—but out of frustration, boredom, and loneliness, she feels a need to hold on to what's close, but I can't be her lifesaver. Now the problem is how to tell her the truth. I can't tell her that now, so instead I launch another blank, a bulletless projectile in her direction hoping that she'll just go away for now.

"I've been very busy, Mrs. Smith,"

I say with as much conviction as a dog-tired soldier volunteering to stand twelve-hour guard duty in the rain; my tepid resistance is pushed aside like the minor obstacle that it was as she stares at me straight in my eyes and solicits my cooperation instead.

"Please, Albert . . . make time."

Then she walks away; Nancy Smith had said her piece, and that was it—she just turns and walks away. But then a split second later, as if she's had an enlightening afterthought, she stops and turns to look at me once more. I can read the looks; all of her looks are known to me—for we have been, despite all of my denials—we have been close enough for me to know her that well. The look reads clearly, so clearly it makes my heart skip—not with love, maybe more with disappointment than anything else.

"I'm counting on you to come through for me, Albert."

And this time she continues on toward the elevator, and as she waits there for the door to open, my heart sinks as I watch her in her aloneness; but I'm not going to be her savior, and God knows she needs one. But this moment of reflective peace is short-lived, for when the elevator door does finally open—which took but a moment's waiting—out comes the Baron Romanovsky with two of his omnipresent thug henchmen at his sides. He is a grand man, a spectacle if nothing else—there's nothing quiet about his presentation, and, like a garish parade float, this ostentatious Russian—flamboyantly, with gesticulating arms flailing in every direction as he regales his legions in idle and inane banter—strides off the elevator. And in mid-stride, he spots Nancy Smith waiting; he immediately modulates his banter to a mere yet seductive whisper.

"Ah, Mrs. Smith, it is good to see you again. I hope you enjoyed yourself last evening at the Metropolitan . . ."

The Baron Romanovsky is no fool; I must say that here and now. For all of his flamboyance and bluster, closer to the core of his real self, he is an efficient observer of human behavior, as he is the slyest foxes,; and his propensity for constructing dossiers on all people that he has even the least dealings with would put Russian KGB and the famed East German Stasi to shame. As he speaks, his eyes dart and pan the space around like a lizard's, and his nose—like a canine's nose—picks up every scent and detail from the lobby. Finally, when his eyes fix—only for a split second—on me, he then in sketchy details fashions a complete and eerily accurate context for our story. He implicates his intimate knowledge of our relationship—Nancy Smith's and mine—with astounding alacrity, and, might I say, with an appropriate operatic allusion, as he continues to address Nancy Smith.

"*Othello* is also my favorite opera, Mrs. Smith."

And Nancy Smith, unaware of his shadowy allusion—she stiffens to a familiar haughty posture as she looks down her nose at the Russian and then replies with a bare and unvarnished disdain, "I beg your pardon, Baron, the opera was not Verdi's *Othello*, it was Mozart *Un Ballo in Maschera—The Masked Ball,* for your kind."

The Baron Romanovsky is too cool and is not swayed to anger by the obviously condescending Nancy Smith; he simply smiles in my direction, and as he looks a longer stare this time in my direction. He nods victoriously as he steps to move away from Mrs. Smith, and then he throws and cryptic yet not-too-subtle jab back over his shoulder, almost as an afterthought—but I think not, for everything that the Baron Romanovsky does seems calculating and as well planned as the workings of a Swiss watch.

"Yes, I know, Mrs. Smith, last night, *Un Ballo*, today *Othello*."

He stops and turns again to face Nancy Smith, and with quite a large smile on his face, he mimes a recollection.

"I tried to get your attention last night, my good neighbor, but I guess you didn't see me."

I must admit Nancy remained as cool as a cucumber, as cool as the baron was, I must say, because I couldn't tell whether his comment had adversely affected her. I know she heard it—everyone present heard it—and understood it for what it was intended, but there was nothing to reveal that, for her countenance remained inscrutable in the face of the baron's indiscreet comment. But still her image never changes as her haughty posture remains intact. The baron—it is clear—is having a bit of fun as he is adding to the pervading air of intrigue in the co-op.

"If I didn't see you, Baron Romanovsky, I certainly couldn't have missed your catcalls across the promenade. Next time, more discretion will render you much better results I think."

Romanovsky is still smiling as he reaches the concierge desk; then he looks at me with a different kind of look—it was a look that, if read correctly, was a signal that we were in cahoots. Wrong, I'm thinking—and he nods, almost as if to say, "I'm freeing you, brother, how do you like me now?" but I don't like him any more now than I ever did, and he wasn't freeing me from anything. He throws what I term as a fake bonding jab at me—you know, like when someone for some reason wants you to feel that they are with you, and you're with them, like you're buddies or something; nonsense, I'm no buddy to a complete stranger.

"What's up, brother?"

I absolutely hate when white men—most particularly when white men that I don't know or have any sort of relationship with—call me brother; it's fake, insulting, and embarrassing. They don't know me, and to call me brother has less than no meaning at all; it's obsequious and rude, and as they used to say, it cuts no ice with me. But he's an owner, and I'm still only the doorman. So I nodded, smiled, and—but in my mind's eye I feel reduced and subservient—I could see myself clearly and sadly as just another servile black man smiling and genuflecting for his white boss for the three billionth time in the history of the world, damn it. In this scenario, I have zero leverage, so I simply say, "Good morning, Baron Romanovsky."

As he turns to leave the lobby for the street, I surreptitiously give him the finger at the same time that I glance in Nancy Smith's direction; she alone catches my admittedly obscene gesture, but she, not surprisingly, approves of its use when she sends me an approving wink and a smile as the elevator door finally closes, and off she goes.

CHAPTER IX

Things are far from back to normal, but some things are as they once were not too long ago, as Mildred and Gladys are back to feeding the falcons, whose nest John has restored to its proper place beneath one of their penthouse balconies. They are like two kids playing in the park at their favorite game to their twin delights. They giggle as the hungry semi-domesticated predators—who willingly take food from them—catch their tosses of chicken.

"I'm so glad Old Blue Eyes is back nesting with his friends. Quick, Gladys, hand me another piece of that chicken before the other birds come back. This little one's been shut out the last two feedings."

Gladys has just about gone limp as she hurries back with a platter full of raw, clean chicken; she almost trips over a chair as she rushes forward to make it in time.

"All right, Millie, just hold your horses now, I'm comin' as fast as I can carry this stuff. All this chicken is not that lightweight, you know."

Mildred laughs, and Gladys laughs after her as the few semi-impatient words of Gladys's were a perfect example of their symbiotic relationship, so close that they were that this was as harsh as it would ever get between them.

"I'm sorry, honey. It's just that I get so excited feeding them. I've missed it so. I was so disappointed when that idiot son of ours so thoughtlessly dismantled Old Blue Eyes' home. He can be such a boob sometimes, Gladys."

Gladys nods in agreement as she steadies the platter of chicken on her one knee; despite her complaining, she is very strong for such a little thing.

"I know, Millie, I missed it too. We've got 'em back now, though, but it still doesn't make this chicken any lighter."

108

Gladys is laughing while she is talking.

"Yeah, and when it's your turn to carry and mine to feed, I'll make certain to be as patient with you as you have been with me."

Mildred rushes over to unload some of the chicken from the platter.

"I'm sorry, honey, I'm just so very excited that's all. This is my absolute favorite thing to do."

As Mildred unloads the last pieces of chicken from the platter, in danger of overfeeding the birds, she sets some aside and then tosses a smaller amount to the side where the smallest of the springtime-born young falcons is nesting. The platter is now empty and lightened by the weight of the missing chicken. With a sigh of relief and a slanted head nod of contrition, Gladys smiles at Mildred.

"I know, Millie. I'm just kidding you, girl."

After they have cleaned up from feeding the falcons, they head inside to the library to relax, read, and ruminate, when Gladys remembers to pose a question about an earlier concern.

"By the way, darlin', did you happen to see the note of apology and the accompanying invitation from the Russian downstairs?"

When Mildred hears Gladys's reference to the Russian, it instantly changes her mood from pleasant to sour. She scowls and twists her face as if she's just tasted something awfully bitter. She doesn't speak right away; she pauses as if she's taking the time and energy to formulate an appropriate response. Finally, her responding ouch equals the pinch of Gladys's query.

"You do mean the invitation to another one of his little soirees in two weeks."

Gladys smiles as she knows this topic of the soiree—or in fact, any reference to the Russian—has hit sour notes for Mildred before, but that can't stop her now because she is so very curious about this devious man, who lives so close to them that they can sometimes smell what he is having for dinner; she's not comfortable not knowing as much about him as he seems to know about them, and she believes that getting closer to him is the only way to do this.

"One and the same."

This time, Mildred pauses little, but she looks right at Gladys with a quizzical gaze that if read properly, it states a very curious "What are you up to, Gladys?" query.

Gladys is having fun now as she smiles impishly like a child that has just snuck an extra cookie when no one was looking. She gets up from her chair and sits on the arm of Mildred's chair; she then leans in and playfully nudges her at her shoulder.

"So what do you think?"

Mildred knows exactly what she is talking about, but she chooses to play unaware; she's almost laughing when she answers her friend back, "So what do I think about what, Gladys?"

Gladys, a little frustrated, harrumphs, "Come on, Millie, tell me what you think about the invitation."

Mildred relents with a big sigh.

"Okay, okay, so what do I think, huh? Well, I think not, that's what I think. I still think he's a scoundrel, that's what I think. Now, if you believe differently, you can go to his little shindig, if you will."

Probably thinking that her refusal would work against an affirmative decision on Gladys's part, Mildred sits back and exhales as if this conversation is over. Gladys, on the other hand, is not quite finished with the discussion; she totally surprises Mildred when she says, "I'd love to go."

Mildred stiffens, and then she folds her spindly arms across her flattened chest as her face stiffens and her thin lips press to a point at the edge of her softly curved chin; she inhales quickly, one short sip of air, and then she exhales three crisp words.

"Well, go then."

Gladys knows that she has upset her friend, but she is determined to have her way, but as always her first order of business is to soothe Mildred's ruffled feathers. Mildred has turned away from Gladys, more in momentary mocked anger than anything deep or permanent. So Gladys has to walk around to the other side of the high-back chair to see Mildred's face. This time she crouches down to put her face right up to Mildred's as she speak consolingly to her, "Now, now, honey, don't go getting upset with me now. You know that I can't go by myself. That wouldn't look right, me going without you. That would certainly draw attention and suspicion from unwanted people and places."

Mildred's normally white-pallor cheeks perk up to rosy red, as Gladys's words have clearly stimulated a passionate response on a completely different topic, "Well, in God's name, why not? You have as much right to be there as I do—more than anyone else in this building has, for that matter. This property is more than three times the value of any in the building, and it's half yours."

This time it's Gladys who's taking umbrage, for she is unwilling to allow others to know their intimate business.

"I know what is and what isn't, Millie, that's not the point."

Mildred is really more frustrated now than she was when they were discussing the Russian's upcoming party; she actually raises her voice when she shouts, "Then, Gladys, what is the point?"

Gladys takes a deep breath as she is forced to air sensitive and old family secrets.

"It's not what everyone else knows, and it's not time for them to know it either."

Mildred harrumphs as she recrosses her now-uncrossed arms.

"That's not in any way fair or necessary, This is your life, Gladys, and you've more than earned everything you have."

Gladys is stubborn as she all but ignores Mildred's plea; she just plows through with her mind made up.

"So we have to keep the walls up on this façade for now—that was our solemn promise to Richard."

That did it. Mildred was almost quiet by then; she had almost taken her usual position of noninterference whenever Gladys decided that she didn't want to reveal the particulars of their arrangement and her vaunted yet secret status in this very exclusive Fifth Avenue co-op. But there was something that Gladys had said that raised her normal docile temperament to fiery ire.

"Richard, hell. You say Richard, right!"

Mildred's boisterous tone gets Gladys's full attention, and in response, Gladys can only stutter out a sibilant yes.

"Richard, my husband, that scoundrel of the first order, he has no rights here, not anymore, he doesn't, and I'm declaring that here and now, finally, his long and torturous reign is now officially over."

Gladys is emotionally and physically shaken by Mildred's words. A devout Christian since birth, Gladys believes in the rules—all of the rules—that govern human behavior. She is aware that many don't follow the rules that are laid down—the poor break them, and the rich make their own. But not Gladys; she has always followed the rules. God's rules have always come first, and then man's rules a close second behind them—"the laws of the land"—as she often calls them. What Mildred is saying to her now has put her emotions in direct conflict with her beliefs, the very same beliefs that have guided her life through the roughest of times. So finally, Gladys—who had by this time walked over and sat down in her own high-back smoking chair—stands up and remonstrates, "No, Millie, no, that's right. A promise given is a promise owed, and we both gave it, Millie, we both gave it to him."

But this time it's Mildred that walks over to Gladys's chair; she pulls a nearby ottoman closer as she sits down to face her friend. This time she speaks in a much more modulated tone. "Yes, but you know, I'm really tired of this ruse, Gladys. You are both of the boys' birth mother, right?"

Gladys stares straight into Mildred's eyes, and the seriousness of this discussion is reflected back at her. She thinks—probably about the boys—and then she smiles a warm, gentle, motherly smile back into Mildred's eyes.

"Yes, that's right, Millie, as right as the day follows the night, right."

Mildred smiles right back at her, and by Gladys's answer, she knew she'd made some headway; and now she's going to push as hard as she can to get what she's for the longest time really wanted for her friend—so she pours it on thick but nonetheless completely true.

"And you took care of all of us—John, me, and Richard, and dragging Albert along, even when times were at their worst, right?"

Gladys stares and pauses as she ponders Mildred's question; she couldn't deny its veracity, and she wasn't about to—that's not her way—but it was clear that she wasn't going to gloat over the facts either. She just nods her head compliantly and says, "You're right, Millie, as right as night follows day, right."

Mildred is destined to make her point stick as she hammers the final nail into the coffin to seal it forever.

"Hell, you are the glue that has held this family together through all of its ups and downs and troubles, and you still want to take the backseat. That's not right. There is nothing fair about that, love, nothing at all. And no, one dead or alive, has the right or a good reason to ask that of you. That old bastard is still trying to control you from the grave, and I for one won't stand for it any longer."

Gladys is a tough cookie; she still—after all of Mildred's words—resists taking her rightful place.

"Listen, darlin', we've been through all of this too many times to count already. You are the one who saved my half-white, high, high yellow that never found a place to fit no place in this world behind roamin' the streets. You picked us up off the streets, my little pale boy, Albert and me. You did that from right there across the street in that lovely park. We had less than nothing, and you found us a home, and you gave me a job here in your home. Even after Richard had his way with me___."

Mildred has no patience to listen to any more of Gladys's litany of things that she did for Gladys, when it is Gladys who has done so much more for her entire family, and that's especially in the light of the abuse of Gladys's at the hands of her now-dead husband, Richard.

"You see, love, that's exactly what I'm talking about . . . had his way with you, huh. He brutally raped you, Gladys. Having his way . . . well, that's just too, too insipid for words, that bastard brutally raped you repeatedly, until you became pregnant, and then he threw you out on to the street again, and that under false pretenses, taking your home and livelihood, that lout__."

"But you came and got us, Millie."

"Yes, yes, I did, my love, yes, I did, and it was the best thing I've ever done too, in this wholly pampered life of mine, it's the best thing ever I've done."

Mildred leans forward and rests her head in Gladys's lap as Gladys strokes her hair as she reflects on their past years together.

"Yeah, and the baby came out as white as an Irish bed sheet. You can always tell when a baby's mixed blood, but John had none of those signs—you remember me telling you about them, Millie?"

Mildred lifts her head from Gladys's lap; she's been crying, and her face is red and wet with tears. Gladys takes out her handkerchief and gently pats her cheeks and below her eyes as she dries her best friend's tears away. They sit like two primates in the wild, one preening while the other luxuriates. Mildred smiles softly as she too remembers; they sigh, and both smile as they speak softly of their pasts.

"Yes, Gladys, I do remember. I remember you showing me the tips of his ears, and his rear end, and telling me that these were the first places that race shows on a mixed-race child. You said you had been told that by your white mother when you were a mere child yourself. I remember the shock of it as if it were just yesterday, love, because that's the day I knew that we would always be together, less than lovers but closer than friends, my dear Gladys. I remember you telling me that that was one of the last things your mother had said to you before she left with her sister and went back home with her forever. I'm so sorry, love, I know that I can never make that up to you, and I know that the only reason she left you was because you were getting darker by the day, and she felt that people would condemn her for having a mixed-race child. I think that white people, and I can speak for them because I am one of them, are worse that way; I think they are harsher on one of their own with a mixed-race child ever so much more than are blacks, for myriad reasons of which the most salient is their assumed superiority. It's all about tolerance and understanding. There is a mental strain in most white folks that believe they are altogether superior to blacks, and it is that frame of mind that makes them so intolerant and unforgiving when one of theirs chooses to be with a black person, instead of the other way around. And besides, blacks are well used to white men creeping around at night taking sexual advantage of black women—if proof of what Richard did to you is not enough, then, I don't know what is, but I'm certain there are many miscreant, self-absorbed, bigoted whites that would still most vociferously argue that point to their graves. But yet and still, it must have been a most difficult decision for her to have made, after all is said and done, she was your mother, and you were her child."

Gladys's face turns serious; she nods at Mildred, and then she takes a deep breath and a long, forlorn look off and up toward the high ceiling of the ornate library. When her eyes and her attention return to Mildred, she smiles at her friend as she remembers the infant John.

"He was moody even back then. I remembered when you said that we should raise him together, and at first I was unwilling, but I knew that it would be hell for me to raise a white baby alone in my world. I could have done it, but it would not have been without problems. But you, Millie, you—that's when you said that we should all come to live with you, you took all of us in to your home, you were never stronger with Richard than you were then, you just told him what you were going to do and that was that, and from then on, you protected me. I was so proud of you, then, Millie. You took our boy in and raised him as your own, especially when Richard saw that his son was whiter than he was. And we spent—how many years was it?—in Florida . . . a year and a half, almost two, and when we came back, nobody ever questioned that John was yours and Richard's son. It was very strange at times, and if we hadn't all stayed together, it would have been an impossible thing to do, but I was there for everything, every important moment: every birthday, every holiday, every nightmare, every scraped elbow, and every bloodied knee, everything—we were both there for both John and Albert, Millie. Oh, I thank God for his mercy and blessings. We've put a new twist on the definition for blended families, I bet we have, Millie, I bet we have."

Mildred smiles with great approval in her eyes, but she does beg to differ with one portion of Gladys's account.

"Not true, love, I never raised him or anyone else—you raised him, just like you raised all of us, Gladys. You know that's the real truth, Gladys, you know that. And that's why you have to give up this charade, hiding around behind an unspoken falsehood. We are all family. There are no outsiders here, and if anyone were to be an outsider, that someone would certainly not be you, love, that someone would be me, for it's your blood that dominates this family tree, if the truth be known, love, it's your blood that dominates here. From the moment you entered our world, Gladys, you changed it, love, you changed it when we were not looking, and you changed it when we were looking right at you. We've always owed you more than we could ever have paid you back for, and what we have chosen to share with you is far less than what you have shared with us. You've shared your life with us, Gladys, and, in truth, life cannot be bought—if it could, all rich men would live to be a thousand years old, and the truly wealthy would live forever. You made us all better, even that scoundrel, Richard—I still can't believe you ever forgave him."

Gladys smiles and says with a sermonizer's twang to her words, "I know you haven't, Millie, and that's why he still owns your feelings and makes you angry; you've never let go of the anger, and that's what keeps you two connected, even though he's in the grave. At some point you have to ask yourself why you keep holding on. Is it him, or is it yourself that you're so angry with for what happened here in this house? Let it go, Millie, let it all go, Millie, let go, and let God, I say, let God have it, he can handle it much better than you can, Millie. But you sacrificed, too, Millie—you gave up relations with your husband when you could have had your own children."

Mildred studies her friend's advice for a long moment, and then she sighs a laugh.

"Love, don't make me laugh, I have had the best of all possible worlds. Gladly, darling Gladys, and you know the truth of that as well. For you more than anyone knows that I didn't give up much, if truth be it well told. To speak quite plainly, he was a little dick, weasel, scoundrel, and I made a wise decision that I've never looked back on. It was the least that I could do. Now, that's that . . . and our John has called me mother for over thirty-five years, and Albert has never acted like less than a son to me. I have your love, and we both have the love of our children, we are indeed a family, and nothing else more is need. Life is good, love, life is good."

Gladys is all but won over as she reflects on her other son's life as well.

"We are truly a family, Millie, even when my Albert got into trouble, you brought him here so we could keep an eye on him, and look how well he's turned out."

Mildred laughs recalling some of Albert's exploits in the building.

"Yeah, and he's really got a way with the ladies, too."

CHAPTER X

The two weeks passed in a flash, and before they knew it, it was time to party. It had not been an uneventful two weeks by any stretch of the imagination, but suffice to say it had passed speedily by. My mother, whom I saw every day during this time as usual, had asked me what I thought of the invitation to the Baron Romanovsky's party. I had seen the baron as regularly as I had seen any of the other owners, and I must admit that, all up, he bore little dissimilarity to the rest of the owners—meaning that he could be as friendly or as aloof and snooty as any one of them. At that particular moment in time, there were many things about the goings-on in the building—especially those movements concerning the baron's quest to acquire the entire building—which I didn't know about; my mother hadn't told me about his threat/ offer yet. And so to me, everything was normal—intriguing, but normal nonetheless. And as far as my advice about Mildred and Gladys attending the party, I thought that it might be a reasonably exciting diversion for them both. They never went anywhere unscripted anymore, with their daily walks in the park and their Sunday brunches at the Tavern on the Green Restaurant on the west side of the park; that along with their compulsive attendance at Broadway Shows, the Metropolitan Opera, and the symphony at Carnegie Hall. You could probably stand on the corner of Sixty-Fourth Street and Fifth Avenue and set your watch to their comings and going like clockwork.

It's funny ironic, and I don't often think about it; it's just a part of our lives that sort of fit together hand in glove. But my mother and Mildred—they're both actually like my two mothers; well, they are of a different era than I. I mean, everything about them has a form, a format, a way of being done that is so ritualized it makes me smile just to think of it.

The baron had sent formal invitations to them to attend his party, and finally—a little later than what may have been expected—they had accepted by RSVP. That was the appropriate thing to do. But, as I personally witnessed, when they on a number of occasions have seen and been close to the Baron Romanovsky in the lobby, they would, the both of them—Gladys and Mildred, who were together 95 percent of the time—barely say hello to him. It was as if the two things were totally separate from each other—the decision to go his party and a desire for a closer relationship or friendship, and they—at least the two women—were keeping them totally separate; they could go to his party, but they refused to befriend him in public. What's up with that? I thought, but of course, the whole thing was more nuanced than I had knowledge of at the time.

And another way that we are different was how they prepared for the party. They actually bought new outfits for the party; I knew they had at least gone shopping for new accessories. To be well-turned-out—that indeed and above all was very important to them, and I guess it is to all women on some level. They, it turned out, didn't even like this man, and besides the fact that they were going to his party in the first place—a decision for which I would later understand—it was important that the proper presentation was made, nonetheless. The supremely important thing was that they were appearing in public, for God's sake, and it was important how they appeared far more than it was relevant as to where they appeared; I don't understand this, and I'll never understand it—it's way too late in my life to be trying to figure that out now.

Well, on the night of the party they two are primping and preening upstairs to get ready for the evening. It's not as if this is a new thing with them; they go out all the time: to the theater, to the opera, to the symphony, and, of course, to dinner. Mildred can't cook, and Gladys sometimes is reluctant to cook for just the two of them. She says it would be too much like being married to each other, and she didn't want to feel that way about anyone ever again. Really, that's what she said; for the love of me, at first I really didn't understand that sentiment, but that was not until I took a long good look at my own life, and when I saw that I behaved similarly, I then knew what she was getting at. But they fretted about up until the last moment; it's funny how symbiotic those two women have become over the years. My mom, Gladys, had a particularly difficult life; I mean she is regarded as an African American woman, simply a black person. No matter how light skinned she is, and she's really light—in this white male dominant society and as they make the rules, no matter how absurd they may sound to ears, or appear to the eyes, she is still considered black. She, as you probably know by now, is half-white and half-black; at least that's the most salient ratio as we don't know her father's or her mother's full lineage. Her father was fair skinned as well; he as well had been the product of a mixed-race coupling—as always a mere fact of human nature, tagged by prevalent nomenclature, and colored negative by ignorance and biases, even though in many cases those two people came together because they really loved each other, but alas, there's no history here.

She never talks about where she was born—at least to me she doesn't—but I know she still to this day hides many scares and hard-to-heal wounds; her devotion to God is laudable, and might I even say miraculous given the trials of her life, but maybe that is why she was given those trials before she was given this magnificent life. It's true that Mildred found her walking with me in her arms in the dead of winter; I could have walked—I was ambulatory by then—but she held me close to her chest to keep us both from freezing to death. After her aunt had kicked her out of the house for having a baby—my father, her husband, had been sent to prison for murdering someone, and this I found out quite by accident, she never told me—they thought that she had had me out of wedlock because she never told them that she was married to a young man whom they abhorred and had banned him from their home and ultimately from seeing her. Anyway, she was in turn asked to leave with her infant child after refusing to marry a boy of their choosing. The entire story, of course, has never been completely clear, and the information that I have garnered was only gathered from bits and pieces from here and there; one day when the time is right, I'll get her to tell me the complete story. But the truth remains that one day, Mildred was walking through the park across the street, Central Park, and she spotted my mother and me. I think the story goes that she, my mother, was sitting on a park bench when Mildred walked up.

It was cold out—of course it was cold. It was the dead of winter, but it wasn't as cold as it had been; in fact, this day was rather sunny. And there she is, Mildred that is, walking by that particular bench at that precise time. And as she's told the story to me—she's always been so motherly and kind to me, she always smiles when she says this part—she says that she was compelled by a force stronger than her ego, for her ego was too concerned with how she looked; she says she was compelled to stop.

"What a good-looking boy," were the first words out of her mouth; Gladys was shocked as she later said, "I could have sat on that bench for three days without anyone ever saying a single word to me. No one ever said much to me at all. So when Millie said anything, and she says that's what she said, but I wouldn't necessarily remember her words that precisely because just the sound of her voice warmed my ear like heat, and all I could do was smile. I remember she had on a fine-looking mink coat. It was as black as night and as long as an oak tree is tall;, it just about touched the ground. I knew then that she was from across the street on Fifth Avenue, and I had seen her before. It wasn't like I was looking for her to speak to me or any such thing, it was just that after you spend so much time in one place, you begin to notice things and people, you know, there's a whole pattern to life if you stay lucid and aware, and I was always aware, as it could save your life out there.

"Sometimes I used to just sit there and stare at those beautiful buildings and wonder what it would be like just to walk into one of them, let alone live there. I don't know why I thought like that, there was no real reason for it; I didn't know anyone who lived there—heck, I didn't even know if I were high enough in my lowly status to know someone who worked there, let alone lived there. Well, when Millie said whatever words she said to me, my ears heated up, and my eyes stretched wider than saucers. I was always a respectful girl, and the baby and the miserable times had not changed that, so when she spoke to me, I answered her reflexively. 'Yes, ma'am,' I said, not knowing what she had said, mind you, but the next thing I do remember, she asked me if I were cold, and I remember I said, 'We are more hungry than cold, ma'am,' and that's when she burst into tears, my dear sweet Millie just started to boohoo all out loud as if someone close to her had died.

"And then, I remember this like it was yesterday, she sat herself and that big ol' black mink coat, down next to me on that cold, cold, old bench, and she said, 'Would you like to come home with me,' and that's when she pointed right at the building across the street—'and we three can get something to eat and warm up a bit.'

"To say I couldn't believe what happened would be a bigger-than-big lie because I had been praying for a miracle, and the next words out of my mouth, even before I thanked Millie, were, 'Thank you, Jesus, thank you, Lord, ' and Millie she just smiled and said, 'Come on, let's go and eat.'

"I remember every step that I took from that point on—I mean from the park to the apartment. Every step, I can still hear each and every one of them. When we started to walk, I continued to carry my baby, Albert, in my arms—he could walk well enough all right, but I didn't want him to—I didn't want him to think anything had changed. If I had put him down, he would just have begun to ask questions about where we were going, and all, and I didn't want him to get nervous and start anticipating anything at all. It's an amazing thing how what you think changes the way you feel. I had walked, literally, every inch of every walkway and trail on the inside and around the outside Central Park by then—that included Central Park South, up Central Park West, across One Hundred and Tenth Street, and back down Fifth Avenue. Having spent so much time there where people tended not to bother you as much as they do on the streets away from the park, it was a good place to get away from the rushing around and the peering eyes of the rest of the city. It seemed that everyone was always so curious about me walking around with a toddler in my arms. I don't know if people stared because of how big Albert was and wondered why I was still carrying him in my arms, but if the truth be known, often I don't know what people are thinking, and I bet oftentimes they don't know themselves either.

"But as I said, I remembered every single step we took on this day because I knew every step was different. They may have sounded the same, and to an onlooker they may have looked the same, but I had prayed, and prayed, and prayed every day that this day would soon come. There is no sense in anyone saying bad things about me here—like I should have done this thing or that thing to salvage my life—or to go now and start accusing me of one negative thing or another because I won't be hearing them. I've always believed—and my faith is unassailable—that God's plan for me has been this plan, and it was my ears and my heart only that could have received his blessings, so don't go treading on my dream.

"Millie is a naturally regal woman, and it's not because of her wealth, but the wealth does indeed frame her natural tendency well, just as a fine frame borders and accentuates a fine painting inside it. She is not a child of wealth—in fact, she's not even from around here; as the saying goes, she hails from the breadbasket, the Midwestern United States, from one of the Chicago suburbs. She lived there and grew up there—that is, until college, when she came east to Barnard Women's College, that's what it was called when she first went there. There's a saying that 'the first things you learn are the hardest to forget,' and I'm sure that is true. That's why when people whom you believe are of a particular type, or, in your limited understanding of who they are, you blithely and freely assign and label them with your biased and subjective characterizations, when they surprise you and behave differently from the person or character you've prejudged and perceived them as being, you then call yourself surprised when they act out of character.

"Well, that was me in regards to Millie—I had seen her often enough on her daily walks through and around the part, and for some reason—that I have never been able to explain to myself—I had avoided her, but I had watched her more or less intently, actually more than less from afar, and it's from this distance that I had formulated my impression and therefore my judgment of her. I was wrong, for as the tree grows from its roots, so does the woman grow from her beginnings, and Millie's beginnings were far, far away from Fifth Avenue. She had arrived here after she had met and later married Richard Smith, who had noticed her when he appeared at a lecture on economics and business in a lecture series sponsored by her college. He had noticed her and had inquired about her, and a meeting was later arranged. The rest, as they say, is history. Too bad so much of her early life with him was his story. Millie was sheltered and pampered at the same time that she was being surreptitiously and cunningly stripped of all of her independence and personal power, and, when I came along, she had as much backbone as a wet noodle.

"So, on this day, and as the winter sun was shining, the confluence of just the right forces, the chill in the air, and the sun on her face must have reminded her, or momentarily thawed a part of her brain that made her respond with her old, nearly forgotten heart. She had come from a warm and loving family living in a small town community, where charity, family, and interdependence were the norm. She was, after all was said and done, a Midwestern girl, and on this day it was that girl—all dressed up in her glamorous mink—that came calling on me, and my boy, Albert.

"'Come on,' she said as we walked across the street as the light turned green—it was quicker to cross in the middle of the block, but that just wasn't, and still isn't, Millie's way.

"'Come on before the light changes, it's a quick light, and I don't want you and the boy, I mean the baby, to get caught on the change.'

"I remember her quickly correcting herself—it was the middle of the Seventies, and people had exhausted the word *boy* when referring to anything male and black, it was not yet the era of political correctness—that public relations scam wouldn't come for another twenty or so years—but there was great sensitivity around this particular issue. I thought it was cute and, of course, very telling that she would go out of her way trying not to offend me, especially where no obvious offense was meant, intended, or taken. She even—in a very warm and motherly sort of way—reached her hand back to guide me forward of her when the light actually did begin to change before we were all out of the street onto the sidewalk. I had to skip a little just to keep up with her, and that's when I first noticed her smile. You know, smiles are funny things—they are like rivers that leave traces where they have been, even when they are all dried up, you know that they have been there. We call these telling signs by a sweet and gentle name; we call them smile lines—sometimes laugh lines. Well, Millie had none, no such tracing evidenced her face, and when she smiled at me, I could see that even the smile was searching for a place to land, it was uncomfortable and new to the region like a guest left unattended in an empty living room alone, searching for the right place to sit. Her face was like the smooth untouched icing on a birthday cake, where no finger has yet touched it to sample a sweet taste.

"It instantly saddened me because immediately I knew that Millie was in pain and unhappy, all dressed up in her finery, and as unhappy as her mink coat was long. But with me and Albert trailing behind her, I knew, or at least I sensed, a new kind of energy in her—as I said, I had watched her from a distance on her daily walks through the park—and I'm sure some of what I see is colored by my relationship with her now, but still I'm sure that she immediately displayed a different, more vibrant kind of energy than she had heretofore upon my observation ever displayed. She was downright jaunty now.

"When we entered the building—actually, before we entered the building, it was right when we reached the doorman—Millie was walking a little ahead of me. We hadn't talked after we all had crossed the street. But when we reached the building, the doorman goes to open the door—it was as if I were invisible—he opens the door for Millie, and then he begins to close it right behind her—he doesn't even say a word. It was amazing as he's closing the door, I stopped—I didn't know the rules—thinking maybe he had that right, but that's when Millie turned around like a mother hen, and without even one word, she put her boney hand on the door, and, like an automaton—and again with not as much as a single word—the doorman reversed the direction of the door. She had power, Millie did, she had personal power, it was not just the power of her position—oh, she had that as well—but her personal power was always there under the surface, which she'd sooner show for someone else—a stranger like I was then—quicker than ever would she use it for herself. The doorman didn't dare say anything, but Millie did, 'Never close the door on them again, is that clear?'

"That was all she said, and I remember that distinctly—it was like she already knew what she had in mind for me, which must have included that this wasn't going to be my last time here, wow, 'Never close the door on them again. She really said that to him, and he never did either. God is so good. From the time that I had entered the lobby and until she—mind you, she brought out an assortment of foods for us to eat, among them included cold cuts and breads, all kinds of fruits, and sliced and chopped vegetables and, of course, milk for Albert—asked me if something was wrong with my mouth and why it was hanging open. It makes me laugh a little thinking back to how she ate. If someone didn't cook it for her—she mostly went out for her meals—then everything was picnic food minus the hot stuff. That marriage of hers—which I was to learn later—had induced her away from any natural will to do simple domestic things. The house was a mess, there were things lying all over the place. It was a tremendous place, but the true beauty of it was lost in the chaos and disorder.

"Once we had completed our meals—still we hadn't talked much save for an uncomfortable pleasantry here and there—and I was readying to leave. I thanked her for her charity, and, as I had not ever put Albert down off of my lap, I just stood up with him still in my arms.

"'Where are you going, Gladys?' she said—of course, by then I had given her my name.

"I immediately thanked her, and then inexplicably, I did something awkward—it was somewhere between a bow and a curtsy—an unseemly bastard of a genuflect. I have no idea where it came from, but thank God it hurried up and went back there never to return again. And as I was about to thank her for her charity and then make my exit, I know, I know what I said about coming back there again and all, but what if I were wrong, and this was it, a onetime meal, I didn't want to wear out my welcome the first time around, and, of course, she knew where to find me if she ever wanted to be charitable again. So I turned, and I hear this screech—and only for a fraction of a fraction of a second did it alarm me, but once that fleeting moment passed, I realized what that sound was, especially when a cascade of them repeated in quick succession one after the other. She was laughing heartily, bordering on hysterically.

"'Gladys, oh, Gladys___'

"She managed to form words between her cackles of laughter.

"'What was that, Gladys? Were you bowing?'

"She could see my face contort in embarrassment, and immediately she became sensitive to my discomfort. She immediately stopped laughing—she stopped on a dime, as it were.

"'Oh no, Gladys, my laughter was not meant to hurt you, it's just that I haven't seen anything that hit me in the funny bone like that in a long time. I'm sorry if my laughing has offended you, that never in any way is my wish or my intention. Where are you going, Gladys?' she says as the level of her seriousness takes over and changes her countenance like clouds moving in front of the sun and darkening the sky.

"'Please don't go, I couldn't stand to know you and Albert were out on the street again.'

"I must admit. I have never seen something so amazing as that—I mean seeing it and at the same time being a part of it. Here I was, this high, high-yellow, white-black homeless woman with a child in my arms, daily praying for such a miracle and believing that it could come true, but when it happened, my wonderment defied and duly challenged my life-long faith, for a fleeting moment. Here was this wealthy Fifth Avenue woman begging me to stay. Stay where? I thought instantly, *I can't stay here*, and that's just what I said.

"'Why not? Look at the size of this place, Gladys, you could wander around and get lost in here, and even though I live here and know that you are here, it could still take a week for me to find you.'

"This time we both laughed.

"'So you'll stay?'

"I just nodded yes. I couldn't believe my great good fortune, but I wasn't about to turn down a warm bed—I assumed I'd get a bed to sleep in. Once I had consented to stay, she was off and running full of ideas.

"'Good, then you can work for me.'

"She caught herself again, and this time she asked me if I'd consent to work for her. I didn't ask her what she would have me do, and she didn't specify. She didn't ask me if I could cook, or if I would clean and run errands, all of which I would have done without thinking twice about it. It was settled then, and then she took me for a walk through the house—she was only half-kidding about that getting lost thing—the house was huge as there were three different floors, there was a lot to get used to. She showed me where Albert and I could stay, and she was very smart. She never tried to separate me from Albert, and she didn't question why I never put him down the entire time until I finally did. Millie has a strong intuitive side, she doesn't force anything that doesn't want to be forced, and she has the sense to know which those things are, and my baby, Albert, was definitely one of them.

"It was several hours later, and we had by that time gotten fairly if not very comfortable with each other. Albert was walking around freely, discovering his new surroundings, while Millie and I were sitting in the library talking to each other. That was about the time that everything changed. Richard came home. Richard Smith was a large man with salt-and-pepper hair. He wasn't fit in today's sense of fit, but he was strong—he had worked construction for his father when he was a young man. He had always been in the construction and real estate businesses, and when his father died, he took over and worked very hard to grow the business. It turns out that it was his father who had built the co-op that we were sitting in, but he always took credit for—and not that he hadn't far exceeded the things that his father had done, but this building, maybe because he lived here, was of some very special significance to him—It made him, and for this and other equally absurd reasons, act imperious and haughty. Although in regards to me, the second he walked in, I could feel his baser instincts clamoring to be set loose on me, that unmistakably boorish presence that hovered just beneath his veneer of refinement, and I knew instantly that I couldn't stay here. No matter how much comfort it offered—and I was sure there was no greater comfort this side of heaven—I knew I would be treated like dog waste on the bottom of his shoe that he would be constantly trying to scrape off. I knew that for as soon as he laid eyes on me, his top lip rolled back like hot cooking bacon in a frying pan; he sneered at me with defiance and disgust as if my very existence in the world of his making was a transgression beyond redemption. I refused to cower, for I had seen worse on the streets, but, I swear, I had never run into someone that was so obvious and willing to hurt me for merely being alive than I felt he was, as if my presence had stained his pristine white world.

"'What is she doing here?' he bellowed like a dockworker unloading cargo in a rainstorm, just after seeing another cargo ship approaching with more to unload. I wasn't impressed by his bluster—I had already read him and knew that I was short for his presence and his world—but I held my tongue and gathered my son. I was ready to go, but that's when Millie showed her mettle—not unlike what she had done when the doorman tried to shut me out—she simply raised her hand, not her voice, in defiance of her husband's rancor, saying, 'She's here for me, Richard; is there going to be a problem?' Speaking of imperious, well, now that was queenly—Victoria, Elizabeth, or Marie Antoinette had nothing on my Millie, with a wave of the hand and a certain authoritative tambour to her voice, she was like a force of nature, natural and precise, nothing wasted but every bit of it effective. It stopped him in his tracks. It was miraculous, the second miracle of the day—she had given him notice, and he had acquiesced without resistance or appeal. Silently he stood there staring, seeming like an elephant digesting a recently eaten meal, still, motionless, and speechless until a small nod moves his head front to back, pulsing ten maybe even twenty times before he spoke.

"Then, he took another long look at me, and says___'Okay.'

"And this he says with an eeriness, a strange sort of resolve that forebodes a hidden agenda. It was still in my mind a want to leave, but Millie took my hand and held it saying___ 'Everything's going to be all right, Gladys, his bark is worse than his bite.'

"And so I listened, it was not such a stretch, but even with that assurance, within days we decided that I should have my own apartment. Millie, after a while in seeing my discomfort, she rented me a lovely one-bedroom apartment right across the park on Seventy-Second Street, where it was easy for me to just walk across the park to get to and from her. Still I spent most of my time with her at her place, but it made me feel a hundred times more comfortable. After a while, things between Richard Smith and me got much better—why wouldn't they have, within a few months I had changed their lives. They were eating at home, and their house had never been so orderly—a place for everything and everything in its place. And Millie, she was developing smile lines. We started going everywhere together, and Richard had become quite civil, even nice toward Gladys—and even Albert for that matter, whom he took a liking, too. It was a good time for a while, and that is until that horrible day.

"Millie had actually taken Albert out to FAO Schwartz, on Fifth and Fifty-Eighth Street—it has since moved around the corner to Madison Avenue—which was just a stone's throw from our co-op. Richard was home early working in his office when he came down to the kitchen to get something to drink, or so he said. I had long since gotten over my discomfort around him; in fact, it had gotten to the place where we could actually hold a pleasant yet short conversation—he really wasn't such a bad sort after he thawed out a bit.

"Millie and Albert had been out maybe a half hour, and I expected them back by dinner. When Richard had come into the kitchen, I was facing away from him. I remember, I had just put a bottle back in the refrigerator, or I would have hit him with it. He came up behind me—he didn't say a word—it was as if he had planned this behavior for a long time, and this was his golden opportunity. I was wearing a dress—I always wore dresses—and he grabbed at the dress and me at the same time, so I didn't know what to do first, whether to pull my dress back down or grab at his arm that had reached and secured me hard against his chest. He was already naked from the waist down—that's how I knew that he had planned his attack. He pushed me forward against the counter—he was just too strong for me and easily overpowered me. He pushed himself inside me, and then he thrust himself against me hard and repeatedly—grunting and cursing, and calling me bad names as he did—until he released himself all over my legs. I never made a sound, and I never turned around—I didn't wish to see his face—until I heard his bare feet slapping against the wooden kitchen floor as he scurried back to his hole upstairs. I didn't move much for the longest moment ever, and I can tell you this, the first thing I thought about was Millie—how was I going to tell her what had happened? I wasn't embarrassed or ashamed for myself because I already knew what men do. It wasn't the first time I had been raped—Albert's father had raped me after we were secretly married, we were so young, and we couldn't afford our own place, so I stayed living with my aunt. I was silly and naïve—I hadn't figured much out yet, but I knew that I couldn't be with him in that way without first being his wife. So I insisted that we get married before I would be with him—he complied, and so I thought that we were on the same wavelength. I think this is just another twist to the idea that a man will say and do anything to get to the getting of what he wants. How disparate and despicable is that?

"After we got married, we were together—intimately—for the first time, and I foolishly thought that everything would flow right for us from there, I was so young and stupid—but it turned out that with our separate living arrangements that we couldn't always be together when he wanted because I still lived in another woman's house. He got angry a lot, and then he started drinking with his friends, and the combination of being drunk and angry—angry at everything, with me, with himself, and ultimately with the entire world, his anger overwhelmed his weak nature. He felt helpless, he couldn't defeat the world so succumbed to the ease of violence when physically he took it out on me, more than once he brutalized me. Albert was a product of his anger, and that's why I protected him so, he deserves no less—his father, he never apologized—he said he didn't have to because we were married. It was a blessed day when he went to jail for murder—I hadn't wished him any harm, but I was glad he was away from me. When my aunt saw that I was pregnant—I tried to explain—she didn't believe me, and I couldn't prove it. There was a part of me that didn't care to prove it, but I never thought that she would resort to trying to force me to marry someone else, and when I refused, she'd throw me and Albert out on the street. He was just an infant then, and back then there were only a few places to go for help—I tried shelters and churches, but they were only for short stays. Finally, I found myself totally out on the street, and that was after I had vehemently refused to give up my child to adoption or child services—they, more than one of them told me, that Albert would be easy to place because he was so light skinned, even though that's one of the reasons my aunt cited for kicking us out—she said, 'That baby is damn near white, I can't have another white child living in this house.' I ended up running away from all of them just so that I could keep Albert.

"And now this bully with his lack of impulse control has ruined all of that. How was I supposed to explain all of this to Millie? She would never understand. I was distraught, worried, and alone. I didn't know what to do. I didn't even have a chance to take a shower. I hand washed myself down with a kitchen towel, and within minutes, they—Millie and Albert—had returned from FAO Schwartz. I wanted to tell Millie right out, but when she came into the kitchen with Albert, and they were all smiles and joy, I couldn't bring myself to ruin her day, and that day—as all bad things unattended to seem to grow like fungus, sucking the life out of its host—quickly turned into ten and then twenty days. A single nation without allies is always more vulnerable to multiple attacks by predatory nations, and so it was with Richard. Seeing as I had made the very foolish mistake of not telling Millie right away, he took this as some kind of perverse complicity—what else would a lout like him choose to think?—and he commenced an all-out campaign to ravage me at his whim and fancy whenever he had a good mind to.

"Finally when I had taken more than I could any longer stand—Millie had gone off to the beauty salon—I fought him off. He was indignant and insulted—acting as if I were his territorial prerogative, he unceremoniously threw Albert and me both out before Millie had returned home. He wasn't even man enough to tell anywhere near the truth as he trumpeted a series of lies, ending with 'She had decided that it would be the best thing for all concerned if she left the premises quickly and completely.'

"There was a tiger lurking inside of Millie, a tiger that would sleep through most feeble efforts to arouse her from her slumber—but once aroused, there was no easy way to resettle her short of total appeasement and satiation. In short, Millie never believed a word that Richard had reported to her about me was true. She as well as I—although in a way and with experiences different from my own—she knew the limits of man's veracity under pressure, especially when the acts for which he is culpable are culprit.

"Before that day, I would only spend some part of the weekend at my little place a stone's throw across the park, but this Tuesday, nearly halfway through the week, I was sitting there alone in my apartment. I was depressed and saddened, to say the least, but I knew I had done little in the way of wrong, and that my greatest mistake was in not trusting Millie, who had by then become my best and only friend. I had no other way to turn, except to my abiding faith in the Lord; I was in meditative prayer, when the intercom buzzed, it startled me. When I answered, I had expected it to be someone seeking a different person, but that when I heard.

"'Gladys, it's me, Mildred Smith.'

"*How formal*, I thought, *she's come to dress me down.* I hesitated, but then I buzzed her in without speaking—I didn't know what to say. I waited an interminably long thirty seconds as she rushed upstairs, and as I opened the door to her, she rushed in and grabbed at me.

"'Gladys, are you all right, what did he do to you?'

"I must admit I was, at that precise moment, feeling a lot of conflicting feelings, only one of which was confusion. It's true, I had confused myself; it was never Millie, she had shown—from the day that we first met in the park, and she had brought me home with her—she had only shown kindness, and given me peace, why then had I grown nervous about her presence in my home. So it was natural then that the first thing I said to her was___ 'I should have come to you, Millie, I should have come to you when it first happened.'

"Millie didn't even pause to have a guess at what my inference was, she knew, she knew all too well.

"'I should never have let things get this far, Gladys, it is my fault, but as God is my witness, it will never happen again. You are my friend, and I love you, Gladys, and I don't mean like some of my contemporaries mean they love their maids and servants either. You are my friend, and I love you as my friend, no, as my sister, Gladys, as my sister.'

"I had wanted to cry for weeks, but I was simply too overwrought to unleash that kind of useless emotion by my lonesome. I had long since learned that crying is a wasted and useless emotion unless you do it along with something useful and productive, and fortunately or unfortunately, as it were, I've rarely found that other thing that it is useful to do it with. But here it is now in Millie's embrace and catharsis is that one time, or at best, one of a very few instances where crying is appropriate, and that's in the arms of a friend, for friendship is about sharing, and what better thing to share between friends than a good cry. After we hugged and cried and cried some more—we are a lot alike, Millie and I, strange but true. I was certain that we both cried for many other things besides the thing we were beginning to discuss, I know that I was. But through it all, I had heard something unsettling that shouted out a need to be pursued by me, so I broached the topic quickly before the moment cooled and good and appropriate timing had passed.

"'Millie, you knew what was going on?' I asked, and this is why—in great part—why I love her so. She answered without a hint of equivocation.

"'I sensed something, Gladys, and neither blame nor understanding entered my mind, but still the energy in the house—as large as the house is—it had changed. You had become hesitant, and even docile, and he had become more the cock of the roost than ever I have seen him, and that's going a bit for his haughty highness.'

"I smiled with a new kind of embarrassment. I knew then that I should have trusted her and told her right off what had happened. She was a deep and thoughtful woman, a special woman in all that she had done for me, and I should have trusted her more. I am so damaged, but will pray hard for God to heal my soul the same way he has always healed my physical wounds. I knew then that Millie deserved to know what more there was to know, and, with that same veracity, I spoke out before I had a chance to think and filter my truth and reduce it down to something more palatable, 'I am pregnant with Richard's child, Millie.'

"There I said it, and I knew there were no more words to say on this topic. We both knew how it had happened, and we both knew now that the mountain to climb had landed in front of us both, or both of us in front of it. There is a part of myself that keeps waiting for this woman to be shocked and outraged against me—why, I thought, *Didn't I know better than to allow all of these calamities to befall me, wasn't I totally responsible, if not at least complicit?* This admission did, however, weaken her legs as she stepped back a step or two to find a seat in a nearby chair.

"'Wow,' she said, but her wow was accompanied by a small yet curious smile. I was next to say wow, and then she totally surprised me with her next words.

"'We have a baby on the way, Gladys, a baby.'

"The world is of God's making, and man is but a subject living upon it and whose understanding of it remains forever nuanced and incomplete.

'We have a baby on the way' is replete with nuance. But far be it from me—especially at this time—to argue with nuance. This woman, whom I have potentially offended and transgressed against by having her husband's baby, has in attitude and word accepted me as we, and my future progeny as ours, who am I to find fault in this. What more was there to discuss—the whys and wherefores where enumerable and illusive as to reason and motive, and as far as solution goes, hell, I was pregnant, and we were going to have a baby.

CHAPTER XI

The party was a grand scene, different from the high Victorian bordello style of previous shindigs. This one was different with high fashion evening gowns and classy tuxedos. The baron has transformed his home again, and this time it resembles the lobby of the Paris Opera—not the new Bastille Opera House, but the ornate old Paris Opera house at the terminus of the Avenue de la Opera; and if you've ever been there, you would see the stunningly accurate reproduction of the ornate classical lobby entrance—although on a much smaller scale—swirling upward to the seating boxes. The marble staircase and all the other ornamentations have been eerily duplicated, and at what cost, just to put a party on; it's mind-boggling—what statement was he trying to make? And that wasn't all; it only began there. As you entered, sitting off to the side was an at least ten-piece orchestra playing Mozart softly as to enhance but not disturb the atmosphere. The atmosphere was all up stunning and compelling. Even Mildred and Gladys—who were already fully intent and set upon criticizing every effort made by the baron to impress everyone—they were both caught off guard and hugely impressed by, in their estimation, his show of high-end culture and style. As they entered the foyer converted into the opera lobby, they pause and are obviously taken aback by the lavish display; and as their mouths are agape, the Baron Romanovsky himself is the first to approach them.

"Mrs. Smith, Mrs. Lawrence, I'm so happy that you are both here. Come let me show you both around."

And while this high-end, oh so *très chic* scene is going on upstairs in the baron's unit, downstairs, a skullduggerous affair is being initiated by a triumvirate of sneaky, if not all completely willing, participants. It seems that one of us—John Smith—has determined that he has been outdone, that he, in fact, has been outwitted by his own family, and he wants to repay them in kind, or at least get the goods on them to make that desire a reality. After he had surreptitiously ordered the peregrine falcon's nest to be taken down and subsequently after being admonished and embarrassed, he was ordered by his mothers to reinstall it, and after being beset by protesters and lectured by the Audubon people, he wanted to have the last word on this thorny issue. And it was without any real—as in hateful—malice, but more in the spirit of giving them a comeuppance and competition that he endeavored to get the upper hand again. So as the party is reveling upstairs at the baron's, he was set along with his two inductees—one a sycophant follower employee, Windler, and the other a half-resistant, half-intrigue-loving pseudo-accomplice—who was, of course, I; all three of us are huddled now in the lobby security office. John is nervous and excited as if we were about to pull off some very risky and dangerous caper, as if we were the CIA doing something terribly nefarious; and if that were true, you could have long ago counted me out. Anyway, so we three are huddled up inside the cramped security office, and John—our fearless leader—whines to Windler, "Have they gone upstairs yet?"

"Yes, sir, Mr. Smith."

And I say, "Your mother and Mrs. Lawrence, they both went up about ten minutes ago."

John has again quickly lost his patience with me for the smallest, most inconsequential reason. I don't have to do much of anything at all to garner this same response from him on absolutely any topic at all whatsoever; he's been steadily angry with me for years now—prison and that one bad thing I did back then—and he's not been able to let it go. So any chance he gets, he lets me know that he continues to be displeased with me. After I spoke, he looked away at Windler, first, and spoke to him, and then he looked directly at me, and he says, "Good, get your stuff, Windler, and let's go up there and get this thing over with."

And then with a look of exasperation, he stares at me with his thin-pursed lips and says, "Albert, why do you insist on calling your mother, Mrs. Lawrence? It's silly and so formal, and everyone knows that Gladys is your mother."

I laughed and smiled because I knew that what I was about to say would put him in his place right quick; it was going to be a small triumph, but I'd take it just the same.

"That's just it, sir. She has earned the right to be called Mrs. Lawrence by everyone, not Gladys, and I'm not about to undermine that honor just because I'm her son."

John is never speechless, especially with me on any topic whatsoever, but here is comeuppance knocking at his door, and he deigns to open it as it was the only way to leave this challenge that he himself had initiated. He clears his throat once, then twice, before he utters a single word, and then a single word indeed is all he utters twice in quick succession, "Touché, touché."

Touché my rear end—he can't even look at me and admit when he is wrong; what's wrong with him? He was so cool when we were kids, and all he ever wanted to do was to hang out with me uptown, but now, and I'm sure he's embarrassed, he looks to Windler once more and then again back at me, and I say, "Now I've got my stuff right here, sir. But are you sure you still want to go through with this right now, Mr. Smith?"

I couldn't resist the final dig by calling him Mr. Smith, but, to be totally honest with you, I don't even know whether he hears it; sometimes he is so haughty, he's so imperious, and in that frame of mind, he must think that everyone owes him a curtsy and the courtesy of calling him Mr. Smith. I really loathe thinking so much about him and his feelings, but being around him is a constant reminder of my own transgressions; it's like I've never left prison, or like I'm on lifetime probation. I know that he knows that I think he has been too hard on me for too long—we were like brothers, for Christ's sake—and enough hostility is enough. I did what I did, and it's done now, long done; I've paid dearly for it, and besides, although he hasn't ever been caught at anything, at least nothing that I have heard about, I'd bet the farm on it, I'm quite sure that all of his real estate and construction deals would not pass the closest muster, or scrutiny either. Look at him standing there all proud and aloof, his lord high and mighty; one day he too will really get his comeuppance, and I pray and hope that I'm there to see it—I really do. He's such a jerk.

"Let's go, you two."

I can only shake my head in amusement as he gets into his secret—agent mode again; it would be more fun if he'd just lighten up a little, as what we are about to do is closer to a practical joke than ever it was to a serious caper of some sort. But still he wants to act like a squad leader instead of what we all are at this moment, and that is three grown men acting like three little boys on a treasure hunt.

"We'll take the elevator to the fourteenth floor to the balcony. We'll install the camera up in the corner of the balcony where I know they've been feeding those goddamn dirty birds from. All I need is the evidence, and I'll be able to get rid of that vermin for good and ever, and fuck the

Audubon people." All I can say is that Johnny Boy—that's what my mother used to call him—is quite determined to make this little escapade amount to something. He's up here messing around with this silliness when he should been downstairs with his desperate, lonely wife, Nancy, taking care of some real meaningful business like keeping his home life together—no wonder she runs the streets and secret haunts of New York City looking for love in all those wrong places.

Now downstairs at the baron's party, the Baron Romanovsky has left the two dowagers standing alone when he almost trips over himself leaving excitedly to visit with one of his thuggish cronies. He had been—in his short yet impressive visit with the two of them—very engaging, even gallant, so much so that he had impressed Mildred, who after all found it very difficult, in most cases, to hold a grudge against even the likes of the Baron Romanovsky, for any length of time. She was, after all, from the Midwest, and Midwesterners are widely known for being confrontation-adverse and nice, and she here on that evening did nothing to alter that well-established, and well-earned impression.

"He's being very nice, isn't he, Gladys?"

Gladys—after some many years living with and around Mildred—has taken on a very similar outward appearance of refinement, high sartorial style, and a very classy demeanor; she mimics well, and it all suits her very well, but lest one be bamboozled by these stellar accoutrements, they would be fooled to look past the original and well-schooled soul of the beast. Gladys's harsh few years on the streets of New York and the rough and unfair treatment she suffered in her youth served well her education on the mind, the ways, and deeds of man—and that this life-altering lesson was continued even while she lived high in the sumptuous luxury and splendor of the thought-to-be-safe penthouse on Fifth Avenue. The multiple rapes and subsequent impregnation must serve as witness and testament to the true scope and breadth of man's depravity, greed, and inhumanity toward other men—and most shamefully taking it an even harsher a step further—toward defenseless women. She, as the unofficially designated protector of all things, Lawrence and Smith, Millie quickly and decisively serves notice that she is—as always—on guard for devious interlopers and bad-intentioned would-be predators, such as the Baron Romanovsky. But she loves Millie with all her heart and soul, and she can't resist a smile as she informs her friend and confidant on the true meaning of his smarmy demeanor.

"Oh, honey, you are so naïve, he's just a big old snake in a sheared wolf's suit. Like Eve's snake, slick, that's all he is, and I want to be as close to him as I possibly can be before he strikes. We've already heard him rattle that day in Central Park. Why do you think I wanted so badly to come to this party of his in the first place, Millie?'

Millie is dumbfounded—at best she is clueless; she shakes her head in dismay.

"You know what they say about keeping your enemies closer than your friends; we, Millie, we are very close now."

Millie is aghast; really, she is quite in shock by Gladys's cold, cunning, calculation in regard to the baron. She titters a squeaky nervous little laugh and gushes, "Oh, Gladys, I'm really surprised at you."

Gladys harrumphs triumphantly as she nods her head with satisfaction, the satisfaction that she hasn't completely lost her edge and critical skills of perception. She has shifted gears; even her speech—before now, much more genteel—changes to a harsher, more serious tone.

"Yeah, well, baby, you can be surprised if you want to, but he's still a snake. You found me on the street, love, and I thank God that you did, but the street is where I received my education. Living in the penthouse hasn't made me forget about snakes; they've too often left their indelible scales and slithery prints on me."

You can hear Mildred suck in the air of shock as she reaches quickly and grabs Gladys's arms.

"Oh, love, I'm so sorry, so very, very sorry, that bastard, Richard, he hurt you, and I know it goes far deeper than I can ever feel or ever know, and I will try to make up for until my dying day."

Gladys tries to stop Mildred in mid-sentence, but to no avail.

"You have done more than make up for it, Millie; you have given me a new life. Plus, honey, look what has come of it, we have a wonderful life, and two wonderful sons, don't we, love, don't we?"

Mildred smiles as Gladys catches a small tear—with her finger—that had escaped from Mildred's right eye, and then she turns to look at where the baron has gone off to in such a hurry; she pans the room with her head on a swivel, and when she spots him, she completes her earlier thought.

"I know enough to know that once a snake, always a snake, so let's just keep an eye on the slithering snake and see where he leads us. Is that okay with you, darling?"

Mildred's face glows like a pearl in water; you can see that she is almost embarrassed by the richness and great, good fortune of her relationship with Gladys and her life in general.

"Okay, love," she says, almost laughing as she sings her words. Now that they know their mission, the party becomes a big game; they get drinks as they nod and stroll around admiring the décor and as they smile and greet—with nods and hellos—some of their familiar neighbors' faces. Their attention, however, never leaves the baron to go too far without them noticing his whereabouts. They had taken notice—at least Gladys had—when the baron had first rushed over to speak with the two giants—Oleg and Borga—who were only a few millimeters difference in actual bulk, big men they are both. And as they stand at the bar talking, their level of animation increases for some unknown reason, and this draws more attention from the two senior damsels, now themselves involved in their own loop of espionage. They watch closer, and when the Baron Romanovsky shushes them both and then he herds the two large men into the kitchen, the ladies take note and quickly hurry across the party-room floor to see what's up. They reach the kitchen door just as it swings out toward them, and that's when Gladys's steely nerves take over. She sticks her foot in the opening between the back of the door and the door jamb to slow down its swing; and when it stops, the door is left just a crack open, and she can still see and hear through the thin opening that her foot—acting like a door stopper—leaves. They stand silently and listen—well, not they. It's Gladys that listens while Mildred stands and frets like an old hen, but she is still useful, keeping her eyes peeled for other, less-determined, busybodies.

While listening on the outside, inside the baron instructs his two stooges, "Okay, you two, I'll keep the two old ladies busy here while you two get up there and take care of this shit once and for all time. Make sure you do it well. I don't want this, as the Americans say, for this to come back and bite my ass. Now go."

The two men start to leave, and one of them, Borga, stops to pick up a couple of tools, and then they both exit by the fire stairs door at the back of the kitchen. Oleg and Borga head upstairs to the fifteenth-floor fire door, where they pick the lock and enter the triplex unit's kitchen. At the same time—one furtive group unbeknownst to the other—John Smith, Windler, and I are stealthily at work on the fourteenth-floor balcony attempting to install a video camera. From the beginning, I didn't like the whole idea of sneaking around on our mothers, but, in the end, I really didn't have much of a choice. When John first came to me and asked me if I would assist him with his plan, I was flabbergasted that he would ask my help at anything at all; he hadn't asked for my help with anything substantial since I had started to work there as the head doorman. John was always so angry with me that he wouldn't dare break the symmetry of his own annoyance; it would have been too much to ask of even for him to defy himself in that way. But here he was early yesterday morning—dressed casually, as it was Sunday. I could tell that he had something unusual on his mind, just by the way he moved. It was a throwback to when we were kids together, and he'd want to hang out with me, but I could see that he was clearly afraid that I would turn him down if he asked. He walked from the elevator to the concierge with his short haircut head tilted to one side; and his feet, as he walked toward me, would slide insecurely, never lifting more than they had to in order to move forward along the floor. I hated that weak, manipulative posture—I used to turn him down just because of it. I finally talked him out of using it as decoy for a more substantive, mature, and honest effort, and subsequently a prolonged close relationship between us followed; he was a good kid, after all. But here yesterday morning, we were back at that weak old place again, but now our positions have drastically changed—mine from ordinate to subordinate—and I'm thinking I must be tolerant and compliant what ever the request; so I listen to his plan.

He stops there right in front of me, and then he looks around suspiciously—how silly he looked, like a bank robber standing outside of a bank with a mask and a gun in his hand—if that's not a dead giveaway, I don't know what it is. Luckily this lobby is not a bank. So he stands there, and after he looks around long enough—I almost laughed in his face, but that wouldn't have been my best choice of behaviors—he speaks his mission: "Albert, we have some business to attend to tomorrow evening as it were, do I have your cooperation?"

Can you believe the chutzpah? He's got a real set on him, doesn't he? But I couldn't go negative on him because he was, in fact, asking me for my help—as cryptic and uncomfortable as it was, it was indeed an ask. So thinking quickly—because he is not nearly the world's most patient man—I nodded in the affirmative, and then he tells me his idea. It wasn't a plan; it seems that I was supposed to come up with that, so we split the difference. Roughly stated, what he wanted to do essentially was to spy on our mothers, and not for any gratuitous or infantile reason, not according to him anyway, but for the sane and reasonable contrivance that they were breaking the law. He said he wanted to catch them in the act of feeding the peregrine falcons, whose nest and home he had felt bullied into reestablishing after having surreptitiously removed it. He whined to me that he was tired of having detritus falling down on his head—an accusation that is totally unfounded as it is I who occasionally cleans up after the falcons, and I must say that I find no great malice toward them in having to do so. But I didn't argue the point with him; I could tell that he had something stuck in his craw, and he needed to get it out, and I knew that even though we would go through with this clandestine charade, in the end, nothing much would come of it. So when we first met tonight, we hadn't discussed it again until then, but I still smirk just thinking back to how much people—with all of their outer and substantial efforts to make change—seldom change very much; he's still that little Johnny Boy on the inside, pouting away about an imagined or blown-way-out-of-proportion injustice that had befallen him it was mostly in his mind that was so often the case. And now that we three fumbling bumblers are up here to do the deed, the deed is just as far from getting done as if we were still downstairs in the lobby. In an effort to get things going and so we can get the hell out of here, I suggested a location, "This corner over here has the best angle, it's well out of the way."

John—who had seemed perplexed as to what to do next—looks up and nods in tacit agreement as to where to locate the camera, "Okay, climb up on this chair."

He then pulls one of the deck's wrought iron chairs over, but it's clearly too short by a mile, and when, Windler offers, "It's not high__," John exasperatedly finishes Windler's thought, "High enough, yes, I see that, damn it!"

We all at that precise moment knew what was required, and simultaneously we all three turned to look for that very solution.

Borga and Oleg were fumbling around in the dark just one floor up when Borga trips over an unseen chair; he struggles to keep from falling, and his pipe wrench falls from his hand and crashes hard on the wooden kitchen floor. Clanking and bouncing, it slides out of reach under the large and heavy Wolf range oven as he cries out in pain, "Oh, shit, I banged my knee__"

Oleg immediately admonishes him for the noise he's made. "Quiet, you idiot."

But Borga snaps back quietly and intolerantly, "There's no one at home, brother, we just left the two old ladies at the party downstairs, remember?"

Oleg takes a second to think and nods his head, but then he thinks the better of their lax attitude.

"Yes, but still there is no reason to be careless—what if they all of a sudden return and find us still here? That would not be good, brother."

Finally, Borga nods in agreement as he finally rights himself and proceeds to look for a light switch so he can find the lost tool and so that they can get on with their bumbled mission.

While looking for something higher and more substantial to stand on, the three of us had stepped inside the unit away from the terrace, when Windler looks at me quizzically. It was clear that I had experienced the same sensation, but I wasn't absolutely certain, so as he was standing right next to me and must have heard the same noise, I turned to Windler and asked, "Did you hear that? What was that?"

Windler nods his head slowly, somewhat like a child who was about to be discovered by a parent while doing something wrong that he had no way to explain; but apparently, at the same time that we were hearing the sounds, John had not quite entered the unit from the balcony, and he hadn't heard what we—Windler and I—had heard.

"Heard what, Albert? What are you two talking about?"

I didn't want to speak for fear of if there were another sound, John would again miss it, so I put my finger to my lips to quiet him, and then I waved him over to Windler and me. We all three listen quietly, and then we all this time hear a scraping noise, like someone is moving a heavy-piece of furniture or something across the floor, and it sounds like it's coming from the kitchen area. Then I whisper to John and Windler both, "Something's going on upstairs."

I can see it in his eyes that same noise that's disturbed me. Windler is cautioned by it as well; it hits John in the same way, but he is too stubborn to relinquish his façade of superiority and confidence and looks first to blame everything on my lack of vigilance in keeping an eye on our mother's' comings and goings. So with that immutable posture and a supercilious look on his face, he subtly moves a step or two closer to me and whispers toward my ear, "Someone's upstairs . . . I thought you said you saw them go to the Russian's soiree, Albert?"

I knew what I had seen, and they had gone and had not yet returned, and also, I immediately knew from the sounds—the squeaking and sliding of whatever someone was moving—I knew that it wasn't the two of them upstairs moving heavy furniture at this or at any other time of the day or night; they would have asked me first if they needed something moved. And they hadn't returned home—I knew that—and besides, the only other way up would have been through the emergency access door in the back fire stairwell. Now, knowing the two of them as well as I do, there's no way—in their glamorous party clothes and all—they would have ever used that escape for any reason short of an actual fire or real emergency.

He can be such an idiot at times, because here we are faced with an unknown that may in fact be a situation that forebodes considerable danger, and he instead is living out his haughty image until the very end—I seriously think of smacking him, a quick backhand bitch-slap across his stiff pink chops, but, then again, what if I am the one who is totally wrong. So instead—as usual—I placate him with the simplest answer I can give him, "I did, sir."

I couldn't lose my disagreeable tone even though I forced myself to use the right words. Besides, I know that he knows that whenever I call him sir, he knows that he has displeased me or that I'm tacitly disagreeing with him. He finally gets it; it's not them upstairs.

"Then who the hell is upstairs?"

He's such a boob, I'm saying to myself as I'm shaking my head from east to west. It's hard sometimes keeping it all in with him, but I do.

"I'm sure I don't know, sir. I'm sure I don't know."

It's, John's turn to be annoyed now that he has joined Windler and me in our understanding of the simplest deduction concluding in that something upstairs is amiss. He bristles back; it seems that I have finally ruffled his feathers.

"It was a rhetorical question, Albert," he says as he then signals for Windler to come over next to the two of us, and then everything changes; he actually gets this twinkle, no, make that a flash or spark in his eyes; I hadn't seen that magic in years. I could tell that he was actually entertaining new thoughts; he was thinking on the fly, quick and decisively, and I was impressed. He actually put his arms around Windler's shoulders and mine as he spoke his extemporaneous thoughts to us both, "Look, you two, I don't know what's going up there, but you two be ready to leave, Albert and Windler, okay. If the two of them are somehow back, you know, in case we've missed their return, I don't want them to find us three here together, it would be too difficult to explain. Now listen, I'm going to call upstairs, and if my mother Gladys or my mother answers, then that's the signal for you two to scurry on out of here. I'll then go up and talk with them and find out what's going on up there. Now, if I call, they don't answer, then the three of us had better get up there and find out what's going on—after all, this is New York City, and it could be anything."

Jesus Christ, I thought I would die listening to him; he is as constipated as a clogged toilet—get to the point already, will you? And I hope that I'm never in a jam where he's the one left deciding what to do; I could be forgotten about before he finishes talking. But finally, Windler, who is as reluctant to speak as molasses is disinclined to flow in the winter, but the hulking man—an ex-military MP himself—finally speaks up, "You sure you want to just call up there to them? What if it's not them?"

John is indignant at Windler's suggestion, and he casts him a look that, if eyes were knives, would have killed Windler; that's probably why Windler is so hesitant to speak around him for fear of having this very same kind of experience every time.

After Oleg helps his brother and partner in crime up from his stumble over the obstructing chair, Borga noisily slides the culprit seat across the floor and out of his path; annoyed, Oleg reminds him again, "Careful, brother, someone might hear you."

Borga is still confident in his incredulity as he scoffs defiantly back at his brother, "There is no one here but us, we both know that the old ladies, who will soon be no more, are down at our brother's party getting drunk. Stop worrying, brother, you are beginning to sound like the third old lady."

But just then, and to defy Oleg's assertions about no one but them being in the spacious unit, they both simultaneously hear John Smith call out from downstairs. It was as clear as a church bell ringing at eleven o'clock on Sunday morning. John Smith calling out for his family.

"Mother, Mother Gladys, is that you, are you two up there?"

Oleg's feet freeze in their tracks, and as he turns to face Borga, he quietly yet sarcastically utters, "Then who is that calling for his mother, Borga, who then is that, is it Boris, do you think it is Boris coming in the front door and calling for his mother? I don't think so, my brother, not tonight it's not, come on let's get out of here."

And the two large men indelicately scramble out of the kitchen, not because they were careless because they were not; they, in fact, took great care in their movements toward the fire door. They tipped toed, but at the same time, they crashed clumsily into things, like chairs and tables; the fact was that under duress—which their scheme was now under—they moved clumsily, if not more so, than they usually did. They were large plodding animals, the brothers Romanovsky were, and the stress that they were now under did nothing to lighten their steps any. As they were moving out upstairs, downstairs—John, the leader of us three—was listening along with me and Windler; it was amazing that they did escape without too much noise, or in fact noise that not one of us three downstairs were willing to admit to hearing without the confirmation of the other two. It was the confluence of fear that had greeted us all at the same time and made us doubt our own ears. So John yells up again, and I could hear in his plaintive voice that he was hoping against hope that one of the women that he called after would finally answer him so that he didn't any longer have to ponder something more dangerous.

"Mother, Mother Gladys," he calls out one last time but to no avail; there was not answer, but there was more sound, the sound of someone leaving the kitchen. Then John turns to Windler—whom he had originally hired because of his size and military police background—and he asks him point-blank, "Windler, did you hear anything?"

Windler pauses and looks around; I can't say I knew what he was thinking, but I sensed that he was uncertain what to say. I know that he knew there was consequence to whatever he said, and Windler—in his relationship with John—had become ultra-cautious and hesitant, unlike his first couple of weeks on the job when he was quite aggressive and territorial. This co-op had a way of changing a person's behavior; it was about expectations—the building's affect was so quiet and sedate, well—mannered, you might say—and it forced everyone who worked there to conform to this same temperament. In short, Windler had lost his edge. But of course, here is a situation where John wanted what he had paid for, and with his lack of patience multiplied exponentially given the tenseness of our predicament, he gave little time and no understanding of Windler's hesitation in answering him. He snapped less than a second following his initial query, "Well, Windler, did you hear anything, yes or no?"

Windler's hulking body stiffens as he mumbles something inaudible, and of course, John snaps again, "What?"

Annoyed, he turns quickly toward me, and in the same voice and excited temperament, he asks me the same question by using one word only, "Albert?"

I knew we were going to do something other than calling for the police—John abhorred having the police anywhere near our building; he thought the police had many criminals in their own ranks and that, individually, they weren't very smart, and that they often made the situation worse than it had been in the first place. I had heard him say on a number of occasions that they—the police—were, in fact, low class, and anyone who dealt with them were tainted by the stigma of having dealt with them at all; seriously, he was very serious about that. And from this I knew that he would rather the three of us deal with whatever was going on upstairs in our mother's kitchen. If truth be told, I would rather have called the police; this is New York City. Who the hell knows what is going on up there. But my thoughts never left my mouth, and that's why I said what I said next; also, I knew for sure that our mothers were still downstairs at the baron Romanovsky's party.

"Nothing, Mr. Smith, I didn't hear anything."

I knew what was coming next, and I hoped that, who, whom, or what was up there making noise was no longer there when we three arrived on the scene. He said it, although he hesitated for a brief moment before doing so, but finally he took a deep breath and said, "Let's get up there."

And we did; we three headed single file up the stairs. I don't think he was thinking clearly, or else he would have sent Windler first, but he wasn't, as he cautiously crept slowly up the stairs, listening for sounds as we went.

Borga and Oleg had left the kitchen, but Borga, he hesitated and waited by the door to listen for whatever might follow them to the kitchen; he waited for a moment, and he could hear us slowly ascending the maid's wooden stairway in the back of the dining room to the kitchen. Oleg was standing right next to him with his head still poked in through the kitchen door.

"Did you hear that, Borga?"

Borga is leaning in as well, although not as far in as his brother.

"Yes, yes, Oleg, I hear them—they are reluctant, but they are nonetheless still coming to greet us. Let's get out of here fast."

When John, Windler, and I reach the kitchen, the lights are not on, so it is pitch-dark except for a stream of light coming through the slightly ajar fire door left that way by the Russians in the speedy escape.

Windler is the one who spots the light as John is reluctant to immediately enter the dark kitchen; he calls out one last time, "Mother, Mother Gladys, are either of you here?"

Even in the dark, I could feel Windler's eyes rolling exasperatedly with incredulity over John's uneven behavior; I'm sure I heard Windler sigh just loud enough to be heard, but not loud enough to distract the now-timid—again John Smith. We both knew that there were no old women in this kitchen, especially when he says, "The fire door has been left open, someone has left the fire door open."

Of course, at this point none of the three of us knew who or whom had left the door open, but we both knew for damn sure neither of our mothers had not left it that way. Finally, John, the timid, spoke up.

"Turn on the light, Albert," he says as he is frozen like a block of ice at the door to the kitchen. It's amazing what happens to people when they are overcome by fear. The light switch was actually much closer to him than it ever was to me, but he was too snake-bitten by fear to even lift his hand to switch it on. So I did, and instantly we could see that things were in disarray. There was a chair lying turned over on its side, and the large and quite-heavy Wolf range had been moved away from its normal position, which was usually flat up against the back wall of the kitchen; it seemed to have been move almost to the middle of the kitchen floor. And then Windler—his eyes all bugged out—states the obvious, "Someone was here, that chair is turned over, and the door__"

Even John loses his patience with Windler's whining as he interjects, "Yes, Windler, we see that, and the back door is open, they'd never leave the fire door open like that . . ."

John becomes brave again when he walks over to the fire door and pulls it all the way open—the hallway is painted battleship gray with a high-gloss sheen to it, so the overhead lights bounces reflecting like a dull mirror off their shiny surfaces. John then sticks his head through the door and listens; hearing a noise, he then turns to us.

"Can you hear that? Come on, Albert, let's go follow the noise downstairs."

This time—I must admit—it was I who paused. I didn't know who or how many persons he was hearing, and I didn't want to run into something that we couldn't handle. We were in the back stairwell of a very secure building, and no one, save the three of us, even knew that we were here; what if something happened and we were overwhelmed by a horde of men, what then, who would know? It was I who all of a sudden had become ultra-cautious. I wasn't about to tell the two of them that, but I was scared; nonetheless I followed their lead as the three of us began to descend the stairs behind the scampering footstep that went before us. And then—after about two steps or so—Windler does something unexpected; he reaches into his jacket pocket, and he pulls out a pistol. John and I see it at about the same time—we were both shocked and speechless at first. The fact is—and this without exchanging as much as a word between us three—we were all buoyed by the presence of the gun; it seemed to boost our sense of security, and we all sped faster down the stairs toward what were now footsteps and music. It was clear to all three of us that the footsteps had entered the Baron Romanovsky's party as a door had opened, and then everything stopped—the footsteps and the music. We all stopped—probably thinking much the same thing.

"Whoever was up here, Mr. Smith, they came from the Russian's' party, I'm sure of it."

John is nodding his head as Windler is speaking; then Windler braces himself with the resolve of an old soldier as if he is going into battle, and then he points his gun in the direction of the offending door. We start down again, and then after a few steps more, John says, "That's exactly what I'm thinking as well, Windler, the Russians' have got something to do with."

An alarm goes off in my head—"*duh*—"as we were approaching the Russian's door; I'm thinking that from the outside, we must appear like the Three Stooges, Mo, Larry, and Curly, the three of us sharing the same half brain as it were. It was a too, too obvious observation to comment on. Here we were the three of us almost at the Russian's door; we could hear the echoes of the party going on inside, and John makes what he must believe is a percipient observation. Oh *vez mear*, I'm in the company of idiots; of course it's the Russians. Who else would it be, and besides, they just ran inside and just about slammed the door in our faces. We reach the door, and we can hear the music even louder now than before; we pause the three of us almost piling into each other, right at the door we three are standing there one next to the other when Windler reaches for the doorknob. John smacks Windler's hand down before he can turn the doorknob.

"Put that gun away, Windler, our mothers are in there."

Windler puts the gun away back into the holster inside his jacket, and then he tries the door again; it's locked, so he steps back while John steps forward to give a try, but it still won't budge.

"Let me see if I can get their attention," he says as he thoughtlessly bangs on the Russian's kitchen door. By this time, inside, Borga and Oleg had ferreted their way through the party to search for their brother, Boris; they find him entertaining a woman at the bar. The hulking two rushed over indiscreetly to Boris's side; he excuses himself, and then he turns, somewhat surprised to see them back so soon. He was at first positive and pleased that they had completed their assignment so expeditiously; he smiles and gloats, and in his anticipation of things going as he had planned, he pans the party with his greed-filled eyes until he spots the dowagers engaged in conversation with another neighbor. He grunts satisfied that all would be his soon, but then he squints a curious thought and then he turns to his brothers.

"Your deed took less time than I had imagined it would, or maybe I was distracted, and time moved faster than I was aware of. So yes, it is all done now, yes? We are, as the Americans say, good to go, yes?"

Boris, although the older of the three brothers, seems oddly out of place now; standing between the two hulking men, he seems oddly disproportioned. His relatively diminutive stature is in part, or in all parts, due to his different parentage—all have only the same mother in common; Borga and Oleg have the same father and share Boris's mother as parent. But like two giant bookends they shade him as they cower in, preparing to recite the bad news to him. First, Oleg stutters a feeble, inaudible mumble, to which Boris flashes a contemptuous scowl; and then in an effort to make amends for his brother's aborted effort and to inform Boris of their failure, Borga quickly offers, "No, Boris, we were interrupted before we got started."

The only thing missing now was the steam coming from Boris's head to illustrate his almost-total anger and would probably have exploded if he hadn't heard—in a moment of quiet, as the music had taken a measured pause—the faint banging at the kitchen door; he was in mid-scold when he heard it.

"What do you mean interrupted? Who interrupted—" *Bang, bang, bang*, and then the music starts up again; but Boris was more than a little curious as to whom or who was banging at his fire door. He turned immediately and headed for the kitchen, and as they are on their way, Oleg—always the young jokester—utters, "I think the interruption has caught up with us, Boris."

Like Queen Victoria, Boris is not amused; as he casts a warning look over his shoulder, he moves toward the kitchen, but Oleg is satisfied that his once-stammering words finally made it to his mouth, and he seems very pleased that their excuse for failure will soon be validated. Boris is incensed; as he heads through the kitchen door, he reaches back and grabs Oleg's arm.

"Come with me," he says as he pushes Oleg forward toward the fire door, where they all stop before they decide exactly how to handle this unscheduled intrusion. But as the three Russians headed for the kitchen, they took scant notice of any of their guests—these Russians were too haughty and arrogant to get caught up in appearances—or their guests' reactions; in point of fact, there actually was very little if any reaction, all except for Gladys and Mildred—well, actually Gladys, who insistently pulled Mildred by the hand toward the kitchen when she spotted the three Russians heading there. She had been watching and alerted Mildred.

"You see that, honey, you see that? Something's going on in there. I knew if we kept an eye on them . . ."

Mildred was always late to the party, but she did pick up quickly once alerted.

"Those two guys seemed a bit excited when they first walked through the party just a little while ago . . ."

Gladys smiles at her, Millie; she did notice things after all.

"And now they've got the Baron Romanovsky all irritated. Where are they going, Gladys?"

That's when Gladys—without even a single word—takes Mildred by her thin and delicate wrist and determinedly guides her across the party floor toward the kitchen. Mildred glides behind her light as a feather. Gladys herself doesn't want to attract attention, just in case someone else—maybe others of the Russians—are watching them as well; so finally, as the two are without a spoken word between them, finally in sync, and on the same page as it were, together they take a circuitous route. They glide hand in hand—as many women are oft spotted doing on this sort of mission—they first head straight toward the bathroom, and then, when they think no one is the wiser, they make a quick turn to the kitchen; they arrive there only moments after the three Russians enter the swinging kitchen door. As they are now at the outside of the kitchen, they both try desperately to huddle up unobtrusively by the door to hear; they play act—they look quite funny miming having a conversation—but they do hear quite well, though. In fact, they can actually hear the banging at the fire door. As the kitchen door has not swung all the way shut, the two elderly interlopers can see a little through the remaining crack; they can see enough to make out that the Russians are standing at the fire door trying to decide what to do. After Boris has knocked away Oleg's hand, he waits trying to decide what to do, but after a while in contemplation, Borga steps forward.

"Should I open?"

Boris pauses a moment more in contemplation, but then as he hears John Smith's voice on the other side of the door yelling, "We know you can hear us out here, open the door inside!" it's then that Boris finally turns to answer Borga's unfinished query; and finally, with his face all ridged and taut with determination, he finally scoffs, "Hell no, let them knock their fists off. We can gas the old women some other day, we still have time as our best ally."

Gladys and Mildred are listening closely enough to hear Boris's fateful words; alarmed, Mildred sucks in a breathy sigh that quickly fills her lungs with a chilling gust of air. The sibilant hiss is almost loud enough to warn the Russians that the women are present to hear their threat. Gladys as well is aghast at what they both have heard, and she too, yet more quietly still than Mildred, exclaims with shock and foreboding as she mimes and whispers in Mildred's ear, "Gas us some other day, what the . . . Millie, did you hear that, that nasty Russian wants to do us in, come on, girl, let's get out of here."

Mildred makes a quick move away from the kitchen, but Gladys again grabs Mildred by her boney wrist, and whispers, "Slowly, Millie, slowly. Nothing is going to happen here, and if they come out of that kitchen before we are out of here, I don't want them suspicious that we have gotten wind of their plans to off us."

Mildred squeaks, "Off us, Gladys, that sounds so grotesque. Off us, I haven't heard you speak like that in years."

Gladys, even in the midst of their plight,—she can't help but to laugh at her modest friend.

"Oh, Millie, Millie, Millie, you can be sure that their plans for us are far more grotesque than my comparatively tame words. I can assure you that these Russians are not reading from the Emily Post's book titled *Etiquette Murders*, or *Murder's Etiquette*. These are bad men, you see, love, we had to come to this party or we would never have known how bad they were until it was much too late."

Mildred smiles as the two old ladies leave the party arm in arm.

CHAPTER XII

At this point my head was spinning. Look, it's very simple: I'm no thug or gangster, or even a good hustler for that matter; and if there was ever any thug in me in the first place, the Hotchkiss School and Brown University had long ago trained that out of me. Yeah, yeah, yeah, I know I spent time in Sing Sing, but that was for bad checks, not for violence; and believe me, in Sing Sing, I saw enough violence to last me two lifetimes and enough to know that I wasn't ever going to be any good at it. So, for me, violence was never a viable option. So here we are, John and me, back at the penthouse—both of us are a little out of breath from the exertion of scurrying up the stairs, that as much from the sheer emotional toll that this at first whimsical escapade of ours, now turned on its ear, has taken on both of us. I think that it's not yet over because our mothers are not yet safe.

As we are now standing in the middle of our mothers' kitchen, for a moment, and for no longer than a moment, the warmth of nostalgia brushes gently across my mind; I'm feeling the peace of old good memories as I stand there in the kitchen with John. I am quietly, and, I might add secretly, lamenting our present schism as I reflect on the past good times in this very same place. Alas and sadly, John abrasively and aggressively, although I'm certain not intentionally because he had no idea what I was thinking about, but he sullies my peace with his abrupt interruption.

"I don't know what the hell is going on," he says—as much to himself as it was said to me. And as my peaceful drift had been irretrievably disturbed, I immediately acquiesced in favor of his charge, and I might add, my own concerns about our mothers. Back in the saddle of the moment again, I say, "I think it's a good move leaving, Windler down there, at least until our mothers are safe at home again."

As the light is on, and we are no longer chasing after some intruder, we both finally take a closer look around the kitchen. I pick the turned-over chair up and begin to look around the kitchen; this kitchen is literally the size of my Upper West Side apartment bedroom plus a half, and so it takes awhile to scan it. We can quickly see what has been altered. A few things had been knocked over, but more alarming, the oven,; that big heavy Wolf range, had been moved far away from the wall. It's apparent, but it's really not as visually distracting as it might have been in a smaller room, but still. When John first sees it, he says, "This old stove is too far away from the wall, let's push it back."

I was a million miles away from here, or so it seemed, but then for some unknown reason, I reconnected, "What?" Even when I said *what*, I didn't look at the stove, or John either; I was still looking off into space. But John turns around, all of a sudden, as I was going to repeat myself.

"I said___"

He interrupts me.

"I heard what you said, Albert. But this stove has never been this far away from the wall, and besides, those two old girls couldn't have moved it if their lives depended on it."

It was a bit hyperbolic, but to make a point I guess because those two old girls, as he calls them, are two very determined persons, and I believe that they can do most anything they wanted if they set their minds to it; so I gave him a pass on that, but he did have a point in there somewhere—the stove was way out of place. So John looks at me, and I looked back at him, and then—as if a witch had just blown her cold breath down the small of my back—I felt a distance and a chill, a kind of coldness emanating from him that I hadn't felt for a while. He was looking at me with this look of blame, and it was clearly a look that I knew I didn't warrant or deserve, not at that moment anyway; but it was there, nonetheless, and I knew this wasn't the time and place to try and discuss it. He was concerned with our mothers, I knew that much, and so was I; so still in formal servant mode, risking little, I asked, "What are you thinking about, Mr. Smith? Because what I'm thinking about is not good."

Maybe I was wrong, maybe I am imagining things—my fall-from-grace guilt or something—maybe it's me that's seeing odd things and drawing the wrong conclusions about John's looks, thoughts, and moods. In truth, even at approaching forty years of age, I want to be a family again; I miss being a family, and I know for certain that there really isn't anything very strange about that. I was probably being far too self-absorbed for the moment, but I couldn't help it. Upon reflection, it turns out that John and I hadn't been together in the house for more than seconds, let alone the kitchen—where we used to spend hours and hours together—in over twenty years; that's why my mind is doing what it's doing. It's not just nostalgia; it's a longing. But John isn't longing, and if he is, he's longing for the safety of our mothers much more than I, in my conflicting emotions, am. I really don't think that they are in any real danger; they're in the middle of a party with all those people around, for God's sake. But he changes all of that thinking and figuring things out with one patented, brusque query: "What the hell is going on here, Albert?"

That was the perfect question as it shocked me from my complacency without further annotation; finally I was appropriately alarmed and alerted. This time, John to his credit was downright unequivocal and forthright.

"Let's go downstairs to that goddamn Russian's party and get our mothers out of there, now."

I know that I sound like a teenager, but how cool was that—I loved it; I never liked those Russians, and from the start, they had made me feel uncomfortable. I had always, from the beginning, felt that either they had something on John or he was simply afraid of them. It never made much sense, but given the tenseness of John and my relationship, I was on no good footing to pry and question his business decisions; and them moving in here was for certain only business because they were anything but friends or even friendly. But now, tonight, it seemed that John had found his gonads again, so we hopped on the penthouse elevator to the lobby; it was at this point inconvenient, but it was the only way we could get there by going down to the lobby to get the other elevators up. We didn't talk at all; oh, John talked to himself ever since we were kids. John used to talk to himself, especially when we, or he, was going to do something scary or difficult, or even dangerous. We'd be walking together or riding a bus or on the subway, and John would be talking a mile a minute to himself. I always used to tell him he was lucky to have me around so that people wouldn't think he was talking to himself. They would actually think he was talking to me and not think that he was crazy. When he talked, not unlike this time, he'd say what he was going to do, sort of like a rehearsal or a trial run; I guess, no, I know that it was his way of psyching himself up.

"If that oversized Russian horde does anything to hurt our mothers, I'll throw them off of their own balcony all together, or one by one. It really doesn't matter which" he says, as he was just getting started. When the elevator reached the lobby, and as it does, John goes steaming off as soon as the door opens. He turns and goes quickly to his right to catch the regular elevator, and who walks off the elevator but our mothers, both of them sartorially splendid and as pretty as cameo brooches—the both of them. John must have been in the middle of a sentence, for when he turned for the elevator, he just about ran into them; his mouth was still moving a mile a minute. Mildred was happy to see us, happier still to see us two together so unexpectedly.

"John, Albert, look, Gladys, our boys together have been up to visit us. How nice, isn't that nice, Gladys?"

This was a surprising scene for all of us for totally different reasons: First of all, our mothers never, I mean never, saw us together anymore. And second, we never are in the unit together. Both of them—Gladys and Mildred—have long since given up on trying to bring us together again.

When I first came home from prison—that still, even after all these years, sounds so totally strange—they both tried very hard to get us two back together. Before I started as the doorman, John wouldn't even speak to me; it was a long time before I accepted that he, John, as an individual, was really, really hurt by what I had done to myself and to my family. We had been family for most of my life and all of his, and I hadn't considered that. When we were kids, he used to talk about how we were going to be in the real estate business together—owning lots of stuff and building like crazy—that we'd be partners; but when I went off on my own to open my travel business, he was disappointed, even hurt, but then he kind of got used to it. He hadn't quite finished school then, and his dad was still alive—ill but alive. The *coup de grâce* was my criminality. There was no forgiving that blunder; I had sullied any opportunity of us ever doing anything together. So suffice it to say it was quite a moment for our mothers to see us together, uncoerced by either of them. John's mouth remained opened, but the tenor of his words immediately and drastically changed from threatening an unseen foe to solicitations of concern.

"Are you two all right?" he stutters breathlessly to change the direction of his speech, as his emotions were doing a halt and about-face all in one breath. Mildred's omnipresent innocence rendered her quickly surprised by his concern, but John stuttered on, "I mean, is everything all right, you're both okay, right?"

Mildred smiles, still caught up in the pleasure-producing fact that the two of us are together again. I'm not trying to imply that Mildred is in any way deficient—in fact, I would say that it is far more the opposite—but she does possess a youthful naiveté that has survived her years. She is far less willing to judge, unlike what most people I've met are prone to doing, and she is by far more tolerant of idiosyncratic behavioral quirks than anyone else on God's good earth; but she is not completely unobservant as illustrated by her question.

"Yes, John, we're all right, we're . . ." She takes a closer look at him. "But what's going on with you two? You're both all sweaty."

After the question, John throws a quick glance in my direction, and I immediately begin to tidy myself up—as if no one is watching me—it was a silly gesture and a waste of time, and it resulted in excoriation from my mother. In a needless and prophylactic gesture, I offered a pittance of a diversion, saying, "Oh, we're fine, Mother, we we're just coming to visit you . . ." I was feeling so exposed.

I couldn't just stand there quietly; everything about that tense moment was wrong, and all four of us from both sides felt it. And as Mother Gladys had not yet said a word, we all knew intuitively that this little developing quadrumvirate had a ways to go before it was completed, and then it came on cue. "You're both lying through your teeth, Albert, John, what the hell is going on? You two haven't been together in the same room—without us two holding your feet to the fire—in fifteen years, and now this. You're both sweating and lying together, and do you really expect me to fall for this thinly veiled charade? I think not."

Just then, to John and Albert's surprise, Windler steps out of the security office into the lobby. "Is everything okay, folks?"

Neither one of us had any idea of how nor why Windler had gotten to the lobby before we had; he was supposed to be keeping an eye on the Russian's' fire door. I must say that in this one day, I had regained a whole lot of the respect back that had evaporated between John and me; talk about quick thinking. John doesn't miss a beat. He knows exactly what I know about where Windler is versus where he was supposed to be; he should still be outside of the Russian's' fire door. At least, if not still there, he should not seem as if he's been sitting in his security office all night. But when John, the quick thinker that he's become, says to Windler, "Windler, I want you to take to the fire stairs and check all of the doors making sure they are all secure and locked," Windler gives John a curious look as do Mildred and Gladys, but he moves toward the fire door without another word. As he's walking away, John adds an unnecessary coda, which exposes him and articulates his nervousness to everyone, "Go now, Windler, and get back to me as soon as you have checked everything."

That did it; even Mildred's lack of curiosity has been reversed and piqued; she then turns a quick head toward Gladys, who still surprisingly holds her own tongue. Mildred—given their location in such a public space, the lobby and all—asks as unobtrusively as possible, "What's going on, son? John, Albert, what's going on?"

I knew then that this was our last good opportunity to escape unscathed. It was the last hint of a chance for us—John and me—to have gone to another corner of the building to regroup and strategize, or stood there and told a lie the size of Manhattan; but it was not to be. It was to be our last chance, but we were too slow and too late because Mother Gladys was not having any of those *Keystone Kops* antics out of us—of the kind we used to pull in concert with each other—and besides, we were out of practice because of our years of estrangement; we no longer had that kind of friendly cooperation and finely tuned timing. Sadly, we weren't even friends anymore.

The absolute end was when John so audaciously used the forbidden word and unalterably sealed our fates; our secret was soon to be revealed as our freedom became immediately forfeit. All families have rules, and we all four knew that he knew better than to use that forbidden word: *"Nothing."*

He had said it with the unbridled confidence of a foolish child.

After that, you could hear in your mind the dramatic music sounding, *dum, dum da dum.* And that's when Mother Gladys's yellow-skin face turned purple with anger—more tepid than boiling, but still hot enough to scald your fingers in.

"Don't you two start with that word: *'Nothing.'* You two turn around and get back in that elevator. We've go to get to the bottom of what's going on here, now, march you two."

I'm nearing forty—that's true—and at forty you'd think that I had seen all of what my mother was or was ever going to be, I mean; I've been around her for all of these years you'd think I'd seen her every mood. Well, wrong I was. It started in the lobby—that unfamiliar sensation—you know, when she ordered John and me back up to their unit. It wasn't the first time I had heard that tone of voice coming from her diminutive self, but in reflecting back upon it, it had been a long time between occasions since I had been scolded in public. And it wasn't so much the voice that is noteworthy; it was more the attitude—it was more determined and forceful—it was that attitude that was more pronounced than I had seen it before, or in fact had ever seen it.

Something or someone had stimulated my mother, and I must include Mildred—the usually mild-mannered—to act more than a little differently. All the way up in the elevator, the two of them huddled and whispered to each other while John and I both stood silent and contemplative. This was new—from the very moment that we four stepped on the elevator together—I didn't know, in point of fact, none of us knew it at the time that things would forever change between the four of us.

As it was, we four had not ridden this or any other elevator together in over fifteen, closer to twenty years, for one reason or another; my arithmetic may be a little off, but it was years since we were together like this, and, unfortunately, it wasn't now the happiest of occasions. For the first five of those twenty years was because of our different schedules; after college I had moved out on my own, and John was still in school, so he wasn't around most of the time. And then for the remaining fifteen years or so, it was my post-prison years, and John was way too angry to ever allow this to happen. When I think back to add it all up, it turns out that it was even more years than I had first thought.

While we were riding up on the elevator, I snuck a long stare at John. It's funny, but when he's quiet, he looks like his old self. I finally, in that one reflective moment—while standing in that elevator with my entire family—I realized how fond I am of him, and deep down, and maybe not so deep down, he as well is still emotionally attached to me; if not, why then would he be so angry with me all the time. I certainly haven't done anything lately—and by lately, I mean in the last fifteen years—to anger him.

By the time we reached the penthouse, our two mothers are standing in the center of the elevator quietly chatting away as usual; they really don't need the company of others to have a good time together. I've never seen two people—women, men, or a mixture of the two—that ever got along as well as the two of them do, and it's a joy to behold.

So we get to the penthouse, and the two of them go about the business of being themselves; but first the order came from, my mother, Gladys, as it often did when we were boys.

"Sit and be quiet, you two, we'll be with you presently."

And don't you know, we did just as we were told; it was definitely throwback behavior, two grown men cowering—not in a bad way, more in a respectful way—A billionaire and an ex-con . . . we both easily relent to the will of the former-homeless single-parent Gladys Lawrence. It would be laughable if it weren't true, even at that it's still quite amusing.

So John and I found our places, and, in fact, strangely enough, it was our old places that we naturally gravitated to; we sat in the same seats we used to sit in when we all sat together as a family when we were boys. At first we sat quietly, not looking at each other while our mothers scurried about doing whatever it was that they do to get ready to reproach us for our misdeeds—or at least that's the way we both seemed to be feeling. The more things change, the more they stay the same—what I mean to say is that John starts to talk to himself, just like old times. Whenever we had done something wrong—which was quite often—and whenever my mother, Gladys, would sit us down to scold us or warn us, as she was always the taskmaster. That's one of the times that John would get so nervous that he would talk aloud to himself; at first, until he got older, he didn't realize he was doing it, but as he got older, he wasn't able to control it—it was his attending behavior—he could hear himself doing it, but he actually thought he was hearing his thoughts instead of speaking them out loud. I never wanted to stop him because it was then that I knew exactly what he was thinking, and sometimes it was quite revealing, if not always funny.

We all knew that he did this, and whenever Mother Gladys was around—that's what, John always called my mom—and she would just call his name, always softly, she'd call his name, and he'd stop talking to himself immediately; she was always gentle that way. No matter what we had done, or had been accused of, she would always be gentle with him and would just call his name.

Today was no different; John and I were just sitting quietly there in the library when he began to talk; let me describe it first so I can put you right there.

When you commonly think of someone talking to himself, I don't know what it is that you might imagine or have experienced, but with John, it's like he's actually having a conversation with himself; he's not attempting to communicate with anyone else. It's like two armies warring, the proper nouns versus the pronouns: John against I, you, we, and a very confusing me, as the battle rages back and forth assigning blame and taking responsibility for one transgression or another. He can become—although not usually—animated, but that usually happens when there is imminent danger, like when we a couple of times got into some hairy situations while acting like we were poor kids when playing uptown and being discovered as anything, but those were times when we had to hightail it out of there on the quick.

We were boys together, and all that entails, and besides that, we were the best of friends. I miss that, and sitting here together for the first time in years, I finally feel the weight of its absence come crashing down on me. And hearing John in his archetypical battle with himself, it makes me wax nostalgic and muse to live a life in the land of what-ifs, and quickly and irrevocably change my life forever from what is. But lament no more, alas and forever, this new moment we do share; for in truth we are all here again together, and in truth this moment has not been ravaged by mistakes and foolishness—not yet any way.

John is talking aloud to himself, and I have yet to listen, as my own thoughts clutter the space in my own mind too loudly and obtrusively to now reckon with his verbosity. I need and embrace only the simple truth now, and that is that we are all together again.

I have again drifted far a field from the purpose of others more senior and centered to their own purpose and am reminded of such when our mothers return to join us. They are both calmer—not that irritating banter and strident noises were ever their signatures—but their demeanors are more grounded and centered now, helped, of course, by their brandies and cigars.

As they take their regular seats between us, her inner resolve belied by her outer calm, when she speaks, Gladys is decidedly quick to the center of the issue with her first point, "So why the sweat and camaraderie, boys?"

Her words ride a stiff blade and pierce the heart of the matter as she then blows the very symbolic smoke that, if correctly read, says that she is the only one allowed to blow smoke in this tête-à-tête this evening. There is a hint of a smile released from her earnest yet gracious nod that intermittent with the smoke presents us with a forum for truth—telling from the first moment—yet we should not be too easily comforted into leaking deceitfully.

I look to John, and John looks to me simultaneously, and it was at that precise moment that I knew we were back, maybe not all the way back but back far enough for me to take the lead and to speak first. How this all happened, I'm not certain; sometimes it's something in the air that changes a thing, sometimes it's in the water, and, tonight, maybe it's something in Gladys's smoke—but whatever the case may be, something has changed.

It has not changed to something foreign, abstract, emotional, or metaphysical; it has changed back to something old, familiar, true, and, most of all, natural. It was always my place to go first in these family meetings; I was the oldest, and therefore, I was the most responsible. It was a funny familiar feeling, for when I began to speak, it was all as natural as natural could be; no one even batted an eye or cleared a throat when I began to speak, except may be my insecure self.

"Well__" I began with the most inauspicious word in the dictionary. "Well, we came up to visit you two—"

And before I could finish my sentence, those two most familiar words, "Mother Gladys," rang from John's mouth, "Mother Gladys, it's on me, Mother Gladys, and you as well, Mother. I pulled Albert into it."

I was surprised, but I paused, and then I gladly gave way to John's interruption; I had no idea what he was going to say. In fact, he looked as if he was going to cry. I'm thinking now that maybe I should have listened when he was talking to himself, and I would have known better what he was about to say, or at least I would have been in the ballpark. But I was really surprised when he extemporaneously broke into the truth.

"Look, it was like this, you two. Ever since you two bullied me—"

Mildred quickly interrupted him with gasp of incredulity at being accused of having bullied anyone, let alone her own son. She smiled and chortled, mystified by the sounds of vulnerability in his accusation.

"Bullied you, John? Why, John, come on, son, the real reason you returned the falcon's nest back to its rightful place is because you knew in your heart of hearts that you had disfavored them out of anger. You've always done that, John, ever since you were a little boy. If you didn't get your way or what you wanted, you'd always find a way to let us know—Gladys and I used to talk about that all the time, and that was one of the ways you were very different from Albert. So go on and tell us what you started with, son, but please be honest with yourself, if not with us."

I don't know, but right then, I had this strange feeling about her words, Mildred's words that is; they were somehow strange to me; they seemed sad, and strangely reflective—somehow they were different, and it was not so much the words themselves, for they were not in and of themselves any different or stranger from the words she's always spoken, but it was something that I couldn't put my finger on yet. It was a kind of feeling that something about her, when she spoke that is, it was that something was different. But maybe it was just me, because, John—who was preoccupied with scripting the answer that he was about to give—he had no noticeable reaction, and I didn't dare look at anyone else until he did produce a response; I didn't know how culpable his answer was going to make me. So I waited and held my breath.

"Well, okay, so I am vengeful at times, I know that, but those birds are hideous creatures. But anyway, let me tell you what happened before you two have a tizzy fit."

I almost laughed, you see; John's always had quite the mouth on him—I hadn't heard it in this setting in years, obviously, but it was kind of fun to hear it again; they—the two of them—were used to it, and I might say quite unfazed by it. So John continues to regale them with his tale.

"So we all three of us take the elevator up after you two had gone off to the Russians' party, and as much as I was at first against you going, I knew that it would be a perfect time for me to institute my plan. So we go up, and we are fumbling around trying to secure a platform to reach a height high enough to secure the video camera in a place where you two wouldn't ever see it—"

That's when Gladys laughs out loud while Mildred—remaining quiet—but she did smile, as she was kinder. Gladys couldn't help chiding John, "Well, it couldn't have been such a good plan, John, if it took the three of you and you still couldn't get it done, now could it?"

John is such a child sometimes; everyone knew that this was said in jest, but he got all perturbed and harrumphed himself into a big pout.

"Well, it would have worked had we not been disturbed by the noise upstairs," he says with his jaws all puffed out in frustration, and then John continues and recounts everything, every detail that happened after we three had heard the noises in the kitchen that in the end had trailed all the way down to the fire door of the Russian's' apartment. The mood got appropriately serious for the four of us as John—long-winded if you ask me—waded through every minute detail of the night; it took him as long to retell as it took to actually happen. But finally, he was done, and from then on for a full thirty seconds, the library was silent; no one knew exactly what to do or say. It was Gladys who as usual was the one who broke the impasse of silence.

"So, John, after you had relentlessly banged on the door for several minutes, and to no avail, the three of you came back here, and that's when you discovered the stove had been moved."

John at first answered yes, but then I interjected, "No, no, we left, Windler downstairs at the Russian's' door—only John and I came back to the kitchen."

John had forgotten that detail, and he easily agreed—and he was quite civil in doing so, I might add. We sat uneasily again, but not as long as we had before, and then John offers a seemingly spurious rejoinder,

"Yes, that's exactly right. Now, we should call the police and have them investigate."

He just said it out of the blue. Now it's true. We haven't had many occasions to call the police over the years; this simply isn't a high-crime area, this oasis called Fifth Avenue, so the police are *de rigueur* in the negative, except, of course, when they regularly drive by on mandatory cruiser patrols, which I must say are quite regular. But I couldn't tell whether John was serious or not, he abhors the police, and the mere thought of their presence at our building, for any reason, and at any time was in the past simply verboten.

I couldn't tell whether he was being serious or merely being sarcastic. But before I was able to discern which it was, Gladys jumped in; she as well had no love for the police, but for a totally different set of reasons. John's reasons were an issue of class and his downright haughtiness, but Mother's was for totally more humanist, experiential, and emotional reasons.

In her younger days, she had several encounters with them, and all of them turned out—not so surprisingly, given where she grew up—to be negative.

Once many years ago—it was when she was homeless and spending all of her time on the streets of Harlem wandering and staying temporarily at one friend's house or another—there were two young thugs who were following her and her infant. That was me, of course. And she was sure they were going to do her and me harm in some way.

She had just been kicked out of her aunt's house because she wouldn't marry some handpicked, ugly, old man stranger that her aunt had selected for her because she had a baby out of wedlock—or so her aunt thought. She was new at being homeless, and as she was trying to get away from these two young thugs and make it to a safe place, a rarely—seen police cruiser was slowly passing by at the time; when she first told me the story, she related that she was very relieved when she saw the cruiser, believing that they would help her.

She ran with me in her arms, and hailed them, and they did stop; but when she told them of her fear, they displayed little concern, and to top that, they called her a junky whore and told her to drop her baby off in the garbage somewhere if she was tired of carrying it around. They laughed and left her to the thugs, who, immediately upon their leaving, attacked and robbed her; she was lucky some other people came along to help her before she had been severely injured. There were other times and other negative police experiences that had shaped her lasting and loathsome feelings about them, but of course, there was none since she had become a resident of the co-op on Fifth Avenue.

It's likened to the real estate adage of priority and importance: location, location, and location. In the eyes of some—far too many—it's the location that turns a pauper into a prince, and yet the person inside these divergent archetypes may in both cases be essentially the same. So Gladys too had no affinity for the police, and so she eagerly steered away from their involvement by stating, in a very subtle way, our lack of need for their intrusion.

"So far, the Russians don't know who followed them down to their unit, or who was banging at their door, right?"

It was then that I looked at John for the first time in a couple of minutes in order to confirm his thoughts on her statement, and he seemed to agree—when he nodded his head—as I did that she was right. They had never opened the door; in fact, there had never been any indication that they or anyone on the other side of the door had even heard us banging. I could tell that John didn't even now—with all that had happened—want the police involved, and that he would quickly regret calling them; so any slight reason, with the thinnest plausibility to the contrary, would be good enough for him to delay including them in our problems.

"They don't know that your mother and me were watching them all of the time."

That was the first John and I had heard of this half of the equation, and we were both very surprised and intrigued. We actually smiled at each other.

"You two were watching them as well."

On that note, Mother Gladys laughs as Mildred's face sports a grand smile as well. Gladys is forthright; she quickly divulges her own best and only reason for ever having attended the Russians' party.

"You didn't think we were going there because we just couldn't resist his invitation, did you two? How do you think you two have inherited your own penchant for sticking your noses where they don't belong, your curiosity as it were? Well, I'm here to tell you that you both come by it naturally—look at your mothers, boys, neither of you dropped too far from the distaff tree."

Both John and I were amused, especially since we are all sitting there in the library together, happy and well, and for the first time in years. We've all had and shared parts of the same adventure—this is true—and it was not yet over by a long shot; we all knew that then, but we all realized as well that we are a family again. This seemingly serendipitous meeting would certainly forge new ones in the near future; we four all knew that then because we four had all been there before.

There was a comfortable quiet—no, not quiet as in silence—but as in the stillness of peace, a peacefully shared moment between us all then; it had been long sought after. In all of our hearts, I will here and now cheerfully project this revisionist thought in my imagination, but now it was in fact really there. And then there was a sound that broke the solemnity of the occasion, when Mildred, of all persons, clears her throat rather distractedly; we all looked up at her, but it was Gladys's look that really told the story.

It was a look of warning years in the making; it was a look that scanned quickly the distance from and in between revulsion to supplication, and when it reached its end, you could tell that it wasn't going to be adhered to. Gladys's face was now drooped and defeated; she knew, and we knew by watching her that her antics had not been successful, and as we both wordlessly and silently turned to her nemesis of the moment, we could see the triumphant and opposite reflection on Mildred's face.

John spoke first, but in fact, he had taken the words right out of my own mouth, "What is going on here between the two of you? What are you two doing?"

We three could hear a barely audible whisper coming from Mother Gladys, and unlikely switch of roles it was, "Millie, don't, not now, Millie, please don't," she says, but knowing Gladys as well as we all do, her faint plaintive leak is wholly uncharacteristic, and it made us both—John and me—want to know more from Mildred than we would have normally wanted to know under these same circumstance if it had not been for that plaintive and uncharacteristic whisper. Since everything that she has tried before has failed, this time Gladys simply clears her throat, and then something amusing happens.

Mildred Smith is the most well-mannered person—woman or man—that you'd ever have the pleasure of meeting; she is indefinable, and she doesn't have a category to tie her down to a neat and tidy frame. You could very well label her nice if you'd like, but that would satisfy those people who believe nice is a euphemism for weak, stupid, or even callow; she is none of those in spades. On the other hand, she isn't stiff or haughty or dull; she is *très, très* unique. So when she does what she was then about to do, you will know why it hits us all the way it did. Mildred gives Gladys the finger—the middle finger—and she forms her mouth around the word suggested by the finger, without making a sound, and then she turns crisply to the two of us—to John and me that is.

"Listen, boys—."

She stopped as Gladys stands up to walk away; then Mildred does something else that surprised us. She raised her voice, "Sit down, Gladys!"

Mildred remonstrated dramatically, and for sure she did get all of our individual and collective attentions. As Gladys froze in place hovering silently above her now-empty seat, she suddenly acquiesced as if surrendering to a certain and deeply studied and anticipated fate that had finally befallen her. And then, without any additional gestures or words, she softly floats back down to gently rest her delicate bones in the seat that she had scant moments ago bolted from. John seemed put out by the whole scene as he squirmed and attempted most feebly to demand an explanation from his two lifelong guardians.

"Okay, what's going on here, you two?" he stuttered insecurely and gulped as if he'd swallowed a premonition that something large is about to break. Mildred then let it out, à la Gladys; Gladys, who is often the one that you might—if you were pushed to frame her sometimes-abrasive demeanor with a title—call it caustic, she would be the one to get right to the point. Mildred would normally imply or make reference to a matter rather hitting it straight on. But this time Mildred just slammed it down on the floor between us.

"You two boys are brothers."

The stillness in the library was deafening; I don't know how long we all sat there. It would have been fairly easy for an outside observer to interject all kinds of suppositions and questions here, but none came to any of our minds—none. But as for feelings and emotions, there was a decided confluence, a recalling of every moment that had occurred in the last thirty or so years that would have hinted that we might have been siblings. I mean outside of the pretend-familial kind of wishing that we were brothers that must have occurred intermittently by one or both of us. I could feel it all now, and I'm sure that John was indeed feeling the same way.

There was always this remarkable resemblance shared by John and me; it really wasn't readily discernable until John's father had died and as we both got older, but the resemblance that we shared was that we both looked like Gladys. You know how an offspring most often looks like both of his parents, and when one is present, he looks like that one more than the other. Well, when John's father died, all we had left was Mildred and Gladys, and John certainly didn't look like Mildred; but when we were all together—and sometimes we'd even all laugh about it—we would say how much he favored Gladys, but they, Mildred and Gladys, would always have an explanation and a way of turning us away from this conversation. But now, those and other conversations and images had all come together in my head, and I'm sure they were caucusing in John's head as well.

You see, we didn't go into this period of wonderment and denial; we were, in our heart of hearts instantly sold on the idea—but all humans are complex, and reflexive denial is often a part of that complexity. After the longest silence, John breaks the stalemate as he physically bucks like a little pony, and in the longest-delayed reaction in the history of man, John finally and loudly exclaims, "What! Come again, Mother, we two are what?"

If I'd been asked to wager a prediction that John would have had this kind of reaction, I would have wagered and won large; he is nothing if not predictable. I couldn't let on that there was many a time in my life that I had thought this to be true, but I had no evidence to support any of my suspicions. Besides, even if he was my brother, I had no claim on anything—and not that that would have ever been a motive that I would have labored under—in the end, it was more curiosity than anything else. I was chillin'; I was totally cool with the prospect. I was thinking that maybe, just maybe, this meant that John would cut me a little slack now; so I cheerfully threw my towel into the mix.

"We're brothers, John, that's what that means," I said, hoping that he would chill and contemplate what this meant, but instead, my younger brother heated up. I mean—what was he worried about? Nothing would change in his life, nothing at all.

Look, speaking of looks, his looks weren't going to change; he's as light as white, and no one is going to look at him differently because he's just found out that he's now really and truly a brother with a brother for a brother. He's got more money than God, and that in this town is all that matters; and as far as his wife is concerned, well, maybe there are reasons why she suspected it all along, and, if not, I know for sure that she doesn't have any problem being with a brother's brother, so why would have trouble being with a brother.

But John's pot has boiled over and all fluids were sizzling on the hot stove.

"What the hell are you talking about, Mother? This is no time for that kind of humor."

We all knew that John was now crying wolf; as a child, in the baby's playpen even his outbursts were heated. We could all see how quickly he was losing the steam in his protest. But now it was Gladys's turn to say something as it was she who tried in vain to keep Mildred from revealing this closely held secret. But John was still sputtering.

"Mother Gladys," he shakily moans through the vowels and consonants to form his pet name for his true mother. But Gladys is more taken with me than she is right now with John's whining antics; it seemed that my quiet and calm are more worrisome than John's tantrum for now. Don't get me wrong.

She doesn't dismiss John; she, in fact, walks over to him and holds him while she speaks to me, "You knew, Albert?"

She questioned me through an incipient revelation.

"You already knew, didn't you, Albert?"

All I could do was to nod; somehow I felt guilty when she said that I already knew, like I had done something wrong against them all. I couldn't speak, so I just sat there quietly until she asked again, "How long have you known, Albert?"

Before I could answer, John stood up and began to pace back and forth and foment, mumbling and talking to himself. We all stopped to watch the show; John was an artist at this; he always was. He never wanted to be upstaged, and right now he wasn't getting the family's full and undivided attention. Stomping around, he pouted and talked aloud, "This is nonsense. You are all crazy. I am white, and he is black. How . . . who . . . what the hell is going on here? Why am I the only one that's having trouble with all of this? Am I the only one with any sense around here? Well, am I?"

If it hadn't been so serious, we would have all been hysterically laughing; but we are family, and we knew that John is sensitive, very sensitive, and needed our support then. But the fact is that Gladys had asked me a question that must be truthfully responded to, and as I looked over at her, she indeed was still waiting for me to do just that.

"I've known for a while, Mother."

Stop the presses; that's what they would have yelled if this family were in the newspaper business, like the Sulzbergers up the block. They all then stopped. John stopped walking and remonstrating; Gladys, who had asked the question, and Mildred, who was already quiet—she leaned forward as I revealed my own secret. It was a secret that could easily bear repeating, and so I did—repeat it that is.

"Yes, you've all heard it right. I have known it for a while. I was wondering if and when someone other than that scumbag Russian would get around to discussing this topic with me," I said, and I was then for the first time in front of them in touch with my own emotions; I was a little angry. Mildred had gasped at my profanity—even the word *scumbag* offended her; it wasn't a word that I had grown accustomed to using in front of her, so I instantly wanted to take it back—but when I looked at her, she smiled and nodded approvingly at me. I was glad because no one was right now thinking about Mildred—Gladys was concerned with what I knew and when I learned it, and John—he was still denying it. But Mildred, she was the one that had let the cat out of the bag. If all were true—which I knew it was—then how must she be feeling right now. It was all very clear already, but I was just sort of thinking it out loud right back then.

That is, if John and I are brothers, then the only person that can be our mother is Gladys, right? So where did that leave Mildred, right? And also, how must she have been feeling if she's been sitting on this secret for all of this time—was over thirty years, thirty-six to be exact. I was looking at her then, and I was at first surprised; instead of seeing sadness on her face, I'm seeing a serene, unburdened face—she'd never looked happier.

And then I thought about it—she must be feeling relieved; she is not necessarily at a disadvantage because whatever happened—and it's clear that something happened at least once—between her husband and my mother, she has had thirty-five years to feel everything that she was ever going to feel about it. After all, it is no longer a surprise to her. And carrying around that kind of family secret, I'm sure it could have weighed a person down; so thinking it through, I could quickly and completely understand the look of relief on her face. And for me, none of this in the end will make a bit of difference in how I feel about these two wonderful, loving, and lovely women, both of whom raised and cared for me, but John—he was still having a hell of a time with it.

Finally after I had said my little piece, the three of them were all climbing through the cobwebs that I had just hurled at them; I guessed it finally hit them all what it meant that someone else besides the family was aware of our secret past.

It was bad enough that someone else knew—if they were normal people that could easily be rectified—but that it was that scandalous Russian fellow was more odious than anyone of us four were sanguine with. John had had one hell of five minutes, and he was suffering every second of it. But as it had finally sunk in then, he began to protest with a new set of concerns., "The Russian knows," he says, not angrily or robustly, as he has said so many of the other things, but more in a tone of disappointment, a certain bewilderment in his voice, almost as if he was strategizing a solution to his new predicament. And Mildred, I had looked away from her when John

167

spoke, but when she as well asked the same question, my head turned on a swivel to look at her again.

"The Russian knows?" she queried the same words, but in an altogether different tone than John's tone had suggested. But before I could attend to her query—as a query it indeed was—Gladys chimed in with an astute observation, "That's what all of this espionage is about. That's why he threatens us equal like when he greets us and talks to us—he knows about my partial ownership of the unit. He wants us both out of his way."

More new news—what an evening—I thought then that John was going to faint; he was taking these seismic quakes very hard. One would have been sufficient to keep him talking to himself for weeks unending, but now there were too many to keep track of, let alone handle emotionally. John walked over and took a seat, his regular seat again. He sat back and put his hands to his face, and then he yelled into them, "God, what more can happen?"

I must say, as cool and as calm as I most often want to be—and pride myself at being—that evening was a bit much for me as well. But in stark contrast to John's outer and my inner emotional tizzies, Gladys and Mildred had settled back in their high-back smoking chairs. They were like two peas in a pod—as they both, simultaneously, as if on cue from a stage director, take a sip of cognac and a puff on their illegal Cubans. They weren't giddy with excitement or joy, but they were decidedly different from both John and me; they were both now very calm and serene. After John took his hands from in front of his face, he lamented, "Oh, Christ Almighty; this is all just too, too surreal, it's just too much. A new mother____"

It seemed he has figured out the lineage all by himself.

"A black brother, and now you're telling me that you both own this unit. Is there any more? Come on, give it to me now, it seems the right time for it."

At least I thought he had until his last words.

"What are you going to tell me next, that my mother is not my mother? Huh?"

It was surreal as John had proffered earlier; we were all living a mysterious life full of secrets and feelings about which we were never fully certain. John looking like me and me feeling like him, but with no connection to the internal truth of it all; it was all indeed surreal. Even when we spoke now—John and me—much of what we said belied both of our substantial education and an assumed level of sophistication.

We were like children playing in the dark, trying to find the light to illuminate the field where our game of chance was now being played out. That's what life had quickly become—a game of chance—in those few moments of truth in that library on that particular night; a dark pall had befallen us that would irrevocably change all of our lives forever, and for the moment, we were groping around in the dark for answers.

So we had questions, not logical or even sensible questions, although some were imminently predictable given the news; we were all riding a very unstable emotional roller-coaster ride now, and until we were able to put our feet on stable ground again, we were bound to be uneven in our thinking.

Laughter is often the only salve to mask old fears, or to soften a new wound, and so they laughed. First, Gladys, unable to hold an errant cackle at bay, she hiccupped a humorous snort; and then Mildred, her soul-mated twin in all things emotional, she as well chortled her own rendition of mirth. Yes, they were both as nervous as they were guilty of holding this vital truth at bay for so long, with good reason I'm certain they both thought; but by any logic, no matter how spurious, it was still held away from us much too long.

Maybe it would have been better for it to accompany them both to their graves, as many a secrets have shrouded the dead from time immemorial. But their twin laughter has recast the mood, and the quickly ebbing emotions of us all quickly took an upward turn.

Now speaking through her laughter, Mildred finally turned to answer John's earlier query; it was difficult because she had begun to laugh so hard that her words sputtered instead of flowed. Through her laughter she said, "That's right, son, that's exactly what we were going to tell you next."

Mildred continued to laugh while she speaks more, "I'm not your mother . . ."

And as she points at Gladys, she says, "She is."

I couldn't help it now because I had less inclination to remain serious than at any other point in the evening; this is all just too funny for words—it truly had become quite humorous. In and of itself the topic was quite amusing, but with the addition of all their laughter, what person with even one remaining humorous bone in their body could have restrained his laughter—their laughter was contagious. We all loved each other so much, and nothing was going to change that. I had not thought about it, and this errant thought didn't come to me all shrouded in logic and thoughtfulness;

it was just there, and so through my own laughter, I blurted it out, "Then who's his father?"

The logic that his father could have been anyone other than my own father had completely and disappointedly disappeared from my consciousness. This entire episode had been subtly traumatic. What I mean is that it was very powerful, but it hit like some stealthy dark disease, like MS, quietly devastating; it was like waking up one morning and finding that your motor skills are dramatically diminished. Not to minimize the real physical devastation of MS, not at all, but what I'm saying is that the effect of the news was quite silent and insidious, and it did affect my logic, which it temporarily destroyed because my emotions feared the truth.

One moment I was going along just fine seeming to adapt quickly to the news and the changes it would bring; and then quickly without warning, I relapsed and fell backward in mental status into the mind of some stranger, an aberrant and sniveling idiot was he, and asking "who his father was" was a clear testament to my temporal insanity.

All three—Gladys, Mildred, and John—all turned to me then and looked upon me as if I were in fact what I have just described myself as being; for the moment, I felt distinctly out of place. But when John turned to look at his mother, Mildred, and he looked at her as if he as well was looking for the same strange question to be answered, I then felt relieved. It was not so much the question—which was, in and of itself, a poorly—formed and ridiculous query—but it was indeed the answer implicit to that pithy question that was in need of the telling. I did, and so did John, want to hear in deed and detail how this very late-arriving secret family history had all come about.

We sat and waited until the looks between Gladys and Mildred were harmonious enough for one of them to speak on the subject dangling there in the air between us four.

When Gladys finally cleared her throat, we—John and me—both knew it was she who was about to tell the tale. Answering the question that I had posed, my mother—or is it *our* mother now—well, she turned to me and said in what seemed like a single long breath; it was to be expressed in an unemotional and thoughtless, mechanical recitation of facts.

"Oh, his father was her husband, and after he raped me, and your brother was born white, as white as he sits here today. Well, we decided that the best thing was to raise him the way we did. And that's the whole story."

That was it. Those were the only words she was going to leave us with; she must have known that they were insufficient. I ponder a guess that she was just being provocative, and that all she wanted was for us to show our level of interest by making further inquiry before she was willing to continue.

I was almost angry that she was willing to share so little without being further stimulated to give more; maybe it was just too painful for her to speak more about it. Maybe she was embarrassed by some culpable behavior on her part; it was probably a bad and wrongheaded supposition, but knowing my mother, I was sure that it was anything but her fault. But if she didn't say more, I was thinking then, then what else would we be left with but to guess about the past. It didn't matter because all of my thinking wasn't anywhere near to the point of asking a lucid and thoughtful question just yet, and before I was able to formulate any particular question, John launched into his own query, "Well, why did you take so long to tell us?"

I knew he wasn't finished with his question, but he seemed to need to pause as he was clearly holding back a torrent of nonspecific emotions—he seemed as if he was on the verge of crying—we had both become little boys again. Then the second half of his question—as he stuttered forward—was even sadder than the first half of his sad rendition.

"I mean, don't you think you should have told us before now?"

My being quiet had allowed me to think and for the most part return to my normal mind, and so as I was sitting there and listening to the answers and questions; I was looking at our mothers, and I'm thinking about what it took for them to have held on to this secret for so long.

It was then that I realized that it had been a mistake—the mistake of habit, it was. You know how it is when you do something habitually, over and over, again and again and again. It doesn't matter whether it's a right thing or a wrong thing; in fact, that has little or nothing to do with it. It really is all about habit, and once you are engaged in a habit, it takes on a life of its own; it becomes a cycle of behavior like breathing. And that's what I think happened here; originally they both felt that they had good reason for doing what they did; that thing about John being white sounds like the reason that guided all of their future behavior and decisions. It is for certain that, at some point, the need for retelling and continuing their habitual behavior had lapsed, but their behavior persisted and took on a life of its own, or something like that, and now here we are. After twitching a little, but not so much that you would've thought that she was going to fall apart or anything like that, Gladys looked at John, and she has this curious look on her face as if she is remember something; I can't read whether it's a pleasant memory.

"Who knows?"

She queries to no one in particular, but then I realized that she was answering John's question; and then she continued to speak the full answer, "But we promised your father we wouldn't tell you until we knew that it wouldn't affect the way your life turned out. You see, all the choices that you've ever made were made based upon who you are in the world, how you saw yourself, and how the world sees you. Do you think that you would have made those same choices believing and in fact knowing that you were the son of a black woman instead of the son of a white woman?"

At first I was aghast, envious, and then I was angered by the sheer noise of her logic; it hit me in so many places at the same time that I didn't know whether I was being pushed or pulled to or away from solid reasoning in the throws of such phantasmagoric logic. The ideas, the switching of parents to make the colors match, and shifting names to make attitudes better to fit the color to fit the parent to fit the desired future outcome. But then quickly I steeled myself; I was able to shift my self-indulging focus to where it really belonged, and that was to John—he was the one that this was really all about.

Sure, I had feelings about it; and even though I had arrived at them quickly, some of them were quite deep and disturbing I must readily admit, but this really wasn't about me—it wasn't my turn. When I turned my head to look at John, I witnessed a look on his face that I had never seen before; in reflection it was not so surprising, the look that is, because he had just heard something—from his newly-discovered mother—that he had never heard before. I tried to clearly discern an effort to read the look on his face, as if I had seen it before, but it was useless; reading facial expressions is about empathizing with someone, and I had no idea what John was feeling then.

And then he began to succumb to the pressure that he was experiencing, and John then started to shake, literally, like he was going to fall over; Mildred started to move toward him. I'm sure it was to comfort him, but Gladys stopped her without much effort; they both knew what this was all about. We had all seen this behavior before. Mildred sat back in her seat, and this time she implored John to answer her with a solicitous query of "What is it, John, what is it?"

John utters a weak retort, "This is too much."

But it was Gladys who responds this time, with a far more robust rebuke; she wasn't having any of that supplication nonsense that Mildred had just doled out, not even for a moment she wasn't having it. All of a sudden, and from the bowels of her deceivingly slight frame, she yells loudly enough to shake the cavernous room.

"Bullshit, boy!" she yelled, and all motion and emotions seemed to freeze where they were; the words were harsh, but it was the timbre of the tone that more stole the moment. It was like she was growling; it had a quaking throatiness to it that I had heard only once before.

In our lifetime she hadn't done it that often—mostly her discipline was done in concert with Mildred—but when she had that one time, the meaning was clear. It was the first time that our mother had ever been stern with us in the very same manner and tone that she had just expressed her displeasure. But today there was a new wrinkle; in fact, it was not until this very day—with all that had already been revealed that evening—that I, for the first time, really understand what the yelling was about all the way back then. All of these years, whenever I've thought back on that moment, I had never been able to wrap my mind around what had happened; it had always bothered me that I really didn't get it.

It was a day like any other day when it first started except we were staying at the winter house in Palm Springs; it was beautiful there, and I think it was there that our mothers grew their closest. We had gone out to a nearby town—I really don't remember the name of it—but it was just John and me with our mother. It's funny. I can say our mother now, but the feelings that I have now are no different from what I was feeling then; we were always the same family—the four of us were.

Mildred had a hair appointment at the beauty salon; I remember that because I remember asking my mother Gladys why it was that they didn't go to the same place to have their hair done. I remember her smiling, but I don't remember the answer; I know better now.

We three were at the fairgrounds of a local fair; we were all very excited. There were rides, lots of fun fair foods, like corn dogs and taffies, the kinds of things that we never ate except at places like that. But it was the rides that were tops on our to-do list.

Once we got there, we—John and I—ran immediately for the big Ferris wheel; it was a giant colorful monster of a thing with lights and music, and I know now that I couldn't wait to get on for a ride. But that's where my balloon got pricked and deflated.

We got to the ticket taker after we had bought our tickets at the booth; we were both so excited. I remember we were both jumping up and down, with anticipation like two Mexican jumping beans. And there we were standing there in front of the man that took the tickets—our mother handed him the tickets—he took the tickets and we both started for the gate to the Ferris wheel. Well actually, we both moved forward as if we were starting for the gate, but the big hairy white arm of the ticket taker reached out across my little chest, and his deep voice rumbled, "Where do you think you're going, boy?"

I was too excited to be deflated—well, not at first I wasn't—but when mother Gladys stepped in, she said something that I didn't understand then. She asked the man what he was doing, and he told her, "The white kid goes on first, and that boy's got to wait until all the white kids get on." It was then that our mother says, "They are brothers, and they must go on together." That's all she said. I heard her but this entire little conversation wasn't about to stem my excitement; and as I continued to agitate excitedly, still bouncing around it was, our mother finally grabbed us both by the arms. I kept insisting that I wanted to get on the Ferris wheel—I'm sure I had become quite annoying—and that's when my mother says in that throaty voice, "You two come away from here with me, now."

Again, it wasn't the words spoken or the pulling on my arm that had alarmed me; it was, however, the timbre of her tone.

I don't know exactly when it was that the two of them had decided that they would raise us two the way they had, but I'm sure that this particular experience went a long way in solidifying their reasoning; at least it did with our mother Gladys.

"You are much stronger than that, and it looks like now you are going to need your brother's help, and I know that's why your mother has told you both about this now. There's danger lurking about in this building, and family has got to stick together."

John is still locked in his emotional battle with all of this, and that's how he answers Gladys with nothing but emotion, "My mother?"

He looks toward, Mildred.

"She's not even my mother."

I heard the words, and they didn't make any sense; I, in my lifetime, had seen the world in all of its extremes. I had experienced its vile, hideous, and dangerous underbelly ugliness in my few years in prison, and in a way—which I'm sure no one is willing to understand without first experiencing my life—I am grateful for having experienced and survived the way I have; it has made me a better person than I ever would have been without it. But I am close to positive that that kind of thinking is way to high thinking for most. I guess you would have had to end up here in a place like this, in a family like this to complete that kind of journey. My body was starting to heave an organic response to John's fretting and belching tantrum of woe is me. Jesus Christ, in point of fact, the man has not lost one thing; all that he ever had is still sitting right here in front of him. All of the love, all of the support, the family, all of the same people—the only thing that has changed is the names. Mildred is not mother, Gladys is; now what can be wrong with that, and to boot, he's gained a brother that in truth he's always wanted.

"Hey, asshole," I said in a very irritated tone, and everyone quiets down; that is, they were already quiet, but they all turned quietly to me and waited for me to continue to dispense my pearls of wisdom.

"She's as much your mother now as she's ever been, John. The only thing that has changed in your life is the last few minutes, that's all. You now have different information, but that still doesn't change your past, John—think about it, what has really changed? The shock, you'll get over that soon enough, I know I did—but what really matters is the lives we've all already shared with each other, not some fantasy about what could have been."

John looked at all of us first, and then he looked cautiously around the room as if searching for something, and then he started to make noises; they were whining, sort of squeaky noises, and I knew instantly that I was not going to take too much of that. It only took a couple of seconds, and I just didn't want to hear another whine, or whimper. I broke up this little developing pity party of his as I raised my voice slightly, "Look, John, you can be a sissy about all of this and keep on whining like a little girl, or you can be a man about it and look at those two wonderful women over there that both loved and raised you like their own, which you are and were. Tell me, John, in your heart of hearts, have you not always felt blessed to have two mothers? Now haven't you?"

I wanted an answer to my question, I really did, and this whining of John's was really nothing new—so no alarm was necessary—he had been known to whine quite a bit when we were younger. Although I hadn't been privileged enough to have heard it in some time, hearing it now again is clear a treat that I could easily have forgone forever. I had gotten my wish because he stopped whining almost the moment I stopped speaking—I love it when a quick prayer is so quickly answered. Well, John was quiet now, and he seemed much more pensive now than he had just moments earlier when he chose to act like a child. We all watched him with great curiosity attending what he'd do next. He surprised us all when he said—and quite casually at that, "We've got a problem, brother Albert. The Russians are trying to move in on our mothers, and we've got to find a way to stop them."

Now, that's what I'm talking about! my mind yelled.

CHAPTER XIII

After our successful family meeting, I needed to get some sleep. Gladys and Mildred both asked me to stay in the apartment with them; it was like old times again, and that was that we were all one big family again. Sleeping over, well even that felt right it seemed, at least for moment it felt like the right thing to do; even John was hardy in his approval.

"I think that's a capital idea that we all live in the same place again, capital, I say," he says as he smiles, and finally in a good mood, he leaves the penthouse for places unknown; we three suspected that he was headed home to Nancy to tell her the news, which would have been great. But unbeknownst to us, John had other plans in mind. After leaving the penthouse, John headed straight for the security office and Windler. John had consented for me to stay at our parents' for what then was an obvious reason, be that as it may, he was also thinking that my presence would provide an additional layer of protection for them as we didn't yet know what the Russians were up to and what their next move would be. Me being close by made us all—however intense the unspoken feelings were—more comfortable than me not being there at all. But John—thinking strategically—had wanted even more assurances of our parents' safety, and that's why he solicited and recruited Windler's expertise and help.

"Any, you can install them on the QT?"

Windler was not familiar with John's shorthand as he sighs a confused huh, and he asks, "What's a QT?"

This little missed communication is John's first opportunity to relieve some of the pressure that he was feeling from that night's consternation.

"*On the quiet*, Windler, *on the quiet*, that's what *on the QT* means."

When John went to Windler in the security office, he went there with his head spinning with all kinds of new thoughts about his life. Earlier I may have seemed to minimize all the new news that had been revealed to us both, but my lack of an even-stronger reaction, of course, had been due to the fact that the Russian had leaked the same information to me sometime earlier and in doing so had buffered my response—fairly or unfairly, I had a longer period of adjustment to digest the news than John had.

But John, fresh from our family meeting, was—to say the least—was still in a tizzy when he'd reached Windler's office. Windler was sitting comfortably alone in his office; he had become very proprietary about his little fiefdom there in the lobby, and it had garnered John's respect that he had become so serious about his charge. And so it was with all seriousness and respect that John had gone and entered Windler's domain to inquire about his expertise and his willingness to assist in his quickly conceived and developing plan. Windler was delighted.

"Yeah, I told you, Mr. Smith, that's what I was trained to do in the rangers, no one will know they're even there, not even Albert, as you've asked."

Windler was pleased, like a good soldier, to have won the respect of his boss, enough for him to be asking a favor in a plan far more than his ordinary duties would normally have called for. And John, never having done anything as stealthy as this, you could tell that he was new at this intrigue of espionage as he labors to make himself crystal clear about his intentions.

"Good then, Windler, obtain whatever devices you need through this dummy account."

John hands Windler a credit card, and Windler looks at it and shakes his head.

"You sure you've never done anything like this before, Mr. Smith?"

John blanches at Windler's supposition and feints complete innocence.

"Why, Windler, what could you possibly mean by that?" he says as they quickly get back on track with the plan.

"I want the best cameras installed—top-of-the-line technology—I don't want to miss anything, nothing obscured. And again, Windler, I don't want anyone with the exception of the two of us to know that they are there; they must be well concealed. You let me know as soon as you've got them all in place and working, do you understand, Windler? The moment they are working I want to know."

Windler's background as soldier comes into full play as he tenders his orders; he realizes John's urgency, and to protect him from anticipated future haranguing, he adds his own caveat to buy him some needed time, "Yeah, okay, Mr. Smith. But you'll have to understand that for me to keep it on the QT, as you require, that it's going to add to the time it takes to do it the right way."

The prescient Mr. Smith—knowing what secrets this new video setup will reveal—is not all that happy with what he is hearing from Windler, but the priority is on doing the thing correctly, so he reluctantly defers to the expert's timetable, but not without his own caveat.

"In all due haste, Mr. Windler;, time is of the essence."

Smith walks to the door of the security office and stands there for a second with his back to Windler; he then turns to look at Windler.

"This thing I'm asking you to do, Windler, is very important to me and all of my family, and I want to thank you for helping us, Mr. Windler."

And then he leaves without waiting for Windler to respond.

CHAPTER XIV

It was another wonderful day in Central Park for friends, lovers, and strangers alike; and as far as lovers go, Amy Dillon and Rufus Kingston had sprouted lovers' wings as they hand in hand glided blissfully along the well-tread paths of one of Central Park's famous walks. They had long ago overcome her father's incipient rage over their budding fancy with one another and, to their youthful yet mature credit, had learned well to bear the occasional stare or errant glances from curious onlookers, and to quickly characterize them as nothing less than admiration for such a harmonious young and fresh union as theirs.

But still, as one could have easily predicted, there were still some who would disagree most vociferously with their private choices turned public. And as their feet in truth, just like everyone else, be they lovers, friends, or stranger, must touch the same pavement as they stroll carefree through the park. But unlike them, and those that respect, ignore, or abide their affinity for each other, this innocent union stirs the churning guts and vacuous minds of some bent on intolerance without good reason or reservation.

"Hey, brother."

The voice and the words had come unexpectedly from a stranger, one of four young white men, white boys to be more specific, who were on approach staring at the young couple walking peacefully and calmly in their own idyllic world. The voice itself had startled Rufus first—not to fright, but to awareness. He knew at once it was not the familiar voice of a friend or fan, he knew that for certain. As he was jettisoned quickly from his almost-total oblivion, he had no recognition of the voice's timbre, which struck a decidedly strident cord. As the appellation *brother* is often a familiar salute to go along with a more personal, friendly, and approving message of favor, this rendition was anything but that. *Brother:* a word that is a salute to friendship or kinship among like-minded and like-cultural beings, a friendly verbal gesture, one that more often than not evokes a sense of safety and comradeship. But yet and still this time was awkward and disturbingly different; the stress in this most recent rendition of *brother* offered only warning that some dangerous interloping was afoot.

Instantly, Rufus's innate sense of danger—albeit arriving a little later than usual—was instantly propelled to alert status red as he spied not one but four suspects angling to arouse his ire. And before he could determine which one had uttered the first words, another of the four young men began to spout off, "Yeah, hey, brother. What all y'all niggers always doin' with our women?"

Rufus, feeling the chill of danger creeping all around him as the four boys fan out like a pack of wolves, he heats up and immediately and instinctively looks to protect Amy. He pulls her close and whispers in her ear, "We really don't need to be dealing with this crap today."

Before he can say more, a third boy—this one is standing right in front of them as the others have moved to their sides and one behind them—adds his two cents and heightens the threat, "What did you say, boy? Hell, we'll kick your black ass and take your white whore bitch from you right now, brother."

Rufus then steps in front of Amy to protect her from the one who has threatened her.

"Why don't you guys go on and mind your own business."

Rufus's words have no effect on the boys; in fact, they seemed to have triggered an action as the boy behind Rufus charges him, but Rufus is ready for the attacker as he steps to the side and uses the inebriated attacker's momentum to throw him hard to the ground; his deft action startles the other three into their own attack. They all go running at Rufus and Amy; Rufus kicks one in the stomach—as he doubles over and vomits,—Rufus then punches another one while the third one attacks Rufus's back; but Amy, who never moved a step away from Rufus's side, she then jumps on the third boy's back and immediately starts clawing away at his face until he grabs her arm, throws her down hard to the ground. Amy cries out as Rufus turns too late to prevent her crash.

He attacks the culprit—hitting him with kicks and punches—as the other three and finally the fourth one as well back off, and then they all begin to run away shouting epithets back at the couple as they run over the grass toward the west side of the park.

Rufus bent over to help Amy, who is obviously hurting from the tussle and the crash to the hard pavement. Strangely as Rufus begins to help Amy to her feet, a small crowd begins to form around them—even people who must have been close enough to have seen the four young men attacking the couple—but all they in the crowd of onlookers asked was if she needed them to call the police on this black kid and what had this boy done to her. It was obviously a socially inbred reflex action to blame the black boy for the white girl's battery.

"It wasn't him, didn't any of you see those four white boys attack us," Amy scolded the onlookers through her tears as Rufus helped her up and to a nearby bench to sit and appraise her physical condition. Chastened and reproached from the mouth of an offended near aristocrat, the crowd finally dispersed; they—Rufus and Amy—then determined that she was going to have to go to the hospital. But Amy lodged a quick and convincing protest before reaching there; they had settled on a story that she had fallen off a bench. Amy made Rufus promise that he'd go along with this story because she didn't want her father to use the attack as some spurious justification and another reason why he didn't want them seeing each other. And as far as the police were concerned, she didn't want to report this to them either; she suspected and feared, given the history of black men and the police, that they would somehow construe that it was Rufus or Rufus's fault that this whole thing had happen in the first place. They planned to stay far away from them as well.

It was two days later when I observed Amy entering the lobby of the co-op, and I was again behind the concierge's desk—I had been away for couple of days catching up on neglected errands and personal business that I had failed to complete in the last little while. So I was totally surprised when I saw Amy's arm in a sling, and not only that; her general demeanor—which was always upbeat and positive—had noticeably changed to a sullen, darker hue.

"Amy? Amy Dillon, what happened to you? Your arm, what happened to your arm?"

I hadn't meant to alarm or embarrass or whatever it was that I had done to make her cry, but cry she did, and that was rare for Amy; she just wasn't a crier, you know, the kind of girl that cries if you look a little cross-eyed at her. Not Amy Dillon—she was as strong and determined as her mother, or, put another way, she was as strong and determined as her father was aloof. So when she cried that day, I, of course, knew that there was more than a little something to it, and from that moment onward, it consumed my total attention and concern. At first—when I called out to her, it seemed from her body language that she wanted to ignore me—she didn't change her gait. But when I changed my tone from friendly and casual to paternal and parental, she quickly paid heed and came over to the desk.

Her head was down as were her eyes—another sign that all was not well with my favorite young confidant. Again I asked, "Amy Dillon, what happened to your arm, and why the low mood?"

She had already started to cry when she approached the desk, so I came out from behind the desk and walked with her to a quieter corner of the lobby; it was a good thing that I had given her a little more privacy than the concierge desk would have afforded her as she then broke into a full scale tearing cry, but only for a moment, and then she checked herself quickly. I reached into my uniform pocket and gave her a daily-fresh, clean white handkerchief—a rarity these days, I know, but there's part of me that will always persist in the old ways of handkerchiefs in the pockets and ascots around the neck; it just feels more like me. Well, I handed Amy Dillon my handkerchief, and immediately she used it to stop the flow of all her facial fluids.

"Thank you, Albert," she said with her little white face all reddened and moist; I nodded and waited for her to say first whatever it was that she desired to say. It was clear that everything wasn't hunky-dory—I didn't need to be hit upside the head to recognize that—and I had already asked my question twice; so I waited. Still sniffling a little, she finally began to speak quietly and frankly about her most recent and most troubling experience, "Albert, oh, Albert, I'm so glad to see you. I wished you had been here two days ago when this wretched thing first happened."

Her little preamble certainly got my attention—not that she needed it because I was already there in full force with her. I'll say it now, just so that I won't have to say it later, as if it only recently happened, but I feel very much more than custodial toward Amy Dillon. You see, I've never wanted children—that I'm not married is no aberration; it is a status not bereft of contrivances as I am so certain of one quickly following the other, and I've never wanted the responsibilities of either parenthood or husbandhood. But Amy is and always has been something different to me in meaning as well as feeling.

I remember the day her parents brought her home from the hospital—she cooed and stole my heart the first time I held her. I watched her like a hawk as she's grown into a fine young woman, and I'm as proud of her as a nonparent could ever be of progeny not of his loins. I am very fond of her.

And now I have a status to preserve—it seems that Amy has trained me well. She has often—in these past sixteen years—told me that unlike her father, and even sometimes her mother, I'm the best listener that she knows and trusts; now that's an honor coming from any child, but especially from Amy. So I indeed stood silently, and I listened well as trained. But after her preamble, she paused, seemingly waiting for my response to her opening statement; finally, I jumped to alert.

"But, Amy, I told you that I had to be out of town for a few days, and look what happens while I'm gone. What did happen, Amy?"

This time she started right in, "What's wrong with people, Albert, what goes through their minds? We're just two people that care greatly for each other, what's wrong with that, Albert, can you tell me that?"

Instantly there was this familiar storm that came in a rush and planted itself inside my head with all the concomitant winds and their howling, their blustering, and their bellowing; it was a storm that I had grown accustomed to carrying about inside myself, and when it spoke words, it too had asked the same questions that my little Amy was now asking me. I was from that moment on afraid to hear what had happened to Amy. With her question, I knew that whatever happened had something to do with her and Rufus being together, and I knew all too well and had experienced far too often the abject horrors of racial enmity that could be inflicted upon the unsuspecting and uninitiated.

In this case I'm sure whatever did happen came as a tremendous surprise because Amy's life, up 'til now, had been idyllic and peaceful. What a sad yet necessary day for all neophytes—it is a humanity diminishing truth—but it is as real as the nose on one's face that the adult world is a harsh and enigmatic sphere far from the great blue marble of childhood games and peaceful fantasies about how life should be for all people.

All the parents in the world, their warning words can neither completely prepare or reduce the natural coarseness of these jolting experiences as the experience itself is the only thing that can give one the experience and sensation of the shock, and now the decision on what to do about future exposure to these demons lies with the next move.

To step up or to step back—it's like a hot pot—cooks handle hot pots all the time, daring their contents to stay put and safely inside; either you deal with it or you find some other more suitable profession. But I knew that my thoughts were at risk of getting way ahead of Amy's story, so I dialed back on my reaction and tried to get the details from Amy before I reacted disproportionately to the actual stimulus.

"What happened, Baby Girl, did someone do this to you? And is it really broken?"

Amy frowned, and I was glad I hadn't said more. Although it turns out that she wasn't frowning at what I had said—the memories were still so fresh in her head that she was reliving them as we spoke.

"Yeah, it's broken all right. We were just walking, Albert. Arm in arm or hand in hand, I don't remember which, but we were walking close that I do remember clearly ever so clearly, and it was a wonderful moment, Albert, as memorable as all of our moments have been. You know like the poet Gwendolyn Brooks says in *The Womanhood*: 'Exhaust the little moment. Soon it dies. And be it gush or gold it will not come. Again in this identical disguise.'"

I almost fell over, this little white girl—whom I love as my own—quoting the poet laureate of Congress Gwendolyn Brooks—and she didn't even bat an eye, sweet Jesus, the world is changing faster than I can say. It is clear to me now that I've got to start spending more time away from this lobby because as Jerry Lee Lewis used to say, "There's a whole lot of shaken goin' on." And would you look at that, this child is channeling Gwendolyn Brooks, and I'm quoting Jerry Lee Lewis.

"We were in the middle of the park, minding our own business, we really just love spending time together, Albert, that's all. And these four white guys started taunting us and calling us horrible names—that's so old school, Albert, I mean, where have they been. And then when Rufus took up for us, they just jumped him and started fighting with him. When I tried to help him—I jumped on the back of one of them—and that's when one of them threw me to the ground, and I broke my arm."

I really hadn't wanted to hear such a story; it seemed that I had been living in this lobby bubble for far, far too long myself. I don't get to hear these kinds of things that often anymore, hardly ever. That thing that happened with my brother, John, earlier in the year, well, that I think had little to do with him being or at least looking like a white man; it had more to do with his attitude, which still doesn't make it right, but it wasn't racial, or, at least, it hadn't started out to be racial.

I was flabbergasted to say the least, or at least I had wanted to be flabbergasted; it was easier than looking the truth right in the face, a truth that was far more unsettling and uncomfortable than I wanted to be feeling right then. So I held back on my response, and like a bad newspaper reporter, I asked a defining yet totally innocuous question, one for which I had already received and answer, "This happened two days ago?"

Amy was all too happy to answer my query again as she was quickly on to expressing her feelings about the whole matter, "Yes, Albert, it was Tuesday afternoon, we had been dismissed early from school, and Rufus and I decided to walk through the park instead of down Fifth Avenue. You know . . . What is wrong with people, Albert? Why must they be so wantonly cruel? There's just no rhyme or reason for it, Albert. Albert, I just don't get it."

I knew she expected, or at least wanted, to hear my take on the whole disorder of things—things are just not the way an idealistic sixteen-year-old white girl from aristocratic Fifth Avenue believes they have the potential of being. I knew what I had wanted things to be like all of my life, and I knew even better that there were many, many people of color—much darker than mine—who have had and were still having a much more difficult time of things than I was; most of my greatest problems in life had been because of my own bad decisions. Hell, I am a lighter-skinned black man—it sounds silly, even oxymoronic to even be saying that, but that is truly an exemplar of the absurdity of race, a subject that our conversation is definitely centered around.

We—the lighter-skinned blacks—have historically had an easier time, or so I've been told. But try telling that to my mother Gladys—who is shades lighter than me—and ask her if her life was easier because of it. But, alas and forever, that is a subject of interest among intellectual and upwardly mobile blacks—or at least during times of high black consciousness when that very and most particular point has been bandied about and heatedly debated as to whose hue is black enough. But I was sure that that wasn't what Amy Dillon was ready to hear on that day. So I gave her the severely abridged but maybe the more to the point of the whole thing version.

"Because, Baby Girl, their hearts are in pain, and they resent your peace . . ."

For a moment, Amy didn't say anything; she just stared at me with her wonderment-filled and innocent eyes stretched wide. And then I wonder if I were the first person she had talked about this issue with; normally—if her mother had been home—she would have talked with her mother, but not this time. She did, however, always manage to talk to me about many if not most things, so this was not at all aberrant. But then I thought, or maybe I was hoping against realistic hope, that she had somehow managed to get closer to her father, and him to her, now that it was just the two of them alone together for a while, so I asked, "What did your father say about this whole thing, Amy?"

Amy almost started to laugh, and I knew for sure then that I was like a half-blind dog chasing a cat and barking up the wrong tree. But then she quickly got much more serious.

"My father! You must be kidding, Albert. I would never tell my father unless I had to."

To me, that meant that she somehow hadn't told the police what had happened because if she had, they in turn would have insisted that a parent be involved since Amy was still a minor. I didn't think that was such a good scenario—she not having told the police or not having told her father the truth. I knew I was showing my age then, but as an adult myself having passed her way once and passed gracelessly, I might add, I understood that if they knew—and this happened again, with these same people—that there were things that a parent or parents could then do if they knew about the first incident.

What if there were further repercussions, what then; what if those boys came back after them again, someone in authority should know about this. I knew then that I needed to find a way to tell Amy how serious I felt this whole thing was, so I said, "Amy, they threw you down hard enough on the ground for you to have broken your arm—that is serious violence, Amy, and still you haven't told the police, that's not good."

Amy's mouth gaped open wider than I had ever seen it before; like an ape she was now standing there and staring at me. She was not happy about my adult posturing, but I needed to let her know how I was feeling about this terrible thing that had happened to her. It was a difficult thing to do for both of us, I'm sure. You see, I'd always been on Amy's side—no matter what—but her side has always been a side that I had found a way of supporting. But this is different; this incident was no minor tiff with her stubborn and often-distant father, or an occasional misunderstanding with her much more available mother, or even a misunderstanding with her friends; no no no, this wasn't that at all, no, not that at all. That's because, and I could see it in her eyes, that she thought these menacing interlopers near tame. Those boys to her were seemingly rakish malcontents having a mischievous day, but I knew that they were from another world and more dangerous than that—they march to a different drummer, and a foreign tune—they are of a different clan of thuggish strangers, and people like those have no set boundaries that they are disinclined to cross; they are all hoodlums and rogues of the first order, predatory like hyenas and vultures that prey on the weakened, the outnumbered, and the unsuspecting.

This traumatic episode, and its emotional aftermath was not going to be easily dispelled from their consciousness—her and Rufus—as living life in the adult world is like walking through a thicket of rosebushes; the thorn pricks and punctures are a certainty, but it's your finesse that determines their severity. It was time for hard choices, and it seemed—to me at least—that Amy was ill prepared to make them, or so I thought. But she flares back at me like freshly oxygenated embers from a brush fire exploding into flame.

"The police, Albert, I'm shocked at your position on this. I know you know better than that, Albert. I've seen the way they disrespect the brothers. They would have probably figured out a way to have charged Rufus with a crime . . . You know, come to think of it, right after it happened, everybody got brave, all of a sudden—not when it was happening, no, not then but after it was all over.

"Rufus was leaning over me helping and tending to my arm, and that's when several people came over, and they were so ready to accuse Rufus of having done something untoward to me. And you and I both know why that is, don't we, Albert?"

It was in reflex, not in thought, that I said my very next words, "Well, to them it may have appeared to be that way."

But as soon as the words had left my mouth, I knew that they were wrong—the benefit of doubt and all—I was prepared to take the sides of the onlookers, even from my remoteness and absence from the scene itself—why was that? Had I subconsciously thought all along that they had brought the attack upon themselves just by being together in their integrated way? I really wasn't sure. But when Amy protested and said her next words, it was then that I had to take a pause and reflect on my own associated thoughts.

This little white girl—because that's what she is—was standing there strong and defiant, right there in front of me, and she was giving me a lesson on perspective, race, and civics.

"I really think you are stretching it, Albert. It only looked that way to them because of the color of Rufus's skin. If Rufus were a white boy, they never would have thought that way at all, do you think? I am a white girl, Albert, I guarantee you that wouldn't have been their first response if Rufus had been a white boy, I know that for sure, as sure as I am sure that the both of us are standing here right now talking about it."

All I could do at first was to nod my head because in my soul and in my heart I knew that she was right. Shamefully I must add that if I had been there, if I had seen she and Rufus together, and him leaning over her after their mishap, my first thought as well would have been that it was he who had done her in; it saddens me to think that was true, but unfortunately it was true.

My interest extended further as I was curious as to what she had indeed told her father had happened, so I asked her. She answered, "And my father, the first thing he would have done was to insist that I stop seeing Rufus—as if that pronouncement would have gone over well—even having met Rufus, and seeing what a fine and upstanding young man he is, he would still have protested our friendship. The only reason now why he seems so normal about it is because of who his boss is."

I didn't even begin to understand what Amy was talking about—as I was still reeling from some of my own truths—but I was more than a little curious as to what she had actually told her father, so I asked her, "So what in fact did you tell__?"

Amy quickly interrupted me before I could complete my tepid query, "Don't ask, you don't want to know what I told him."

I took her warning seriously. I, the lone member of the hoi polloi in this conversation, had for sometime—much longer than I cared to admit—thought about how much I knew, or someone more devious than me might say, how much I had on all the renowned, the upper crust, and the super wealthy in this building. I would have hated to have gotten hauled into court and had to spill the beans on all of them; as the saying goes, I could write a book about it all. Yet with that said, I continued to engage in a form of optimism that I must in hindsight characterize as pointless.

"I don't know, Amy. I've learned recently that people can change, even those whom you least expect change to come from . . ."

As Amy's face reflected a frown that made me quickly abandon that untenable position in a hurry, I, in turn, quickly change my direction.

"By the way, how is Rufus? I'm sorry I didn't ask sooner—my bad, I should have."

Finally a smile, just the mention of her beau's name brought a huge and welcomed smile to her pretty little face. Relieved, I then smiled as well.

"Oh, Rufus, he's a guy, Albert, he's fine."

She pauses to think and reflect for a moment, and then she adds, "He's fine minus a couple of scrapes and war bruises—that's what he calls them anyway. He said they were just a bunch of drunken punks that couldn't have hurt him if their lives depended on it. Besides, he said that they weren't very strong."

She paused again and then she asked quite inquisitively, "Albert, what's that all about . . . you guys will never admit weakness, or rarely if ever, what's that all about, Albert? I know Rufus is very strong with all of his muscles and martial arts training, but . . ."

I attempted to finish her thought, as I said, "Yeah, and there were four of them too."

It was what she was thinking.

"Yeah, that's what I was going to say, but he said he was more worried about me than he was for himself. He said—and he was a little annoyed when he said it—that he could have handled them better if I hadn't been there to worry him. He was very upset about me having gotten my arm broken; I think he blamed himself for that."

I understood exactly where Rufus was coming from if that, in fact, was his position. I gained a lot of respect for the young man; he's going to be a good man real soon. I didn't want to continue defending him to her, as I understood that it's a guy thing, and all of the explaining in the world was not going to make her understand that now.

Finally, I queried her well—being to change the subject.

"Well, are you going to be all right?"

"Yeah. Albert, I'll be fine, but I'm glad you're back. I missed you terribly. I'll see you later, okay?"

Amy left and headed for the elevators; she was, if not happier, less sad than she had been when she had first entered the lobby. And as one elevator door opened to take Amy away, out popped my brother, John. I haven't said it as much out loud, but inside my head it rings a fashionably pleasant ring—as in any time is a good time to have your brother as the co-op president.

When he sees Amy approaching, he smiles and greets her pleasantly, but when he speaks, his words reveal that he is way ahead of me in the gossip department.

"Hello, Amy. I heard what happened to you and your arm in the park. They should give a really large fine for having your dog off leash in the park, the bigger the dog, the bigger the fine should be. Feel better, Amy."

Amy knew that I had heard all, and she turned a sly-headed glance, and her eyes instantly caught my eyes; so that's what she told her father had happened in the park. She then nodded in my general direction, but I knew it was for me. As she headed into the elevator, her steps quickened, and she skipped a final step as she responded to my brother, John—I'm starting to like the way that sounds, even if he's not all that certain and sanguine with it.

"Thank you, Mr. Smith, I will," Amy says as the elevator door closes on her. Then John walks over to where I'd moved back again behind the concierge desk, his face was wrinkled in serious thought—I wondered what his concern was besides the usual. It wasn't at all long before he had apprised me of the reason for his consternation.

He nodded to me to walk him to the front of the building where we would have the greatest amount of privacy, so we did. He didn't speak until he was sure no one could hear us. We hadn't made any formal announcement about our newly discovered siblinghood—it wasn't as if either one of us was hiding it, but in the end, what kind of announcement was it that we were supposed to make—it wouldn't have changed anything for the better in the building. And besides, I was determined for my life to remain just as it was, but, apparently, John had other plans. Once we were alone outside the building, my brother, John, came gushing forth with plans.

"I'm not going to give up, Albert__"

John had already asked me several times to come and work with him; it was a generous offer, even if the particulars somehow escaped his offer—but still, and more to the point, I was not yet impressed by the tenor, tone, and the real honest reason for the offer. It at first seemed more about his image—you know, like doing the brotherly right thing—than ever it was about my welfare; at least that was what I was feeling.

"I don't want my brother working as a doorman for the rest of his life. Now, there's a place for you in my company, we have a lot of things to work out financially. I'm not going to stop until you accept my offer, or better yet, when you learn the business, you decide what area you want to work in. I'm serious, Albert."

For the first time, John did seem more serious than ever before, and that was good. I might have been disposed to changing my life someday, although my life was already pretty good. I liked my job for now, and of course, with our mothers in the penthouse, they were as safe as could be, and now having my brother here as the co-op president, job security and healthy remuneration would never be an issue—not like it had ever been an issue in the first place. I liked my place—probably owing to my innate lack of initiative and industry—and I knew I could stay here forever, or return if I so chose.

So giving John's ideas a chance was no big risk, but even with that said, there was something I needed to see through first, so with all this in mind,

I said to John, "I don't want you to stop, John. Keep the fires burning hot for me. But right now, I just don't want to leave here until we've figured out what to do about the Russian threat. Me staying this close to our mothers is a good thing for right now."

John was already nodding his head in agreement before I had finished my reasoning for staying put for a while.

"I hear what you're saying, and I don't disagree with your sentiment, but there must be a better alternative—you're no kind of cop. What, in fact, would you do against a really serious threat?"

It seemed for the first time John was totally sincere, or maybe he had been sincere from the beginning and it was me who wasn't reading it correctly. I was buoyed by his persistence, and my response to him I hoped let him know that.

"Well, when you think of a better solution, John, you let me know, but for right now, this is what I need to do."

For the first time in a long time—and I mean for almost twenty years—John smiled at me with that generous warm smile that he used to smile at me with; it was heartwarming, and I knew that we had connected again like old times.

"Well, if I can do anything more . . ."

He paused before he said my name, and this time he surprised me with his words.

"My brother, Albert. Okay?"

If he had been a girl, I'd have kissed him smack on the lips, but I demurred—and I'm sure if he could have read my mind, then he would have thanked me for my discerning discretion. So instead, and with better judgment, I smiled a blushing, father-of-the-bride, loving smile and said, "Yeah, okay."

It felt real good standing there with my brother, and finally that constant aching in my heart that had shadowed me like an ominous ghost for all of those years, it simply and not too precipitously disappeared. As Amy would have said, if she were feeling the way I was feeling, "I was stoked."

Later, as I was standing at the concierge desk musing a bit over the grand scale and magnitude of change that had so recently inserted itself into all four of our lives somewhat like the proverbial elephant in the middle of the room, but this time, in a providential twist of fate, everyone had acknowledged that it was indeed there. As I mused and drifted elsewhere, none other than Nancy Smith—my now-new sister-in-law—smoothly and quite surreptitiously planted herself right in front of me; if I hadn't been so surprised, I would have been chagrined, because I knew for sure that she was certainly up to no good.

Well, it was too late for me to adjust my mood; she was there, and so I simply smiled. It was her time to return home from her yoga class at the club, and she was exhilarated following her class as per her usual demeanor this time of the morning. She had a little glow about her, and her smile was a tad more mischievous than usual.

"So, brother Albert, your dilemma persists."

She didn't waste a second's time, or a calorie's effort, as she started right in on me. She posed sultrily, if not seductively, in her expensive gym tights and Masai walking sneakers; actually, she did sway back and forth almost imperceptively while querying me. like an annoying mosquito buzzing around my head on a hot summer's night in the park. I was not going to let her sting me, or so I thought, so I swatted back at her attempt and with my best charade with an air of pretend nonchalance as I feigned surprise that she was even there.

"Oh, good morning, Mrs. Smith."

My intended slight did nothing to dampen her quest; it was clear from her next words that she was on a mission.

"Maybe I'm being selfish, Albert, but I don't care. Just because your status has changed, it doesn't mean that I should be the odd man out."

I couldn't help but laugh inside—God forbade me to laugh aloud in her face; it would have been the height of rudeness and unnecessarily insulting, and, besides, she would have unabashedly on the spot ripped me a new one. But inside I was quite amused with her referring to herself as the odd man out; it just struck me as funny, that's all, just a funny way for her to have referred to herself. I knew it was just a turn of a phrase, but, still, there was nothing manly about Nancy Smith, and that in fact was the major part of the problem—she was and still is a very appealing and attractive woman. I could easily be disposed to calling her stunning without a second thought or question in my judgment. I swear that brother of mine was an idiot for neglecting her. But there she stood staring in my face waiting for me to make sense of her life for her. And then I said, "Oh, Mrs. Smith, by no means are you the odd man out, you are in like Flint."

She doesn't hesitate or miss a beat as she answers me quickly and somewhat haughtily, "Very well, Albert. You seem to be getting your sense of humor back, how nice. So when am I going to get all of you back again, Albert? You know, Albert, all the stakes are higher now, I mean, your new status and all. What if our 'Golden Boy' found out that his brother was having an affair with his wife . . . Hmm, I wonder."

Of course, my first impression was correct—I was right—she was there to do mischief; the scent of her deviousness had been more than hinted at by the strength and aroma of her pheromones. She was what my mother used to call a pip—it was an old slang terminology for a wiseacre; she was quite a pip. And I didn't want to go down that road again, not in the first place; I had had enough long ago, but certainly not now, not after the now widely known discovery of familial entanglements. She was just being bad now, and I told her so.

"Mrs. Smith, you are being very bad now," I said while hoping against hope that I'd make an impression, a plea if you will for caution, self-discipline, and restraint, which it was immediately clear that I hadn't. As she said, I think it was almost playfully, while standing quite aloof and defiant, and with a minor pause of hopeful—for me—equivocation.

"I know, Albert, I know."

But I, in point of fact, it was I who was getting nervous about things that before now had not moved me at all emotionally—or maybe they had moved me emotionally, but never in a positive direction before now. I can see more clearly now that I was very angry with my brother, John.

At first, when I had come home from prison, I felt exceedingly guilty, and if I had had other better job opportunities, I had really known much better than ever to come here to work. But two things changed my mind: I had nothing better, and this was my home, where my mothers were demanding me to return. John's coldness at first I felt I deserved. I admittedly had done wrong to myself and toward them—as they had grubstaked my future, and to profit them only in my doing well with their largess—and with little good reason I had failed us all.

I blew it, I who had all the advantages—a black man with an Ivy League education—was almost as uncommon as a black cantor at Shabbat service in a temple on Passover. I blew it like a compulsive gambler with his paycheck at a crap table trying to increase his bounty, not a good bet, but in fact, I had paid my debt—overpaid it if you'd asked me. I had done hard time, for a soft white-collar crime, and having survived the iniquity of an imbalanced justice system, I was chastened, and humbled.

Hat in hand I took the job, and I thought that in time all would be forgiven if not forgotten, and mostly it had, all except for John; his truculence had lasted and seemed as if it would last forever, although thankfully his disdain was mostly passive-aggressive. And that's what I became in retaliation; I too became passive-aggressive in my behavior, ergo Nancy Smith. Admittedly, I didn't have much leverage in the situation, but charm I had in spades—no pun intended. I could have easily said no to her seduction, but I didn't for a number of reasons, not the least of them was that she was John Smith's wife. A man whose cold shoulder I had been feeling for more than fifteen years now, who once was my best friend, and now with a reflex of great ambivalence, we've all discovered that we are brothers.

As Nancy was clearly up to no good, I for the first time was feeling protective of my brother, John. It was now my aim and desires to tread the course on a lighter foot than before in an effort to leave no impression. I wanted to beg her for a stay from future entanglements and hope that the past would not soon if at all catch up with the three of us, her and me as the dreaded antagonists. I decided to execute my warning without blame on either of us.

"But, Mrs. Smith, what if he already knows?" was my plaintive whine, but she was doggedly resistant to it, giving an only slight concession with her next and immediate comment.

"Well, Albert, that would take some of the bullets out of my gun, but not all of them . . ."

She paused for a moment's thought, and then she uttered, somewhat desultorily and as if her mind had wandered off to a distant planet, "Does he know, Albert?"

There need not have been necessary for something to have entered to break the mounting tension of the moment, but if there needed to be, and a choice was within my realm to choose, I could not have prayed for a better diversion than what was in the very next moment to befall us all. For in that very moment, striding through the lobby like a peacock dressed in a tuxedo came in the presence of a very handsome Hispanic man, whose arms were filled full of colorful packages and shopping bags, all being carried for Mrs. Sarah Peters, who followed closely behind the young man.

She was equally tanned and colorful in her flamboyant and garishly vibrant sundress, hanging sultrily off her one shoulder. When she sees me talking to Mrs. Smith, she nods dutifully at her contemporary in all things, and then she immediately goes for me with a gush of energy and bravado.

Approaching the concierge, steps closer than necessary or courteous—as she proceeded, probably not with the intention that the action exhibited—she cuts Mrs. Smith off without another nod to her presence and effusively lavishes me with praise: "Oh, Albert, thank you, thank you, thank you. That was the best idea you had sending me to Puerto Rico."

She was like Sarah Bernhardt remonstrating over the body of Essex in her 1912 silent film version of Queen Elizabeth; she was really hamming it up. She hammed it up so much that she even brought a smile to Nancy Smith's face when she could have easily taken offense. But she could see that the woman meant no harm; she was just excited about her breakthrough and had wanted to share it with me, whom she pleasantly charged for the inspiration.

I remembered it now; all I had said to her was, "Sarah, you're too lovely a woman to be chasing around after Puerto Rican delivery boys. If you are so inclined, why pick one boxed and battered from the store when you can go to the source and pick one ripe from the tree ?" But I must confide that I never saw my words as advice; it was my way of telling her that she should lay off of the delivery boys. It's so funny to see what words can do.

After Sarah had finished thanking me, she turned and pointed at her plunder in the form of that handsome Puerto Rican young man, who I'm sure knew little of what he was in for.

"Juan, come, come now, my little greasy spoon," she says as she motioned the young and compliant man toward the elevators.

Juan, his name might not have been—for she called all of her conquest either José or Juan out of habit, maybe, just maybe out of a hint of discourtesy. But the young man she called Juan, he did obediently follow ever so blithely along as he smiled and tiptoed lightly behind her.

"*Sí, sí, señora.*"

Sarah smiled as she now led the way, calling back as she reached the elevators, "Isn't he lovely, folks? Quite lovely, yes."

I smiled, and Mrs. Smith smiled, but I was certain our duo of smiles were for totally different reasons. It didn't take long for Mrs. Smith's words to reveal the effort of her smile.

"Now that's a woman after my own heart, Albert. She went out and got what she wanted. She's my hero, Albert, I'm studying her very closely."

I bet she was too.

CHAPTER XV

While just thinking about them together, their images and influences on my life are so strong that I can experience the pungent cigar smoke wafting through the rarified air of the penthouse triplex as the two middle-aged spinsterish damsels—that I've learned to interchangeably call mother—languish in their staid, luxurious peace. And they did, in fact, at that moment sit in each of their usual chairs doing just the thing that I had imagined them to be doing, smoking illicit Cuban cigars, sipping rare and expensive brandy, and talking openly of the mischief—intended or not—that they had caused.

"It's funny, Gladys. You know, ever since I told the boys the truth, I actually feel lighter and younger."

Gladys smiled as she reflected on her feelings as well.

"No need to explain that feeling, Millie, so do I. It's really nice to see them getting along, and our Thursday-night dinners—"

All of a sudden, Gladys began to cry; she clenched her delicate fists and calmly brought them up to and placed them softly against her chiseled elegant chin. She then swayed her head ever so smoothly from side to side as the poignant words eased themselves slowly and ever so gently from her full pink lips, "They are happy tears, Millie, tears of gratitude and love. God is great, God is good . . ."

Gladys pauses to reflect as she remembers certain important moments.

"Walking in that park, cold and alone, with baby Albert, all snuggled into my dry bosom, but thank God it was still warm enough to keep him from freezing to death. How could I have ever thought that our lives would end up here, like this of all things possible, why like this? Oh, Millie, you are forever God's angel on earth. I love you more than my tears can express or ever prove. Thank you, thank you for my life, and the lives of our children, thank you. God has clearly shown you his face."

Millie's azure blue eyes were already now red with tears that had by then scurried quickly and delicately down her angular glacier-white cheeks, and had managed to escape the hollows of her pointed face. She twitched nervously to speak and escape the torrent of accolades and thanks, which clearly made her a wee bit uncomfortable.

"I love you too, darling, and I could not have had a better life. Thank you, Gladys, for giving me all the love that I've ever wanted, or could ever need, thank you, for sharing Albert and John with me and completing my life."

CHAPTER XVI

Time surely flies; it's seemed like John and I had never been anything other than brothers as exampled by the gravitas his old countenance had borne for so long in his dealings with me has totally disappeared, and in effect, it seems that he does indeed feel lighter. And that's not only evidenced with me; it is with almost everyone that I've seen him interact with lately. He is freer and more spontaneous with them as well; in comparison, he is far more effusive in words and relaxed in manner than ever I have seen him, since I started working here. I would deign to say that he has flashed a bit to the excessive side of flattery, fulsomeness I'd say—as when he compliments the elevator operators on the splendor of their attire—but for now I'll take it, and besides, "me thinks" in time the pendulum will work its way back to a more harmonious center, where his flow and cadence are forever normalized.

Again standing my post at the concierge, I spotted Amy entering the lobby still with her soft blue cast over her arm; I realized that today was the day that she gets to lose that cumbersome thing altogether. I was, needless to say, in a pretty good mood all up. There had been nothing further with the Russians, and my family was happy and intact. Amy's mind was elsewhere as she didn't even look my way as she entered the lobby, so I called quietly out to her, "You get to take your cast off permanently today, Amy."

Amy turned to me; as she heard my voice, she stopped and smiled weakly before she made a full turn and walked over to the concierge. It was then that her smile brightened.

"Albert, I can't believe you. Why do you always remember exactly what's going on in my life when at the same time my father is always completely clueless? You know when my birthdays are. You know what's happening with Rufus—"

Suddenly, Amy breaks off her words, which are instantly replaced by a face full of tears. Of course, I didn't immediately know why she was crying, but now I knew why she was avoiding me. I was immediately sorry that I hadn't let her go; maybe she really wanted to be alone, and I had interrupted her privacy. But now it was too late for that, wasn't it? Now I had to know what was going on with her, why was she crying?

I am not really any good at this, so my cautious thoughts led me directly to inept words.

"Don't cry, Little Ms Sunshine, everything's going to be all right," I said, and I knew as the words left my timid mouth that I didn't have a clue of what I was talking about. But when she said her next words, "He's a Lucy," I went quickly to anger like some kind of doting parent, saying with some degree of annoyance, "Oh, I'm so sorry to hear that, Amy. He seemed like such a classy young man, I'm very surprised with him."

Amy's face instantly flashed a look of confusion before she caught up to what I was saying, but then she got it, "No, Albert, not Rufus, Rufus has been great. No, it's my father, my father is a Lucy, Albert . . . Albert, I have two mothers."

With her sudden change in direction, I put the breaks on; I had to restrain myself as I almost laughed out loud. I didn't recall hearing the name Lucy before that moment, but I instantly knew what she meant, even if she hadn't followed it by saying she now had two mothers.

I couldn't laugh because I could tell that she was very serious, but the name Lucy did strike me in a funny place. I decided to play a little dumb for the moment. I wanted her to start from the beginning to explain this seemingly wild accusation to me with all of its accompanying and incumbent details. So I said, "What are you talking about, Amy? Why are you calling your father a Lucy, and I'm assuming I know what you're referring to?"

Amy then looked askance at me; I can't explain it, but it was almost like she had just discovered something disturbing about me that she had not seen before. It was like maybe I was no longer "chillin'," like I had suddenly become a real bona fide adult in her eyes, and at that particular moment for me, that may not have been the best thing to be. Happily for me, the stare lasted but a moment, and then her desire to explain to me just what was going on with her father pushed its way again to the front of her consciousness, and that's when she spoke again, "Yes, Albert, you assume correctly, my father is having an affair with another man. No wonder he's been so tolerant of my personal choices lately. It wasn't just the pressures from his job, or solely Mr. Kingston taking over his law firm——, he was afraid that he might be discovered, it was an unspoken *quid pro quo*, he didn't want the light to shine on him, so he eased up on me."

Wow, now that sophisticated analysis seemed to have come straight out of a Psychology 101 textbook, but when it was so deftly and seemingly very accurately applied to this particular case—and if it were all true—it was difficult to deny. I had never talked down to Amy; she was always quite percipient as a child, and now as young adult, her intellect had continued to steadily outstrip her chronological years. So in this case, as always with Amy, I strived to do the best thing, and so instead of engaging in some highbrowed intellectual discourse—which would have served no good purpose at all—I asked for evidence, "Oh, darlin', how do you conclude that? Maybe you're mistaken?"

Amy was calm and unmistakably adult in her demeanor and her response. She was like some highly paid trial lawyer standing before the court giving evidence. She started her dissertation slowly; it was an opening statement that made me first look at our long relationship. She took a very slight step back away from me, almost so that I would see her as a whole person; it was a bit theatrical, but it worked to a T, because it had been spontaneous and truthful. And then she took a short breath and began to speak, "Albert, you trust me, don't you? You have known me since I was born, you even said you held me on my first day home from the hospital, so that means you've been there from the very beginning. We have been through and awful lot together, you and I, and that's not about traveling places and seeing things—for we have never shared more than a walk across the street in the park in that way—more than that, Albert, it's been about sharing things, important and personal things, right, Albert? I'm the one you trusted enough to answer any and all of my impertinent questions about your time away from the world with, and my mother and I have always felt so blessed by your wit and candor on that painful subject. "

Amy was doing really well; whatever it was that she was doing, she was doing it with aplomb. She had my full attention or, in other, more famous words, "she had me from hello."

"I've never lied to you, what that I didn't eventually tell why I had lied and revealed the truth to you anyway. So with that said, Albert, I am imploring you to trust my veracity now, and believe me when I tell you that my father is a Lucy."

Well, she had said a mouthful, but I got it.

"Of course, Amy, I trust you, it's just so difficult to——."

Amy was anxious, and this time her youth did show itself again as she cut me off like a city cab racing another cab for a fare.

"Then, Albert, believe me when I tell that my father is a *"fudge packer."*

I was aghast; the language was clearly inappropriate and callous, and I wasn't going to stand for that.

"Amy Dillon, I'm surprised at you."

She knew she had said the wrong thing, and I didn't then know whether she meant it in the way it was said, but I was not going to participate in this scathing and ignoble language by being complicit by my silence. I didn't share the language in sentiment or taste, and I needed to let her know my feelings.

Whatever it was that her father had or had not done, I would gladly comment on that, but to deride the entire gay community would not be the province of this discussion. Hatred and bigotry were anathema to me, and I would not countenance it for anyone; I had personally had my fill of it. It was far more my facial expression than it was my words as I could feel the skin at my cheeks grow hot and taut with displeasure.

"I'm sorry, Albert, I don't really mean anything bad about that . . . I mean, he is, but . . ."

I thought she was going to cry again, for which I would have had less patience than the first time she cried earlier; I would have felt like she was trying to manipulate me, and that would have pissed me off. But happily she didn't; she just gathered herself for a moment and then she explained what she was going through.

"It's just that now I'm all alone, and that's not because he's gay or bi or whatever he is, Albert. It's because he has abandoned any relationship at all with me. If he can't be honest with me, how can he parent me? You're the only adult person that I have to talk to anymore, Albert. I just feel so all alone, that's all. Albert, it's not all those other words and ideas you suspect me of, I'm just hurting, Albert, that's all."

I, for the love of God, didn't, for once, know what to say. I was feeling a bit over my head, as if Amy was looking now to me as a parent, and I'm not worthy of being anyone's parent, not with my track record, I'm not; so I panicked, and the first thing that came to mind was her mother.

"I'm sorry, Amy. I'm so sorry, but your mom will be home soon, Amy, and then you can talk everything over with her."

It wasn't what she believed would be soon happening, or necessarily what she wanted to hear, not from me, it wasn't. So she snapped back willfully and incredulously, "No, she won't. Why would you say such a thing to me now, Albert?"

But this I knew for certain as the truth; as I pulled the postcard from my drawer and showed it to Amy, I said, "Yes, she wrote me that she, she'll be home on the fifteenth of this month."

Immediately upon seeing the postcard, Amy abandoned that restive world between her post-pubescent and incipient adult façade and turned into the wonderful child again as she squeaked, "She wrote to you, Albert? You see, Albert, why can't you be my father? That would be so chillin'? You already know everything about me, and I know that you already love me. And Mother—she really respects you. It would be perfect, Albert, wouldn't it?"

As she was talking—like an encroaching army—Amy had come around the desk, and as she finished, she hugged me as hard as she could, and I could feel her sincerity of spirit radiate through me; she was indeed serious. It was too much for me, and again I froze. I said, "Now, now, Amy Dillon."

I didn't know what else to say; she was serious, and I was seriously afraid. She sensed it; I knew she had—I think I was sweating. But she was so kind; she is such a prescient soul, but still I could tell from that impish, devilish smile that she then flashed that she had unspeakable future plans for me. She then chuckled as she spoke, "Don't you now, now me, Albert. Come on now, Albert, wouldn't it be perfect? I mean, I could change my name to Amy Lawrence, you would adopt me first, of course. You could live downstairs with us—of course, it's not as fancy as the penthouse, but it's no shack either. And of course, if you so desired, you could continue to work down here just like now. You'd never be that far away, right? That would be chillin', right, Albert?"

I couldn't make light of all of what she was saying even though it was all completely absurd, for I could see that the child was hurting badly.

It's funny; it is often thought—and I'm sure it's thought by people with little money—that people with money don't have problems, at least not serious ones. But look at this child. Amy Dillon, a little rich girl—who was born with a platinum, diamond-encrusted spoon in her pink little mouth—is blowing in the harsh winds of confusion and doubt as her irresponsible parents have abrogated their parental duties, both pulling in opposite and equally selfish directions. In doing so, they have allowed their charge—their gallant and lovely daughter, Amy—to fall through the crevasse that they, in pulling apart their marriage, have created. What a shame, there is no reason for this child to be in this type of unwarranted pain. No no no, I can't now laugh and make light of her fantasy, a fantasy constructed out of grit and her sheer will to survive and conquer her fears, and set her disheveled life right.

Finally, after thinking all of this, I hugged the little darling back for all she was worth, and I said, more softly than usual, "That's right, love."

Almost, as if on cue, the elevator door opens and out walks none other than him, Dennis Dillon. As the saying must go—for I'm sure in anger, many, many have felt this very same way—"If looks were daggers, the man would now be dead"—as I scathingly stared him down. Alas, my eyes were never as effective as I could have wished because the man barely looked our way. With a cursory glance, he had assessed our intimacy, and with a few pithy words, he scurried off to God knows where in the world. In his affected voice, he lisped a sibilant farewell.

"Oh, it looks like you two are having a little tête-à-tête. I won't disturb you."

I had never much been affected by his sibilance—which I must admit seemed far more prominent now than I ever had noticed before—but because of my ever-increasing ire, it now reverberated ever so loudly in my ears.

His lisping alone would never have aroused me—I was never that intolerant—but it was his utter abandonment of his progeny that I found totally offensive and inexcusable. And concluding from the child's inference that an alleged homosexual affair was central to his reason for the most bodacious, as in remarkable, and confounding behavior—if it in fact were all true—then it surely made me steam. I was in fact steaming because I believed Amy's pain much more than I was willing to question its veracity and the indefinite proof of its origin. After all, she was my friend, and her father, Dennis Dillon, had done little in the past to assuage my already-skewed tendency to believe everything this child told me about his aloof and unparent-like behavior, no matter how farfetched I initially considered it to be. As he walked out of the building and before I could respond, Amy beat me to the punch with her predictably sad words and reaction, "You see that, Albert, he didn't even ask what was wrong or anything. I'm his daughter, Albert, or at least I think I am, and he barely knows I'm alive."

I had never desired to be in the middle of anyone's family squabble, that was sure one of the worst places in life to be for several reasons: First, you're never on the right side because there's only one family. Second, they, the family that is, always have a way of making up, and then you become everyone's enemy for seeming to have tried to break them up. But for some reason, I didn't really feel that this was one of those cases. But even with that thought in mind, I still was not ready to take sides for or against; diplomacy was the right course, I thought.

Besides, Amy was very young, and I didn't want to seem to be carrying water for her alone, especially not before she had exhausted all of her options in an effort to getting this whole thing right. I did my best as I cautioned her.

"You know, Amy, everyone has their own story, and very few get to know the entirety of the other person's story—mostly I bet it's because they never ask. But I'm willing to bet if you and your mom sat down with your dad and had a heart-to-heart talk with him. I think that you might all come away with a better understanding of and for each other. Whatever is or isn't going on, I bet you'd all feel much better if you could do just that."

This was one of the happiest short moments of my relationship with Amy, ever. It was because I realized that all these years we had spent talking, laughing, and playing with each other had not in fact been wasted. I knew as certain as my name is Albert Lawrence that Amy was listening to me and taking my counsel seriously. This pause was about that, respect and trust.

"You think my mom already knows he's gay, Albert? No wonder she went to Africa. But, Albert, why did she leave me alone with him? Adults are funny. I'll see you later, Albert."

I hoped—maybe against hope—that I had done all the right things, said all the right things because I was feeling that I had. I'm not a stupid man; I know what goes on in the world even though I spend most of my life in the lobby of this co-op. And I know that Amy Dillon will get through this, with a few scrapes and bruises maybe, but she'll get through; she's made strong that way.

CHAPTER XVII

It had already been a long day when the Russians returned from wherever they had been. If I had been born blind and deaf, I would still have known that they had returned. The lobby quaked as they entered—they were, none of them small men—and then there was the smell of perfume. The only good thing about it was that it was not cheap—if my nose did not deceive me it was in fact Chanel No. 5. Both Gladys and Mildred wore the same scent—it's pretty stodgy for two young ladies their ages, if you ask me—but at least Gladys and Mildred don't take baths in the stuff.

The lobby smelled like a roving perfumery, all of a sudden. Luckily, there were only two of them—floozies that is, there were only two—but I was sure, from past episodes of this very same kind, that there would be more coming. The baron was as effusive and gregarious as ever as he yelled across the lobby floor at me.

"Albert, what's happening, my brother, how goes it?"

I was mortified—my brother, I've got you're my brother right here, Baron—but that didn't slow him down; in fact, given the look I shot his way, it probably egged him on a bit further as he continued to harass and abuse the staid air of this once-regal lobby with his boisterous, flamboyant, and ill manners. He yelled again, "Did you miss me? Business called, so I had to leave abruptly, but I'm back now."

The baron and his thugs had been away for a while, but I must say I had longed for this peace just broken when they were here last, and now their return had quickly resuscitated the animus I held for them that I had easily forgotten in their absence; I was surprised at how quickly it returned. He laughed as I responded in the only proper way left to my thinning and remaining civility. I said, "Good afternoon, Baron Romanovsky."

The baron then let out a high-pitched laugh—no, it was more like an evil cackle, like something a warlock would make before embarking upon some heinous, dastardly, evil deed. As the two ladies and their equally sycophant male counterparts continued to giggle through the entire episode, Boris then steers himself closer to the concierge to give me his private message; and as he does, for some unknown reason, he modulates his tone down to a normal speaking voice and says, "Let the parties begin."

As he approaches, but once there in front of me, he almost whispers by comparison, "Albert, you must come to my 'Welcome home, Boris', party tonight. Come, Albert, don't be shy. I give one or both of these lovely ladies to pleasure yourself with, come, come, Albert, come to my party."

Then the baron turns to walk away, but he then—like in the movies, he does a double take, as if some random thought had just become relevant—turns back and says, "Or bring your Mrs. Smith, if you like—we all have our little secrets, Albert, don't we now?"

I was far less shocked than I was annoyed; the baron was as sneaky as he was loud, and ever since he had hinted to me that he knew of my familial linkage to the Smiths, I knew that he had dug deep into the history and the lives of everyone in this building. He was no idiot; he played the role of buffoon far too well to be in any way that stupid. He was the worst kind to have as your enemy.

I thought it was all over as he and his retinue reached the elevator doors, but then he turned again and walked all the way back from the elevator to the concierge. This time he leaned in and whispered almost in my ear, "By the way, brother—."

Hearing that one word come out of his frozen pink Russian lips made me cringe, but I withstood the affect while I listen in hopes that he would speak quickly and then finally go away for good.

"My offer still stands, the two million dollars is still yours, if you can encourage your mother to sell me her shares to the penthouse."

Nothing surprised me, and this offer was just another trip down one of memory's dirty little alleys, as it was maybe the fifth time he had proffered it. I didn't even think the topic was worthy of discussion, and it was clear by his repeated offer—especially this present one—that he had not been apprised of the latest news, and that was that everyone now knew that John and I were brothers. And when he said, "Think seriously about it, Mr. Lawrence, things could be worse," I almost laughed in his face. I was never close to taking him up on his offer in the first place, but now, I was even farther away from that less-than-remote possibility.

CHAPTER XVIII

If you already loathe parties, as I so very much do, you would think that any one party would breed as much contempt as any other party, as in that they are all the same.

Well, the fact is that I have found that the Russian's' parties are far more contemptuous—given the normal decorum of this building—than any I've ever loathed before. It's not that they are loud, which would be cause for sanctioning and eventual eviction if the case warranted; I have not yet figured out why my brother, John, has not had more to say on this particular matter.

It's true the Russian's had been away for a while, but I'm certain that with all that has gone on with them in the not-so-distant past that in their return his ire, not unlike my own, has been stimulated again. As I ramble on, I must not neglect to mention that this last party was not nearly as lavish as some of the others had been; actually, by comparison, it was quite sedate.

The room is full of people; some are sitting and talking, others milling about, while several couples slow dance in the center of the floor to the DJ-spun music. Boris and Borga stand talking near the bar in its usual place off at the side of the large room.

Boris seems a bit melancholy as he reflects.

"I am really tired, Borga. It's a long and worthless trip now, all the way back home. Mother Russia is a hovel compared to a place like New York. It really makes me to want this building to be mine now, now more than ever before we went back home."

Boris had been quite desultory and complacent in his ruminations and reflections on their lives and recent trip back home until now, but it seemed that he had suddenly become stimulated again as he returned to a more concrete plan that had just aroused his dormant sensibilities as he turned to look at Borga.

"Borga, why don't you go upstairs and invite the old women down, just to be social with us. I'm thinking it would be good for them to know we are back and thinking of them."

Borga smiles mischievously before he responds to his brother, Boris, and then he shakes his head incredulously from side to side.

"They won't come, Boris. If I go to them, I will have to drag them out."

Boris begins to shake his head calmly as his brother's comment has enlightened him to comment more perceptively and with a twinge of sarcastic humor, "No, no, we must be nice to them again. Besides, I'm thinking now that they won't even let us in unless we break in."

Boris then smiles wickedly while Borga begins to chuckle.

"Boris, you are very funny."

But then, Boris's tune changes abruptly to a mild yet clear annoyance.

"Funny, I want that place. I want this complete building, now more than ever. We'll make my New Russia right here on Fifth Avenue."

Out of the corner of his eye, Boris sees Oleg walking toward him holding a silver tray in his extended hand and with a note of some kind resting upon it.

Boris smiles at Oleg, who is acting like some sort of servant, but he responds more quickly to the letter than his brother's antics. Before Boris can speak to ask about the antics or the letter, Oleg informs him what it's about, "Look, Boris, here's an invitation to our first co-op meeting, and look where it is being held . . ."

Oleg then points up toward the ceiling indicating the Smiths' penthouse above them. Boris quickly answers him saying, "I know that place."

Boris then smiles, devilishly and immediately, Borga begins to laugh.

"Ha-ha, Boris, make good joke. Ha-ha, you know that place."

Boris wants to see the invitation with his own eyes as he snatches it from the silver tray.

"Give it to me, Oleg, let me read—."

Oleg quickly interrupts his older brother.

"Boris, I have read it already, you, no, your reading English is not good."

Still with his brother's admonishment, Boris carefully and intently peruses the invitation. Then there's a sudden burst of excitement and an exclamation to follow.

"That's it, I've got it. When is the sixteenth, Borga?"

Oleg can't resist.

"It says the meeting is on the sixteenth."

Boris hears his younger brother, yet for some reason, he is annoyed with his brother's lack of understanding for how his mind is working. As Borga has calculated in his head the date of the sixteenth, Boris scolds Oleg with a few words in his Russian bearlike heated tone, "Yes, Oleg, the sixteenth."

Then it was Borga's turn to speak, "The sixteenth is on Thursday, two weeks from tomorrow, but this same day we have this meeting with Ivanov, Boris."

Boris smiles and begins to nod his head with an attending smile of satisfaction.

"Good, then you two take meeting with Ivanov, I will go to this meeting here alone."

Oleg becomes a bit more animated, as it seems that this meeting with the Ivanov person has some degree of importance. He smiles at the prospect of having an important meeting without his brother present.

"But the meeting with Ivanov is very critical, Boris."

Oleg's tone is hopeful as he wants to attend this meeting without his boorish brother, but he needs to make certain that is really his true understanding and intention. Boris smiles again as he turns to his brother.

"Yes, Oleg, the Ivanov meeting is very important, and you will take good care to represent our family with distinction and honor, yes?"

Oleg is clearly surprised and gratified as his smile and response both indicate.

"Yes, Boris, we, my brother Borga and I, will do the family honor."

Boris nods and turns slightly away in thought, and then he speaks words that indicate where his mind has drifted off, "Good, then you two will take meeting with Ivanov, and I will take meeting here."

It was quiet for the next two weeks, and if it hadn't been for all of the take-out Russian food being delivered to them, I would not have ever known they were still at home.

CHAPTER XIX

I had, for several continuous hours the day before and into that next morning, thought of nothing else, but all of a sudden, things got busy and distracting later in the morning, and before I had time to think about her again, the limousine carrying her had quietly arrived at the curb. I hadn't thought about how much I'd missed her until I saw her face, and that unmistakable grace with which she moved her athletic body confidently and slowly, shifting from one very steady leg to the other as she walked toward the trunk of the vehicle. I always thought and admired her confidence and independence, although in my heart I had disagreed with her leaving her daughter here virtually alone for so long. I hadn't lodged any formal complaints because it wasn't my place, and besides, no one had asked me for my opinion.

She was her usual enigmatic self-dressed as she was all in well-worn working khaki—, not Madison Avenue fashion khaki, but the real stuff—along with dusty hiking boots;—comfortable and appropriate, as she had come straight from Africa to home. As she headed for the back of the car, she flung her tattered backpack over her steady shoulder, along with a glance toward the building entrance—it was clear she was looking immediately for help with her things. I'm saying all of this in my mind as I hurriedly head out to help her.

As the trunk pops open, I can see her take a long, thoughtful stare at the building, and I wondered, almost aloud, what she must be thinking.

"Mrs. Dillon," I called out to her as I rushed outside to help. She turned and with her sun-baked face, she immediately gave me her biggest, most sincere smile, the kind that I had been bereft of ever since she left—that is, from everyone except from her daughter, Amy. And then she spoke, and god, how I had missed that confident, throaty tone; it gave me goose bumps.

"Albert Lawrence, what a sight for weary jungle eyes, man, it's good to see. Now don't you be all formal with me. Come over here . . ."

Believe it or not, but my legs began to shake as my knees buckled a little—boy, this woman certainly has a powerful effect on my body, but I finally made it all the way over to her.

Once there, she grabs and hugs me—it wasn't the first time she had ever hugged me, but that was usually around Christmas or for some rare and special occasion—I wondered what the occasion was this time. The hug felt good after the shock of it quickly dissipated; it was—not surprisingly coming from her arms—a strong hug too. I told you she was athletic. She says in my ear as she is holding me, "How are you, Albert Lawrence? Did you get all of my cards, and my letter?"

It made me smile to think of the letter as I hadn't let on to anyone what was in it—except to Amy—and that was only about when her mother would be coming home. I smiled proudly and said, "Yes, yes, I did, I received everything you sent. It's good to have you home, ma'am. It really is."

I didn't want to call her ma'am, but I dared not call her anything else before she had given me permission. I didn't know exactly what to expect from her, even after her letter. A letter is one thing, but now here she is in the flesh, and I knew it would be prudent on my part to wait and see what really gives. So instead of risking overstepping, I took the road more frequently traveled and continued to call her ma'am.

"Thank you, Albert, it's so good to hear those words in an American English accent for a change."

It was clear she was taking visual and mental stock of the world around her as she—only half attentively speaking to me—looked carefully around herself and me, like some kind of tourist on their first visit to New York. And then finally, she turned to me and looked me square in the eyes and says, "How's everything been going around here, Albert?"

After a pause, but before I could answer—and she still hadn't taken her eyes from my eyes—she says in a totally different lower voice with in a much slower cadence, "How are you, Albert?"

I didn't know whether to be flattered or alarmed, and again I stuttered to answer her appropriately, "I'm doing fine, ma'am . . . Well, ma'am, to be perfect and totally honest with you—."

Before I could finish my sentence, Mrs. Dillon had stiffened like a petrified tree—I had somehow hit a nerve—it seemed I had begun to relax, and I must have forgotten myself, and my speech in that breach had become a mite too sloppy and familiar. I had known far too well and long before this moment that Mrs. Dillon had been on a lifelong crusade to bring back personal honesty and integrity to people in their everyday lives and in their relationships; that was the one thing she and I always talked about in our more serious conversations. And it indeed was one of her pet peeves; it simply irked her that little catch phrase, "to be perfectly honest with you," the very same phrase that I had just so thoughtlessly used.

She had often said—in our sometimes heated—but—friendly exchanges—that it was always a tip-off that when someone used that phrase that they were absolutely used to being dishonest, and that the phrase was a tip-off that they were finally willing to engage in telling some minimal part of the truth to help them manage or manipulate a situation.

That was often a point of contention between us two; I saw it as just a habit, like saying uh, uh before and between sentences. We'd go 'round and 'round about this all the time, but it was funny:; I never before in my memory used the phrase "to be perfectly honest with you," not before now. So when she immediately said, "I would expect nothing less from you, Albert," I knew that she was back and as sharp as ever; I actually touched her on her hand as I looked her into her eyes—this time it was me who had taken the initiative to be close. Without saying a word, I reassured her of my relentless and steadfast veracity in all things between us.

"Well then, ma'am, quite a few things have changed since you were away."

I watched her body soften again, even while her face did take on an extra frown of concern.

"Are you trying to give me face wrinkles on my first day back, Albert?"

She wasn't smiling either when she said that.

I immediately looked to apologize.

"Oh no, ma'am, not at all."

"Well then, have you been looking after my Amy as usual?"

This was a predictable question that really didn't need to be asked.

"As I have since the day she was born."

This time, Mrs. Dillon did smile.

"I know, and I am sure you have, Albert. That was the only reason I was able to leave this place behind the way I have. You know I counted on you, and she has counted on you as well. She's an exceptional human being—young, but nonetheless exceptional. This sojourn has saved my life, Albert, and now with my head clear, I can do what I've needed to do all along."

213

She had lost me with the "saved my life" part. I thought I knew what she was talking about, not so much what she was talking about, but in the way she was talking about it, I knew what she meant; but save her life, what was that all about? It was clear, though, she was back with a new resolve; she was ready to do something demonstrative, I was now certain of it. All I could say was, "Yes, ma'am."

Well, it really wasn't all I could've said, but it was definitely all I was going to say then without being seriously prompted and pressed for more. She wasn't having any of that.

"What's wrong, Albert, you seem distracted?"

I tried to cover; I knew that if I continued to talk, the questions would soon get around to me and maybe prompt her to ask about things that I didn't want to talk about standing there in the middle of the street.

"I'm sorry, ma'am, I didn't mean to drift on you."

Finally, she had had enough of my calling her ma'am, and come to think of it, so had I.

"Albert, if you call me ma'am one more time, I think I'll scream. Before I left for Africa, we were good friends, Albert, and now 'ma'am'—, that just won't do . . ."

She paused and got this devilish twinkle in her eyes.

"Speaking of friends, Albert, is that gym-rat hussy, Nancy Smith, is she still chasing after and frequently catching you, Albert?"

You see, just what I was worried about; it didn't take her very long, now did it? What am I supposed to say now; I can't lie, I won't lie, no, not to her, I won't.

"Now don't you go, young boy, and get all quiet and uncommunicative on me now, Albert. I'll take that as a yes, then. And how about Sarah Peters, is she still ordering bodega takeout?"

She is as feisty and sharp as ever, maybe even shaper—I couldn't keep from smiling.

"We'd better get your things inside—."

That twinkle I spoke of, well, it hadn't yet left her eyes, and as I moved one of her bags out of the trunk, she pulls on the arm of my uniform jacket—just like her daughter has mimicked a hundred times or more from the time that she could reach my sleeve—and she says most mischievously, "Go ahead, Albert, go ahead and say my name the way you were saying it before I left for Africa, go ahead."

I was cornered; I didn't know why I had resisted saying it. I know, I know, I all too well remember how I used to say it sometimes when she wasn't even standing there in front of me; I'd find myself saying it to myself. I had seen this woman almost every day for sixteen, seventeen; you know, I don't even know how many years it's been from the beginning until now. She was warm to me from the beginning.

In the beginning, when I first returned from Sing Sing Prison to start work here as the doorman and then as the concierge, she always had time to talk to me—personal like—it's funny, after she asked and I told her why I had gone to prison, she laughed. No, no, she wasn't laughing at me; she was laughing at the irony of the whole thing. I remember her exact words. She said, "If every man and some of the women in this co-op were all prosecuted for their criminal offenses, there would be an overabundance of doormen living on Fifth Avenue alone." And she added, and I paraphrase, "If ever you decide to do another crime, do it for far larger than a couple of thousand dollar checks like the rest of your neighbors do, and you'll be rewarded far more handsomely."

She never judged me; I guess she could see that I was already judging myself harshly enough. Then when Amy was born, well, it's funny but in a way I became her stand-in or surrogate father as Jessie began to rely on me more and more. It started out innocently enough with Amy wanting to come down and sit with me at the concierge; that's when we really got to know each other very well—as she began to share her thoughts with me—to this very day.

It's funny, but when she started school, I was the first person that she would share her day with when she arrived home. It makes me smile how she loved spending time with me, and I with her. She'd often even try to get her mom to take me on trips with them.

It's funny now, I guess; I hadn't thought much about it lately, but they—meaning the three of them, Jessie, Amy, and Dennis Dillon—rarely if ever took their vacations together. I guess their whole family thing was not working from very near the beginning. And now things are finally crumbling. I wonder if Jessie was waiting for Amy to reach her current level of maturity before she decided to make a move. *"I can do what I've needed to do all along."* Isn't that what she said? That sounds to me like something was being calculated all along, and now she's back, and Amy has discovered a truth that her mother may have long been aware of or must have at the least suspected before now.

Wow, relationships can be complicated, and those are the good relationships that I'm referring to as the bad ones have no real chance of success. Things are not always as simple as they may seem, and I didn't even know that I had all of this going on inside my head, and my reflex not to say her name was, I'm sure, based on all of that stored and pent-up information and the feelings that go along with them. So finally, I looked at Jessie, and I simply said, "Jessie."

And then I picked up her suitcase and headed for the building. I could hear her say as I walked away.

"That's very good, Albert."

CHAPTER XX

The ambient noise combined with the human chatter hums and bounces off the book-filled shelves and walls of Smith's library; it is all friendly, happy, and conducive to this pleasant evening's festivities. Almost every unit in the building is represented by at least one guest including the newest one, in the imposing presence of Baron Boris Romanovsky, who stands alone in a corner holding a plate of food in one of his clawlike hands. The co-op board meets monthly, but this little get-together happens less frequently, often enough for the neighbors to look forward to it, but seldom enough for them not to rue its approach.

It is, however, an important evening for the two falcon-feeding spinsters as Mildred and Gladys sit center stage in their regular positions—in their usual high-back smoking chairs—Mildred taps her wine goblet to bring everyone to attention.

"Gladys and I are so glad you could all make it to our little buffet. Let me first say that it is so good to see Mrs. Jessie Dillon back home safe from her extended African safari. I can't wait to hear the details firsthand, direct from our lioness'es mouth."

Never bashful, Baron Romanovsky waves his hand to be recognized by Mildred, and indeed as Mildred looks in his direction, he blurts out, "Don't forget to introduce me to the returning Mrs. Dillon. I have not yet had the pleasure to make her acquaintance."

But you knew that he wouldn't wait for an introduction; he didn't have it in him to wait for much. As almost every head turned to look toward the corner where the baron was standing alone, it was as if their turning heads were a signal for him to move forward, and forward he did move toward Jessie and me.

Jessie had called me and invited me to attend the party with her as I had finally moved back to my West Side apartment, as it seemed that the heat from the Russians had diminished substantially enough for me to do so. In fact, nothing untoward at all had occurred since they had returned from Mother Russia.

Finally, when the Baron Romanovsky had arrived in front of us, Jessie was the first to speak. Jessie was taller than the baron, so when they were face-to-face, she actually had to look down at him.

"So you're the Baron Romanovsky that I've heard so abundantly about?"

I could immediately see that the Baron Boris Romanovsky—who is used to being out in front of everything and everyone—was taken aback as it was clear Jessie had beaten him to the information punch. I laughed as he stuttered his way through his first couple of moments with Jessie.

"I see, you've already heard about me."

I loved that Jessie was back—she is fierce and competitive, and her tongue and mind are as sharp as a tack—it is quickly clear that the baron's boorish behavior and Russian wit are no match for her. "Oh yes, Baron, my friend Albert Lawrence has told me everything about you." The baron doesn't so much turn his body, but his eyes followed ever so slowly behind his head—like an arthritic tortoise in a headwind—as they both finally drifted slowly toward me as I stood there next to Jessie. I almost laughed as in only a few words; he had been stripped of his cloak of secrecy and first knowledge—which were both his stock in trade.

At that moment, I didn't really care that much as I was too, too thrilled just to be standing there next to Jessie. God, it's funny, but you sometimes don't really know how much you have missed someone until they return; I know it almost doesn't make sense, but it is nonetheless true.

I had thought about Jessie while she was away, but that was always in regard to her husband and daughter, never did I think of her in regard to myself. And before she had ever gone on her safari, I was just so totally used to having her around that the thought of her not being here was a distant, if any, concern at all; everything then was just normal. We were all just one strange blend, not a family, but a strange blend of co-op compatriots.

But after all that has gone on in the building since she was away—and all of these changes I would most certainly have talked, discussed, and debated with her about—we had missed that, and I was in a strange way too busy to have missed her as so much of what went on directly affected me. And now that's she's back, I realized that I did in fact miss her, her presence, and the opportunity to share everything as it all happened with her. I know, I know, I know, you don't know what you have until it's gone. Well, in this case, I didn't know what I was missing until she returned.

Jessie is totally impervious to the baron's presence—for the first time since I'd first met him—he has nothing more to say as he begins slowly and quietly slithering all the way back to his corner, like the stomach crawler that he is. I could see that Gladys had been watching him as well; I watched her as she leaned toward and whispered her observations to Mildred, "It's an old-street move, honey—he wants everyone to get a stomach full of keeping an eye on him, but we won't."

As the baron is moving away, he turns to ask a parting question, "Everything?"

Jessie, without pause, answers him back, "Oh yes, Baron, everything."

The baron nods as I could see in his face that those Russian wheels in his head were turning and churning out more devious thoughts and plans for us all.

"Good to have met you, Mrs. Dillon," he says as he finally slithered back into his corner. I looked again toward Gladys and Mildred as they keep their eyes on him, and then I turned all of my attention to Jessie; she was fully in the game now, as if she had never left.

When I said to her, "I haven't told you everything about him, why did you tell him that?"

Jessie—with her battle face on now—says, "I know his kind, Albert, and he deserves to live every second of his life in the discomfort of uncertainty. Besides, Amy and I stayed up all night talking, and she told me all about him." I almost smiled when Jessie said that she had been talking with Amy because I could not remember even one time that she and I had spent more than a minute talking about the Russians in general, and more specifically about the Baron Romanovsky himself; what would she know about it.

And that's what I immediately postulated. "But what would she know about the Russians? She is just a child?" I said, with all the confidence that I had garnered from Amy's and my relationship, very close relationship. I never thought—as wonderful as she truly is—that she had concerns or knowledge about anything except her own circumscribed life.

I mind you, I wasn't down on her for that, it was just that she was a teenager, and teenagers—no matter how highborn—are selfish, egotistical, and self-centered. Most of them don't know that anyone else exists except himself or herself. It seems, apparently, that I have misjudged Amy Dillon.

Jessie's smile this time was a different kind of smile; it was a satisfied kind of smile that I couldn't decipher until she added words to elucidate it. "In a way, Albert, I'm glad you see her that way because most men, whenever they see her now, would only see a nubile, ripened piece of fruit hanging low from a tree. Thank God for Rufus."

I was, to say the least, flabbergasted and at the same time heartened that Jessie knew all about and in fact seemed to approve of Rufus. It is clear from what she's just offered that Amy has told her all about everything, and included in that I must assume they talked about Mr. Dennis Dillon as well. But at that particular moment, I was stuck on Rufus.

"You know about Rufus too?" I said as my eyes stretched widely. I was embarrassed the moment the words had totally escaped my mouth. They were no longer hidden; they were now revealing free radicals drifting in the space between her and me, words almost too revealing. But the mistake, or shall we call it a faux pas, had already been made, and I was just going to have to take my lumps and deal with the concept of consequence.

It was clear that my question, and more than the surprise with which it had been asked, was because Rufus is black—because that's exactly what I was thinking; it's what all black men think at times like these, how accepting white people will be when finding us black men in unusual and unanticipated places. What will white people think? And in this particular case, what will Jessie think about her Amy going with a black boy.

It's not a given—no, never is that the case—in my experience. And the stories that I've been told by people who look like me, no matter how close you are to someone or however close you may believe you are to someone of another race—they may even call you family—race is always the third rail when it comes to intimacy, that is, just one touch can desiccate an otherwise-sanguine and thriving friendship.

Friendships and social glad-handing—to the neophyte—are one kind or part of a relationship that are most often separated from other parts, and they often are good, and they feel so good that they may lead one to believe that they in fact are a mirror or a reflection that must encompass the totality of the relationship between friends, but one would most often be mistaken.

You know how you often take for granted that if someone accepts you as a friend that they are accepting you as an equal, a complete and absolute equal with no hidden conditions or caveats; but don't you dare go messing with someone's progeny, in particular someone's daughter because that is a whole different ball game, and the rules that govern this risky flirtation upon violation will often change abruptly the heretofore-sedate and normal part of the relationship.

And so, no matter how many talks, hugs, and handshakes we've had, or intimate conversations where our souls have meshed and measured the length and breadth of each others hearts, that is Jessie and me, it is still an unknown quantity what the dimensions of one's heart really measure up to when it actually comes down to it—down to the real nitty-gritty, as Gladys says—do you know anything at all about how this person will react when you touch that metaphorical third rail? And that's where I now stood out of balance, and leaning perilously over the third rail waiting for Jessie to respond.

And respond she did, not missing a beat. I'm standing there all nervous and childlike, waiting to be scolded, for the slip beneath my black armor is showing, the slip of insecurity that is lodged somewhere between my thoughts and my words that always seem to transform my anger into compliance, and my peace into rancor—as black men are inherently insecure about just about everything (it is a racial-gender hazard that transcends money and social status)—from birth, all black men are made aware of the tenuousness, the motility, and volatility of their existence as their power base is miniscule at best and illusory at the saddest and worse, so much so that they wear it like a second skin.

Meet a black man, any black man—biracial, young, or old—talk to him about anything, and I do mean anything even the most innocuous subject, and within a short time the conversation will turn to race, and if not, you will feel the tension of him avoiding the topic of race altogether.

For black men, the subject of race—theirs and others'—is like an immortal mosquito that no matter how many times you swat it, it always finds a way to sting you and take a little of your blood. But Jessie doesn't cooperate; I don't know why, but she bypasses my anxiety like an express train passing a local stop.

"Of course, Albert, thanks to your counsel, Amy has been quite forthright with me. Thank you for looking after her, Albert." I could do none other than smile, even though my brain, for all the permutations, configurations, and anxieties was figuratively sweating profusely inside my scull, all for naught.

I told you that my insecurity could sometimes run amuck for no good reason at all, or at least I should have told you so. I was relieved, to say the least, not to have had to confront some of my worse demons right there at the social. "You never know what people see," I said—a double entendre if every there was one—but it was of no interest to her then as she took the manifest and not the latent meaning in stride and continued her train of thought unimpeded.

I had meant that I was concerned that she had spied my insecurity showing, and either she had and took no notice of it or she hadn't noticed it at all. In either case, she didn't let on, and I must admit I was glad she hadn't.

We stood quietly for a moment, and then she said, "I hope you haven't underestimated Amy, Albert. She sees more than she lets on. She adores you, Albert, and she has nothing but good things to say about you."

What could I say? I had done the least that I could do; Amy had already said it to me some days ago when she told me that I loved her. She may have been being flippant when she said it, but it was nonetheless true; I do love her, like a daughter, of course, but it's a real love, as true and as real as the nose on my face—it's real. I thought as we continued to stand together quietly while watching the rest of the room.

Mildred had the floor now, which, of course, immediately lent our gathering a more serious tone. As she started to speak, my eyes wandered the room from one rich white face to another rich white face. Some of these faces I've known most of my life, and as my life had come full circle—from the penthouse to the basement, and back to the penthouse—all in front of their eyes. It is truly amazing that life can be—admittedly more for some of us than for others—a veritable roller coaster of surprises and unfathomably, unpredictable occurrences that boggle the mind.

From a nearly frozen babe in my mother's homeless skinny arms to here now listening to Mother Mildred declare my rank and station in this aristocratic and wealthy Fifth Avenue family—wow! She says, "I hope you all have read the note in your invitations concerning the Smith and Lawrence family tree intrigue.

"It was released simply to apprise you all of our legal status—that's in case one of us old girls should survive the other beyond your willingness to fathom and or accept this unique possibility, and then lend itself to unnecessarily and pointlessly negative speculation. I, through said missive and court-filed legal papers, documents, and such, have made it clear to all pertinent and legal concerns alike what the true story is. It was not in the least bit given for cocktail chatter or gossip's fodder. We are one family, of that there should no longer be concern or further question."

Wow, I thought; I hadn't read anything, as my invitation was probably still sitting somewhere waiting for me to open it. I had made a habit of never opening them as they—Mildred and Gladys—had made a habit of sending them to me every time they held one of these social gatherings. So, in hearing Mildred, I was more than a little surprised, though not at what she said—that I already knew all about as they had sat both John and me down and told us as much—but that she had made an announcement in writing, and now in stereophonic sound in her presidential-like address to all of our neighbors. *Wow!*

If I were deaf, dumb, and blind, I would still have expected and noticed Jessie's attention coming immediately my way. But I am—thank God—none of those things, so I could see clearly the look and Cheshire Cat grin on Jessie's face as she turned to beam her blue eyes on my brown face. "Albert," she says, as she speaks through her smile, "I haven't read anything since arriving home yesterday. I left my last pair of reading glasses on the plane. Would you be so kind as to give me a summary of Mildred's missive?"

I had no idea what the contents of the letter was, no more than what Mildred had just alluded to.

I must admit I was more than a little tickled by the whole thing; my status had just been publicly elevated. It's one thing to know something within the small family circle—which the four of us, Mildred, John, Gladys, and me were—it had leaked out, but that was still in the realm of gossip. But now to have it announced in front of this august body of various and very influential Fifth Avenue people was the sociable elevation of all social elevations, what next—the *New York Times* social pages, a coming-out party, a cotillion, a debutante's ball?

Well, I'll be the toast of Fifth Avenue, the first doorman to live in the penthouse. It was a bit much, I have to admit as much myself, but Mildred's heart was, as always, in the right place, and for that I must forgive her for any residue of embarrassment it may cause me now and in the future.

Now the question is, how will they all now treat their socialite doorman? But answer, Jessie, I must: "I have no idea what the note says because I never open those invitations; if I had, I would have tried to discourage Mildred from making this announcement."

Jessie was quick to rebuff my assertion and concerns,. "Why, Albert, why?"

I immediately responded, "Because it's embarrassing, that's why."

Jessie wasn't about to listen to me whining; I knew that well already. Then she says, "Well, I think you ought to read it anyway—for what it says, not for what you think it says. It seems to have an awful lot to do with you—good things, Albert, and that can't be all bad." I thought for a moment, and then I mumbled, "That seems to be the case. I guess I've got some catching up to do."

Here's what happened then. As I continued to talk with Jessie for a while, and then she and I alone and separate from each other did walk around visiting with other residents of the building.

While talking to this one and that one, I found that many of them wanted to and did congratulate me on my newly revealed and now-elevated status as it were. But the evening was a far-from-perfect colloquium by any stretch of the imagination—several of the old-timers, who, having over much of my lifetime witnessed this entire odyssey, were quick to express to me that they believed that they knew all along what was going on up here in the Smith penthouse for all these many years. I had suffered their slings and arrows in silence for many years, and it was then that I thought to myself, *Like who really cares what they think*. I almost laughed in some of their jealous and insincere faces. And what is it that they have to be jealous about? I ask that question. I quickly admit that I can't fathom them concerning themselves with me.

Stumped, I concede that only heaven knows as I looked around the library festivities because these are, every single one of them wealthy people—each one wealthier than the one standing next to him or her, wealthy wealthy, filthy wealthy to the most ostentatious and obscene degree—multiple houses, yachts, privates jets, jewels, art collections, and cars, and not to mention the seasonal million-dollar wardrobes and vacations.

Why would any of them be jealous of me? And then again, I thought maybe, just maybe, it wasn't simple jealousy—because collectively my mother and I still had nothing on a relative basis compared to all their vaunted wealth. But maybe, just maybe, some of them felt in a perversely niggling way threatened that their vaunted and exclusionary walls had been so easily breached by an interloping black doorman and his high, high—yellow mother.

Maybe it was that they felt duped, hoodwinked, and bamboozled in the light of day, in plain sight, as it were; maybe they were just feeling deceived and betrayed by the Smiths and found me vulnerable and easy prey to vent their repressed vitriol upon. I could see that being true because this place is, in its very exclusive and highbred way, special and way out of the ordinary; it may sit across the street from the very public Central Park—and as such, you can walk by and in front of it a hundred times a day, if you like—but in truth, it's a million miles away from you and anything that you may understand and fathom as being normal.

In this most exclusive case, looks are anything but what they seem to be; they are tumultuously deceiving, and far from the newly and recently conceived notion that in our increasingly egalitarian world where everyone dresses and behaves like everyone else—the so-called hip-hop generation of rap music money there is a merging of wealthy cultures—all these people are as rich, watch how they live. They are, in fact, birds of a feather, and, in fact, themselves reshaping the wealthy of the hip-hop culture, as the hip-hop culture influences them—if you'd simply take a quick trip to Long Island and check out all of the Hamptons in the summer, you'll see exactly what I mean.

These days, in this new tech-dominated world we live in, where one out of ten reads books anymore, it logically follows—more now than ever before that you cannot tell a book by its cover—everything and everyone comes in their own self-designed package, or at least a package that in truth reveals so little about its content that you just don't know what it is that you're facing anymore, but not here. This place and most of the places along this august and venerable avenue are an oasis far apart above and beyond normal standards of living, and is for certain a complete and utter enigma to the common workingman and woman.

It is indeed a veritable conclave of the rich, and most of them with no desire to be famous, in particular and especially the older money. Everything about their lives makes them different—it's true; they see and experience the world differently from the ordinary person. And with that perspective dominating their thinking, they have grown very used to seeing me in my station, in my place one and the same way for years unending. And there is a haughty carryover that imbues our occasional conversations whenever it is that they may deign to speak to me.

In those cases, it matters little what the topic is, or the circumstance that arrives freshly in front of them; a few certain people always strain to give the impression, however childlike and infantile it may be, but they insist through their behavior and attitudes that by some inexplicable power, or mere prescience, they know everything.

Now standing in front of me, they say, "They knew"; they often say those two same words when trying to insinuate their superiority, but I say that they knew nothing, and yet I must confess in all honesty that even if they may have suspected something similar, or maybe even if they were spot on and got it exactly right with their hunches, guesses, and suspicions about exactly what did happen up here; well, I don't care—that all means less than nothing to me because it's still none of their damn business.

225

Many of the residence—in particular, some of the older residence—never liked the relationship that Gladys and Mildred had with each other all of these years. I know this because for years, especially and exclusively in the years after the senior Mr. Smith had died, I would hear them saying nasty things about my mother and me specifically, and the Smith's in general, and they were always said purposely and loudly enough for me, and sometimes Gladys—whenever she was alone without Mildred—to hear them.

Jealous people can be so cruel, and envious people can be downright evil. It wasn't any of their business how the Smiths choose to live their lives, and when I was younger and Mr. Smith was alive, they wouldn't have dared say any such horrible things as they had begun to freely say after he had died; alive, he was way too scary and powerful.

So alas, and somewhat sadly, I presently lament that this co-op was never Camelot, and I was no Galahad, and Gladys as well was never any facsimile of a Guinevere. But yet and still, this co-op here on Fifth Avenue, after all was said and done, and not to everyone's liking or favor, this co-op is still our home.

CHAPTER XXI

He must have done it before everyone had turned their attention to him again, gone into the kitchen, and unlocked the back door. Because even for him, it was strange behavior, as out of the corner of my eye, I saw him dart in and just as quickly out of the bathroom like a child playing mischievously and trying to get the attention of the adults at a grown-up party. He just darted in, and immediately he darts out, and then he calls out in his inimitably coarse Russian voice.

This Russian is a fox in a bear's suit; as he gets the full attention of the guests, he calls out, "Ladies and gentlemen—." I know he's up to something; I wonder what. "I would like to propose a toast to our hostesses."

It's an old trick; he wants everyone's eyes on him, and my sense is it is to allay any suspicion from some devious plan or act that he has already committed or is soon to take place, and he is setting us all up as his alibi. He's a fox, all right. But, of course, no one can resist his toast, as all of the glasses in the room lift in a joint celebration of my two mothers. What a snake. I have to laugh because already in the span of a couple of moments, I have called the Russian three different animals. I must admit that I have probably done those animals a disservice by naming him after them, but he is a sly one.

His silky and gracious words belie his true intentions, I was sure, but with no obvious evidence, I, along with everyone else in the room, could do nothing less than respect his obvious charming ways, if not his actual charm. "Thank you for a lovely evening of food, conversation, and the pleasure of your company. Good night, and good evening to you all."

He was smooth as silk, and I'm sure he had accomplished all that he had set out to accomplish. And as he left the room and subsequently the apartment, I wondered what his obvious gloating from a not-so-obvious victory had been. He had done something, but we'd have to wait to find out what it had been.

In the end, it couldn't have been such a monumental thing because no one was presently aware of it. Everyone was at the height of his or her mingling—talking, laughing, drinking, and eating—that after he left, no one seemed to question if he had done anything untoward while he had been there. In fact, no one had any real reason to suspect him of anything, as, of course, he had from day one, pursued them all with his charm and his flamboyant parties.

It's a funny thing, but, in comparison to me, this man—no matter how shady people thought or knew he was—they treated him, in most part, like one of them, and this treatment was accorded far more readily than they were willing to treat me in the same way; go figure that. But there were still two who were not so fooled by his charm, money, status, or obvious manipulation, and they were—immediately upon him leaving the apartment—off to check out where he had been and what possibly he had done. "What did he do behind the door to the kitchen?" Mildred turned to and asked Gladys as soon as the Baron Romanovsky had left the apartment. "He wasn't in there long enough for anything." But by then, Gladys was already out of her chair and headed toward the kitchen door.

"Sure he was. Let's check it out."

And so they were both quickly up and on their way to the kitchen door that leads a short flight of stairs to the fifteenth floor kitchen, as the vaulted ceiling library spans two floors—both the fourteenth and fifteenth floors. They flip the light switch on at the bottom of the narrow staircase as they eyed intensely the walls and steps and investigate every inch of the stairwell leading to the kitchen. It is a most unique kitchen design and location, but it was the one thing that Mildred wanted most; she had always thought that no one should know what was cooking in the kitchen when they walked through the entrance to her home, and she believed that by locating the kitchen on the top floor, and at the far end of the apartment, that all of the aromas would lift toward the roof and sky rather than descend to annoy or unfairly entice her guests.

As the stairwell was totally empty, they were able to scour it while moving fairly quickly to the top and to the kitchen itself. The door to the kitchen was wide open—normally it was closed—and that was their first hint that the sneaky Baron Romanovsky had ascended all the way to the kitchen.

Reaching the top to the open door, now suspicious and a little frustrated, they both realized that their task had quickly grown and become that much more difficult; as the kitchen was large with many appliances, tables, shelves, and what not, all places to hide things and make general mischief on behind and around. But they both knew that the Baron Romanovsky had only been there for a short while and that there wasn't much he could have hidden or actually done in that amount of time.

"Millie, stop," Gladys calls out as Mildred immediately becomes a bit frantic as she begins to move about the kitchen like a chicken without a head moving and looking around under and behind things.

"I hate that he was here in our kitchen, Gladys, I just hate that."

Gladys is patient only because she is trying to think clearly about what he might have been up to and was able to accomplish in such a short visit to their kitchen. Then she thought and remembered their last visit—the Russians that is—and she then headed for the place that was now very obvious. "The door, Millie, what about the door?" Gladys says as she heads across the room to the back door. She tries the handle lock to check and see if it had been tampered with. It had; the little button that unlocks the door had been turned to the lock-off position.

"That's it, Millie, they are coming back tonight, I'm certain of it."

Mildred was aghast by the notion that their home would be invaded again like before. "We should call the police if you are certain of this, Gladys. Let's call them now." Gladys was quiet for a long moment as she put her hand to her chin in a thinking posture; Mildred relaxed her inquisition as before this silent moment, she was revving up for a quick rescue from outside their little circle, but before very long, she started up again, "Then if not the police, at least we should tell the boys about this nervy intrusion."

Gladys had been interminably quiet—probably more frustratingly than interminably—which only stoked Mildred's nervousness. But then Gladys finally spoke, "You know, Millie dear, sometimes people have just got to take care of themselves because when people don't respect you and think that they can push you around and that you won't push back—it doesn't matter what kind of help you recruit from other people. They will just keep pushing until you push back.

"We need to push back, Millie. We needed to push back as hard as they are pushing us."

CHAPTER XXII

As soon as the last guest left the apartment, Gladys and Mildred got to work. Gladys had concocted an elaborate yet simple plan. The elaborate part was the intricate stringing of the eighteen-gauge wire—fashioned after a spider's web—throughout the kitchen. She—with Mildred's help—had anchored it around the base of the heavy industrial Traulsen refrigerator, and on the opposite side of the room across from it on the legs of the equally substantial and heavy Wolf range.

Everywhere in between, the wires lurked—especially in the darkened kitchen when the lights were turned off—like muggers in a murderous shaded alley. That this was a purely defensive move; it left them little time or room for fancy embellishments. It was Gladys's simple yet unmistakably direct way of serving notice that they were not going to be intimidated by this bearlike Russian bully.

"Are you sure this is going to work, Gladys? Don't you think we should just tell the boys and let them handle it?"

It seemed that through all of this, this series of threats initiated by the Russians, including overly suggestive and heavy hints and the bungled break-in of many weeks before and everything in between, it seemed that Gladys had not reacted forthrightly—that is, strongly and openly—she had been, it seemed in a word, intimidated. But something had changed to spark an old and heretofore dormant and long-since-cooled fire inside her—the same fire that had kept her and me alive on the harsh streets of New York some many years back.

Maybe it was the announcement that Mildred had made at that evening's little party that was the catalyst for her new aggressive resolve in an effort to protect her home and friend; even Mildred was surprised to see her react that way again. So, after Mildred's nervous inquiry, it was full circle that she had come, and now with a few stern words, she rebutted her dear friend's nervousness, "To answer both of your questions, Millie, yes and no. Okay?"

Mildred loved Gladys as much as Gladys loved Mildred, and they trusted each other implicitly. There would be no debating or arguing that, or any other point from there on out. Mildred had long ago shown that she could assume a leadership position in Gladys's life when Gladys was down on her luck and needed a hand. It was clear that the roles were reversed, and that Gladys was taking the lead position now, and Mildred, to her credit, was willing to follow.

On the way down from the party, it was Jessie and I alone in the elevator; we had waited and were the last to leave the party. I was feeling kind of lost and alone for the first time in a long while. Maybe that old feeling was creeping back for me. I had decided, most seriously since my release from Sing Sing Prison, that I needed to stick close to Gladys—you know, in case something went wrong and she needed me—I owed her that much, especially since I had so disappointed her.

I don't want to get all Freudian and psychological on you now, but maybe I actually needed to be close to her a bit more than she needed to be close to me. But alas, the time has passed by quickly, and whatever meaning or explanation you would need or like to give to my life so far, I am without question or equivocation nonetheless still here, still present, and I'm feeling sad and probably acting sadly.

Then, too, maybe it was the little speech that Mildred had given this evening, all in an effort to give clear and distinct understanding to those who would spread misinformation and scandal concerning Gladys's legitimacy of title to the penthouse; I had tried to avoid its clarity, for in it's clarity, I was now released from my umbilical cord of worry. The tie that bound me to her, as it were, had been ritually severed. After all these years, I was now free to pursue my own life, and the immediate pall of sadness that now hung over me like a coffin floating over my head was a testament to my feelings of lost purpose.

I was hoping that Jessie wasn't feeling me now, for if she tapped in to my morose mood and mind, she might flee fast and far away from me, too fast to catch her and too far to touch her. But when she spoke, I knew immediately that my cloud of gloom had not yet reached her sunny shore. "Well, this was an interesting evening. So, Albert, what are you going to do with your new status?"

My brain sweats instantly stopped, chilled by her cool demeanor and response; I was instantly comforted and now so confident I was that I leapt much further than intended—as the adrenaline rushed its ardor to my much-too-compliant lips, I spout out like a young geyser words that my lips could not close fast enough to stop or reach far enough to take back. "Maybe I'll become Amy's new daddy," I said, and my heart sank like a stone dropped in a hundred feet of dark ocean water; I thought I would die. But then again, why was I having this emotional upheaval, all of a sudden?

Jessie had only just returned from Africa, and until then my emotions were just fine. *What the hell was going on with me now?* I thought, almost out loud, I thought. I was nervous, a little sweaty, and I was acting like a high school nerd on a first date.

Before she went on safari, I wasn't like this around her; I was chillin', and I was calm. Am I that smitten with Jessie? Jesus! I'm all in my head now. So I kept my head rigid straight just so she couldn't read the utter craziness I'm feeling in my heart that she most certainly will, if I allow her to see my eyes. But only a second later I can't help it—I peek at her as I cut my eyes I slid them as far to the corners of my eye sockets as I could, without turning my head; it hurt a little)—just so I could see her reaction to the foolish thing I've just said.

I can immediately see her reaction is far from what I might have expected it to be; I thought she might've heated up, but she did nothing of the sort. In fact, she did the opposite. I watched as she did something she must rarely do because it's a fact that I've never seen her do it. She dropped her eyes, and with that, she also dropped her head. I was chagrined that I had elicited that kind of powerful and negative response from this titan of a woman. I immediately began to apologize, "I'm so sorry, Jessie. That was extremely thoughtless and rude of me to say a thing like that, even though I meant it as a joke, it was a bad choice to have made."

I had made my amends quickly, but I still felt that I needed to explain myself, "I was thinking about Amy, she—."

I was unable to finish my pithy sentence excuse before Jessie interrupted me, "I know—I know, Albert." *She knows what?* I was thinking. What does she know? Here I am stumbling over my feelings and words, and in the midst of my contrition, she informs me that she knows. Well, if she does, I hoped she was about to tell me what she knows.

"She's already made it clear to both me and her father—as he was on his way out the door for good—just whom she wants to replace him. Now, I know that she is hurt and angry, but she is as levelheaded and clear thinking as I am—of course she is, after all, she is my daughter—and I believe she knows what she's saying when she says it."

Now it was my mouth that I had to close with my hand, as my jaw was in danger of falling completely off. I didn't know what to say. I mean, was there anything that I could say that would carry any weight or make any difference at all? For, of course, the answer was a resounding no! But still, I had to say something, something that would show that I wasn't aloof and unfeeling. "I'm so sorry, Jessie, I didn't know."

Jessie actually smiled a laughing smile at me as she says, "I know, Albert, how could you have known when the final decision was made only a few hours ago before we went upstairs to the little party? It was a *fait accompli* years in the making, I might add. It took a trip to your ancestral home in far-off Africa to set my home in America right."

I guess most women have got it right when they lament that most men just don't get it. I mostly want to be that different sort of man that does in fact get it, but, sadly, standing in this elevator, I'm feeling bereft of that fleeting and rare satisfaction simply because I know for sure that I'm not getting it. And as if my unspoken thoughts weren't enough, I had to speak and reveal my innate yet completely honest shortcomings when I asked, "So what are you going—?"

Jessie was right there again anticipating my all-too-feeble response, "Going to do?"

I still thought it was a reasonable, if not timely, question, and I guess so did Jessie because when I asked it again, uninterrupted and in its entirety, "Yes, Jessie, what are you two going to do now?" she was quick and solid with a answer.

"We're going to be just fine, Albert. We're going to do what we've been doing ever since Dennis first left us emotionally a long time ago, Albert. We'll be just fine."

Of course, they were, I thought immediately. Jessie had always seemed so much more self-sufficient than any of the other women in the building—there were women, like Susan Smith, who were independent, but Jessie was self-sufficient—she had more of a sense of purpose to her behavior, no dilettante, she. She owns her own business, and she has done quite well at it. *No,* I thought, *she'll be just fine, but what about Amy, what about how she will take being a single-parent child from here on?*

Before I knew it, I was speaking my mind quite openly again, and as I was feeling strongly paternal, I said, "I'll keep an eye on Amy as usual, of course."

Jessie sighs and smiles—what I thought then was a curious-looking smile—right before she said, "I had hoped, Albert, that you'd keep an eye on us both, as I know you've always done."

I was elated by her words and the feelings that they engendered in my heart must have made me blush as she continued, "Are you going to stay on here, Albert? I know with all that has recently changed for you, that you'll have better opportunities elsewhere."

Jessie's words sent my mind spinning as so much had changed over the last little while, and now with Jessie's return, Jesus, there's so much to take in. My new status, huh! My new status is wrecking havoc with my life, and my feelings about everything having been altered, some things more substantially than others, but nothing has gone untouched. But even through all of that, I knew that I wasn't going anywhere; this co-op was my home, and these people were, in a very untraditional way, my family. It's Jessie and Amy that I'm speaking of now.

"I'm not going anywhere right now, Jessie. All the things that are happening here now compel me to stay. And, besides, Jessie, I think there's no better place to stay than close to my ever-growing family."

Right before the elevator doors open, Jessie's biggest smile yet lights up and outshines the amber glow of our somberly-lit elevator. And as the elevator doors open, we both stepped out and were both now walking forward on a much-different path than we had when we first entered the little box hanging precariously from strings.

CHAPTER XXIII

All they had ever wanted to do was to assert their independence, their rights to live free and safe, unencumbered by fear or the threat of harm in an otherwise civilized environment. And here and now—wires rigged, and ready with video camera—they waited, poised and confident in the knowledge that the things they've done and were about to do were a direct extension of their attitudes and intentions to address these issues and to redress their grievances in person with that person or persons whom would transgress their sanctuary, their home, for God's sake. They took these actions in order to repel said interloper—to detain, discourage, warn, and finally thwart this would-be attacker forever.

They stayed huddled together in the dark—sitting, as it were, in a chair inside the darkened stairwell that led from downstairs into their kitchen—they were both as nervous as two little girls pulling a questionable prank on an unsuspecting stranger. Their hearts were racing with anticipation and hints of uncertainty.

This, after all, was a serious thing that they were doing here. The Russians were men—bad men—and the two of them were not little girls; and if things were to go wrong, anything at all, they had no backup because they had informed no one what they were up to.

"Okay, you've got the strobe light, and I've got the video camera"—Gladys then pats the side of her leg where she has wrapped John Smith Sr.'s old .38 snub-nose pistol. "—and I've got the gun."

That's when Mildred gasped, as if the reality of this dangerous and questionable escapade had finally sunk in. "You think wrapping all that wire around things all over the kitchen was a good thing, is it enough of a deterrent?" Mildred questioned her partner in crime as she squirmed to make herself more comfortable in their shared seat inside the doorway.

"Of course, it is, Millie. That much wire would stop a raging bull from plowing through our kitchen, much less the force of a fat Russian bear like the Baron Romanovsky poses to it. Whatever happens, it happens because he will have violated our home, Millie. Sneaking through the back door to harm two old girls like us. Shame on him, he deserves to get scared out of his wits, and maybe a little banged up, for good measure as well."

Mildred was so nervous; you could tell because she was asking question after question, something she would only do if she were indeed nervous, "You think he'll see the wires, Gladys?"

At first Gladys harrumphs as Mildred's questions were clearly upsetting her own resolve. But she resisted her heartfelt desire to give in to Mildred's ambivalence as she steeled herself and spoke resolutely to her best friend and benefactress, "Look, Millie, I have never done anything like this before, and, in my heart, I am as nervous as you are, and with every breath I am questioning my own actions. But, that said, I had learned long ago—in my life on the street before you rescued us—that you just can't allow people to push you around, because if you did, the insidious nature of it had a way of gathering its own momentum until it had crushed you. People, or should I say bullies—and the Baron Romanovsky is a bully—they have no off button because they have no hearts; they will stomp you beyond submission. It's the kind of depravity that exists most exclusively in humans and tigers, I'm told. And I am not going to allow us to fall victim to it without a fight. My god, Millie, we are already his prey, but I'm not going to allow us to become victims. We are going to fight back against this depraved Russian bear together because he won't stop unless we make him stop. I owe us that much and more, Millie, that much and a lot more."

After Gladys's heartfelt appeal, Mildred was almost done voicing all of her concerns, but of course—as a product of her compulsive and fastidious nature, that one last concern remained: "What if he turns on the light first, Gladys?" This time Gladys smiled brightly, having anticipated that possibility; she was glad to share with Mildred how she had already dealt with that eventuality.

She smiles and answers, "I double clicked the three-way light switch so the light won't go on from over there. He'd have to first cross the room to use this switch to turn the lights on by resetting the distant switch. And besides, Millie, he'd have trouble seeing all this thin wire in the daytime, let alone in the dark. It'll work. All we have to do is to catch him on camera in the act of illegally intruding our home, and we have him where we want him. And this gun,"—she says, as she again pats the gun's holster—"is our insurance, just in case he's not so easily persuaded . . ."

Gladys smiles shyly as she pauses., "He has no idea that I've never shot it or any other gun before in my life, but I'm certain that will be the thought farthest from his mind as he'll be squirming to loose himself from all this wire we've hung."

Little did this dynamic senior duo know, but as they themselves were scheming in the penthouse, the Baron Romanovsky was plotting in the stairwell; in fact, he was actually in the act of skulking his hulking self up the stairs toward the penthouse that very moment.

Once he had reached the kitchen level—having moved very carefully and quietly not wanting to disturb the absolute peace and solitude of this echoing backdoor stairwell egress—finally there, he could hear no noise from within; he paused stealthily outside of the kitchen fire door exit. He was prepared to leave no evidence or trace of his having been there, so he had already dressed his hands and feet in prophylactic covers; on his hands he wore plastic surgical gloves and on his feet he wore paper hospital operating-room booties.

And then, as he pressed his one ear to the door to listen—he heard nothing, no human sounds as it were—only the heavy humming of the Traulsen refrigerator sang back to his ear's inquiry, which made his heart echo in thankful harmony, glad that the coast seemed clear for his intended misdeeds.

Yet and still he continued to move slowly, and cautiously, as his large fat fingers slowly uncoiled from their nervous defensive fists, like sunflower petals preening and awakening in the noonday sun. And as he extended his heavy hairy arm, his gloved hand reached for the doorknob.

Solidly in his fingers now, the cool metal excited him. Then slowly gently and quietly he turned the doorknob, hoping that it was still bereft of its former resistance, as he himself had left it some short hours ago, and indeed it was, as it did turn happily and easily in his sweaty glove—covered hand. He then moved gracefully forward—quite nimbly for such a large man—and as he quickly and quietly stepped inside the spacious kitchen, he saw nothing unusual for the short moment that the hallway light flashed into the darkened room.

He then closed the door behind himself just as gently quietly and quickly as he had entered through it. Still moving as gracefully as an aging ballerina, he reached for the wall where he had in the light from the hallway spotted the kitchen light's wall switch. He reached, with the supreme confidence born on the total success of the evening so far, and flips the switch, but nothing happened. Undaunted by this minor inconvenience, it was clear that the Baron Romanovsky had decided to move forward through the kitchen, probably toward where he had flipped that light switch on earlier in the evening, when he had thought he had secretly and, unobserved, unlocked the fire exit door.

As the baron was a large and confident man, every forward step that he took was strong, purposeful, and weighty, and it was this weightiness that would be his undoing. For as he strode, one, two, maybe even three strong and fairly large steps forward, he surprisingly encountered his first obstacle wire. It surprised him as it hit him right across one ankle and then the other, and before he could stop his forward motion, his momentum had hurdled him forward and downward faster than he was able to recover his balance to right himself.

He toppled over like a felled logger's tree, crashing straight down in one stiff unsectioned piece. As he fell, his powerful arms and hands began to flail in the air as he struggled to grasp something that might impede his tumble and break his now-panicked and rapid decent toward the dark kitchen floor.

Crashing downward fast, his body quickly encountered and went speedily into the mesh of spider's web strung eighteen-gauge wire, or as it were, it went speedily into him, tearing and slicing through his clothes around his chest, and then through the flesh of his exposed neck—his muscles veins and arteries—deep and rapier-like all the way to his spine as he flailed and struggled to free himself. A strange and eerie swishing sound came with his methodical and powerful descent. And in the midst of the fall, he squeaked a sigh, a gush of air, a breathy high-pitched sigh, just as the Traulsen refrigerator and the Wolf range—the heavy anchors for the meshed wire maze—they both joined in squealing and squeaking as they too weightily lurched quickly forward toward the center of the kitchen in one sudden motion.

The weight of his fumbling, falling body—ass over dingle berries—having been caught up in the tangle of wires, had pulled the heavy appliances, like an entourage of fat men, following him straight toward his ignominious ending.

In the end, there was no thud as his lumbering body—caught between the two weighty sentries—had not quite reached the floor. No, not quite there, as he hung dangling only inches from a final splat as his now-cascading red blood washed down in liters to land in silent splashes on the burnt orange Mexican tile floor.

It was over quickly. And still while his death was not a contrivance of design, it was indeed the consequence of an abysmally incompetent and failed attempt at ad hoc security; put more simply, it was indeed their fault.

Stunned and shocked at this unforeseen result and still standing in their secure corner of the kitchen, they upon this sudden and eerie silence, both Gladys and Mildred instantly knew that their plan of catching this rotund Russian interloper in the act had backfired eons beyond their simple and most tame expectations. But even before the horrible result had been finalized, on cue, as the noise of the Russian's tumble had begun, both Mildred and Gladys had managed to pull the triggers on their respective devices—the video camera and the strobe light—and as the scene itself was horrible, they nonetheless caught it all, from start to finish, on tape.

When Baron Romanovsky had first entered the inordinately large kitchen, and the light had flashed in from the back hallway, they both ducked their once-brave heads behind the wall where they had planted themselves. Once the door was closed and the baron flipped the light switch, in the quietness of the room you could hear it all the way on the other side of the kitchen.

Mildred was now shaking in her shoes. "Did you hear that?" Mildred whispered in a birdlike chirp to Gladys.

"Of course, I heard that, what do you think, I've gone deaf, all of a sudden?"

"What should we do, Gladys?"

It was clear Gladys was ready to do battle, and she said so, "We do what we're here to do, Millie, shine your light on him while I videotape the bum." As the light flashed, the Russian fell, or did the Russian start to fall before the light had flashed? Who would ever really know? They shined their light and pointed their camera from their distant dark corner. Had it startled the Russian? "It sounds like he's falling down, Millie. We should get in there and turn the camera right on him before he gets up."

Gladys figured quickly and rightly that the baron had indeed tripped over some of the lower strung wire, but she really had no idea what she was doing with her video camera; neither one of them—Mildred, or Gladys—knew how to work it that well. It had been sitting in the box that it had come in since Christmas—it was a gift from me—and they had only taken it out that evening to use as part of their rushed security plans. But as she spoke and instructed Mildred to turn her strobe light on, Gladys simultaneously pressed the record button on her recorder; she didn't even look through the handheld camera's viewfinder. She just pointed in the direction of the noise and basically hoped and prayed she was filming what the noise was all about; in that same identical way Mildred had also pointed her strobe light.

Believe it or not, they were both too scared to watch the calamitous carnage of the Russian bear; not until long after the many sighs squeaks and other assorted and unfamiliar noises had erupted and aroused their frightened curiosities to bravery did they finally look to see what their mischievous plan had brought.

"Did you hear that, Gladys, what was that sound?" This time Gladys wasn't so quick to answer because the foreign sounds of a man dying, although not often heard, were only distant to her, but not totally foreign. They—the sounds—instantly sobered her out of her ardor as their temporary security expert with all the plans. She in fact was very silent as she and Mildred now stood staring at the dangling baron's body caught in their deadly spiderweb turned suddenly into a ghoulish mangled bird's nest.

The strobe light made the scene appear even more macabre than necessary; it would have been quite eerie enough had all the overhead kitchen lights been on, but they could see everything just fine, and what they both saw at the same time was a dead Russian in their kitchen. It was instantly clear that he was dead as from his incised and torn-flesh body, the blood was pouring onto the floor as he dangled motionless in his slightly swaying squeaky trap, only inches from the floor. He hung there like one of the many freshly-killed deer—minus all the blood—that had hung not far away in the other side of he kitchen, where Richard Smith used to hang them before he butchered them in his little butcher shop.

Gladys had only seen Richard slaughter deer, but Mildred had seen many a deer slaughtered as a Midwestern girl—after a hunt, her father used to hang them bleeding from hooks in the barn back home—but they both recognized the same stark image; they recognized quickly the similarities. "Jesus, Mary, and Joseph, Gladys, what have we done?" Mildred pronounced—in a voice cracking in near panic, as she turned and grabbed at Gladys, but Gladys stays calm as she continued to point the video camera at the dangling Russian. Mildred begins to emotionally decompose, "Oh my god, Gladys, we've gone and killed the Russian. We could end up in a Siberian gulag for this. Oh my god! Oh my god. What are we going to do now, Gladys? What are—?" All through Mildred's panic was in full force, Gladys's outside demeanor remains calm, but her mind is racing like Secretariat at the Belmont Stakes—way out in front of everything and everyone.

Finally she stops filming, and she turns and takes Mildred's shoulders—one shoulder in each of her boney hands—and she shakes her friend, once, and then again. "Calm down, Millie, the first thing we're going to do is to calm down."

Mildred quickly answers her friend through her frightened tears, "But you're already calm, Gladys, it's me that's falling apart."

Gladys is back in control now; she smiles and calmly responds to her friend, and she throws her arms around her, she says, "Neither you or I are going to jail, or any such place. The only place we're going is right here where we live."

Gladys stares again at the Baron Romanovsky's dead body, and then she says, "First, we've got to figure out what we're going to do with this dead Cossack."

This reference makes the frazzled Mildred respond with a curious rejoinder, "I didn't know he was a Cossack, Gladys, how did you know that?" Gladys is a little taken aback as she senses that she and Mildred are not on the same page; far from it, they may not even be reading from the same book as it were.

Gladys proceeds forward, hoping to get them both on the same track.

"I don't know that to be true either, Millie, I was just trying to make light of the situation. You know, to make it easier to handle."

Already shaking in disbelief at the horrible sight of the dead Russian floating precariously and strangely in the hanging wires that they had strung across her kitchen, Mildred wasn't nearly ready to venture a guess at what Gladys's inference was supposed to lead her to conclude. She stiffens as she recoils in a huff, "Oh, I see . . . Easier to handle, Gladys, what do you mean easier to handle? What if—."

Gladys makes like she doesn't even hear Mildred's heart pounding in her chest; she is determined to get them moving as fast as they can to liberate themselves from this awful mess. Because all the while Mildred was talking, Gladys was scheming on what to do with the Russian's body. She never thought even once—well, maybe once—about bringing anyone else into this intriguing debacle. And then, when she had figured it out, that's when she chose to interrupt Mildred's little tirade. "Listen, Millie, there are ten thousand what-ifs to choose from, and the only one that should concern us is the what if we don't handle this situation cleanly. Now, go get some bleach and those heavy plastic garbage bags from the utility closet while I get some paper towels. We've got to get this hulk in the freezer."

Curiously, Mildred begins to compliantly and quietly walk away, but then—I'm guessing when the words actually hit her brain in the right spot—she stops dead in her tracks, and on a dime she spins around to face Gladys. "Did I hear you correctly, Gladys? You're not going to do what I've just heard you say you're going to do? Tell me I'm mistaken, please tell me so."

Gladys stands her ground, "Ha, and I suppose you have a better idea, Millie? Millie, please don't tell me you're thinking of involving other people in this, like the police, maybe? We hung him, Millie, look at him. I know we didn't mean to, but we did, and do you think that anybody is going to believe we just wanted to stop him or scare him? I don't think so, Millie, I really don't think so. And besides, you heard him say that he was alone tonight, that his goon brothers were out of town. So who even knew he came up here to harm us besides the three of us, and one of us is dead."

Mildred pauses as she ponders Gladys's determined effort to bring her to the dark side; she wanted to rid them of this mess, and it seemed that the dark side was the only place she was immediately able to find solace and solution. Gladys waited not another moment before she grew impatient with Mildred's hesitancy.

"Now don't get all swirly on me, Millie. I need your help, and what we are going to do is exactly what we need to do."

Mildred seemed immediately annoyed at the accusation. "Swirly, Gladys, what do you mean by that?" Her comment made Gladys laugh out loud.

"You know, I don't think I've ever used that word before, it just came out like that, darlin'. Hell, Millie, I'm as nervous as you are, but I'll be damned if I'm going to let us get railroaded into some drawn-out and highly public imbroglio because some nasty man wanted to hurt us. We were just defending ourselves, and it just happened to have worked out more effectively than even we planned it. Why should we be penalized for that? And I know what you're thinking—that the law and justice will be on our side because we are innocent in our intent, but I wouldn't want to bet on it. And also, Millie, the building doesn't need that kind of publicity, this would be the last place anyone would be looking for a missing Russian thug because that's all he was—Baron Romanovsky, my foot. I never ever believed he was any kind of royalty anyway."

The plan was certainly a go when Mildred's response was, "But where are we going to put Blue Eye's chicken from now on?" The ladies had clearly switched back to their cool, calm, and naturally rational selves as Gladys's response was on message.

"That's the least of our problems, Millie. What I want to know is, how are the two of us skinny things going to get this Russian into the freezer?"

CHAPTER XXIV

While the intrigue between the Baron Romanovsky, Gladys, and Mildred was settling in upstairs, Windler was testing and checking the security system downstairs in the security room. The truth of this was that even before the baron had started his assent skyward, Windler had his eye on things. It wasn't like he was sitting there watching the monitor, as if he had expected something to occur that very evening; it was the case that he had actually returned to the security office from his dual post in the lobby. As the evening traffic was very low, there was no need to have more than him working.

At that particular moment, he causally walked into the security office to check on the monitor, and, at first, he sees that everything is clear, except for the little flashing light that signaled that something had passed through the camera. This indicator would last until he manually turned it off. Usually, it was the camera recording one of the tenants putting out their trash for pickup, or even taking the back exit to the garage, or some such mundane activity. Every time one of those or some other such thing would happen, the light would flash until Windler would switch it off. He would sometimes check to see what had occurred, but sometimes out of boredom and the monotony and banality of back stairwell nonevents, he'd just turn the flash off without checking. But this was the middle of the night, and this little amber flash, this time piqued his almost totally dormant curiosity.

This job he could do in his sleep, so most of the time, he was, in effect, sleepwalking. It was a long away from the military, but good jobs, any job was hard to find. Windler had a criminal record—he had a number of petty arrests and one misdemeanor conviction, but the-military had let him in anyway. The military was desperate for men, and, besides, the conviction was many years ago when Windler was just a mere pup. It was, in fact, his MP duties in the service that had secured him this job in the first place. So his curiosity now piqued to act, Windler recaptures the images from the beginning that set off the amber signal in the first place; this was done by simply clicking a rewind switch. And lo and behold, what does he spot? He spots the Baron Romanovsky seconds after he leaves his apartment dressed like an orderly from a hospital surgical floor. He watches him at first moving suspiciously in front of his own apartment door, and then as he moves toward the stairs and then skulking, as it were, up the stairs.

It wouldn't have been so noticeable—maybe he could have been persuaded to believe that the baron was going upstairs to borrow a cup sugar—but when he noticed how weird the gloved hands and the booties on the baron's feet really were, especially as he engaged in this curious and furtive behavior more than just a step outside of his own apartment—he was convinced then that the man was indeed up to no good.

Immediately, Windler checked the recording time against his own watch—to see exactly how long ago the baron had been engaged in his suspicious and devious behavior—and it was exactly an hour ago that this scene had taken place. Windler's heart immediately began to race because he knew that all manner of bad and harmful things could occur in a tenth of that amount of time, and that, indeed, he might be much too late to intercede successfully. Windler watches intently—he can't believe his eyes—and so, just to make certain he's got it all right, he replays the replay. Of course, the thing comes out exactly the same—he had to check it twice because the baron is a bad man, and he doesn't want to get caught on the wrong side of him and his thugs—the images don't lie; the baron is up to no good. He watches 'til the end, two times, he watches until the baron—after listening at the penthouse door—enters the apartment. Then he waits, but nothing, no more amber lights; all the tapes are clear from that time until the very moment that he is standing there watching them in real time.

Windler is now stoked; he's all pumped up, but now what does he do? Does he wake up John Smith and tell all that he has discovered? What if it's something innocuous going on between the baron and the spinster sisters? He could lose his job. What about calling Albert? No, he decided. He decides that he can't tell anyone before he knows exactly what to tell if anything. He decides, thinking, *I'll go up and investigate this thing for myself, by myself.*

His heart pounding like the timpani in the finale of *Tchaikovsky's* "1812 Overture," Windler takes to the penthouse elevator, and as he's riding up he breaks into a mild sweat, he knows his job and his well-being are clearly on the line, and whatever he does now will determine whether he keeps it or not. When the elevator reaches the penthouse, a ring at the locked entry automatically alarms the ladies inside. Only through receiving their direct orders or someone with a passkey could get up to the floor by elevator without approval.

Gladys, by this time, had successfully cut away the wires that the Russian's body, falling hard, had entangled itself in. Mildred was too grossed out to participate in this gory task, allowed Gladys to go at it alone, but still the bulbous body was much too heavy for them to lift with any effectiveness and was still lying most obtrusively in the center of their eerily morbid kitchen when the buzzer rang.

Their speed diligence and determination to clean up the mess they had made for themselves had not been nearly enough to contain their culpability in this mangled mess; when the door buzzer sounds, they immediately turned to each. Mildred first. "Who could that be?"

"It's one of two persons, or maybe it's both of them." Mildred quickly answers, "It's Albert, or John."

Gladys pauses for a quiet moment as she thinks of what to do; she decides that it's neither of them. "No, Millie, something in my gut tells me it's neither, something tells me it's Windler."

"Windler!" Mildred squeaks.

Gladys responds quickly, "Yes, Millie, Windler."

Mildred hesitates, and then she asks herself mostly, "What does he want up here this time of night?"

Gladys mumbles something inaudible to Mildred's ears, "God works in mysterious ways, his wonders to perform."

"What was that you've just said, Gladys?"

Calmly, Gladys responds to her friend in a new more subdued tone than just seconds before, "Oh nothing, sweetheart, I was just thinking how things fit together in my life when I need them most, that's all, love, that's all."

"Let me answer the buzzer, Millie. I don't think that he's going to go away if I don't. I'm sensing something innovative here."

Mildred was totally perplexed by Gladys's remark. *She's sensing something innovative, now what on God's earth was that cryptic sentence supposed to mean?* she thought, but she didn't question Gladys right away, and she didn't follow her to the door either; she was too nervous to see anyone now.

Gladys finally arrives at the elevator—which is through a separate door into another room outside of the kitchen itself—she takes a deep breath, and then she unlocks the lock, and the elevator door opens slowly. Standing on the other side—as she had most percipiently anticipated—was Windler, all swollen and panting.

Gladys—doing her best Sarah Bernhardt impression—feigns surprise at seeing Windler standing there. "Oh, Windler, I thought you were John. Is there something wrong, Windler? What are you doing up here at this time of night?"

Windler is nervous, and he begins to stutter indistinguishable non-sequiturs—a pitiful sight for sure for a man of his physical stature—but he quickly rights himself to finally speak a full short yet lucid sentence. "Are you two all right, ma'am?" he questions; all the while, Gladys's furtive and fertile mind's wheels are churning milk into butter.

Gladys is quickly jolted from her thoughts as she too stutters a word or two, "Why . . . why . . . yes, yes, we are . . . why do you ask, Windler?"

It's real cat-and-mouse game they're playing, and they are both keenly aware of it. It's simply a matter now of who will give in first and break this silly stalemate. It continues. "Are you sure?" Windler whines as he attempts to soften his naturally strong demeanor in an effort to coax a different response from the resistant spinster. But this only makes the cautious Gladys stiffen her resolve not to move too quickly forward.

"Of course, I'm sure. What is wrong with you, Windler, what do you think is going on up here at this time of night?"

With all of Windler's years of dealing with recalcitrant soldiers in the service, he can easily and with the aplomb of a trained bloodhound smell a lie from this close-up, and now he's determined to make sure everything is as it should be. He had checked the video more than once before he made his move to the penthouse, and he knew that something untoward had or was currently taking place. He was glad to see that Gladys looked all right, but then, too, she had remained mostly in the darkened vestibule outside of the elevator—she had not yet invited him in—where he would never step all the way into unless invited. And so it remained that he really couldn't see yet all there was to see. His incredulity, supported by video evidence, forced Windler to act like what he had been hired to do, and that was security. "What about the kitchen?" he asked this time more forcefully than any of his previous questions had been uttered.

This time, he could easily see that Gladys's resolve was not as strong or as resistant as before, and even she does stutter again. "What . . . what, what about the kitchen, Windler? You want something to eat?"

Emboldened by the stutter and her waning resistance, Windler blusters harder, "No, I don't want nothin' to eat, ma'am . . ." Windler pauses in order to gather the nerve to ask his most intrusive question yet, "When was the last time you was in the kitchen?"

It was her last try as Gladys's thin-muscled body defines her skeleton by tightening every inch from head to toe, and yet there was still something pointless about this effort because she had long since decided that she needed this man's help. She then speaks equally deceptive words as before, "Windler, what's this all about?" But her tone gave her away as her earlier resistance had obviously weakened.

Feeling more confidant ever since in his mind he had decided that he was indeed doing his job, Windler says, "I'm sorry, Mrs. Lawrence, but I need to check your kitchen." Windler finally steps uninvited into the apartment from the elevator as Gladys takes a step back; she doesn't try to resist him. "You stay right next to me, Mrs. Lawrence." The elevator door closes behind them, and nervously they both turn to look at it. And then Windler takes a cautious step forward before he stops and asks, "Where is Mrs. Smith, Mrs. Lawrence, is she in the kitchen?"

Gladys lies, "She's downstairs, why?" Windler answers quickly, "Because, ma'am, I think you have an intruder in your kitchen." He pulls out his gun. He doesn't notice, or maybe he ignores, Gladys's lack of surprise when he announces to her that she has an intruder in the kitchen. Gladys knows that the gig is up, but what she doesn't know is how and what Windler knows, but she knows enough to follow him through the vestibule door into the kitchen.

The kitchen lights are off as they step through the door. "Wow!" Windler says as he coughs from the strong smell. "It smells like someone spilled a tub of bleach in here, what's going on in here, Mrs. Lawrence?" Gladys remains quiet as she knows they—she and Millie—are only seconds away from their mischief being discovered. Windler's muscular arm reaches as his thick fingers clicks on the light switch, and his eyes are immediately drawn to the center of the room where all of the heavy appliances had gathered like a crowd in a stadium watching a ball game. He was about to ask, but when his curious and wondering eyes went without instruction next to the floor between the gathered appliances, he quickly discovered and answered his own yet-to-be-asked question.

As the flaccid bulbous corpse of the Russian Baron—the very same person whom he had seen, in the playback of the security tape, surreptitiously enter the spinsters' apartment on the creep—now lying in the center of the kitchen floor bloodied and for certain dead.

"What the . . . Holy shit! You guys killed the Russian. I knew he didn't come back out of here . . . Holy shit! Look at him. What did you guys do, I mean how did you manage to do it? I mean, he was a bad man, a very bad man, and you two old girls bumped him off." Windler breaks into a short yet hardy laugh. Quietly Gladys is encouraged by Windler's reaction as her eyes quickly find Millie sitting nearby in one of the kitchen chairs; she sits motionless with an implacable look on her face and a bleach-soaked bloodstain towel dangling from her hands. Windler turns and looks at Gladys, and without saying a word, he stares.

Gladys after a moment's hesitation meekly replies to his silent yet obvious inference, "We thought he was coming back after the party to hurt us, so we took some precautions."

"Precautions, no shit! I'd say they were pretty good precautions at that." Windler had tried to make a joke and make light of the situation, but the two old girls were having none of that. They wanted to know what was coming next; after all, there was a dead man lying in the middle of their kitchen floor, and they were the ones who had killed him. Mildred was still too stunned and overcome by the horror of this whole thing, and so both she and Gladys knew that it was Gladys who was going to have to do the negotiations with Windler.

So after a dithering moment of uncomfortable silence, Gladys spoke up, "So, Windler, what are you going to do now?" Windler was a bit taken aback by the question.

"Me, it looks like you ladies have already gone and done it, don't you think?" ·

Finally, Mildred speaks up, "We're in big trouble now, Windler, aren't we?" Windler finally gets their drift as he looks around at all the paraphernalia—the large heavy black plastic bags, the towels, the containers, and the overwhelming smell of bleach—all surrounding the baron's corpse.

Quickly, Windler's mind shifts to himself; he knows—which was different from just a few moments ago—that he is now in a position of advantage, if not in fact actual power. He likes his job, and he knows that if he does anything to displease these ladies that his job for sure is forfeit; but they have killed a man, a bad man, but a man nonetheless. He doesn't yet know exactly what they are thinking of doing, so he decides that he will find out first before he commits himself to anything. "Well, what had you ladies planned to do? It doesn't look like you were about to call the cops or anything even close to that."

Gladys's heart screams with elation; luckily no one could hear it, or it would have surely frightened them. With that energy jolt, and now apparently an answer to her silent prayer, she does get right to the point, "Well, Windler, we were just about to put him on ice. How about you giving us a hand." Mildred is shocked by Gladys's ease and amazingly forthright and some might call it flippant candor; she looks askance at Gladys while Gladys stares straight at Windler.

Windler is beyond shock; he's numb. He had anticipated poorly, thinking that if he remained compliant and solicitous that he would surely have gotten off easier in terms of job longevity and security. He had sucked it up for the old broads—he hadn't judged them or scolded them; in fact he had been quite placid under the circumstance—and yet, he had no idea that these two old biddies had this kind of steel, this kind of deviousness hiding, lodged deep inside their senior bones.

Windler's shocked nerves allow him to say very little; all he can manage is this. "You've got a freezer?" he says with more than a tinge of hope in his now-nervous voice. Hoping that the answer was no, and that the idea was purely in jest, but neither wish would be rewarded with a granting because the old women were as serious as a heart attack.

Gladys was no fool; she out of the three of them had lived the fullest life, and she knew by her hard-earned and well-garnered old wits that she had Windler right where she needed him and certainly wanted him. But she understood well that the tenuousness of this man's recent conversion to allegiance could be easily severed through a personal display of arrogance and hubris; she instinctively knew to treat him like a rescuer and savior, which in fact he would become if he deign to stay the unsteady coarse that she had just laid down before him. So she then responded carefully to his timid query; she says softly—in her best Nell Fenwick to his Dudley Do-Right, the archetype of a damsel in distress, "Yes, Windler, we have a freezer."

Immediately that soft, fragile woman's voice incited something inside of Windler; something clicked, and clearly, he now felt a part of something—and he quickly forgot about law and consequence—he was a savior, these two women needed him.

Gladys had skillfully played him like an old player piano—hitting every right note—sounding the right tone and playing the right tune. Now completely on board, Windler had his own pithy query. "Is it large enough to hold something his size?" Windler says as he points at the dead Russian on the kitchen floor.

"Large enough to freeze a full-grown ten-point buck larger than you," Gladys retorts confidently, all while Mildred's head is on a swivel back and forth between the two of them as the two of them coldly engage in this unbelievable conversation. Windler is as resolute as his final response is positive.

"That sure oughta work."

CHAPTER XXV

It was much more toward the later part of the morning, and being that it was Sunday, the decided and equally appropriate flow of the building's tenants leisure attitudes drifted benignly from languid to lazy. The night before had been a long night for some, but still, as this sunny Sunday sister slowly waddled along toward her more robust masculine and muscular brother Monday, Windler was quietly back at his usual post in the security office; he was nestled up to and behind the security desk, cloaked in for him, an unaccustomed seriousness—hoping no one would bother him—while watching the newly functioning security monitors.

Actually, he was more resting than ever he was watching as the night before had been a physical as well as emotional drain on him. If the absolute truth was to be known—and as it was only truly known to three—Windler's demeanor was scarcely one of great concealment. In fact, he was indeed more nervous than anyone—anyone who knew him well enough by now—if they were to set fresh eyes on him now, they would have discovered a personage of their security guard they had never seen before. He now was attempting to rest quietly—as he had not slept a wink last night—and surreptitiously, as it were, trying to hide any signs of his wrongdoing and guilt.

Unfortunately for him, his semi-dulled state had reached only the height of a bumbling ruse—comical at best—a failed contrivance to hide his dubious and dangerous complicity in the past evening's intrigues. And he knowingly, and before his freely chosen and culpable entanglement, could have and should have rightfully walked clearly and guilt-free away from. He also knew, however, this mammoth man, whose true heart was as big as his sizable head, he knew, he knew all to well that he had scuttled badly that last golden opportunity to walk away, to walk away from a deed that he would forever be a culpable part of, and yet and still and in fact because of that very same heart, he knew that he had done the right thing. This was the archetype; this was the morning after, and he would just have to ride out his transitory nervousness, and to hope that no one disturbed him with inflammatory gossip or rumors of last night's misdeeds.

That last night—once he had made the fateful decision to lend his large hands in assistance—he delivered his help with the zeal and zest of a new convert to a worthy cause. And being, from his military training, somewhat of a detective himself, he had learned about evidence in the military. He knew all too well what had to be done at the scene of the crime—there was no doubt in his mind that a crime had taken place there in the spinsters' penthouse—what needed to be cleaned up and how the cleanup needed to proceed; so he took over.

As soon he had gotten the particulars from Gladys, he knew well what his course of action needed to be if he was going to be on their side. He knew to make the scene of their kitchen appear as if nothing more untoward or more benign than a poorly cooked meal had ever taken place there.

"Okay, ladies, let's roll," he says with an adolescent head wiggle and a sheepish smile. Windler had always remembered being bigger and stronger than most other people, men in particular; he often basked in the glorious rays of his muscular and physical difference, almost always except when around or in the presence of the opposite sex, the ladies, as he'd often and fondly referred to them. With them, he always feared that they would fear him—because of his size, of course—and so most often in their presence he would try to diminish the effects of his obvious dominance through humor, self-reproach, and self-deprecation, and it oft times worked to perfection; that of course, would have been the reason that he had always used it for most of his large-size life. But as soon as he tried that same tactic with Gladys and Mildred, they balked; they were—neither one of them—having any of it as Gladys was only inches away from him as he took his first familiar steps down that warn-out and low road of self-ridicule.

"Oh no, you don't, Windler," Gladys immediately scolds after him—as soon as his adolescent behavior cropped up again—and upon getting her first whiff of him turning on himself, she remonstrated vigorously, saying, "You stop that right now, . . . Windler. I've seen that in you for some time now, son, and I don't like it one bit. God made you strong the way you are, and there is no reason for you to cower and attempt to reduce your gifts. Be proud, son, stay strong, son, always stay strong."

Mildred as well came to the caucus. She had finally come around; she was finally out of her seat from the corner of the kitchen and up on her feet standing next to the now-dynamic twosome. "I wholeheartedly agree with my sister here, Windler—we are now, and will always be, indebted to you for your help and obvious kindness. Do not reduce yourself because you are strong and more virile than most others, son, bask in the glory of your specialness, and keep your head high."

Gladys chimes in again, "We both know that this is not some joke to you, and that you are helping us out of the goodness of your wonderful big heart. It's a rare human quality that you possess, the rarity of being there when a friend needs help, as we now need yours."

Mildred then grabs Windler's and Gladys's hands and says, "Friends to the death, friends for all the days of the rest of our lives." The three all smile heartfelt, warm smiles at each other.

Windler was, of course, dumbfounded by the support and praise of the two thankful spinsters; but I'm certain that they already had him at "hello." Even still, he was taken by their warm and encouraging words. After a quick moment of basking in the rays of their verbal largess, or maybe because of it, Windler knew that it was time to get back to the business at hand. He smiled, sheepishly, but much more radiantly and self-assuredly than before, and he then took charge. "Let us begin by bagging the body. I'll lift him and sit him up while you two ladies slide three bags, one inside the other over his torso."

Mildred hesitates as Gladys immediately starts to pick up the thick black plastic bags and put one inside the other, just the way Windler had instructed them to do.

"Come on, Millie, you heard Windler, let's roll." The three of them all smile as it's Gladys this time who breaks the palpable tension. They go about wrapping the large man's body in plastic and cord; it turns out they have a dolly that Windler finally places the body on and wheels it, quite handily to the front of the freezer. "Luckily we are running low on chicken—we most times fill it half the way full with free-range fowl."

Mildred had become totally comfortable with Windler, so comfortable that she lost her inhibitions about revealing heretofore-private information about her and Gladys's little secret. Windler was nonplussed as to why they would use or need so much chicken, or was he? As Gladys quietly gives Mildred a bump of the elbow, Mildred squeaks with and gives Gladys curious stare.

"What?" she says as Gladys tries shushing her, a big mistake because neither of them can abide being shushed by anyone for any reason at all; they both believe that it's the height of rudeness to shush another. "Don't you shush me," Mildred asserts more loudly than can be ignored by Windler.

Windler smiles a knowing smile and says, "Are you two worried that I have discovered your secret chicken stash for the falcons?" They both gasp, and then he says, "Well, I think this secret by far trumps that one." That did it, friends forever the three of them would be as they all—standing over the bagged corpse of the dead Russian—in as a macabre scene as you ever want to see, they three break into hearty and pressure-releasing guffaws.

After a moment of needed humor, the seriousness of the task at hand returns. "Okay, ladies, I'd say the best thing is for us to empty the chicken from the bottom of the freezer and replace it with the Russian on top."

They three have a little giggle as Mildred under her breath utters, "It sounds like we're making a salad." As the ladies are emptying the freezer of its chicken, Windler begins to frown a frown for the ages. So dour is his scowl that it makes the ladies stop in midstream their flow of emptying the chicken.

Gladys is alerted, but only slightly more and little before is Mildred, but she is the first to ask, "What's the matter, Windler?"

Windler hesitates as he studies the wrapped Russian all nestled up on the dolly there next to the freezer, and then he simply says, "He won't fit." The Russian bear is at least 330 or 340 if he's a pound, and six feet four inches tall if he's an inch tall. On the other hand, the freezer is all of four feet, maybe four and a half feet long. It is deep, but not that deep, and it had become increasingly clear, as he had for the last several minutes been studying it, that the freezer was indeed too small to fit the Russian's whole body inside it. And as both Windler's head and eyes jumped—like at a tennis match intermittently arching back and forth between the two, the Russian, and the freezer—as the ladies watched him, they all finally came to the same conclusion, and that was that he was absolutely right. There was too much Russian for the freezer, at least that was their initial and sad conclusion.

"What are we going to do now?" Mildred asks to no one in particular. The pensive three all stood solemnly and quietly for the longest and most painful moment in history; they all knew if they were discovered now that their own individual fates to be clear and as foreboding as the hulking shadow of this once-menacing Russian's had been. This same dead Russian, who had entered their home to harm them, would now finally in death get his wish if they were forced to suffer the whims and vagaries of the criminal law's codes.

But it wasn't more than a moment more when Gladys says but one word, "Deer."

Immediately, Mildred answered her, "Yes, love, what is it?"

Gladys responds by saying, "No, no, Millie. Deer as in John Deere, or reindeer, not you, love."

Windler smartly gets what Gladys is talking about when he says, "The animal, the deer that people kill in the woods, deer."

And that's when both Gladys and Mildred answer simultaneously, "Yes."

And then Windler responds in this every increasing circle of words, "Yes, then what about them?" And that's when Gladys puts down her hand full of frozen chicken that she had mindlessly been holding, and then she walks over to a large pantry door and opens it wide.

Both Mildred and Windler turn to look. Mildred already knew what she was going to see, but Windler was totally awestruck, well, totally for all of two seconds because he got it quickly enough—the message that is—as more and more of the pantry's gifts were revealed as the door opening widened to reveal all neatly hung on thick black hooks and heavy equally dark wire hangers were rubber gloves and big black rubber aprons; and from the hooks hung an assortment of cleavers, saws, both power and manual, and pliers, more hooks, wires, and ropes of all kinds, as well as all kinds of other paraphernalia that he had never seen before and had no idea of what to do with them.

Windler can't help but to say, "Wow."

"Jesus Christ in heaven, Gladys, we can't," Mildred calls out in shock and horror as she knew exactly the depths to where Gladys's mind had tumbled and bottomed out.

And at just about the same time that Windler realizes what's going on, Gladys, not one to hesitate making up her mind, or one to hesitate once her mind is made up says, "We must, we must, we must, we must, that is unless either of you has a better idea where to store this disaster."

Mildred is beside herself; she throws her hands forward and high into the air, like a parishioner in the church of the Holy Rollers, and shakes them hard, once, twice, three times as if she is trying to detach them from her wrists, while all the while saying, "No no no. I can't do that, I just can't."

Gladys moves quickly in to hug her, and as she does; she whispers into her friend's ear, saying, "You don't have to, Millie, I'll take care of you now the way you've always taken care of me."

All the while, Windler is watching the two of them; he is figuring just how much cutting they are going to have to do. And after it quiets down a bit, he finally says, "I'm going to need a large tub, a sink, or maybe a bathtub for all the—"

Gladys interrupts him as she points to another door on the opposite side of the room, and she says, "There's a butcher's block and a huge sink in there where Mr. Smith used to carve up the deer." Mildred can't take it as she pulls away from Gladys's grasp and heads for the door out of the kitchen, and down the stairs she scurries.

For a short moment, neither Windler nor Gladys say a word, but then Gladys says, "What do you need me to do, Windler?"

Windler then walks over to the other pantry on the other side of the room; he opens the door and again he exclaims, "Wow!" But he doesn't stop there when he says, "This is like a full butcher's shop."

As he opens the door to what amounts to another room, it's not a pantry at all, and that's when Gladys says, "Mr. Smith built everything to his specifications—, he was a very dominating and exacting man. Now, Windler, what do you need me to do?"

Windler looks inside and sees a tape measure. A short while later, and after he has measured the inside of the freezer and the body of the Baron Romanovsky, he decides what cuts have to be made, and there are quite a few. Between the two of them, they get most of the job done before Mildred returns to the kitchen. Mildred walks in on them just as they are removing one the baron's lower legs, and she says totally out of character for her, "Wow, that certainly is a big one."

Both Gladys and Windler stop what they are doing to turn to Mildred. It is all business now; after draining the blood and after the first cut, it was all just meat, and then Gladys says, "I'm glad you came back, Millie." Windler nods in agreement as the three of them finish the job and pack the Russian in the freezer with room to spare for the remaining chicken.

Once they complete that task, they finish cleaning up the kitchen. Windler moves all of the appliances back to their proper places and bags all of the telltale cleanup debris and sets it by the back door. "Ladies, leave this here until I return. I need to go to the security office first."

Gladys was much more curious than Mildred as she inquired as to why Windler was all of a sudden acting so distractedly, "Why can't you just take the stuff out right away? It's late, wouldn't this be the best time to expose of it?" Windler answers her quickly but nervously, as if he were hiding something. "Oh yes, it is, and I will, but first I have to go downstairs. I'll be right back." Gladys, not one to hold back, is persistent in her inquiry. "Why, Windler__?"

Before she can complete her question, Windler nervously answers it, "I just got to turn something off before I go out there with this stuff."

"I think you just answered an unasked question, Windler, but I think your answer reveals all. That's how you knew he"—she points in the direction of the freezer—"was out there and came in here, isn't it, Windler?"

Mildred's head was again on a swivel, but this time she had no idea what they were talking about. "What is going on, you two, what are you both fussing about now?"

"Tell her, Windler, tell Millie what we're fussing about." Windler gives them both an aw-shucks drop of his head accompanied by a little feet shuffling as he hesitates a moment, but Gladys is as unimpressed as she is impatient. "Go on, Windler, tell her," she insistently demands as Windler, after a stutter or two, finally gets it out.

"Yes, ma'am, you're right, that's how I knew he was up here, I saw him on the monitor." Gladys is clearly unhappy hearing this; you can immediately see it. As her coiled wire body tightens with anger and disappointment, she barks at Windler, "How long have you been watching us, Windler?" Windler smiles, "Oh, not that long, maybe three hours before all this stuff happened."

"Three hours!" enraged Gladys yelps. But Windler is no longer as afraid as he was only moments ago; it was as if his spilling of the beans, as it were, had released the pent-up pressure of his secret.

Proudly in a figuratively chest-pounding pronouncement, he boasts in his sweet baritone voice, "Yeah, that's all. I just got the system working this evening."

But Gladys is still not amused about being secretly watched, incensed about their privacy having been invaded, yet in the brief interlude between his words and Gladys's reaction, Windler discovers new strength in an unlikely ally. He can see out of the corner of his eye—because he still dared not turn his full head away from Gladys's intense glare—that Mildred is all for it as she then sprightly intercedes on his behalf; she then says to Gladys, "It saved our lives, love."

Totally surprised at hearing her best and most loyal friend's words ring out in Windler—supporting tones, Gladys's harsh stare increases now to a scowl of incredulity, knowing full well that it was her plan to wire the place that most certainly saved their lives, even though it's the same plan that also led them to their current predicament.

Undaunted by and following Gladys's disapproving scowl, Mildred's position remains unchanged as she immediately counters Gladys's stubborn position with, "Then if not that, his intrusion did still serve us well, it indeed did save our tails because without it, Windler would never have come up here, and—."

Gladys knows her position is untenable; as she quickly relaxes her stubborn stance and abandons her temporary little huff, she then turns back to Windler—she had already turned braced to quarrel with Mildred—and as she does, she interrupts Mildred in midsentence as she speaks directly to Windler, "So I'm guessing you have to go downstairs to turn that thing off before you open that back door and get rid of the evidence?"

This time Windler doesn't dare smile first; he simply nods his head in a compliant childlike, yes, and as Gladys's face relaxes and cracks a little smirk, only then does a small smile likewise warm his round brown face. Then playfully Gladys mouths, "Then go go go go." She mildly and in good humor scolds Windler away.

It only took a short while for Windler to return to the penthouse kitchen, and as he entered, the lights were still on. His initial observation was that the kitchen looked perfect, and that made him proud and at ease that a hard and terrible job had been well accomplished, and what had once been a strange place to him felt now like a second home.

The ladies had left the kitchen for parts unknown in other corners of their baronial Fifth Avenue triplex, but when they knew that Windler had returned, they likewise ascended the stairs again.

"Windler, you're back," Mildred called out as soon as she cleared the stairs, and it was clear from the timbre of her voice that nothing had changed in their society, that Windler indeed was still their friend.

Windler was likewise buoyed by this splendid woman's presence as he answered her in high spirits, "Yes, yes, of course, I am back, and now I will be taking this garbage to where no one will ever know that it came from this building."

By this time, Gladys was also present; she too was happy to see Windler, and she says with a bounce in her voice, "We can't thank you enough, Windler, we really can't. I know this has been difficult for you as well, but we could have never, ever done this alone. We owe you forever, Windler."

After their little congratulatory session, Windler loads the cleanup debris onto the aforementioned dolly and rolls it out into the hallway toward the freight elevator. Mildred and Gladys stand at the still-opened door—like two little girls they were—watching their hero and savior stride strongly away pushing the remaining residue of their once in a lifetime night.

Once inside the elevator, Windler takes the debris down to the garage and loads it into the bed of his little Toyota pickup and drives it away. As he left the garage and headed uptown on Madison, he knew exactly where he intended to dispose of the garbage; restaurants and large freestanding garbage bins were the best places. As he knew that if the cops or anyone else for that matter stopped him that it would appear that he was indeed scavenging instead of depositing garbage, and besides, at this time of the morning, the cops were busy keeping their eyes on the late-night revelers and partygoers going home or to their last watering hole of the evening, not lowly scavengers.

He knew that restaurants were good because they always had bloody garbage from meats and fowl to throw out—or even sauces and gravies that looked like blood—and that no one would question him if he actually got caught with something bloodied in his hands; he knew he'd just act like he was going through the garbage. And then there were the freestanding dumpsters, well, no one really bothered much looking into them, and hopefully no one had been murdered and missing near where one of them was sitting.

Slowly he drove uptown, the streets were mostly quiet as he went weaving in and out of the blocks, stopping and dropping, until he had reached near the Tri-borough Bridge at 155th Street in Harlem, right next to a gutted-out redo, and it was there that he found a large freestanding garbage bin and is where he drops in his last deposit of evidence. He had clearly lost count of how many deposits he had made—all were little packages, and not enough to put the entire puzzle of the night's mayhem together—but it was at least ten, he thought. And when he was done with his mission, instantly he headed straight back to the co-op; in a way he was much relieved that he had been successful in getting rid of the evidence, but the feelings of culpability and guilt he could not lift as easily from his heart as he had lifted the garbage from the bed of his truck.

"Windler." It indeed was his name, but hearing it jolted him from his semicomatose state. He immediately thought, *Had I been dreaming? Had I fallen to sleep?* He wasn't sure, but now wide-awake, he knew he hadn't been either when he heard his name called again, "Windler, are you in there?"

It was John Smith who had called him, and his heart's alarm rang with a calamitous gonging that shook him like a punch to the chin; he sat straight up and answered reflexively, "Yes, yes, Mr. Smith, I am in here, sir."

The only thoughts that weighed on his mind was the fear that the ladies had panicked and had told John Smith everything that had happened last night.

So before he came out of the office, he braced himself for that supposed inevitability. And he thinks, *Mr. Smith has been itching to see the security system working, I'll distract him with that.* And indeed, as John Smith approaches the office, the very next thing he asks in a whisper is, "Windler, have you managed to get that system going yet? These Russians have been quiet far too long, and I don't want them doing something devious and we not be ready for them, caught with our pants down, so to speak, you know?"

Windler's relief is palpable; John Smith's inquiry about the security system was, well, it was like throwing water on a burning bush and instantly dousing the incipient flames. John Smith's question was right in Windler's bailiwick; it was what he had wished so desperately for and was handsomely requited. Giddily he responded, "I've got it working, Mr. Smith. I got it working late last night." Not realizing how very tired he was, Windler then let out a big yawn, right in John Smith's face.

John Smith easily recognizes that Windler is very tired and says, "You're a good man, Windler, staying up so late to get this thing done, a good man you are, sir."

Windler could only smile and thank God in his heart, but Mr. Smith he thanked aloud, "Thank you, Mr. Smith, I'm glad that I finally got it done."

Smith is excited to see it work; as all boys want to play with their toys, he says, "Let's go inside and get a look at this thing, shall we, Windler?"

Windler's mood has jumped the fence of his heretofore stalled emotions as his exuberant posture takes on a heightened tone that mimics Mr. Smith as he says in answer to his employer, "We shall, let's take a gander."

Ever since, John had discovered our relationship—that we are indeed siblings—his demeanor has changed significantly; it is much lighter, and he's much more approachable. I'm not just talking about with me either; I mean with people in general, and mostly I'm talking about the building staff. Every one has been commenting about it lately, especially Windler.

If this were months ago, Windler would never have been having so much fun with John, and making this last comment would have been a total anathema.

John laughed out loud at Windler's words as he says, "That's funny. 'We shall, let's take a gander.' I like that, Windler, that's very funny." As they two enter the office, and Windler clearly relieved that they are going to talk about his security setup, but just the thought of it makes him in his head instantly hearken back to the last evening's debacle, but now with something physical to do, he can more easily distract his selfish worrying over last night.

He gets on with it, showing Mr. Smith how the system works saying, "Right here, Mr. Smith, are the buttons that control the replay . . ."

CHAPTER XXVI

While the showing off of the security system was going on inside the security office, I was at the concierge, at my regular post. Sundays are always more relaxed, and might I say the atmosphere is a more than a tad friendlier as most business endeavors are normally suspended for this day of relaxation and family. And although my particular position, and possibly my fortunes, in time, would change, the same people that were always haughty and noble acting toward me, well, they are still haughty and noble acting toward me. I know, they think—as their eyes too often reveal their not so hidden hearts—that I'm just an opportunistic interloper, and that they are better than everyone anyway, and even more so better than me. The only thing I bet would ever change their minds is if I had to one day save their lives; then and only then might they ever tip their hats to me. I think I'm rambling crankily because I don't really know what to do with my life right now. Ever since Jessie returned from Africa, I've been more jittery than ever. Oh well.

To this point I had no knowledge of last night's remarkable events, so that lack of information never figured into my next encounter. Because as I'm standing there behind the desk, Fricke and Frack, the Russian behemoth brothers noisily—as usual—entered the lobby.

Talking arrogantly and loudly obnoxious, as usual, they approach the desk; again as per the usual course of behavior, when they arrive without their beastly brother Boris, I must first intercom upstairs as I do with all guests, no matter their association or relationship to the owner of record—unless, of course, they live here permanently, which the brothers don't.

I am by now quite used to restraining my own personal feelings and attitude—it is a well-practiced ritual here—so when the two approached the concierge and, my cordiality is well rehearsed, I say, "May I help you, gentlemen?" The larger of the two—although that statement should not in any way diminish either of their mammoth sizes—Borga speaks first, and I had to pinch myself to distraction to keep from venting my distaste for his epithet. Spoken from his mouth to my ears, the word *brother* could be nothing less than a curse.

I can still hear it ringing in my ears, him saying, "Hey, brother, it's us, Borga and Oleg."

I stared at them as if it was the first time I had ever laid eyes on them; it was my only civil defense. Then giving just a little, or risking being totally absurd, I said to them both, "Yes, I see who you two are, but the question still remains, may I help you?" Obviously I want to make them ask for what they want.

Then the other one, Oleg—obviously annoyed—he chimes in, saying, "Come on, brother, it's us, you know who we are, it is us, Borga and Oleg. We here to greet our brother, Boris, go on call on up to him, and tell him we are back from our business success."

I knew that I couldn't, nor did I want to keep this charade going, so finally, I relented and called up to the Romanovsky apartment. The telephone rang at the other end several times, but no one picked it up; I was surprised because the baron usually picked up after two, maybe three, rings and answered, but not this time.

I put down the receiver and turned to look at the two massive men, and I said as matter of fact as I could, "There is no answer, gentlemen."

Oleg quickly renders his disappointment, saying in a surprised and somewhat frustrated tone, "Then, where did he go?"

I had no idea, and I said so: "I have no idea, but you gentlemen are welcomed to wait until he returns. Please, if you will take a seat over there." I pointed to the very comfortable sofa across to the other side of the lobby, but Oleg, he wasn't hearing any of that waiting-around nonsense.

He huffed at me saying, "Then we go up and see him now."

I didn't make a move from behind the desk, but I was firm in my denouncement of their plan to storm the Bastille as it were; there would be none of that behavior here, and I said as much when I announce to the two of them saying, "That's not the way we do things here."

The Russians looked askance at each other, but their bullying stalled and for the moment they were both calm, figuring that wherever their brother had gone off to, he would surely return shortly and this whole matter of their entrance or not would be alleviated when he was again present.

So the two men proceeded to sit on the sofa; they were so large and out of place there, leaving so little room for humanity; they seemed as out of place as two beer barrels sitting on a glass bar shelf—in the right room, but in the wrong place—as they sat quietly and motionless for some time, the twin pictures of Russian asceticism and discipline.

While the Russians were sitting stoically repressed, and for certain steaming on the inside, Windler and my brother, John, were still busy in the security office playing with the new security system. As they watched and played with the monitor, Windler was having a good time showing John what the system was capable of.

Flipping a switch, he says, "It's really sensitive, Mr. Smith. You see, look, that's Mrs. Peter's boy toy setting out the garbage." Windler was feeling very good and relaxed by then, but he thought maybe he had gotten a bit too relaxed with his last comment as he moved quickly to redeem himself, saying, "Sorry, Mr. Smith, about the boy toy comment."

John laughed and commented back quickly saying, "Well, that is what he is."

Not wasting much time on the small talk, Windler gets excited as the monitor splits when someone else enters the hallway at the same time as the boy toy; then he says rather proudly, "Look, you see how the screen splits, Mr. Smith, there's Mrs. Lawrence putting out a trash bag." Windler smiles broadly as the system he's installed is beginning to flex its technological muscles; overnight it has become his baby.

He continues, saying, "It will split over twenty times, depending on how much activity there is at the same time." John Smith was happy with the results of his investment; he too had become increasingly animated, full of spirit and energy, like the adolescent boy he had all of a sudden found inside of himself and become again.

He couldn't and didn't feel the need to restrain himself any longer as he asked more questions to acquaint himself even further with this new envy's functions; excitedly he asks Windler, "And it records everything, right?"

Like two boys, they hovered over the control board and the monitor exploring all of its features; Windler is slow to answer his boss—maybe there was an errant thought blooming that harkened back to last night, but quickly he got himself back on the safe and right track—because by then they both sound like old friends. But Windler finally gets to the answer of John Smith's query about its recording capabilities, "You've got that right, Mr. Smith. I actually had it working yesterday, but I wanted to check out if everything was working properly before I let you see it.

John was very happy with everything that he had so far seen, but of course, there was more; after all, he had invested quite a lot of money in this thing, and he certainly wanted to get his money's worth. "And what about the individual alarms, Windler?"

Windler smiles as he is equally excited about installing them as he says, "I've already started installing them, sir, they should be done in the next two, three weeks, sir."

As the two continued to talk shop in the confines of the security office, I had gotten back to my slow Sunday business as usual behind the concierge desk when I felt a now-familiar presence insinuate itself in front of me. It was none other than the foreboding Russian brothers shadowing my Sunday *New York Times*, all spread out before me on the desk. Without looking up, I inquired, saying, "May I help you?"

"Call him again," is all one of them said; I couldn't tell, if not looking at them, which one had spoken because they both sound so much alike, but if I had to guess, I would have guessed Oleg only because he seemed to have the better grasp of the English language of the two. I really didn't want to get into anything with the two of them, so I simply picked up the intercom and dialed the baron's number.

Again, it rang several times without answer. This time I looked straight at them and said, "He's still not home, gentlemen." This time Borga growls something in Russian, but even at that—the foreignness of the language and all—I knew it wasn't something complimentary. They had lumbered over to the desk again. They were already heated up. I wondered for a second why they hadn't just bypassed me and tried to take the elevator, and it was then that I thought, *They don't have his keys. Their brother doesn't even trust them enough to give them keys to his apartment.* And now, they were fit to be tied; they were really angry, probably with me as well as with Boris for not trusting them with keys. So they rumble and grumble, but this time I am unable to shoo them away to the sofa of Siberia; they stay at the desk to menace me.

And all of a sudden, we are having ourselves a confrontation in the lobby as the bigger one, Borga, says in a throaty Russian huff, "We do things that way in Russia . . ." I guessed his response was harkening back to an earlier comment I had made about the way we do things here. He continues after a brief pause in his sentence, "Let us go, Oleg." And that's when Windler—hearing the commotion—steps out from the door of the security office. I never really thought much about it, but Windler is—or is it that he can be—a scary-looking, brother.

In the beginning—when I was ever so haughty and mischievous, and maybe even a little jealous of him—I had called him stumpy. He hadn't liked that then, but I had long since abandoned that thought and the kind of thinking. Back then when first dealing with Windler, I used that transitory name *Stumpy,* it was never meant to have been used as an unflattering inflammatory moniker as in truth, I was just throwing a little joke at him and his impressive muscular form. However, looking at him walking toward the concierge and the three of us—as he strode with determination and bad intentions—his dander up and all, I thought, whoa! That's a big hard tree stump of a man, and he was every bit as large but much harder than the two Russian bears were, but still there was something about him—in this present incarnate—that was far more foreboding than the two of them together.

We all felt it radiating—I could see immediately by the nervous looks on both of the brothers' faces—as Windler approached the desk. I hardly noticed my brother, John, trailing in his wake and shadow behind him.

"What's going on here?" Windler growled; I had never seen him like this. He looks at me hard for one of the longest seconds in the history of mankind, and then at the brothers Karamazov, but this time there was no patricide to contend with, as with Fyodor's boys. The death or even the missing of Boris Romanovsky was nowhere in the conversation, not even a hint of it. And yet Windler knew more about everything than anyone would have ever dreamt, and his mercurial ascent to anger—although based upon that secret and well-hidden knowledge—at the time seemed more gallant than in any way defensive.

As he came to my rescue, he had this fearsome scowl on his face—totally serious he was from jump street—and then he says in his revved-up, sonorous voice, "What's happening here, Al?" And after a quick turn of the head to the big Russian boys, Windler finally addresses them head-on, saying in his deepest baritone yet, "You guys going somewhere?"

Immediately the two Russians were put on the defensive—they were instantly reduced—and started to act like children playing in the sand. Their feet began to shuffle, and their erstwhile composure totally abandoned them in the heat of Windler's forceful visage and demeanor. Oleg this time seemed almost apologetic as he whined, uncharacteristically for him, saying, "He big guy, like Russian black bear, aye, Borga." He elbows his much more stoic brother in the arm.

No one moves as the silence deadens the staid lobby-turned-ring of fire and testosterone—testosterone so thick you could have bottled it and sold it in place of Viagra pills. But it was Borga this time that broke the silence as he grumbled low and somewhat sheepishly, saying, "We be back, black America, we be right back soon."

The Russians turn, crestfallen and defeated, and they shuffle their two large body selves off, lumbering across and through the lobby and out of the building without so much as another word between them or to anyone else for that matter. That's when I finally noticed my brother, John, now standing next to Windler. He sighs as if he had actually been a part of the standoff, saying, "Wow, that was a close one, you think they'll be back anytime soon?" I laughed because if anyone had asked the Russians if they had even noticed him, I bet they would both have said that they hadn't seen him.

Standing there now, it reminded me of old times again when John and I, as young pups, used to get into trouble hanging out uptown in Harlem with the brothers of another color.

Johnny—that's what I used to call him then—he would always be handing out these wolf tickets that he had no way of cashing, and then he'd hide behind me for cover and protection. We'd always end up running back downtown to the safety of our own neighborhood and the far more exclusive environs of Fifth Avenue. The uptown brothers didn't dare venture that far downtown to bother us there because in those days the cops—who were very protective of our exclusivity—would've had their heads; they still are, but I'm not a kid anymore, and I long ago stopped playing those games.

We, John and me, engaged in this kind of youthful mischief for a short while only; that all lasted until all of that adolescent intrigue and those raging hormones were absorbed and gotten under reasonable control; then we both settled down to understand and acknowledge just how privileged we in fact were. It all got old—that wanton mischief and all—and we got older and more serious and strategic about other pursuits, and finally we both just stopped going uptown anymore. My mind harkened back to those times because of this near rumble with the Russians. It simply tickled me; that was all it was worth, a little tickle.

It had been a tension-filled couple of moments there in the lobby, but after the Russians had departed, everything went quickly back to normal. As quiet as Sundays get, well, this Sunday, after the furor, was the quietest ever. Afterwards, John skulked out and had left us for parts unknown and unnamed, and Windler had quietly disappeared back into the sanctuary of the security office, probably to take a nap. Windler, by the way, all during this very secretive period, while he had been clandestinely installing the building's security system, well, he had quite boldly made the security office off-limits to everyone; the co-op board president, my brother, John, of course, approved of his seemingly independent move. It really wasn't a big deal as it was a small cramped space, and besides, there was a regular building staff lounge in the back of the building anyway, which meant no one was in a clamor over his new cordoned-off—figuratively, of course—space.

As I had said, it was quiet, and the quiet had allowed my mind to drift freely, and in that drifting I seriously wondered about Windler—something just didn't fit. And as I was presently standing behind the concierge desk, I needed to go to where he was. So I went, without trepidation and a modicum of curiosity, to the security office to personally see how Windler had experienced the earlier ruckus. Not that he was or had ever been the emotional type, but he had seemed, upon reflection, to have been a tad bit angrier than the earlier situation had warranted; I had felt that he was just inches away from getting into a physical confrontation with the two Russians, which would not have been good at all. And so I thought, *Why was he so committed to that limited tactic? I had never seen him react that way before.*

Windler is a very powerful man, and until this past morning, I thought that indeed that was his abiding strength; it was the thing that gave him the most confidence in dealing with difficult and uncomfortable situations. But this morning, I had seen something totally different, another side of him as it were. So unannounced, as I arrived at his office—the door was ajar—and I walked in. As I had said, Windler had made this place off-limits, and therefore I had not been inside it for some time; apparently it was long enough period of time for the office to have totally changed from what it sometime ago had been. It now looked like a command center at some sort of lockup—and I know lockups when I see one.

At the desk in front of a large monitor, there is this panel with several switches and knobs; it's not a large panel, but a panel nonetheless. And sitting at that desk is Windler. I was surprised, if not shocked, and I guess I overacted as I squeaked a womanlike shriek of "What the hell is that?" Oh, I knew what it was, all right, but my query was not so much a query as it was an exclamation.

Windler was quick to react; his head was down on the desk when he heard me enter the small room, and he immediately sat up and reached for what apparently was the turnoff switch, and he clicked on it, and the monitor turned that grayish black color; I think they call it opaque.

Windler was funny as he tried to feint a sheepish reaction, saying, "What was what, Al?"

I laughed; it was not like I was in some kind of pain and was unable to find the humor in all of this—him trying to hide the obvious and all—and his reaction to my screech. But it was, after all, a serious and truthful reaction that I was having to a big surprise, and I wanted to know what it was all about. So my course was set, and I would not be deterred, and I said as much. And as I was no longer squeaking and screeching, my newly modulated tone let Windler know that I was one hundred percent serious, saying, "Don't you what was what me, Stumpy"—the name slipped out of my mouth as I had been thinking it for quite some time, but Windler didn't react negatively or otherwise, and then I quickly corrected myself—"you know what I'm talking about, Windler."

Windler's head drops uncharacteristically, but I was hot, and I continued my inquisition. "It's a security monitor, I know what it is but, who . . . When did you install this thing? I never really figured it out. I knew you were up to something, and I knew that my brother, John, was part of whatever it was you were up to, but I hadn't thought of this, not even once. You were acting strangely there for a while, but John can do that to people. So, Windler, what's up with this?"

Windler seemed relieved as he relaxed a bit and raised his head and eyes to look at me and mine, saying, "Yeah, well, it was supposed to be a secret. Mr. Smith—."

I so rudely stopped Windler in mid-sentence, as I had wanted to complete his thought with my own perceptions of what had taken place between him and my erstwhile thorn in the side-turned—brother, John. John was a very independent sort, a kind of do-it-his-own-way maverick, and if this had been his idea—which it now was clear to have been—then it was most like him not to have told or consulted anyone.

I should have guessed as much ever since he first decided to sneak the video camera onto our parents' balcony to catch them surreptitiously feeding the falcons. So I said, "No, let me guess, Windler, Mr. Smith had you install it to keep an eye on the penthouse, right?"

Windler, who seemed happiest with me doing all of the guessing, says, "Yeah, that's right. How did you guess?" I was cheered on by Windler's lemming-like cooperation, but I should have been quickly wise to it.

Alas, I wasn't that quick, as I was still so headlong focused solely on the singular track, and that was understanding the functioning of and purpose for this new security system. I smiled broadly as I was feeling quite pleased, like some sort of parvenu Sherlock Holmes breaking an important Fifth Avenue criminal case wide open. Ha! I knew little then how much truth there was to this haughty and errant emotion. Pleased, huh? So I turned to Windler and asked him if he was all right; I had initially come to his office to inquire after how he was feeling after our little near dustup with the Russians. I asked, "How are you feeling, Windler, that's really why I came in here in the first place."

For the first time that morning, Windler actually smiled at me; I could tell that I had reached his heart. I cared—and I guess it showed—I really did care about the way he was feeling. I had sensed him out over the months that we had been working together, and despite his size, and maybe it was because of his size, Windler was really a very sensitive man, and I knew that the commotion of earlier that morning had affected him; I just didn't know how much at the time.

So Windler smiled a long, deeply felt smile, and I got it—it was his way of saying thank you for caring enough to ask—but then he just mouthed, saying, "I'm good, Al, I'm good." I was glad, but now my mind shifted quickly back to the security system, well, not totally. I was thinking about the Russians; I intuited that they were going to be trouble. I knew that this was the first time they had come to see their brother and were not allowed in.

Initially, I was just trying to rancor them as they had been a royal pain in my haunches for some time now, but now—upon reflection—I as well was wondering where the baron had gone. So I asked, Windler, with just hint of sarcasm in my question, saying, "Hey, Windler, is the system set up throughout the building, or is it just for the exclusive safety and security of the penthouse elite?"

In response, Windler laughed almost derisively before he said, "No, no it's all over the building, including the garage." I was surprised as I squeaked—my squeaking when surprised was becoming a regrettable habit of late; I was going to have to check that new tendency—as I said, "The garage as well?"

It was then that I saw how proprietary and proud Windler was or had become about his installation of the security system and the system itself; he had wired and installed the entire system throughout the entire building in secret and possibly alone—although no one would know whether it was done alone or not as it was done in secret—and he had done it well. So I was glad to say, and I said it quite readily in my most robust and sonorous TV news anchor announcer's voice, I said, "Well done, Windler, well done." And I really meant it, although I could have lost that silly voice before I said it.

Windler nodded his head upon my approval; he had no idea where I was going with all of this butter and flattery, and at first neither did I. But then I thought more about the Russians, and the baron in particular, and I asked, Windler, saying, "So then what you're saying is that it has recorded since it was installed the comings and goings of all our residence, and if I were to look at the recording from, say early this morning, or in fact late last night that I would—that is if he left the building—see the Baron Romanovsky's movements?" It was a very precise and detailed question that I had just asked—not tautological, but pretty damn close to it—I know. And it was then that I saw something that I'm sure few persons have ever seen before, or will ever see again.

Now let me say this: Windler is not a dark man; he's what African Americans call brown skin, not too light and not too dark. He, historically, is a most favorable hue, somewhere in the midrange of complexion and tone for us, a happy medium if you will, between light and dark. I bring this all up because of what was about to happen, or as in what happened next.

Upon me completing my thought to have been a fairly innocuous query, Windler's entire muscular frame stiffened, as if some sort of electrode had been applied to his testicles; and his skin suddenly changed from that sweet golden brown color to an ashen pallor of bed sheet white—I swear. For one full second, Windler was a white ashen shock of a man. If I hadn't thought that I had caused this miracle to occur, I would have bolted from the security office in panic. But I didn't; I knew it was somewhere inside my query that the ghost that had so suddenly ravaged my associate had emerged to set this new tone for our shared moment. He lightened up brightly like some sort of neon sign on Broadway and me standing there witnessing it with my own two eyes.

It was gone in a flash as his color and life returned to his massive form, but we both knew that this moment and its uniqueness could not pass without notice or discussion.

Yet the only thing that could follow that mercurial if not miraculous transformation was silence, a moment of awe and silence. You see, I knew then that there was something in the moment of what I had just witnessed that happened—a confluence of associate particles in space and time that caused a miracle—that would possibly never be repeated, and that I had seen it, only I had seen it. It's true, it had happened to Windler, but he was the one that it had happened to; he felt it, but I was the only one who had seen it. That was that; we were a newly-minted coin, each of us was one side, and in this way we would be joined in this singular and unique coupling forever.

I looked at Windler, and he stared back at me; he spoke first, and surprisingly he didn't try to deny the experience, saying in as flabbergasted voice as one could imagine, "Did you see that?" Now I'm guessing that he did in fact see some of it himself.

We were like two kids just having exited a haunted house at a carnival, I said, "Yeah, shit, what the hell brought that on, Windler?" I could see that he knew—instantly—he knew what the hell had brought that on. And at first he equivocated, not in words, although I could see it in his eyes that he wanted not to speak on what was there; he wanted to tell me anything but that very thought that was lurking anxiously, running from his brain quickly to his mouth.

I caught him trying to snatch it back, and I said quickly before it could retreat, "Don't you dare lie to me now, Windler, I'm watching you."

And that's when Windler gave it up, it was clear that something very traumatic had caused him to transmogrify earlier; there was no escaping that fact, and I had been there to witness it. So I said, "Look, man, you didn't just turn white for no good reason, what gives."

I knew he was already on the verge of giving something up, but I had just wanted to give him a little push to make sure, and then he said, "They killed him."

This was good, a murder, I thought, and my mind went straight to the Russians. "A-ha!" I said, again thinking in the Sherlock Holmes mind, "They did, didn't they?" I thought there was a lot of bluster this morning over nothing. "Great! Watson," I then said, and again Windler gives that look of his that read clearly, *What the hell is going on with you, Al.* But then I focused my attention on Windler, and I took a longer look, and I read something completely different from my own selfish and just as errant an assumption in Windler's eyes. Windler wasn't joining my party of celebration. As I hadn't yet blamed the Russians by either of their given names, but it was clear that I was already mentally and emotionally blaming them for having murdered their own brother. But to my sudden horror, I could see in Windler's eyes that my deduction had been faulty, and my conclusion was amiss. It stopped me cold, as I knew instantly that I was wrong.

"If the they, you believe, are the Russians, you would be wrong by a mile, Al," Windler says as his voice quivers and dithers like an cranky old car trying to start up in the dead of winter; it was quite a transformation from that sonorous tone he had used before. To me now, that crackled sound was the voice of some great foreboding doom; I knew instantly that the truth would be far less palatable than my earlier and cheerier assumptions had been, that the Russians had done it; I wished then that I had never come to his security office sanctuary. But alas, we had both fallen too deeply into the crevasse of details and confession to turn about now, so I awaited his ominous revelation, and when it came, it did not disappoint my rapacious fears, for they as well craved and demanded satisfaction.

"Your old ladies did it." The simplest of words, I'll admit—he had no reason to lie. I knew that they were truth before their singular flights—each word landing separately and heavily—had all reached fully inside my ears. The suspicions of our farthest-away fears are sometimes easiest to hear when they have come true and arrived at our hearts, but still the impact is not buffered. Those few words had hit me with their fullest possible force, and I could bear them not.

I nearly fainted as I then stumbled backward as the words' impact finally landed just as Windler rises and pulls a chair under my steadily flexing and weakening legs; I sat hard backward with a flopping-plopping sound, so disruptive that it at first made me look around thinking that someone other than the two of us had just entered the small room. I immediately discovered that it was still only Windler and me. And as my mouth—with my bottom jaw seemingly unhinged—hung wide open, I was in shock and dismay at the news so distant from any guess that I wouldn't have come up with it in a million tries; it hit me like a sneakily thrown punch in the jaw from a thug in an ally, and it had just about floored me. It probably would have if it hadn't been for Windler's chair rescue.

I could only manage to squeak out—still squeaking as I now finally had good reason to—three brief and barely audible words, saying, "Are you sure?" I needn't have asked as Windler, sitting quite stoically in his seat at the console and monitor, did not answer; we both stared as we both knew the horrible details were about to come.

Only a moment passed when Windler says softly, "They are both fine, I've taken care of everything."

For that longer than brief a moment, I was happy to hear they were fine, and that he had taken care of everything. There was a sizable part of me that right then had wanted to leave the room and scurry for the cover of anonymity. I wanted to turn the ignorance on and the clock back to an hour ago, and then choose and take the road most often traveled, the one that would have ninety-nine out of one hundred times led more times than not to all possible places other than to this dinky little security office where I had just had my life unalterably changed forever.

I was not chomping at this bit now dangling like a soulless ghost in front of me, but I knew, and Windler knew, that I was about to bite down ever so hard on it. One last pause, and then I bit, saying, "What the hell happened, Windler?"

With less pause than a blink of the eyes, Windler was quick to turn to the monitor, and as he clicked that fateful switch to rewind to last night, I intuited that it was indeed the switch to throw my life in a tailspin. He had already said who had done the deed, and now I was going have to bear some kind of witness to its origin and outcome; I was nervous, but like at the scene of a horrible car accident, most dare not look away.

Once it was set, he stopped and said, "You watch this now, and you will know all that happened before I acted, and why I acted at all." So I watched aghast at the nerve and sleaziness of that Russian bandit. I was angered, and I wanted to intercede—so aroused I was that I physically stood up, readying to head for the elevator to rescue my mothers from harm—but Windler, by word only, cautioned me that what I was seeing had already taken place. In my head, I knew immediately that he was right, but it was in my heart that I continued to panic.

I could see that Russian snake entering my family's penthouse apartment by then, and my heart almost stopped. "That's where I came in." I heard Windler say through my fearing and loudly thumping heart, and he said, "That's where I came into the office and played back this very same scene, and then I rushed upstairs to your—."

"To my mothers," I remonstrated as I stood up again readying to head for the elevator to the penthouse.

This time, Windler placed his ham hock of a hand on my shoulder as he then says, "To your mothers, yes. I told you already that I've taken care of things, there's no reason to rush there now, they are both of them fine."

I turned to look at Windler as he spoke his instructive words; it was clear that he had more to tell before I bolted out of there and made a fool out of myself, or a complete mess of things. I sat back down, and then, he began to explain.

After taking a deep breath and letting out a big sigh, he started to explain last evening's fiasco. "By the time I had seen what you just now saw, it was already over and done with," he says, to my total surprise. Even though he had already said in no uncertain words that they had—meaning my

275

mothers—had killed him, I guess the idea and the image of that happening really hadn't sunk in yet; I must have assumed that he, Windler, some how had a hand in it. But when he said that by the time he had seen what I had just seen that the thing had been done already, I was aghast all over again.

"You mean he was already dead when you got there, is that what you're telling me, Windler?" Windler was clearly nonplussed by my seemingly obtuse query as he had already told me as much. But instead of making me appear more foolish than I already was, he instead looked me off with a grammar school teacher's pedagogue's eyebrow flash and then continued on with his account of last night's travails.

"He was already very dead when I arrived on the scene. It was a bloody mess, but we three cleaned it up and got rid of all the evidence—." As it was my look this time that stopped him in midthought, he paused and nodded, and then he continued, saying, "Yes, the body too. No one looking for it will ever find that body."

Now, unlike before his explanation, I felt stuck to my seat; I couldn't move, and I didn't know what to say. But Windler did as he says, "I'm telling you all of this, not so that you can go running to your mothers to give them the how-could-you-have-done-such-a-thing third degree. I don't think that it is necessary for you even to mention it to them—they were just trying to defend themselves, and clearly, they were pretty damn good at it too. But that's not it at all. I will destroy the recording showing the Russian entering their apartment, which will clear them of all suspicion forever. Even if his bumbling brothers knew that he was sneaking there, they would never say. And plus they in a million years would never suspect that those two old gals were able to off him the way they did. I know that I wouldn't have suspected them if I hadn't seen it with my own eyes. But that's all I'm telling you about what happened. You don't need to know any more than that. And when the brothers and/or the cops return, which I'm sure they won't ever report him missing to them, they'll find nothing."

I wasn't completely sanguine with the notion of not speaking to Mildred and Gladys about all of this, but there was still that very selfish part of me that wished I had never walked into the security office at all. I stood up and looked at Windler and said, "I've really got to go now, Windler—thanks for everything, I think."

I walked out of the office into the lobby, and just as I did, Amy jumps sprightly off the elevator all bubbly and cheerful. She calls out to me in her unmistakable voice, saying, "Albert, Albert Lawrence." Even though I had stepped only two steps out of the security office doorway, the sound of her voice instantly carried me miles away from there. It was easier than it may at first seem possible, but I was already in flight and looking for an excuse, any excuse to free myself from the crushing weight of recent knowledge now weighing me down.

Her voice was like the rescue basket settling in around me, sent by God to lift me from the waters of the swirl abyss of a certain drowning. I had fought it—ever since Windler had unleashed that dreaded news upon my head—but I knew that soon I would lose that fight and succumb to its demands for my attention. But here now was the distraction for the moment and a welcomed respite from my ultimate fate. She continued, saying, "Mom and I want to invite you to have lunch with us this coming weekend. And, Albert, don't even try saying no."

I smiled in more ways relieved than she might ever know. I had no intentions of saying anything of the sort. In their cases, no was anathema to me. So—as the biggest thank-you, for the rescue smile wiped across my, what must have been otherwise panic stricken face—I said, "Just let me know where we're going, Sunshine, and I'll be there with belles on."

It's amazing the things that one morning or is it one moment in time can bring about.

Here I was thinking that it was just another lazy Sunday morning—just the way I liked it—and then, almost literally, all hell breaks loose. But I guess I need to count myself lucky. The fact is I personally haven't done anything wrong this time. I don't know what the brothers Karamazov are going to do next and what really happened to their brother leader. Hell, I'm not really sure what really happened. After all that Windler told me, I still don't know that much. He said he took care of things, and I really want it to remain that way. I know they are my mothers, but I've been to prison already, and the closer I get to knowing exactly what happened to the baron, the closer I get to prison again.

I hope for now, like he said, that they have taken care of everything. I guess I can live with that for now until it becomes too much for me to handle without needing to know more.

CHAPTER XXVII

Only a few days later, my brother, John, approached our building as he was returning home from the gym—I had finally gotten him to start taking better care of himself, and not just work, work, work all the time—when he spies, with his new set of bright eyes, an unfamiliar figure standing posted at the façade of our building. He was perplexed at first seeing him as he at first thought that he had arrived at the wrong address, but then he smiles disarmingly broadly as he was a bit embarrassed at his mental faux pas when he finally recognizes the familiar figure of the man he wasn't at all ready to see there.

It seemed that this was one change among the several recent changes that had taken place in his life and now at his home that he had recently been greeted with. He had decided to step back a little from his dictatorial leadership style, as the co-op president, and allow others—like Mildred and Gladys—take to handling separate projects in regard to the running of the building. They had planned to redo the lobby, as well as other landscape and detail alterations around the property. It was nicer now seeing him in a much better mood, and looking better as well, and not so consumed with the details and minutiae of co-op presidency life.

"Windler, I thought I was in the wrong place for a moment, you standing there like a Greek god and all." Windler and John were getting along very well, unlike his earlier days when he first started, and John had mentioned several times in passing that he could see in the future Windler standing out front representing our co-op just fine. Well, we made it happen, without telling him; we gave Windler a permanent shift as the doorman and concierge.

Windler was so proud of his new position, and it seemed that day that everyone else was also pleased to see him there out front. After John's comment, Windler looks smartly over to John, and he says, "An African god, sir. The Greek gods are a bit more northern, I'm certain."

John roars with a good belly laugh, saying through it, "Touché, Windler, touché, an African god it is then. It's good to see you here out front like this, Windler, it very good to see you out front." The both stand for a moment in silence as they gaze across the street through the sparse Fifth Avenue traffic into Central Park. After a moment almost too long for my type A brother to stand still, he asks Windler in what was now a totally different, somewhat more worrisome tone than could at first have been anticipated, saying, "Have you not yet seen any signs of the Baron Romanovsky, Windler?"

Windler immediately gulped, guiltily; he was not at all prepared for that level or weight of inquisition. But he languished but a New York second there as he quickly and smartly recovered, saying, in a matter-of-fact and professional voice, "Not a hair, sir." It was an indeed very humorous comment given the history of recent events, but it was totally lost on my brother, John.

"Well, keep an eye out for him, and let me know as soon as you do see him."

Windler is quick to respond, saying, "Sure thing, sir. You'll be the first person I tell as soon as I see the Baron Romanovsky again, you'll be the first to know." As John walks away, Windler can hear him repeating to himself the words "Strange, very strange him disappearing like that."

As John entered the building, our mothers—Gladys and Mildred—were exiting their elevator. They both smiled and greeted John with warm hellos, kisses, and hugs. "Mothers, good morning to you both. Are we going for our Sunday—morning constitutional?"

Mildred was happy to see her son happy as well, says, "As a matter of fact, son, we are, won't you join us?" For some reason unknown to either mother at the moment, John's face lights up like a Christmas tree on fire.

Proud he was to announce, "No, some other time, thank you. I've just come from the gym, and I'm having brunch with Nancy—she's prepared it for the two of us all by herself." And with that, John turns and heads off to his elevator with an obvious—once lost, now found again—spring in his step. Both Gladys and Mildred turn, and both with gentle and identical waves of their delicate hands, they see him off.

As soon as the elevator door closes, they turn to each other, hug, and squeal like grammar school girls seeing a heartthrob up close; Gladys first, followed imperceptibly and closely by Mildred, they say, "I'm so glad things are working out for them again."

"So am I, love, so am I, brunch together at home, how grand." They giggle together as they as well approach Windler at the entrance to the building. He's standing facing out as he should. The door to the lobby is closed, and as the two ladies approach it, Windler turns—on cue as if from some invisible and silent signal—and opens the door as they've reached it.

They both step through at normal speed, and then they each nod politely in Windler's direction before Gladys speaks, saying, "Hello, young man, and how are you doing this very fine morning?" Windler's mood is totally different and deferential, quite a contrast to his more manly demeanor when dealing with my brother, John, or any other man for that matter.

He smiles warmly and says, "I am very well, ma'am, very well, thank you." Gladys pauses as she takes a look at Mildred, who stands silently and patiently right next to her. Mildred is looking toward the street; in fact, she is staring, but for the moment, Gladys ignores her friend's elsewhere gaze as she completes her conversation with Windler.

"You look good in Albert's stead, son. I understand he's off having brunch with Amy and Jessie Dillon?"

Windler had already noticed the car parked down away from the building with the two men sitting in it sometime ago, but he hadn't let it unnerve him any. He continued to pay full attention to Gladys as decorum and good manners demanded, and besides, he has a great fondness for her in the first place. As he answers her query, saying, "Yes, ma'am, they are dining at the Tavern on the Green, ma'am."

Gladys smiles warmly again at Windler and says, "You stop by soon to see us, son, you hear?"

Windler responds happily, saying, I will, ma'am, soon I will."

But still Mildred stares, and finally she speaks as she anxiously offers her few nervous words of query, "Why are those two Russians sitting there staring at us here?"

Windler knew he must answer her and at the same time reassure her security in their secret without bringing the words to his lips that would make direct reference to it. He also knew he needed to respond quickly, and so he did, saying, "They don't pose a threat to anyone here, ma'am. I am here as always to protect all that might be harm from any unlikely investigation or intrusion. So you ladies have at your constitutional, and be as light as the breeze." Windler's poetic words—every bit as surprising to his own ears as they were to the ladies—were nonetheless the ointment for Mildred's sudden ailment. For she was suddenly calm again as her errant malady disappeared as quickly as it had arrived, and off they both went, crossing the street at the light to disappear into Central Park.

But for Windler, the two men were still on his mind as they remained seated in their big black car, watching, ominously staring and waiting. From his point of view, they were like two oversized forlorn sinister puppies—of course at his own formidable size he had the luxury to designate them as such—but still even at that they were beginning to annoy him.

Sitting in the car, Oleg has clearly become the most impatient of the two brothers as he grumbles to his brother, Borga, "Maybe we should give money to the black bear, if he let us in to Boris's apartment, yes?"

But Boris is not so inclined as he grumbles back, "*Nyet*. We wait to hear from Boris."

Across at the Central Park West side of the park, at the Tavern on the Green restaurant, in the famous Crystal Room sit Jessie, Amy, and Albert having brunch. Amy is her usual effervescent and ebullient self, even more so than in the last several months, and that's clearly because her mother has returned and certain family problems have been resolved. In many ways—Jessie and her daughter Amy—are so much alike, although today, Jessie has put a lid on her own innate exuberance. There is something more serious than usual in her tone—not that she is in any way morose, but she is obviously more subdued than usual.

Alone with me, it wouldn't seem so dire, but the contrast is more obvious when Amy—all animated and perky—offers in a ladylike squeal, saying, "This is really chillin', the three of us here together, huh?"

But when Jessie counters with a unpredictably cool response, it reminds both me and Amy of most of the women that live in our co-op; it was almost snooty in affect as Jessie says, "Yes, it is quite nice, don't you think, Albert?" We—both Amy and I—could have gagged at the haughty tone. As proof we almost simultaneously looked at each other, and then we mimed—like we always had done at the concierge when one of the *Snooties* (the name we gave them) would high tone us and stick their uppity noses high into the air—with our single fingers into our open mouths and pointed into our throats as if to induce a gag reflex. At first, and in the span of a second, Jessie was baffled, then stunned; and finally she got it as she began to laugh out loud in her usual uninhibited, not-at-all-high-class cackle. And still dithering through her laugh, she asks, "I sound that bad? Oh my god, I'm sorry you two. I was distracted with some heavy thoughts, please, I beg both of your pardons for me being such a bore. I'll quit it right now." And did, as she immediately dropped her haughty airs.

I, on the other hand, had brought my own distractions to our brunch. *Jesus*, I was thinking, *my life lately has been full of so much change and trauma that my head is still spinning.* It's a small wonder that I can sit still at all, but I did so much want to be right where I was, there at the Tavern on the Green for Sunday brunch with Jessie and Amy Dillon. I'm not really complaining, but the problem was, though, I hadn't had much time to adjust to one thing before another change event or circumstance had already been heaped jumped or was placed in front of me that I had to deal with. And now, it looked like I've just got to deal with all of them at the same time; as the saying goes—it's an old saying but totally apropos—when it rains, it pours. But Amy had asked a question of us both—Jessie and me—and she deserved an answer as I finally said, "Yes, it is very nice us all here together, Amy." But now it was Jessie's turn to inquire after my mood; she could see that I was distracted as well.

"Is there something wrong, Albert? I must say that you seem distracted as well."

I didn't want to begin our little brunch outing, us three finally out together in such a lovely place, on such a lovely day, and start it off with an ugly lie, so I took a full gulp of courage and I said, "There's nothing wrong, Jessie, but I do need to clear something up . . ."

I paused, and Amy instantly got the hint, and on cue she says, "I see some people I know over there, I'm going to make a visit. I'll be back when you guys have cleared the air. And besides, I have to go to the bathroom. Would you both please excuse me." She leaves the table, but not before she gives me a little wink first.

At first, I thought that Amy was being so terrific giving her mother and me time alone, but when she added that little verse about "when you guys have cleared the air," I became a little suspicious. But, oh well, I thought, maybe it just was a random choice of words that really didn't amount to much of anything at all.

Jessie got right to the point—she wasn't at all distracted by anything Amy did or said—she immediately put all of her considerable attention on me. I was buoyed by the force of her presence; it was singular and strong, oh so strong, and it made me feel really special. And then in her most solicitous tone, she says to me, "So what's bothering you, Albert?"

I unhesitatingly charged right in, saying, "I told John about me and Nancy."

Jessie stared implacably without emotion or reaction, and without a single word, but she intuited—from her attending behavior—that there were words to come; there were to be many, but until then, she waited. And then I said, "I apologized to him, Jessie. I told him that I was sorry."

She continued to stare, but this time she did utter one word, and that word was a simple yet solicitous: "Yes." She had the attending behavior of a good psychotherapist; I now I was committed to being a good patient, so I continued.

"He was so calm." I continued, "As if he already knew."

Then she finally did speak a full sentence, saying, "He probably did know, Albert."

I was aghast by the thought of him having known all the time. "You think?" I asked her with the voice and mind of a clueless child.

This is the point or time in a conversation where learned people will often say about someone as clueless as me, "He just doesn't get it." And if I never knew or had an example of what they meant by someone not getting it, well, this is the perfect time for that perfect illustration. You think?

Then Jessie says to me, "I knew, and I've been in Africa for months." She laughed, and I got it. But still I was saddened by it all, not just because I had cuckolded another man, but that he was as well my own brother, that really hurt. And then Jessie adds the *coup de grâce*, saying, "You can't hide secrets in that bird's nest, Albert. So what did he say?"

"It was strange, Jessie," I said.

And she says, "How so, Albert?" And when I thought of what he had asked me, it hit me again; just like when he first asked it, it hit me like that again.

And I said, "Well, he asked me what were my plans in regards to her."

Everything that had come before this moment between Jessie and me was pretty run—of-the-mill stuff. I mean, she already knew about my longtime fling with my brother's wife—although at the time we didn't know she was my brother's wife because we didn't know that he was my brother. But somehow this last little part of the whole sordid episode was of great, great interest to her as she perked up after she had heard me repeat what John's question had been.

"Yes, yes, and you said in answer to his question?" she asked as her back had gotten very straight in her seat, and she had leaned forward so as not to miss a word and any nuance of behavior coming from me. Staring me hawkishly in the eyes, she waited. It's funny, I knew this was an important moment for both of us, but there was no way that I was going to fabricate something that wasn't there naturally. I knew then that I wanted to be closer to Jessie, closer now than ever I had allowed myself to think about before. But still, I could only tell her the truth and let the cards fall where they might.

And so I said, "I didn't really know what to say at first. And then, I realized what he was trying to say to me, that he was telling me to step up or step off. So I told him that I had no plans, that it was over forever." Then I looked directly at Jessie—as during my recounting of my conversation with John, my eyes had been unfocused in thought and recall—and in an honest and hopefully encouraging appeal to her, I said, "I didn't want to add insult to injury, but there had never been any wish for future plans with Sandy—it wasn't ever going to go any farther than it had gone, and that was only as far as her bedroom."

Jessie is a true chameleon of the first order—nothing negative intended by that assessment—she changes mercurially heeded and advised by her own cues, of course, from one thing to another to suit her varied needs; now she is a detective as she sits and stares and slides a sibilant and totally manipulative yes through her clenched teeth. Then she nods her head attentively as she encourages me to speak even more on the topic.

I quake with anticipation of doing the right thing. It's truly amazing when meaning meets message and every word carries weight. So I continued with the particulars of my tête-à-tête with my brother, John, saying, "Then, he looks me square in the eyes and says, 'Then it's over—.'"

"It wasn't so much a question as it was a statement of him reclaiming his wife. I looked at him and said, "'Yes, it's over.' He then shook my hand and thanked me for coming clean, and that was that."

Jessie then let out a sigh, as she says, *"Okay, okay, okay."* I quickly wondered what those three okays meant, but I wasn't about to ask—the timing just didn't seem that right. But I need not have anticipated waiting long because Jessie was on the move, in more ways than one. Because then, Jessie—who had been sitting a seat away from me as Amy's seat was between us—then moved into Amy's vacant seat next to me. She then says my name twice, "Albert, Albert, I have something I want to share with you. It's obvious that we care for each other, and where it will go from here, now that Dennis is gone for good, only time and God's good providence will tell. I have had all of Amy's life to get to know you, and I am certain that you are a good man. You know, Albert, that's the first thing one wants to know about another in any relationship, and that is that the other person is a good person."

I could tell this was going to be a long one as I could feel the formation of a dissertation coming on as she reached into family business to explain, "Dennis, with all of his shortcomings—that have nothing at all to do with his sexual orientation—is a good person, he's just not very strong. That the people around you are good people is truly the greatest gift of humanity, all other things, possessions, and acquisitions, they all pale greatly by comparison. The way you are with Amy, God knows that we all could just be friends forever, and that would truly be a great blessing. But I sense you want more, and if I'm not risking too much by saying this prematurely, so do I.

"We all have our many secrets—some frankly carry more weight than others, of course. Dennis had his, and I had mine, or as it is, I still have mine. If we are to go any farther, it is important that you know at least this one that I am perched maybe too eagerly on the edge, that figurative precipice of telling you—it might explain some things, but it may not be what you need to hear, given your proclivity and predilection for white women like Nancy. I know it does matter to me that you know this about me." Jessie pauses, and of course, this cessation piques my interest even more than it already was aroused.

She seems more hesitant for a moment, but then she continues, "I don't know, Albert, but maybe I'm just feeling excessively vulnerable, connected, or altruistic, I don't know which. I bet none of those words seem to fit together, do they, Albert?" She was right; at first I thought I was following her, but then I got lost again. Jessie's not a frivolous woman, prone to excessive chattering and maybe, like she says, just maybe right now she is feeling a bit more vulnerable than usual. I knew now to do what I had become accustomed to doing over the last seventeen years; she needed my support and understanding now, and of course, I knew how to give it.

"Why don't you just slow down, Jessie, and tell me straight out what you're trying to say, you know, like you usually do. If there's any doubt that I'm interested, well, you can put that to rest. I've been interested in you for seventeen years, Jessie, ever since the first day that I met you. You have shared your good heart and your inordinate strength with me whenever I've needed you to, and I've loved you and respected you for it. I don't need to wait for God's providential hand to tap me on my shoulder—I've been waiting here the whole time. So go on and spill it, girl, I'm here to catch, hold, and caress whatever falls from your lovely lips."

It was then that Jessie lets go of one of her brightest smiles ever as she beams and glows from ear to ear, and then she says, "Oh, Albert, it was never anything bad that I had to drop on you, it was more a crisis for me in my life than ever it would be for you. For you it is just something unexpected that you have, in your gentle, loving way, have made seem so small and trivial, but here it goes." She did exactly as she said as she jumped into her elucidation with two feet.

"I am not what I appear to be, and let me say this. It is central to why I've just spent so much time in Africa. I am biracial, Albert. My father and mother both were biracial, and when they married, they didn't know what to expect, but they had me, and I came out like this. I spent most of my life in ignorance of that basic fact, and in point of fact, I didn't learn about it until right before I met Dennis, and we made our pact."

I knew before she said it what it was that she was about to say. This racial flip-flop, this duplicitous skullduggery borne on the frustrated wings of the class-status-seeking American bald eagle, done out of necessity and the desire to escape the disadvantage of having darker skin; as she offered it up for my consideration, it seemed like something new to her, but I had witnessed it on my side of the racial chasm—the darker side of things—more times than it would seem possible to say and be believed.

I could see in her worried eyes that she wasn't at all certain how I might react to this news, even after she had professed how in my expression of love, desire, and commitment toward her that I had demoted it all to a less-than-trivial status. It was clear in her telling of this secret that she hadn't revealed this clandestine history to many if any people at all before this as she waited with baited breath for me to respond; but I paused quietly, and at first, I said nothing. I had learned, from being with her, I'm sure, to hold my thoughts to first allow her to complete her own.

So as she had done many times with me in the past, I hovered patiently while she decided what to say next. She didn't take that long to speak again as she says, "I, at first, upon learning the truth of my father's race . . ." She paused to think. "I was proud, but also I was sad. You see, he had spent so much of his life in racial and social conflict—he had passed for a white person most of his life—no, check that. He and my mother had started new lives after they were married and left New Orleans. It happened when they moved from New Orleans to New York."

As Jessie was telling the story, I could see that she was becoming more and more comfortable talking about it. Maybe it was because it was a story—I don't mean as in a lie; all of it was true, I'd swear to that. But she was now telling a story that was not about her, but about her father, which for some would be easier to tell; I know it would have been true for me.

286

I listened while she continued as she said something that made me smile, saying, "You know, Albert, for years and years in New Orleans, blacks got lighter and lighter. The people down there noticed it too. It went something like this: because New Orleans had that very French heritage, its social fabric was enigmatically different from much of the rest of the country. At first, there was a lot of intermingling between the races. That's not to say that there was no racism. There was as much there as anywhere else—but there was not as great a taboo on miscegenation. It was rights and freedoms of the darker people, like throughout the rest of the country, that were unequal. And the births from those unions, obviously the skin tone and the dominant features, were skewed differently than they were on either side.

"That's when passing for a white took on a fashion. It was widely accepted that the lighter you looked, the whiter you were considered. And as the natural result and progression of that racial phenomena, it followed that the lighter your skin was, the better your opportunities were. So the lighter skinned—octoroons and quadroons—began to take advantage of their natural gifts."

This is when Jessie became very pedagogical, as she explained, saying, "By the way, mulatto, mixed, biracial were some of the other names used to describe the so-called new races. But in my father's papers, he always referred to us as 'roons,' and then he'd designate—in his words—how 'roonish' we were."

"By the way, I am the child of two octoroons, and both my grandparents themselves were quadroons. There is great racial complexity to the most mind-boggling and absolute absurdist degree, but it is nonetheless true as it is well documented and can be followed all the way back like a well-drawn road map. I've done all the reading of his notes and other research, and I know the complete history. Mother hid all of this from me until I got a hold of my father's papers after he passed. He was quite a fastidious man, and he had documented everything."

I sat there stunned at the detail and length of Jessie's explanation more than I was surprised by its content. I knew this happened all the time; I had heard many stories. I am what other blacks call high yellow, or simply light skin; on the other hand, Gladys is probably at least a quadroon. She could always pass for a white if she ever really wanted to. If my father had been a lighter-skinned man, even as dark as me, then maybe I too could have passed, as I may have come out light enough to have done so, like my brother John.

Jessie was on a roll now, and I didn't want to interrupt her flow; as she continued, I watched her closely.

"Finally, after I had discovered my father's papers, my mother then told me that they had always planned to tell me the truth. But they had kept putting it off until it was too late because he had died. It was then she sat with me and gave me the verbal history of my family. You see, it all started with a slave named Becka—now, mind you, this is on my mother's side of the family because I already had my father's writings about his side of the family. And Becka, she must be my great-grandmother." I wished at the time that I had a tape recorder because I knew I'd never hear this story told in this way again; Jessie was filled with such passion and pride just to have the complete knowledge of her ancestry.

"Becka was bedded by her master, Pierre Moreau . . ." Jessie begins to laugh, and I smile because she has a beautiful engaging laugh; and also, for the first time, I am allowing myself to fall deeply in love with her—but I have no understanding for what reason she is laughing. But then she explains. "I'm sorry, Albert, it's rude to laugh and not share the humor. But Master Pierre Moreau—well, his name *Moreau* in French, it means dark complexion." I stared at her without smiling. I didn't feel the humor; oh, it was funny all right, but I just didn't feel the humor. Jessie understood, without necessarily having to understand my reluctance to engage in a fit of laughter just for laughter's sake alone. She's an adult and an honest broker, and I don't have to pretend with her; that's why I love her so.

So without much hesitation over trifles, she continued, "Well, Pierre Moreau and my great-grandmother Becka, they have several children—girls and boys both. But one of them, a girl name Louisa, he gives to his brother Charles Moreau. Louisa and Charles have a daughter, and that daughter is my grandmother, the octoroon Justine, for whom I am named.

"My father's family and my mother's family, they all knew each other intimately." Here she pauses and waits, and I see there's a sadness that washes over her countenance as it is clear her mind is reveling in deep thought. And then, as suddenly as she stopped, she starts up again, saying, "Albert, it was a success. They, we all—as there were a total of twelve of us, six boys and six girls—we all passed. My mother's family married my father's family, and like ghosts, we are living white in America. If you ever wanted to document an experiment, this one worked to perfection." This time, I was flabbergasted. I had no idea where she was going with this, but she had arrived, and I was dumbfounded.

I didn't at first even know what to ask her, but I started just to reel off question after question without thinking much about what the answers might be. "Had they planned this, Jessie? Did your mother say that they had planned this from the beginning?"

Jessie smiled; it was almost a disappointed smile, but she remained patient. Finally, she answered me, saying, "No, no, Albert, nothing like that can ever be planned by ordinary people. It was just that the families were so close, and after the children became lighter and lighter, it became a pact to marry each other and escape the innate physical shackles of race. It has always been a clear impediment to forward and equal progress in our society, so why not take advantage of something that came quite naturally? No, Albert, it was never a plan. But at some point—and that point was arrived at pretty damn early—it became a contrivance of opportunity, a tremendous opportunity. And besides, Albert, as light as we all had become, what would have been the use of fighting to stay black? No one would ever have believed us anyway, would you?"

I just stared. I couldn't believe what I was hearing, "You mean there are more like you out there? I mean, your cousins, brothers, and sisters, and now nieces and nephews?" Jessie stares at me as if I've lost my mind.

"Didn't you just hear what I've just told you, Albert? Yes, the rest of my family is out there looking white just like me."

"Do they all know who . . . I mean, what they are?" I asked.

And then she shook her head, but this time, it wasn't in any way derisively. "No, they don't, Albert. Some of them know nothing about what their history is. And before you ask, yes, I know who and where they all are."

I know, I know, I already said that I was flabbergasted. Well, I was a lot more than that. I felt like a bone china plate dropped on a ceramic-tile floor. I felt shattered. There were pieces of me that were angry, others that were envious, some were sad, and still others that were completely and unreservedly joyous.

Picture them, Jessie's clan, all of them defying racial relevance and relativity; how archaic our thoughts, how primitive our legacy, how persistent our fears are in the light of such possibilities.

Before we could continue, Amy returned to the table all bubbly and bright-eyed. By then, Jessie and I were holding hands and gazing into each other's eyes.

"Wow, I'm so glad I went away. I wouldn't have missed coming back to this for anything in the world," she says as she sits down next to her mother in the newly vacated seat. "I've been wishing for this scene for years, and it's finally here. Yahoo!" she yelps. We all laughed at and with Amy's expression of joy. I looked at Jessie and then at Amy, and my first thought harkened quickly back to the conversation of before Amy had returned to the table.

I guess my eyes betrayed me because before I could speak, Jessie says, "Yes, she knows all that I've just told you and more."

I was stoked. I don't know why I felt so cheerful knowing that Amy had knowledge of her heritage, but I was. I guessed part of feeling that way was because I cared greatly for Amy, and I thought that it was only right for her to know about her family's remarkable history. I had watched Jessie's face closely when she was telling me about not having known her past for most of her life, and I could see that she was hurt by it. "She knows?" I said.

And Jessie repeated again, "She knows."

Amy didn't have to turn her head because we were both within her eyes' frame of view. She then repeats us, saying, "She knows, she knows what? What are you two talking about?"

Jessie then turns to Amy and says, "About your heritage, sweetheart, you know about your very unique heritage."

Amy smiles broadly as she could immediately tell that her mother had told me their story. "Wow, that's so cool. Right, Albert? I'm black like you now."

I smiled because she still looked as white ever to me, so I said to Jessie, "Well, what does that make her? She, the granddaughter of two octoroons and the daughter of and octoroon mother and a white father. Now, that would make her an octoroon divided by half, or some such thing."

Jessie smiles because she immediately knows where I'm going with this line of questioning, and she says, "Yeah, but if this was in the 1850s in New Orleans and other such places, she and I would still be considered black. You know of course, Albert, the one-drop law."

Jessie was right of course, and I did know the one-drop law, which stated that it took only one drop of black blood in a person's body to make them black. I laughed to myself as I was thinking, *If one drop of black blood makes someone black, Jesus! They must have considered black folks very powerful.*

Jessie just looked at me with this knowing smile; it was a warm smile indeed, and then she said, "Yeah, Albert, they are quite powerful indeed."

But then Amy—I guess she was feeling left out of the conversation—answered quickly as she had already figured it out, saying, "I am a quintroon . . ." She breathily sighs with delight. It was clear that not only was Amy happy that I now knew of her heritage, but she was in fact very proud of it herself. I could tell that it was a recent acquisition; and so far, she was wearing it like a new favorite winter's coat, well and proudly.

Quintroon, now that was a word I recalled only having heard years ago in one of my college anthropology courses in that single lecture on race categorization and social class in the old South. Wow, that really took me way back! It was good to see them both embracing their heritage; but like with my brother John, there was so little risk involved, for the truth was not obvious, and what was obvious was still to their social advantages. It was indeed a fascinating and elucidating revelation of this family's history. My own family and I had fallen just short of their journey, John being more like them than anyone else in the family.

I was not at all chagrined or jealous; I bring that up because I certainly could have been. Living in this building since I was a child and now working here, some things have been out of my reach just by a mere fingertip, and the color of my skin is clearly the reason why. My personal transgressions not withstanding, my life has walked a path not common to most men of my same hue, and yet I still feel the heat fanned from the nearby flame of resistance to persons of my kind. But still, all up, I haven't had it so badly at all. So I smile and acknowledge my own gifts and good fortunes and blessings as it were. I smile at Jessie, and I smile at Amy—both of them more family to me than any save my own: my mothers Gladys and Mildred and my erstwhile brother John.

Then as I smile, Amy gives us both a candid bird's-eye view of youth's innate honesty and inhibition when she says, "You see, now the two of you can get together without reservation, if ever either of you had any at all in the first place." We three smiled as our brunch orders finally arrived.

CHAPTER XXVIII

So many things have changed in the last six months since everything has changed. The Russians are finally gone; they were forced to sell when their brother never returned. There was no real investigation; the police did come around, but they—as always—were quite intimidated by the surroundings, the wealth, and the high social and political status as many of our owners has an undeniable leverage. They—the police, that is—would never say it out loud, but the people on Fifth Avenue are treated by and held to a separate set of rules. They in fact have their own precinct. I would know this as I am in that august and unique company by which I have been accorded the treatment in both sets of rules—there's the set for the rich and the set for everyone else and lastly theirs, the set for black males—albeit by different precincts and different police.

When they saw me here at home in the penthouse as one of the Smith family, there were more "I beg your pardon, sir" and "Mr. Lawrence, sir" thrown at me than pitches are thrown in a nine-inning baseball game. Usually, on my own, I'm lucky—when accosted by them, and that's for simply living as a black man in New York—there are many more, if I'm so lucky, "Hey, buddy," "Look, fella" addresses than "Any one, sir," but I digress.

The missing Russian case was put to the most cursory investigation in the history of missing-person investigations, I bet. And I would also bet that John Smith, yes, my brother, John Smith, had a little something to do with that. I'm not saying what he did because I don't know what he did, but the fact that the brothers Karamazov protested very little must have helped to dull the quest as well. They all in the end were just a bunch of thugs who got the tables turned on them, and I guess that losing one of their numbers was the high cost of doing business. I hope that somewhere down the line, we don't run into them; for a bunch of tough gangsters, they did go quite quietly and mysteriously into that good night.

And then there's John and Nancy, my brother and sister-in-law; they have adopted a new baby. She just arrived last week; she is biracial—her teenaged African-American mother was raped by a white Catholic priest, who is now serving time in jail—six weeks old, and she is beautiful. That ought to keep Nancy busy for a while, although there are presently more nannies in this building than there are children; she won't have any trouble at all finding help. Speaking of help. I thought at first that I was going to need help because when my brother, John, first asked me and Jessie to have dinner with him and his wife, I thought he was setting me up for some kind of harsh retribution, and that made me very nervous.

I had wronged him. And for most men, no matter how you shape it, turn it, or couch it, being cuckold—by no one less than your own brother—is a difficult thing to live down. It was the kind of experience where everyone knowledgeable thinks you've been duped and destined to feel just one way about you. And all of those feelings are everlastingly negative, no matter what you do or say—it doesn't matter. And with this cloud hanging over John's head, a cloud that his wife and I put there, he still insisted on us going forward like everything was normal.

I continued to be nervous until our first dinner, and it was nowhere near what I had feared or expected. In fact, we've all had dinner on several occasions over the past number of months. At first it was strange, interminably strange, but John insisted—he really knows how to turn the tables. I can't say that I could have blamed him for a little retribution, but it never came. And all up, I felt it was a very small price for any of us to pay; and if payment for all misdeeds and bad judgments were this sweet, I'd rather prefer a life of crime.

In the end, we all got along just fine—as Nancy and I had gotten along for years before we started with our silly sexcapades—the two guilty always knew what they had done; and the other two knew as well, so there were no secrets to hide, and no intrigue to skew things to the abnormal and negative side of relationships.

And now we turn next to me—Jessie, Amy, and I are a family now; they both finally talked me into moving back into the building. I'm living with them now—the quickie uncomplicated divorce was not at all contentious—and we are all very happy with the arrangement.

And Windler is our new concierge. It all seems so normal now, this life of mine, I'm thinking this as I ride downtown with my brother, John, in the back of the corporate limo; but John interrupts my train of private thoughts, saying, "You know, Al, I'm really happy to have you as my partner.

293

You learn fast, and this West Side project is really going well. A whole lot of things have changed in six months. You have a new job, a new family, you're a new man, Albert."

John has loosened up, really, really loosened up. Oh no, he's not been calling himself a brother yet; in fact, I don't think that's in the offing, and by no means is it necessary to me or anyone else. We are who we are because of what we do, not because of whom we're born, if that makes any sense at all. John is doing just fine, and for him to pretend all of a sudden—because of this new information about his heritage—change and start to act in some false stereotypical way would be repugnant and repulsive.

So I smile at John and take it all in slowly. The change in my life moved as gradual as the creeping southward of a North Pole glacier, so when it finally came, I was imminently ready for it. And then I said, "Thanks, John. You're a huge part of all these positive changes in my life, and I thank you, as a brother and mostly as a friend."

John smiles and says, "We're family, Al, maybe not a traditional one, but nonetheless, we're family."

I laughed and said, "Yeah, we're all pieced together like a patchwork quilt. Something old something new, something borrowed . . ." And as usual, the final word goes to John, his only regret is that he so much wanted to be the older brother.

"That's quite all right, Al, we've managed to come through the fire to meld together, and that in the end is all that matters."

In the end, there's Windler standing under the awning when a new thudding sound echoes from the pavement next to him. Windler's hulking frame turns slowly and ambles over to where the debris has fallen to the gray asphalt pavement; he sees what had landed and is chagrined. He hurries to pick it up in his nearby trusty silver shiny utensils, and as he sweeps a large fat man's bloody finger inside the dustpan, he looks up toward the heavens, the falcon's nest, and the penthouse balcony; and he says, "You really need to be finishing up on this sometime really soon."